Secrets

of

Moonlight Cove

Secrets of Moonlight Cove

a romance anthology

Nicobar Press

Riverside, California
http://www.NicobarPress.com

Nicobar Press
http://www.NicobarPress.com

First publication, October 2016
First print edition, March 2017

———

———

ISBN 978-1-938125-43-0

———

Cover image © Glenn Nagel | Dreamstime.com
Cover design © 2016 Shauna Roberts
3-D box set design: dhananjayaeffec | Fiverr.com
All rights reserved

———

Dedication

This book would not have existed without the inspiration of Kathleen Rowland who invited us all to visit a sleepy little town somewhere on California's coast...

Thanks for the opportunity to live there for just a little while through our stories.

Table of Contents

Mr. Valentine Comes to Town

by

A.G. Reid

Chapter 1

The problem with being immortal is that you can't vacation in the same place very often. Usually, a couple of weeks every decade was all Valentine allowed himself. More than that, and people started asking too many questions.

Moonlight Cove. His research told him this location was ideal for his needs. A coastal city with a Mediterranean climate, extended dry summers and short wet winters. The structures, though old, were well maintained. Best of all, Moonlight Cove had a transient tourist population.

Valentine observed Erica and Brett, who had just come out of the hardware store across the street. His research indicated their paths would converge here over the next few days.

It was obvious they had just met. She was in her mid-twenties with reddish-brown hair full of long, unmanageable curls. Valentine smiled as he watched her push some loose strands of hair into place. She was a little nervous but not in a bad way.

Brett was a little taller than Erica, he still maintained the muscular tone that he'd had in the military. His black hair was combed straight back to touch his shirt collar. Brett helped Erica with a stubborn lock of hair that would not stay in place. Valentine's smile grew as he watched them. They had potential. They just couldn't see it yet.

Valentine took the last sip of coffee. The waitress stopped by his table. "I'll have another cup of this." His gaze remained fixed across the street on Erica and Brett.

"You must really like coffee. This is pretty strong stuff, it's called Fisherman's Lightning. Most people stop at two, that'll be your fifth cup."

Valentine, realizing the waitress was speaking to him, shifted his attention to her. She was young, a year or two beyond twenty. Her hair was reddish blond, so light it reminded him of the blush of apricots. He studied her eyes for a moment, they were hazel and he could not decide if they held more green or brown. He glanced at her nametag then returned her smile. "I find it invigorating, Mindy."

"That, I can guarantee." She reached for his cup and saucer.

Valentine watched Mindy return to the counter. Her ponytail bounced in rhythm to her footsteps. A group of staff had gathered in front of the TV monitor near the coffee station, watching the morning news broadcast. Mindy stopped to join them.

Valentine glanced again towards the hardware store across the street. Erica and Brett were gone.

Mindy returned with the coffee. "Did you hear about Is Brea, that village in Ireland? Everyone there is getting married." She set the coffee near his hand. "It's been in the news all week."

Valentine swallowed, then cleared his throat. "It has? All week?" His last assignment had been there. The outcome was complicated.

Mindy's cheeks flushed bright pink. "My friend and her fiancé are flying there to get married. It's so romantic."

Valentine swallowed again, then coughed. "I'm happy for you, I mean them. Well, for everyone."

"While I was at the counter, they were reporting on the first tour bus to stop in Is Brea. People are flying in from all over the world just to get married. It's so amazing, don't you think?"

"I really don't know what to say," Valentine said.

The cashier at the counter called to get Mindy's attention.

Mindy glanced over her shoulder at her work mates still huddled around the TV, then returned her gaze to him. "There must be another bus. Do you need anything else?"

"No, you have been quite thorough." Valentine picked up his coffee cup.

Valentine was halfway done with his coffee when Mindy returned. "Humm, Mr. Valentine?" She looked up from the name printed on a sealed envelope she held. At his nod of acknowledgement, she handed it to him. "There's someone at the counter who asked me to give this to you."

Valentine glanced past Mindy. A Cupid in standard uniform, light gray suit, white linen shirt, thin black tie and black mirror-polished shoes perched on a stool. Cupids were, in physical appearance, androgynous. The Cupid leaned back on the counter with one elbow resting on the edge and gave Valentine a relaxed two-finger salute.

Valentine returned a curt nod to the Cupid then looked at the envelope. He raised it to his nose. He breathed in its scent, the barest hint of fresh-cut lavender, and behind that, a fading tingle of cinnamon. He'd recognize her handwriting and fragrance anywhere. He opened the envelope and unfolded the crisp white paper inside. The letter was short, succinct.

Valentine

    My office, now!

        Venus

Valentine smiled, he loved the way she wrote his name. He returned the note to its envelope and secured it in his inside jacket pocket. He placed two large bills under the saucer and strolled over to the Cupid.

"Valentine." He extended his hand in greeting.

The Cupid clasped his hand in a firm grip. Valentine had forgotten how strong Cupids were. He was sure some of the bones in his hand had rearranged themselves.

"Marcella," she said glancing out the door at the main street. "Just passing through town?"

"No, vacation," he said.

"There's a large city to the south not far from here, Los Angeles," she pointed out.

Her statement felt like an unspoken question to Valentine. This meant Marcella was young as Cupids went, maybe a thousand years old give or take two hundred years. The young did enjoy places full of distractions. Of course that could just be the nature of a Cupid as well. He decided to answer her question, unspoken or not, and provide her with something to think over.

"I prefer small towns, they're more intimate." Valentine considered his preference and why he held them. "Time is a funny thing and you should prepare yourself for it. Somewhere down the length of that long path you become not the same person you started out being."

Marcella tilted her head to one side. "That's interesting, your second statement. As you put it, time could be a stand-in for life."

"True," Valentine said. But, what changes would life have without time?

"And the length of the path is life as well," Marcella added.

Valentine tapped his chin with his forefinger. "I like to think of it as an accumulation of experiences."

"So, in the end you change."

"Consider it an achievement and there would be no end," Valentine said.

Marcella smiled. "If that's what you meant you could have used fewer words. Time, Experiences and Achievement."

"I prefer the longer way. It has more imagery."

"I'd still prefer Los Angeles."

Valentine only smiled in response. He straightened his jacket. "Shall we go then?"

"The limousine is to the side of the café." Marcella gestured over her shoulder with her thumb.

Valentine followed her outside, then around the corner.

The car she led him to was, as expected, nondescript, with no markings or emblems to indicate make or model. A brief glance would register in the mind of an onlooker as unremarkable, though luxurious.

Marcella held the rear passenger door open for Valentine.

"I'd rather sit in front," Valentine said.

"The back is more comfortable, sir," she said.

"Yes, it is. All the same I'll sit up front. Also, please use my proper name." Valentine opened the front passenger door himself and got in.

Marcella's habitual routine interrupted, she paused, then closed the back door. She walked around to the driver's side and got in.

"Though it's a short drive I like sitting up front to watch the Transition," Valentine said.

"I never get tired of seeing it sir. Sorry, Valentine," Marcella said, as she smoothly turned onto the main road.

The limousine crested the hill outside of town, then dropped out of sight into a small coastal valley on the other side. Marcella squeezed a button recessed in the steering wheel.

A bright purple orb of energy shot out of the front grille of the car, landing on the road five hundred feet ahead of them. As they sped towards it, Valentine watched with admiration and a bit of wonder as the orb expanded into a large translucent purple bubble. The car pierced its surface and the bubble popped out of existence, taking the limousine and its two passengers away from this world.

Chapter 2

Before Valentine entered Venus's office building, he turned around to look at the courtyard. It was always spring here. He breathed in the fresh scent of new grass. Birds were busy with the activities that would create mating pairs, the trees alive with their distinct songs. Bees carried pollen from flower to flower fulfilling their bargain to bring forth the next generation of flora. It all made sense, he mused. He was glad that humans were not this trouble-free.

Venus: now that was more complicated. Could she not be aware of how he came to feel about her? Her actions hinted she did but they were subtle yet flirtatious. No words were spoken to make it real.

Valentine considered what he knew about her past relationships. Loves had come and left or been killed. No one began a relationship without hope, not even a goddess. Each disappointment and heartache became a stone in a wall she stayed behind. He could understand that. That didn't make it easier to stand outside searching for a weakness in its construction.

He pushed the large wooden door open and walked in, following the hallway to Venus's office. The rose-streaked marble in this building had the unusual property of allowing the sunlight to pass through it, immersing the interior with a soft pink light. Valentine stopped when he reached the receptionist stationed in front of Venus's office. The desk, a curved semicircle of polished cherrywood glowed richly in the rose-tinted light.

Venus's receptionist, Angelo, was an organizational genius and was one of a handful of humans who worked here because they excelled in their particular vocation.

He looked up as Valentine approached his desk. His natural blue eyes looked violet in the pink light. "She's expecting you," he said, trying to stifle a yawn.

"Sleep well last night?" Valentine asked.

"Overtime, lots of it." Angelo folded his arms across his chest.

"When did that start?" Valentine asked.

"Hmm, recently." Angelo leaned forward. "Can I ask you something before you go in?" He rested one arm on the desk .

"Always," Valentine said.

"You are on vacation, correct?" Angelo asked.

"You know I am. I gave you the request weeks ago," Valentine said.

"You do know what being on vacation means?" Angelo leaned back in his chair.

"Yes, it is a time to enjoy yourself. It can be difficult at times to define exactly where work ends and a vacation begins. Especially if it is a fascinating assignment or, something out of the ordinary presents itself on vacation." Valentine said.

Angelo rubbed his forehead then ran his hands through his thick black hair. "I'm not sure I understand."

"In principle, with work you are assigned a project at a specific location," Valentine said.

"Precisely." Angelo nodded.

"With a vacation you are free to pick your own location." Valentine said.

"Of course." Angelo tried to lean further back in the chair but it was already at its limit.

"And to enjoy the time there. So, if any likely romantic situation could be helped along then the vacation becomes more pleasurable." Valentine smiled as he thought of Erica and Brett.

Angelo let out a breath he had been holding as a light on his console started blinking. Venus's line. Angelo pushed the button. "Yes, he's here," he said into his headset.

Looking up at Valentine he said, "Go right in, Valentine, she's expecting you."

Valentine entered Venus's office. Her taste clearly ran more towards Italian Renaissance than the Classical Greek of the exterior. A tiled mosaic floor stretched from wall to wall, dominated by a large yellow-gold sunburst in the center. The rest of the floor provided the impression of a field of flowers nurtured in the light of the sun.

At the far end of the room Venus waited for him. She sat at a simple rectangular refractory table that had four sturdy oak legs, which served as her desk. Silhouetted in the light of the window behind her, Valentine thought she looked as delicate as a glass vase. He knew appearances could be misleading. If Venus were made of anything it would be diamond, or better yet, titanium. Not glass.

Her dark black hair was braided with a golden ribbon that glinted in the light from outside. The braids were pulled back and fell to the middle of her back. She looked up from her computer screen and smiled at Valentine as he shut the door behind him.

He returned her smile. His sight seemed be absorbed gradually into her dark rich brown skin that held an aura of a reddish blush. Valentine rubbed his chin trying to remember why he was here. He heard the rasping sound of whiskers. He winced at the realization that he had forgotten to shave. He smoothed back his wavy brown hair as best he could. He pulled on the corners of his jacket to smooth out the wrinkles.

The matched pair of Dantesca chairs in front of the desk had a distinctive X profile from his point of view. He crossed the room and took a seat in one of them. "Is there an emergency?"

Venus held her hand up, signaling Valentine to stop talking, "Yes there is." She reached into a desk drawer and placed a golden apple on the desk between them.

"Is that, The Apple?" he asked.

"It is. I find it useful to look at and remind myself of unintended consequences," she said.

"Do you require my assistance with a project?"

"Can you recall what we talked about the last time you were here?" She tapped her finger on the desk as she looked at Valentine.

"You mentioned my high numbers of completed cases," he said.

"Actually, I said I should demote you for incompetence if you did not have the highest number of completed cases," she said.

"There was that," he agreed.

"You are on vacation," she said. "But, you spent the weekend in the library."

"I mean this with all respect, Venus, technically my vacation didn't start until *today*."

"With anyone else, and I do mean everybody but you, spare time in the library would not concern me. But I do not want any more surprises."

"I confessed my surprise to you as well about the last case, if that's what you mean," he said.

Venus pressed her lips together, then spoke. "Our statisticians still haven't calculated the extent of the fallout from that action."

"Action, yes there is that as well."

"A whole town…" she began.

"It was a very small town," Valentine added.

Venus placed her hands flat on the desk and leaned towards Valentine. "Everyone is getting married."

"Except for those already married," he offered.

Venus closed her eyes for a moment and took a deep breath, "Two individuals, love at first sight, easily explained or at least not questioned."

"Of course," he said.

Venus clenched her hands into fist on the desktop. "This has never happened before. There is no way this could have happened."

"Yes, well I agree…" Valentine began.

"It has gained worldwide attention." Venus tightened her fists hard enough that her knuckles turned white.

"Yes, but…" he said.

"It has generated too much attention. Human scientists are looking for an explanation."

Valentine was silent for a moment. "Are you planning to undo this?"

"No. We are not in the business of undoing love," she said. "Also, we are not in the business of instantaneous love affecting a whole town."

"I have offered my help," Valentine said.

"We do not know how you did this. You do not know how it happened. So, you will help by doing nothing." Venus sat back in her chair and folded her hands, "Which brings us back to the library."

Valentine leaned forward in his chair. "During my research of Moonlight Cove, I noticed a couple, Erica and Brett, they will be wonderful for each other."

"Valentine." Venus pinched the bridge with her nose, slightly shaking her head. "I want to show you something. I learned this at a seminar given by a human resource consultant."

Valentine tilted his head to one side, "You took a class?"

"Yes, I wanted to gain more insight into humans but found some of the techniques can be applied here." She paused before speaking again. "Normally enthusiasm for one's job is an asset. For you, right now, there is too much potential for unintended events."

"Yes, I did not intend that particular outcome."

"I have a demonstration of what I am trying to get across." She lifted a pitcher of water and poured some water into a crystal glass to the halfway point. "Valentine, tell me what you see."

"I see a lovely glass. Lead crystal would be my guess. See how soft the light molds around it and…"

"Describe the amount of water you see," she said.

"Well, it is half full or you could say it is half empty," he said.

"Wrong to both answers," she said. "What we have is twice as much glass as we need."

"But, a smaller glass would not be as magnificent as this one. Even the empty space above the water is beautiful in the way it captures the light. Now notice the shift as the glass and water come into contact.

The whole of it, the glass, the water, and light are an elaborate display of the parts achieving more significance than each alone," he said.

A red flush crept up from Venus's neck to her face. She was taking deep breaths through flared nostrils. "Valentine, that is not the point."

He loved how the shade made her violet eyes stand out, deciding they looked as pure as amethyst. Then he wondered why it only happened occasionally. "Do you think we need an even bigger glass?" he asked. "If twice as big is this impressive, then a larger glass…"

Venus sat straight up in her chair. "You will take vacation; you will do nothing."

Valentine swallowed hard. "Vacation, uh, do nothing?"

Venus leaned forward, her hands still folded in front of her. "Think of this time as a sabbatical. Observe humans and compare that against what you have learned."

Valentine rubbed his chin. "Um, observe, yes."

Venus stood and walked around her desk towards Valentine. The interview was clearly over. He rose and followed her as she continued to her office door. "Good, now enjoy your vacation," she said, the sweep of her arm indicating that he should exit. "I'll keep you informed on your last assignment as soon as we learn more."

Valentine stepped out of Venus's office and heard the door close behind him with a solid click.

Chapter 3

Angelo entered Venus's office. "I sent you the update on Is Brea before Valentine arrived."

Venus tapped her fingers on the desk as she stared off into the corner of her office.

Angelo waited a moment, then asked, "Have you seen the report from this morning?"

Venus turned her attention toward Angel. "Yes, I finished it before Valentine arrived."

Angelo cleared his throat. "May I ask you a question?"

"I already know your concern so please sit down." Venus pointed to the chair in front of her desk.

He took the indicated chair. "Do you think it's a good idea to have Valentine in Moonlight Cove?" Angelo rubbed the back of his neck, "It's a small town as well."

"For now, yes. The preliminary data on Is Brea told us nothing, but this update gives us a place to start." Venus turned her computer screen around so Angelo could see it. "This is from a webcam near the center of the village. There are a few more in different locations but this one is the most clear."

Angelo scooted forward, leaning his arms on Venus's desk to get a closer look at the image on the screen. "It looks like a good replica of the Anikythera Mechanism."

"Originally, we called it the Vehementem. Before, what happened in Is Brea, I would have agreed with you, a good replica. I thought the only remaining device was destroyed more than two thousand years ago," Venus said.

Angelo sat back in his chair. "I'm not sure how an ancient astronomical instrument could cause what happened there."

"Think of it as a portable megalithic monument. True, your ancestors tracked the heavens with devices like this, big and small, but they also served a magical purpose in the right hands." Venus turned the computer screen back so it faced her.

"What magical principle could a box of gears possess?" Angelo asked.

"What sort of magic did a structure of stone have?"

Nodding, Angelo crossed his arms. "I see your point."

Venus leaned forward in her chair and folded her hands on the desk. "The Vehementem amplifies human emotion, love, jealousy, greed and envy. It has caused a lot of problems in human history."

"Just by turning gears?" Angelo asked.

"And blood. Some human magic used blood," Venus answered.

Color drained from Angelo's face. "How much blood?"

"A stone shrine, quite a bit, but the Vehementem is compact. A drop is all it needs."

Angelo began to rise, "Should I retrieve Valentine before he leaves for Moonlight Cove?"

"No."

Angelo remained standing, "Umm, does Valentine know?"

"No, and I intend to keep it that way, for now." Venus leaned back and tapped her chin with her finger. "That Valentine was in Is Brea was no coincidence. His methods are not conventional. Whoever did this was depending on that as cover, and it worked until we found this photo."

Angelo nodded towards the computer screen. "A glaring error on their part."

"Or unfamiliarity with human technology," Venus said.

"What are you getting at?"

"The Vehementem use was deliberate. That it produced love on a grand scale was an accident. Whoever is using the device is still trying to learn how it works." Venus touched her computer screen to open a file, "Valentine's vacation to a small town is a convenient situation."

"Are you sending resources to Moonlight Cove?"

"Resources? No, too conspicuous. I'd rather not reveal our hand just yet. I have something else in mind."

Angelo tilted his head: "What does that mean?"

Venus ran her finger across the computer screen. "I see that a Cupid is driving Valentine."

Angelo raised an eyebrow. "Yes, Marcella, there and back. I don't see how that could be useful."

"Let's see," Venus looked into Angelo's eyes. "Arrange for Marcella to meet with me before she retrieves Valentine."

Angelo twirled his pen in his fingers before placing it behind his ear. "I need to point something out. As a friend."

Venus leaned back in her chair and put her hands on the armrest. "As a friend I'll listen."

Angelo gave her a quick nod then leaned forward, "Can you remain objective with Valentine in the current circumstances?"

"Don't be silly…"

Angelo held up his hand, "You request his reports from the field to be delivered to you as soon as they are submitted."

Venus smiled. "It's just business. His methods end up being unique. I'm trying to see if there is anything that can be applied in other areas."

Angelo bit his lower lip before speaking. "I'm not sure how to say this so I'll just state it. You do look forward to meetings with Valentine, and allow him to extend those meetings beyond the time you schedule."

Venus rubbed her hands back and forth on the chair's armrest. "Again, just business. I'm clearing up some points that aren't fully developed in the reports."

Angelo laced his fingers together and rested his hands on her desk. "And you always seem distracted after he leaves."

Venus glanced down at the desk. "I'm assimilating new information."

Angelo rested his hand over his heart. "Tell me you weren't distracted when I walked in."

Venus looked up from the desk's surface and said nothing.

Angelo held her gaze. "You need to come to terms with your feelings for Valentine."

Venus pressed her lips together. "All right, I understand your concern but it's not going to happen."

Angelo tilted his head to one side and waited.

Venus shifted her gaze again to the far corner of her office. "I want predictability in my life. Nice, calm predictability. That is not one of Valentine's qualities."

Angelo remained silent.

Venus tapped her computer screen and opened her schedule. "After you call Marcella, get my car ready. I'm clearing my schedule and going to Moonlight Cove to check the situation."

Angelo smiled, "Of course."

Chapter 4

Marcella should have returned by now according to Valentine's estimate. He sat on a marble bench near the pond in the courtyard where he could watch for her to drive up. This also gave him extra time to think over what Venus had said.

The meeting hadn't gone well. Is Brea had become another obstacle, this one of his own making. Maybe her flirting was a game.

He had a passion for Venus, the kind of feeling that grows into love. He didn't enjoy the thought he was being trifled with. *The next time spent with her, this would end or go onto something more resolute.*

The immediate problem was the information he needed from the library. That was off limits. Though if he had the information, being confined to observing, what could he do with it? *There must be something else.*

Valentine heard a sigh. He looked around his surroundings when he heard it again. Bending so he could see beneath the bench he saw a Cherub sitting among a few blades of grass. It was hugging its knees that were drawn up to its chin as it stared off across the surface of the pond.

"Hello. Am I disturbing you?" Valentine asked.

The Cherub jumped, almost standing at attention. "No sir, I'll leave so you can have the bench to yourself."

"This bench is certainly big enough for both of us. Please call me Valentine."

The Cherub's wings moved too fast to see as he darted over and up to settle on the end of the bench. He was a little bigger than the blades of grass he was sitting in. His small form was powerfully built and the muscles of his arms bulged as he smoothed his tightly-curled hair back. "My name is Sahayak."

Valentine noticed the Cherub's stooped posture. "Sahayak, are you troubled?"

"You wouldn't understand. Nobody understands." The Cherub pulled a flower petal as it drifted by on the air and wiped his eyes.

"I will try, Sahayak. That I can do."

Sahayak threw his hands above his head. "Everybody thinks Cherubs are too small to be on projects, but if I don't get experience I'll never grow and be useful."

Valentine rubbed his hand on his chest. He knew that feeling and he pushed it aside. "I am on vacation but I have a side project I need some discreet help with."

"A project?" Sahayak asked, his voice hopeful, his posture upright and his wings fluttered a little that caused a soft purring sound.

"Not a full project, only some research in the library," Valentine said.

The small Cherub's eyes widened. "A real project," he said.

"Very part time," Valentine added.

Sahayak bounced on his toes before shooting up into the air above the trees. When he came back down he hovered right in front of Valentine's face. "Tell me, tell me," he said.

"All right," Valentine began. "I need some information from Venus's library."

"Yes, yes, what is it?"

"Confirmation on an early summer storm that is to arrive by nightfall in the area of Moonlight Cove." Valentine opened his hand.

Sahayak landed on Valentine's hand. "I can do that."

Valentine smiled, "Remember, you must be discreet."

The Sahayak smiled back. "That'll be easy, nobody pays attention to Cherubs." He then flew away faster than Valentine's eyes could follow.

———

Marcella finally arrived driving an SUV, having taken twice as long to return as Valentine had expected. When he got into the vehicle he noticed a suitcase on the back seat.

"Going somewhere?" Valentine asked.

Marcella was rubbing the back of her neck as she drove, "Apparently, on vacation."

"Are you going to that city you mentioned earlier, Los Angeles?"

Marcella brought her hand to her throat as if trying to loosen a tie that was not there any longer. "No."

Marcella had been more talkative earlier; maybe she had something on her mind. Well, more conversation would bring her out of it, Valentine thought.

"So, where are you going?" Valentine asked.

Marcella grasped the steering wheel with both hands. There was a crackling sound as her knuckles popped. "Moonlight Cove."

"Yes, but where are you going after you drop me off?" Valentine asked.

Marcella kept her eyes forward with a momentary look to the rear view mirror, which she then adjusted. "Moonlight Cove."

"It does have its charms but I thought the city to the south was more to your liking," Valentine said.

"Actually, Venus suggested it." Marcella reached to adjust the mirror again.

This was a new complication, Valentine thought. Also, for a Cupid, a town the size of Moonlight Cove would not have enough leisure activity. He could understand her displeasure.

"I apologize," Valentine said.

Marcella looked at him. "I could have said no, but there's more."

Valentine was silent. They both glanced at each other.

"Look, I'm not a baby sitter so don't think that," she said.

"I am listening," Valentine said.

"Actually, I'm your apprentice," she said. Marcella again reached to loosen the tie that wasn't there. She then switched to running her fingers through her spiky white hair.

This qualified as a complication and a surprise, Valentine thought. He had never had the responsibility to train another. He decided to start by being honest.

"This could be a short apprenticeship," Valentine said.

Marcella sat up straight in her seat. "Don't make up your mind just yet."

"No, it's not that…" Valentine began.

Marcella gripped the steering wheel tighter. This time the crackling sound came from the hard plastic giving under the strain. "I can do this, I will apply myself. Like I said, I could have said no." Her voice had a lower steady tone now. "You're running projects in a way no one expects, but you're getting it done."

"I was thinking about Venus and what she could decide about my last case," Valentine said. Though being assigned an apprentice, he might be around a bit longer, he thought.

Marcella bit her lip, "Oh, that." Then she smiled: "Wait: you'll accept me as your apprentice?" She pumped her fist into the air.

"Yes, Marcella. Shouldn't you have pressed the Transition button by now?"

"Right." Marcella hit the button, and the interior of the SUV filled with a purple light as the energy orb shot forward. "So, what are we going to do in Moonlight Cove?"

"Besides vacation, Venus has instructed me to only observe humans." Valentine said.

Marcella's shoulders drooped a little, "Observe?"

"Observe is a verb, you know." Valentine smiled.

"Ok," she said.

"Verbs convey action," Valentine said.

"Yes," Marcella said.

"So, we will actively observe," Valentine said.

"I'm not sure what you mean," Marcella said.

"I will explain." Valentine said as the SUV pierced the expanding translucent purple sphere that would hurtle them back to Moonlight Cove.

A.G. Reid developed a love for romance books while serving in the military. The stories reminded him of a part of the world he had temporarily left behind. He now lives in Southern California with his wife and their one-hundred-pound puppy, Cinnamon, writing stories about love.

You can find him at http://www.WhatIsLove.zone.

Or email him at AGReid@WhatIsLove.zone.

Maggie's Mystery Man

by

Barb DeLong

Chapter 1

"Well, that's just—seagull poop."

Maggie Henderson closed QuickBooks and shut her laptop with a sharp bang. She forced her stomach to settle its pitch and roll. She'd recalculated her weekly newspaper's financials a half-dozen times. Reviewed assets and, thanks to her late uncle, a long list of liabilities. She laughed. What assets? The plus column was absurdly short. At least she had the rent money due in five days.

The aged printer belched out a sample copy of the tabloid-sized next edition of the *Moonlight Cove Gazette*, the last one for the month of June. Was that rude sound a commentary on the quality of the output? Probably. Not much news in this small, coastal burg right at the moment. But the touristy town held promise for July and August. What she needed were big stories that sold lots of newspapers.

Maggie swiveled in her squealing chair and looked around the front office with its stacks of newspapers and magazines that probably housed a slew of silverfish. She'd get Noah, her intern, to sort and clear all this out soon. How ironic that she had a slight allergy to paper products. The smell of processed wood pulp had her constantly on the verge of a sneeze.

Maggie gazed out the office windows to the trendy shops and restaurants across at the marina. A familiar tall silhouette strolled out onto the sidewalk from the jetty. She jumped up from her chair and parted the slatted blinds. Yes. Mystery Man. He was renting a room at the Moonlight B&B at the seaward end of the long, rocky spit of land. He wore a baseball cap pulled low on his forehead, glasses, plain beige shirt and faded blue jeans. He walked head down, hands in pockets. The investigative reporter in her flared to life. She wanted to know the five W's of Mystery Man. Who was he, really? What was he doing here? Where was he from? When was he leaving? Why was he so, well, mysterious?

Very few facts were known about MM, who had arrived in town two weeks ago, but the scarcity of details only fueled the rumor mill. The ladies at the Scissor Happy Salon speculated he was CIA on secret surveillance. Lily from The Lily Pad bistro thought he might be newly divorced and nursing a broken heart. Well, Maggie was going to find out. She was born a newshound, and her sensitive nose was twitching. There could be a breaking story here, one that could sell a ton of newspapers.

She grabbed her bulging tote bag and hurried out the door. MM had disappeared but she knew where he was headed — The Honey Bee Coffeehouse. Rumor had it he could be found there most mornings in one of the corner booths brooding over a cup of joe and his cell phone. She couldn't wait to see him up close.

Maggie breathed in the tangy salt air sailing in on the ocean breeze — so fresh, so uplifting. She let the promise of another gloriously warm June day chase away any thoughts of impending financial disaster. As she reached the coffeehouse door, the tickly sneeze caught up to her. *Bless you*, she thought. *Finally*. The intense relief was as close to an orgasm as she'd gotten for months or was going to get in the foreseeable future. Maggie savored the moment.

Once inside, she waved to the Moonlighters Book Club members who sat at a round table at the back. The two ladies and one man all waved, then resumed talking in low tones. She glanced at the man in the corner booth by the front window before lining up at the counter. MM had his coffee but was reading a paper, not his cell phone.

OMG! My paper. He's reading the Moonlight Cove Gazette.

Why her heart banged against her ribs, Maggie had no idea. Wasn't that why she published newspapers? To be purchased and read? Well, at least she had her icebreaker.

"Your usual?" Chloe asked.

"Oh, hi, Chloe." Maggie urged her nerves to settle down. "Yes, Arabica. Straight up to go." She stole another glance at MM.

Chloe tucked her dark hair behind an ear and leaned closer. "His name is Nick."

"Nick what?" Maggie whispered.

"Don't know. Asked him so I could write it on his cup."

Maggie nodded. Smart girl. Chloe, with her straight, shiny hair and hunter green Honey Bee apron was always so pretty and put together. Unlike herself.

When she had her coffee, she hung her bag on one shoulder, took a deep breath and let it out slowly. Maggie approached his booth. "Excuse me. Nick?"

In those short few seconds before he looked up, she took in the New York Yankees logo on his blue cap and his mousy brown hair sticking out at odd angles.

Hmmm. A wig? Yeah. His dark brows don't match.

He lowered the paper and met her eyes through plain black frames. She could tell right away he was ill. His face was well sculpted, but flushed. Strong chin with at least a five-day growth, a straight nose as red as his bloodshot eyes. Setting his cold symptoms aside, he was ruggedly handsome and looked kind of familiar to her.

No hand shaking today. "I'm Maggie Henderson. I've been meaning to introduce myself, to welcome you to the town. I own the *Moonlight Cove Gazette*." She nodded at the paper in his hands.

She thought he was going to just stare at her, but then he cleared his throat. "I'm sorry." His voice was raspy.

"Sorry? For what?"

"That this is your paper."

Maggie blinked. A slow burn licked at the corners of her self-control. Instead of dumping her coffee over his head or bopping him with the I'm-sorry-this-paper, she decided to be the bigger man and find out what he didn't like. "Can you elaborate?"

"Not enough time."

"Then let me take this offending rag off your hands." Maggie snatched the paper from him and stuffed it in her tote, leaving one ragged corner in his fingers. His cell phone tweedled as she wheeled around and stomped to the door, but Andrea from the book club blocked what was going to be her grand exit.

She clutched Maggie's arm in a death grip. "Maggie, you're going to want to hear this."

Andrea dragged her to the club table, where she was forced to lean in to hear their frantic whispers.

"He's a serial killer." Dave nodded his head solemnly. Dave was head of the drama club at the local high school, so…

"I'm sure of it. I think I recognize him from America's Most Wanted." Hermione tortured a curl of fire-red hair in her fingers while shooting quick glances at MM on his phone. "He's hiding out there at the lighthouse while he scopes his next victims."

Maggie blew out an exasperated breath. She picked up the book they'd all been reading this past month. She already knew what it was because she'd used the club and their book list to fill in a good-sized gap on page two of this week's edition. The very one she'd torn from MM's loutish hands.

"*The Silence of the Lambs*." She looked at each of them. "I suppose if you'd read a Jason Bourne book he'd be a spy with amnesia."

"Shhh. He's leaving." Andrea laid a hand on hers.

Three pairs of eyes followed MM out the door. She refused to look up. A collective sigh rose from the trio when the door closed.

"Listen, I'll find out who this guy is. He looks familiar to me too, but believe me, he isn't a serial killer." At least, she hoped not.

———

Two days later, Maggie sat at her kitchen table going over her notes on MM. She was no further ahead at identifying him, although she did know a few more facts about the guy besides him being a rude ignoramus. She'd contacted the out-of-state owners of the Moonlight B&B and found out he'd rented the entire B&B for two months under the name Nick Carraday—all paid in cash. He definitely wasn't a serial killer, or any kind of a felon. He came highly recommended. That's all they would divulge. The book club would be disappointed.

Maggie Googled the name and turned up nothing, but figured it was a false name anyway. Just in case the B&B owners were wrong about MM, she talked with Officer Swinton from the MCPD. He did a brief search on the name in his database for California and New York only because she agreed to bake a pie and bring it in. He'd throw in a call to Interpol if she'd go out with him Saturday night. Maggie assured him that wasn't necessary. Oh, Officer Swinton was nice enough—tall, lean, and who didn't like a man in uniform? But he didn't ring any of her rusty chimes. She'd find a way to learn MM's true identity on her own.

The timer pinged on the stove. Her Swinton apple pie was done as well as a pot of home-made chicken soup. The kitchen smelled like the old days back home in Sunnyside with her mom and dad—homey, loving, and delicious. As an only child, Maggie had been the sole focus of two doting parents. She wanted the same soul-deep bond with a man her mom had found, except she wanted at least four kids. A houseful of joyful noise.

A bell went off in her head. Chicken soup. She'd take him chicken soup for his cold, and maybe stifle the urge to lace it with laxatives.

As a matter of fact, Nick hadn't been seen in town these past couple of days. Maybe he was sick in bed. She'd be a good citizen and do a wellness check.

Chapter 2

Carter Culhane sat up on the sofa and grabbed another tissue. He blew his nose, adding the damp wad to the pile on the coffee table. His head felt like he'd stuffed all those tissues inside his nose and packed them in with a battering ram.

His stomach growled. Nothing wrong with his appetite. He really should get something to eat, but instead he lay back down on the sofa. He loved this beachy-inspired suite, but so far this getaway to find his muse had been a bust. He'd written maybe five pages in the two and a half weeks he'd been there. Five lousy pages. His deadline loomed like a date with the executioner. Writing seemed harder and harder lately. Maybe it was time to cash out.

He'd picked this place on the California coast from the dozens his assistant had shown him online. The rustic B&B was attached to an actual lighthouse. Waves crashed against rocks. It even came with its own resident black cat a lot like Felix. Damn. He still got misty-eyed thinking about Felix's last days. The place was isolated at the end of a seawall jetty, and since Ivan had secretly rented the entire four-unit B&B for him, he would be ALONE.

His disguise of chestnut wig, black-framed glasses and brown contacts was lame. He'd never let one of his characters try a getup like that. He hoped he hadn't been made at the coffeehouse the other day. *A book club. Jeez.*

And the newsie. He had to admit, Maggie was very—he wouldn't say beautiful. Unusual. But in a striking way. Great cheekbones. Big brown eyes. Sun-kissed ash blonde hair tied back in a simple, messy ponytail. Maybe pushing thirty. He'd felt a momentary quickening of interest. *Bada-bing.* She was New York, just like him. He heard it in her voice. Same strong-coffee preference.

Then she said the sad news rag was hers. *Bada-boom.* His only excuse for being mean was his disappointment that he for sure couldn't start any relationship with her, a reporter, as irrational as the idea was anyway. And he felt so crummy. And maybe a dozen other reasons he didn't want to think about right now.

Carter sat up to sip some orange juice. Karma rubbed against his ankle and mewed. "You hungry too? Just a minute." He blew his nose again. Now he felt worse than ever, and not just physically. He'd been uncharacteristically insulting to the woman. She was only trying to be friendly and he bitten her like a mean dog.

The doorbell sounded.

Christ. What had he been saying about isolation?

"Go away. No solicitors." What about a closed barrier gate didn't they get?

Carter tried to make out the muffled words through the thick oak door. Sounded like a woman, and she wasn't leaving. She knocked.

He got up, grabbed the wig from the table and shoved it on his head. He had no plans to go anywhere today so he hadn't put in his contacts. He slipped on dark sunglasses to hide his eyes. He still had on his baggy lounge pants and old Yankees t-shirt. He knew he looked rough but he'd hide his body behind the door.

More knocking.

"I'm coming." His voice squawked like a throttled gull.

He opened the door a crack and peeked out. Maggie what's-her-name stood on the step, looking so perky, bright and shiny that he was glad for the sunglasses.

"Hi, Nick." Then she frowned. "Oh, you look terrible."

"Thanks." He started to ease the door shut, but she put a foot inside and shouldered her way through. "You know, you are really pushy."

"Comes with the job." She shot him a toothy grin.

Carter thought about manhandling her back out the door, but his curiosity got the better of him. Instead, he followed her to the kitchen, where she put a large container on the counter and her huge tote bag on the floor. She stooped to pet Karma, talking to her in one of those cutesy-coo-kitty voices girls use on small, furry creatures. He dragged over a stool and sat down. He quickly scanned the open-concept room to make sure he hadn't left out anything incriminating. His laptop on the built-in desk by the window was closed. The shelf full of books held only one of his.

She looked him up and down and then shook her head. A half smile tugged at the corners of her mouth. "I have just the remedy for what ails you."

"A shotgun? Poison?"

"Homemade chicken soup." Maggie removed the lid and put the container in the microwave.

He salivated. Couldn't help himself. Neither could Karma. The cat jumped on the counter. Carter whisked her off into his arms.

"Can I trust that brew?" he said to Karma.

"Hey, I was tempted to mess with it, but I'm hungry."

He felt bad. Here she was trying to be nice. "I'm sorry I was so rude at the coffeehouse. I have a bunch of excuses."

"I'm sure. You felt miserable. I bothered you. You hated the paper, and you're the brutally honest type."

Maggie was New York all right.

"Correct on all four counts."

She threw him a withering glance and handed him a box of tissues when he reached for the paper towels.

"Just being brutally honest." Carter dabbed at his nose.

She went about searching the kitchen for bowls and spoons. He didn't help her out 'cause he liked watching her. Whenever she stretched, the action lifted the edge of her little pink t-shirt just enough for him to catch a teasing glimpse of flesh. He wished he could take off his sunglasses and appreciate the true color of her skin. She wore her long hair in a ponytail again with one of those colorful scrunchy things around it.

The timer went off on the microwave. She transferred the soup into two bowls and took the stool beside him. Carter put the cat on the floor.

He took up the spoon and tried the soup. Thick chunks of chicken, carrot coins, flat, wide noodles. "Man, I wish I could really taste this." He dug in anyway.

"My mom's recipe…" She paused, a weird sound working in her throat. "You know, if you don't take off those dark glasses and that ridiculous wig, I'm going to die laughing and snort soup out my nose."

Carter let his spoon clatter into the bowl. "Now who's not being nice? I have light sensitivity and premature male pattern baldness."

"Right. Well, better bald than —" she reached into her tote, fished around and came up with a small mirror, "—this."

She held it out for him.

Carter looked at his reflection and felt the wig. Some kind of molting creature had curled up and died on his head. He snatched it off. His own dark hair didn't look any better.

"Glasses?"

He shook his head.

"Okay, Nick uh, Carraday."

"Oh, you found out my last name." So she hadn't recognized him. It shouldn't have come as any surprise that she'd ask around about him. She was newspaper, paparazzi light. His head started to hurt.

"Not yet."

Damn. Time to deflect. "So, what's your last name again? Maggie —"

"Henderson. And that's my real name."

"Not married?"

"No."

Good. "You're from New York."

"Yes, same as you."

Not hard to figure that one out. "What brought you out here, Maggie?"

"The newspaper. I inherited the *Moonlight Cove Gazette* from my uncle a couple of months ago."

He smiled. "You should have let me finish reading it. I might have changed my opinion." He began eating again. His nose had cleared a bit and he savored the rich taste of the broth.

She sighed and tucked a wild strand of hair behind her ear. "Not likely. It's probably boring to outsiders. The residents love it." Her shoulders slumped. "I think."

Where was the spunk and spirit that forced its way through his door? He should just end this, thank her for the soup and send her on her way. If she knew his true identity, she'd splash it all over the paper. The news would go viral. He'd have to leave in a hurry. Start those five pages all over again somewhere else.

No. He loved this place. He really liked Maggie.

"Why don't you leave me a copy? Let me read the whole thing. As an impartial outsider, I'll give you an honest critique."

Maggie straightened. She licked a drop of soup from her full bottom lip. Carter almost groaned out loud. Yeah, he liked Maggie too much.

"Are you sure you have enough time?" She raised a brow. A wry smile tilted one corner of her mouth.

"I'll make time."

She shrugged and fished in her bag again. "Here you go. This week's edition, hot off the press." She handed him the paper. "Now tell me, what brings you here?" She got up, collecting their empty bowls to place in the sink. He noticed the way she took in the whole room with a sweep of her sharp eyes.

"I needed to get away from work for a while. At least physically. I check in now and then." *A half-truth at best.*

"What work do you do?"

He laughed. "You *are* nosy."

She came back around the counter and grabbed her bag. "I call it friendly. But, to be honest, I have a purpose. I like to interview tourists. If they have an interesting story, I write about them for the paper."

"My story isn't interesting."

"Okay. If you say so." Maggie headed for the door with Karma close behind.

Carter followed. He wanted her to stay, but he was afraid she'd chip away at him one false factoid at a time until he slipped up or spilled his guts. Anyway, she suddenly seemed to be in a hurry to leave. He picked up Karma, cradling the cat in one arm.

She turned at the door. "If you change your mind, Nick Carraday, give me a call." She pulled a business card from her pants pocket and handed it to him.

On the card the *Gazette's* logo of a crescent moon over a curve of rocky coastline was—okay. A bit romance-y for his taste. He heard the door close.

"Hey, wait—"

Forget it. Let her go, Culhane.

He should have thanked Maggie for the soup. He could breathe through his nose now. Smiling, he returned to the kitchen. She forgot her container. He'd take it back to her tomorrow along with his review of the paper. Just to be nice.

He stood for a minute stroking the cat's shiny black coat. For the first time in three days, he felt like writing. He let the ideas flow. Seemed Maggie Henderson was good for him. Heck, she might even be the muse he'd lost somewhere back in New York between killer deals.

The trick would be tapping into her energy, using the muse for as long as it took, without Maggie guessing who he was.

And without falling for her.

Chapter 3

Maggie couldn't wait to get to the office. She was sure she knew the identity of MM, aka Nick Carraday. If she was right, this would be the biggest story in *Moonlight Cove Gazette's* history. She hurried through the door. Her nose instantly closed up in self-preservation from the onslaught of paper dust in the air.

Noah straightened, hefting an armload of binders he'd picked up off the floor. His well-muscled arms strained. A varsity quarterback at the local high school, Noah was not who she expected to show up for her intern position. She thought she'd get some skinny nerd with little round glasses. Turned out Noah had a passion for journalism and a raw writing talent she was eager to nurture. Plus, he exhibited exceptional initiative.

"Got the stuff sorted into stacks, Mags. These binders and pile of old *L.A. Times* are going to the recycle bin."

"Thanks, Noah. Great." She sidestepped a pyramid of paper and grabbed her laptop and notes from the desk. "Just label the stuff you think I might want to look over. I'm going to work upstairs and dodge the dust." Plus, she wanted to keep the MM project a secret for now.

Maggie climbed the back steps to the second floor and shouldered her way through the door to the flat. The scrumptious aroma of apple pie still lingered in the air. She'd dropped the pie off at the station first thing that morning. Thankfully, Swinton had been out on a call.

She'd grown to love her small place in such a short time. The three-room flat above the offices came with the lease. Her uncle had lived there for years. With what little extra money she had, she'd made the place bright and airy and fun. She'd painted and hung cute curtains. A shelf held her favorite books along with a collection of seashells she'd picked up on the beach.

Maggie loved all the windows, especially the one in the living room looking out to the marina and lighthouse. She'd shoved her small dining table under it and set up her laptop. She lifted up the sash. A warm breeze laced with the wildness of open ocean ruffled the gauzy curtains.

Within a couple of minutes, Maggie brought up the website.

"Yes!"

Carter Culhane.

Maggie sat back in her chair. There he was, a very nicely cleaned-up version of Nick Carraday. Dark, wavy hair, swoon-worthy handsome face, clean-shaven. Those signature eyes: one turquoise green, the other sapphire blue. He must have been wearing contacts at the Honey Bee. His online photo album pictured him with his black cat Felix. She recognized the photo from a gossip rag. Seeing him with Karma, along with the certain way he'd smiled, clinched it for her. She'd hustled out of his place as soon as she could to check if she was right.

Wow! Culhane, *Celebrity Magazine's* Handsomest Man of the Year and Most Eligible Bachelor. Bestselling author of dozens of thrillers, many of which had been made into movies. His latest, *Lost and Found*, had been number one on the *N.Y. Times* bestseller list for twelve weeks. He was the subject of countless gossip rags with a different beautiful woman on his arm for every fancy party. The website showed his trendy glass and chrome New York penthouse apartment—a far cry from where he was now.

Maggie got to work outlining her article. Front page. Huge headline. She'd have to think about what angle to take. She worked for a couple of hours, filling in known facts about the famous author. Thirty-four, younger than she thought. She wasn't surprised to learn he'd been a reporter back in the day. Yes, this was going to be ginormous. Maybe she should think about selling the story to another publication first. Didn't some rags pay ten thousand dollars for celebrity news?

Wait. No self-respecting writer who called herself a journalist would do any such thing. She'd do this the proper way. She'd interview him and ask his permission to run the story in the *Gazette*.

Maggie's hullabaloo balloon burst. Culhane was obviously here incognito, his laughable disguise aside. He was probably telling the truth when he said he needed to get away. Was he burned out? Were his cold symptoms related to a more serious illness? Only one way to find out. She'd ask him, even though she knew he'd never agree to an interview.

Something else besides having to ditch her paper-saving headliner dug at her subconscious like a determined little sand crab. Something to do with Nick Carraday. A vague—disappointment.

She'd begun to really like Nick while they shared soup. He was funny, apologetic. Generous to offer his critique of the paper. And anyone who talked to cats was prime in her book. She had hoped he'd turn out to be just as he said, a guy who needed to get away from some kind of high-pressure job. No one special. A guy she could maybe get to know better while he was here. To vaca-date.

Really, Maggie? Are you that desperate?

She hadn't thought she was desperate at all. She put dating and romance aside while she licked her wounds from her ex-boyfriend Traitor Trevor and got the *Gazette* back on its feet. Her bio-clock tick-tocked, but at twenty-nine she still had plenty of time to find Mr. Forever Right and future father to her four kids.

Maggie heaved a sigh. Right. Plenty of time.

She heard someone calling from downstairs. Noah.

"Mags, your landlord is here."

The rent wasn't due for three more days. Maggie dragged herself from her chair. No good came from a personal visit from Leonard. What could he want now?

Carter checked in the mirror, tugged his wig in place and then jammed his Yankees ball cap over it. He fussed with the hair that stuck out until satisfied he looked somewhat human. His eyes watered with the new brown contacts. He regularly wore blue ones to even out his eye color, but coupled with a cold and a new lens supplier, these contacts felt like he'd picked them up off the beach and stuck them right on his eyeballs. He donned the Clark Kent no-prescription glasses.

Last night he'd rinsed out Maggie's container. He went through the paper, jotting in the margins, circling columns, redlining some prose. He hoped she wouldn't be insulted. Again. Since he felt a whole lot better this morning, especially after writing a pretty decent scene last night, he decided to deliver both to her. Besides, he wanted to see her again. Just for a Maggie Muse fix, of course.

"So, what do you think? Acceptable?"

Karma gazed up at him with adoring eyes. "Meow."

"Yeah, that's what you always say." Carter stroked her sleek fur. Karma arched her back in appreciation. "Let's hope this cheesy disguise still holds."

He gathered the newspaper and container and opened the door. Maggie stood there with fist upraised, ready to knock.

"Hey, good timing." Carter noted her long hair all sexy-messy loose and her wide-eyed surprise. "I was leaving for your office." He waved her in with the newspaper.

"Oh yeah, my container." Maggie walked past him and put her bag on the sofa.

This time she wore navy capris with a white tee. God, she was cute, but something was off about her. Her sunshiny self had gone behind a marine layer.

"Can we sit and talk?" She perched on the edge of the sofa beside her bag.

"I hate that question." He sat across from her in the armchair. His heart did a slow ka-thud in his chest. Karma jumped up on the wide arm and rubbed against his shoulder. He gathered the cat in his lap. "What's up?"

"A bunch of things. But let's start with the most important. Well, not sure it's *the* most important, but it sure is…"

He waited a moment to see if she'd continue. "Let's start with that anyway."

She blew out a breath. "I know who you are."

Damn. "Who am I?"

"Carter Culhane."

His heart rate shot up. A dozen thoughts raced through his brain. Find another getaway spot. Pack. Leave on the next stage outta town.

Leave Maggie Muse.

"I can see you're upset."

"You think? But, hey, you don't have to tell anybody. You haven't told anybody yet, have you?"

She shook her head.

"You're saving the big reveal for the *Gazette*. Big, splashy headline."

"I was. But I was going to interview you first, get your permission and write an in-depth article."

"Was." His heart settled back down.

"I realized you're in disguise for a reason. You don't want anyone here to ID you and let the world know where Carter Culhane is." She sighed. "So I'm pretty sure you're not going to want to do an interview."

"You're right. To tell you the truth, and this is off the record, I hit a brick wall with this book. Damn writer's block. Never had it before. I decided to get lost for awhile and find my mojo again."

"It happens, Nick — er, Culhane."

"But you said I wasn't the most important thing on your mind."
Disappointing.

Maggie fidgeted with the strap on her bag. "Just the usual with a small-town weekly — finances. The paper barely breaks even so there's nothing left over for new equipment, my living expenses. My savings are almost gone."

"And this big story about the infamous Carter Culhane in their midst would help sell newspapers."

She nodded. "But all this might be a moot point. The owner of the building wants to sell his prime location. I don't blame him."

"Sorry, Maggie. I saw a couple of vacant storefronts in town you could check out." He mulled over her problem for a moment. Should he? *What the heck.* "Tell you what. For keeping my identity a secret, I'll help you whip the paper into shape. Not that it sucks, but I have some ideas that'll help your bottom line." He waggled the redlined paper at her.

Her eyes lit up. "Really?" She reached for the newspaper and scanned it. "Oh, doesn't suck, eh?"

"Nah. Your actual writing is great. If you have time now, we can go over some ideas."

"What about *your* writing? Or are you still blocked?"

Carter smiled. "After you left yesterday I had a breakthrough. I think you're my muse."

"Me? That's—great. Glad I could help." Maggie looked at her watch. "Let me call Noah, my intern. I'll tell him to start setting up the next edition. Only the two of us are on the payroll. Well, no payroll, since we both work for nothing."

While Maggie made her call, Carter took a minute to go to his room and remove his wig and itchy contacts. He ran a hand through his hair. *Ah, utter relief.* At least now he had a greater appreciation for what he put his characters through when he disguised them.

He grabbed a couple of water bottles from the fridge and joined Maggie at the kitchen table. She looked him over. "Isn't that better, Culhane?"

He nodded. Unscrewing the cap from one of the bottles, he took a swallow.

"I was hoping the scruffy beard was fake."

"Sorry. I planned to scrape most of it off tomorrow."

She continued to stare. "Your eyes are so beautiful."

"I blame my mom."

"She did good." Maggie smiled, and then sighed.

"What?"

"Nothing. Let's do this."

For the next two hours he went over everything he'd marked in the newspaper. He shared ideas for generating more revenue while she wrote on a large yellow notepad. They discussed the wisdom of going completely digital except for a free, ad-enhanced handbill for tourists with a provided link to subscriptions. He found her to be bright, receptive, funny and self-deprecating. She was unlike most of the women he dated, who dangled their assets from their earlobes and wrists.

She pulled her chair closer as they worked. Her knee brushed his every few minutes. She was a fidgety little thing, driving him crazy in a strangely erotic way. Under normal circumstances, if Maggie were like those other women, he'd have made a move long before now. But she wasn't, and he wouldn't, and knew he'd pay the price tonight in a cold shower and sleeplessness.

Soon they were done. Maggie talked about growing up as an only child in a loving family. Of course, perky Maggie was from Sunnyside, an old-fashioned middle-class Queens neighborhood. He talked about his large, boisterous Irish-immigrant family in Woodlawn, the Bronx.

"So Maggie, what did you want to be when you grew up?"

"A brilliant, respected journalist. I was thrilled when I got a job at the *New York Times*. Wow! The *Times*. I started out as a cub reporter grinding out puff pieces, but I never moved off that desk. I thought I'd come a long way when I inherited my uncle's paper." She laughed. "Here I am in Moonlight Cove writing puff pieces again. You?"

"Big dream—a television news anchor. I settled for being a reporter for *Newsday*, handling the NYPD until the fiction bug hit ten years ago. I loved all the publicity after I hit it big and loved the sweet life in the celebrity limelight. But, for the last year or so all the fast living has seemed to sour on me."

"Really? You tired of the parties, the beautiful women?"

"Not to mention the relentless paparazzi."

Karma took advantage of an available lap and jumped up on Maggie's, circled once and curled up with a purr so loud that they both laughed.

"Any heartbroken boyfriends you left behind in New York?"

"Hardly. I dumped my almost-fiancé after he stabbed me in the back. The traitor went for a feature writer's position he knew I desperately wanted. I know I would have gotten it, but he lied to my boss, then called me a hack."

"The moron. He didn't deserve you."

Maggie smiled. "Thanks. I'm an expert at reading people, analyzing them. I don't know where I went wrong with him." She stroked Karma's back in a way that had Carter all hot and bothered. "So, why do you think you're experiencing writer's block now?"

"Don't know. I have this great premise I sold to my publisher about a crooked cop who masterminds a bank heist of six million dollars. Wrote a general outline, so I knew where the book was going. I got into the first two chapters then my words just dried up."

"How long ago was that?"

More knee kissing under the table. Did she just rub her leg against his? On purpose?

"Culhane?"

"Uh, yeah. About the time I found out one-time friend Jack Buckney had the exact same idea and was going to publish a week before me. My publisher moved up my deadline by three weeks."

"Buckney. Wow! He's such a big name. Coincidence of course." She raised an eyebrow.

"I'm not so sure. In any case, I'm under the gun to get this done within the next six weeks."

Maggie tapped her pen in a steady rhythm on the table. She was deep in thought with furrowed brow. Carter didn't interrupt her process. He loved looking at her.

"Okay. Let me lay this out for you."

Maggie moved closer, disturbing Karma. Did she know she was now within lip-kissing distance?

"A, you hit it big with your first book. Boom. Instant success. B, the parties, the fame, the money and the women were great. You loved it all."

"The women—yeah."

"Three—"

"C."

Maggie narrowed her eyes at him. "C. Three years in the fast lane made you jaded, the pressure to perform grew and grew until you—"

"I can still perform." Carter waggled his eyebrows.

"—reached the breaking point. Your creative juices dried up."

"I hate when that happens. The juices—"

"Culhane, I'm serious." She cuffed him on the arm. "Your problem is not the story you're writing or Buckney. It's your lifestyle. You've realized the way you've been living is artificial. It's not authentic. Your subconscious is rebelling. Think about it."

"And you know this because, uh, you're good at analyzing people?"

Maggie blew out a breath. "Exactly. You are a simple man. No offense." She laid a hand on his arm.

"None taken, I guess."

"I can tell you're elemental in the way you live here. The way you dress here. Your relationship with the cat. And with me."

"And what relationship do I have with you?"

"I'm pretty simple, too. Uncomplicated. Low-maintenance. Good candidate for a muse." She squeezed his arm and gazed at him earnestly. "You've begun to loosen up. You're back to writing, right?"

"Yeah." But he was far from loose. In fact, he was on the way to rigid. Lucky his bottom half was under the table. "What if I wanted a complicated relationship with you?" He covered her hand with his own.

Maggie's eyes widened. She ran the tip of her pink tongue around the seam of her mouth and then bit her bottom lip. Carter's pulse shot up.

"With—me?"

"If I didn't have this damn cold, I'd kiss you right now."

Maggie smiled. "Too bad. I shoulda brought more chicken soup." She leaned forward and kissed him on the cheek. "Will that keep you for awhile?"

"Hardly."

She got up and gathered her notepad and pencils. "Your muse is ordering you to get back to your story, Culhane."

He saluted. "Aye, aye, Cap'n."

After Maggie left, Carter sat at his computer considering what she said. Maybe the burnout he felt about his crazy fast-paced lifestyle was the cause of his writer's block and not the story itself. Maybe a major life change was in order, and just maybe he'd like Maggie to be part of it.

Chapter 4

When Maggie returned to the office, Noah was gone. He had left a small, neatly stacked pile of folders and binders in one corner with a note asking her to look them over. He'd either file or dump them, depending. The room looked like an entirely different space—clean, tidy, spacious. She took a deep breath. No sneezing and wheezing. Maggie would enjoy the place while she could, and start looking for a new one this week.

She intended to get to work on the next edition right away, eager to use some of Culhane's suggestions about increasing ads and revenue-generating content, but she found herself with chin in hand, daydreaming as she gazed out the window. She was so attracted to Carter Culhane. Her stomach did a double flip when he came out of his room all de-Calladay'ed with tousled dark hair and magical eyes.

But what had her walking on sunshine was that he seemed interested in her, and more than just for her muse-ability. He opened up about himself, shown her his vulnerable side. But in the end, Culhane was a world-famous writer, a hot babe magnet. He was out of her league. What did he see in plain old Maggie Henderson? She never fussed with herself. Preferred comfy clothes over trendy. She wore little makeup, hair either loose or tailed. Life was too short to waste time in front of a mirror.

Well, she'd see where this summer fling-thing took her. That's all he could be looking for. She wouldn't be the one to initiate any make-outs, though. She was not desperate. Culhane would have to be the cheek—or wherever—kisser next time. And she'd love it to be *wherever*. Meantime, while everything was fresh in her mind, she'd type up her notes about him. Maybe by the time Culhane was ready to leave town, he'd allow her to run a feature story on him in the paper.

―――――

For the past couple of evenings, Maggie had gone over to Culhane's place after dinner to have him look over the draft of the next *Gazette* edition. On more than one occasion she wanted to be like Karma and curl up in his lap and purr, but restrained herself. She even kept her touchy-feely hands and knees to herself. Dammit, so did he. Had his interest cooled?

Apparently not. She danced around her tiny bedroom. Last night he asked her out to dinner at The Lily Pad bistro. Maggie had a date. A real date. Now was the time to spend an extra minute or thirty on her appearance. She blow-dried her long hair, upside down at that, until the blood pooled in her brain. She left it loose because she'd had a dream of Culhane sensually running his fingers through it. She wore a short, sky-blue skirt, dynamite blue striped t-shirt with a V-neck that showed a teasing hint of cleavage. Maggie ran a blush of lipstick across her lips and test-kissed them.

Take that, lady-killer Culhane.

At least she wouldn't have to worry about the paper tonight. She ran out of time, so she'd arranged for Noah to come to the office later and pop in the front page *Bikini Babes* feature story she just finished, do some final edits and run copies for morning deliveries to the local stores and eateries. It was just precautionary in case she got food poisoning or got run over or Culhane whisked her away to his lighthouse lair for a night of hot sex. All equally improbable, but you just never knew. Had she read too much into his announcement that his cold was gone?

Her cell phone tinkled with a text message. Culhane was outside. She grabbed a white shawl and her purse and floated down the stairs. When she saw him her pulse jitterbugged. He wore khaki pants with a tropical Magnum PI-inspired shirt. He'd sort of shaved. Oh, yes, he wore that stupid wig and those mud-colored contacts, but even as Nick Carraday he jingled her bells.

She took the arm he offered.

He paused to gaze at her. "You look…"

"Awesome? Gorgeous? Delectable?"

"Yes."

"Ditto."

He smiled at her as they walked the short distance to the trendy marina shops and to Lily's. "For a pair of writers, we sure are short on vocabulary."

"Okay, here's something I've always wanted to know. How do men actually shave yet leave a constant five o'clock shadow?"

"It's a secret art form."

"Uh-huh." Maggie was a sucker for the ruggedly handsome, shadow-jawed type.

Feeling the strength of his arm in hers and bumping hips heated her skin. She slipped the shawl from her shoulders. The ocean was quiet but the gulls squawked as the last of the fishing boats drifted in for the evening. A squadron of pelicans in precise formation soared low over the row of shops and dropped out of sight behind them. The competition for fish scraps would be fierce.

The Lily Pad was crowded even at 7:30 on a weekday. After all, it was almost July and the tourist season had begun. But, surprise, Culhane had made a reservation. They were shown to a table at the back and soon were enjoying glasses of pinot noir after ordering the special of the day, abalone with ginger butter sauce. So, he'd noted she'd loved abalone when they talked about the ad for the local Barrell Abalone Farm. It took more than a day's advance planning if you hoped to enjoy the delicacy fresh. He'd thought about asking her out before yesterday. Interesting.

"I'm glad it's hopping in here. No one pays attention. Half of them are on cells." Culhane hunched over, but there was no way a guy like him could make himself small and inconspicuous.

"Wait till next week. There'll be more crowds. The TV show *Bikini Babes* starts filming at the beach for the summer. At last, something fun for the paper every week."

"I'll have to stay out of their way. I'm sure I know some of the crew."

"We'll have to find you a better disguise. Maybe a large old lady with a widow's hump."

He laughed. Maggie thought he'd best tone down that smile. Signature Culhane.

Their food arrived all steamy and savory. Culhane took up his fork. "You know, I'll be only too happy to work on the *Bikini Babes* stories with you. Especially sorting through the photos."

"I'll bet. You didn't get to see the announcement story I just finished writing."

"Only saying."

Darkness had fallen by the time they finished eating. He suggested a stroll along the marina. When he took her hand, Maggie felt like a teenager on a first date with her crush. Hyper-driven nerves and excited anticipation had her keyed up. A nighttime party cruiser full of tipsy tourists caused the docked boats of all sizes and social status to bob in its wake. They stopped to watch as the happy sounds and festive lights disappeared around the cove.

Culhane turned her to face him, taking both her hands. "This is a beautiful place."

She nodded. Maggie felt the railing at her back. *He's going to kiss me. Just be cool. Be cool.*

When he bent and covered her lips with his, cool evaporated in the heat. She closed her eyes, tasting coffee and the chocolate sundae they shared. Her two favorite flavors on lips to savor. And she did. At some point he dropped her hands and put his arms around her waist to pull her closer. She moved her hands to his broad shoulders, deepening the kiss. Maggie's brain ceased to think. She gave in to the swirling, swooping sensations arcing through her, the excited stirrings, the toe-curling arousal. She pressed her body against his. Strong, warm, hard. She couldn't form a coherent sentence.

His fingers were in her hair, lifting, sifting just like her dream. Delicious goose bumps erupted on her skin.

Culhane whispered against her lips. "Maggie, come back to my place."

Hmm, his place. Maggie's brain cells chugged into gear. She opened her eyes. Oh, his place. "I—okay."

He laughed. "Are you sure? 'cause you don't sound sure."

His eyes were watering with a slight redness in the corners. "You need to take out your contacts."

He gave her a quick hug. "That, and I have wine. Really nice wine."

Culhane looked boyishly eager when he lifted his brows and cocked his head to the side. Maggie could hardly resist. What had she said about improbable? Happens sometimes. He held her hand as they walked the length of the marina and the walkway to the Moonlight B&B. Maggie didn't think her feet touched the ground once.

Chapter 5

Carter evaluated his appearance in the mirror. Dead animal on head: check. Itchy contacts somewhere on eyeballs: check. Did he really just put on such an ugly green t-shirt? Must have. He was on autopilot this morning. He got zero sleep last night after walking Maggie home at 1:00 a.m. and here it was 6:00 a.m. He was headed to the Honey Bee for a killer coffee and a New-York-style bagel.

Ah, Maggie.

They'd barely made it through the door last night before the clothes came off. Maggie's body—curvy and soft and willing—had felt so right in his hands. He was no Boy Scout, but when it came to safe sex, he made sure he was prepared. In bold Maggie fashion, she helped him put on the condom, and made the action a killingly sensual experience for him. Making love to her was like mainlining paradise.

They never did get to the wine. Maggie didn't want to spend the night. Fine, he guessed. The streets were empty when he walked her home. The kiss at her door—mind-blowing and full of promise—had him hot all over again. Somehow he sensed that the promise was temporary. She gave herself completely on a physical level but seemed to hold back a piece of her personal self as if she didn't want to invest mind and soul along with body. Maybe he thought she was remote because she wasn't all cuddly afterwards. Didn't want to spend the night with him. Was she protecting her heart? Did Maggie think of this—this thing between them as just a summer affair?

Didn't *he*?

Karma curled around his legs. He bent and picked up the cat. "Karma, all I know is I can't think straight in the morning until I have my coffee. Let's go."

Carter set the cat down outside the door, shooing her off to do her mousing. If he could whistle, he would've whistled all the way to the Honey Bee. Maggie Muse gave him a definite lightness of being. He was writing again, had his mojo-flow back.

The place was empty at this hour except for Chloe, who served him his Arabica and bagel with cream cheese right away. He added a *Gazette* to his bill and sat at his usual table by the window. He was eager to read this new edition, see what she did with his suggestions. He laid it on the table. His face stared back.

"What the—"

The huge headline read "Carter Culhane Lost and Found."

He scanned the article, reading about how celebrity gossip circles wondered where he'd disappeared to, his disguise, and how he'd chosen Moonlight Cove, how the famous *New York Times* best-selling author had lost his muse, and on and on.

Goddammit, Maggie. Carter closed his eyes. A dull throbbing started in his temple. It was nothing compared to the ache lodged near his heart like a near-fatal bullet. She'd done it. Gone ahead and run her article to sell bloody newspapers.

It wasn't that now everyone would know who he was and his peace would be shattered. It was her—betrayal. Yes. Betrayal. This hurt more than, well, more than the 368 rejections of his first book. That's why she seemed to hold something back, why she insisted on going home. She didn't want to be with him when he saw the paper.

Carter stood on stiff legs. He left the Honey Bee and his coffee and bagel. He had arrangements to make. Might as well return to New York and hope his Maggie-less muse went back with him. He knew the hurt would. Against his better judgment, he had fallen for the sparkly newspaper girl.

———

Maggie chomped on her buttered toast—well done with a little char, just the way she liked it. She checked the coffee maker again. Still dripping. She hadn't remembered to set it last night when she'd come in. Now she had to wait.

It was no wonder she didn't remember. She was sure she'd lost a few brain cells between dinner with Culhane and her place at 1:00 am. Jeez, she'd never been like that with a man before. But no one had turned her on like Culhane. Her need was fierce and powerful and seemingly unquenchable.

Maggie smiled. Culhane was up to the task. Her body warmed all over again. His hands and lips were capable and experienced and did masterful things to her body. At first, they both were all hot and frenzied, throwing off clothes, sinking to the plush carpet. Later it was the soft tangle of sheets, the pleasure-pain of sweet, drawn out lovemaking, the moans, the sighs. She only hoped her unsophisticated style satisfied him. It sure seemed to. Again and again.

He seemed surprised she didn't want to spend the night. Oh, she wanted to. But waking up beside him in the morning, both of them languid and sleepy-eyed, bed-head hair and tangled limbs, seemed so—intimate. Like lovers. Real lovers. Weren't they casual summer flingers? She was sure Maggie Henderson was just an amusement for him while he was here. An a-MUSE-ment. She laughed at her play on words. She would treat him the same. That had been her plan right? Maggie was afraid her feelings went way beyond casual.

Coffee done, Maggie grabbed a cup and headed downstairs to the office. She wanted to see the final printed edition that Noah had put to bed last night. He'd been a quick study on the publication program she used. She had every confidence in him that the early vendors had their copies already this morning and the on-line subscribers had access so they could enjoy *Bikini Babes* with their breakfast. Maggie grabbed a copy from the stack by the door. And froze.

Oh. My. God.

She squeezed her eyes shut and opened them again.

Oh. My. God.

No. No. No.

Her heart crunched into a tight bristly ball. An elephant sat on her chest. *Can't breathe.*

Culhane.

How? How did her lousy first draft about Culhane get on the first frickin' page? Any page? *Gah!* It was full of stuff she had no intention of using.

That bristly ball worked its way up to her throat. "Noah, what did you do?" She squeaked out the words.

Maggie grabbed her cell and placed a call. It rang and rang. "Pick up, Noah."

"Hello?" His sleepy voice whispered through the line.

"Noah, it's Maggie." Her own voice held an edge of hysteria. *Calm down. Calm.*

"Oh, hi, Mags. What up? It's only, uh, 7:30."

"Um, okay." She could finally take a deep breath. "Where—why is there a story about Carter Culhane in the paper?"

"What? That's the story you said to fix and put on the first page."

"I—no. I said *Bikini Babes*. The one I sent from my laptop."

"You said to print the big story—you emphasized big. And attached was the Carter story. And man, I have to tell you, what a big story. I left you a text message kinda late."

Maggie tried to get her chaotic thoughts in order. Text message. She hadn't heard it. He'd probably texted her between stupendous orgasms.

Big. She thought he'd get it. Big, as in big boobs. Girls in bikinis. Weren't girls and sex all seventeen-year-old boys thought about?

The one I sent. Omigod. She didn't. Did she? Did she send him the Culhane story instead of the *Babes* story? She rushed to her laptop on the desk and brought up the attachment. There he was. Culhane, so handsome, so rich, so—*furious if he sees this.*

"Noah, get up. Go to every vendor that gets first deliveries. Grab every copy. Rip it out of people's hands if you have to."

"Why, Mags? Did I—"

"My fault. Just hurry." She clicked off and rushed through the retraction process for on-line subscriptions.

Her heart thrashed in her chest. *This is what panic feels like. Don't panic. Maybe he slept in because—well, because I overworked him.* She had his cell number but decided calling was cowardice. She had to go see him in person.

Maggie rushed out the door and plowed right into Leonard. He was nothing but skin and bones and thinning hair. She sent him flying. "God, sorry, Leonard." She gave him a hand up. "Gotta run. I'll talk to you later."

She hurried out to the sidewalk and heard him call after her, "I sold the place, Maggie. But I gotta tell you—"

"Great," she tossed over her shoulder as she crossed the street. Great? She was screwed.

Karma was outside Culhane's door. Maggie took a second to compose herself while she petted the cat. She felt the rumbly purr under her fingers. "At least *you're* glad to see me."

She knocked. Nothing. Rang the bell. *Oh please, oh please, don't let him be at the Honey Bee. Reading.* She knocked again.

"Go away."

Those two words were like a slap in the face. Her heart skittered and fell to her toes. He'd seen it. "Culhane, let me in. Let me explain."

She tried the door. Unlocked. She entered the room just as he came out from the bedroom dressed in blue jeans and collared shirt, carrying a duffel. His hair was mussed, his real hair. In those few seconds she pictured them in bed, her fingers in his hair, clutching and pressing, her body arching into his.

He stopped and stared at her with those incredible eyes. His jaw tightened. "You have nerve. Gotta give you that."

He set the duffel down beside his laptop case. He was leaving. Her heart shattered. She hadn't realized just how much she cared about him until this moment. She couldn't lose him. Not like this. "I didn't intend to publish that article, Culhane. It was just a draft. Noah—"

"Blaming Noah? Isn't he like, sixteen?"

"Seventeen, but—"

"Maggie, you told me you were doing a story. My mistake was believing you when you said you'd ask my permission first before publishing it."

"I was going to, but Noah went ahead and put it in." Maggie went to him and touched his arm. He took a step away.

Culhane blew out a breath. "I could sue, you know." He held up a hand when she opened her mouth. "But I won't. You don't have the money, anyway." He laughed a bitter laugh. "I hope you sell a ton of newspapers."

He turned his back on her and left the room, closing the bedroom door behind him. He called, "I'm in a hurry. I have a plane to catch in Santa Barbara in two hours."

Her cue to get lost.

Maggie wanted to either curl up in the fetal position or flail her fists against the bedroom door. Neither would get her the result she wanted. She headed out the door and down the walk. She stumbled on the rough path, swiping tears from her eyes. No crying. She'd shed a gazillion over the old ex-almost-fiancé. And what was Culhane? A boyfriend? Lover? One-week stand?

He had just become another ex.

Maggie reached the office and realized she'd left in such a hurry she hadn't locked the door behind her. Soon this would be her ex-office, her ex-home. Too many exes in her life. Noah had been there and left little piles of *Gazettes*, each pile marked with where he'd grabbed them. Maybe no one but Culhane had seen the article. Didn't matter. She fell into the chair and it shrieked in protest. A large, hand-scrawled note sat on the desk in front of her. "I'm so sorry! Noah." She would have to call him. It wasn't his fault; it was hers. All hers.

She pushed her hair back with both hands. Holy cow, what a mess! How had she looked to Culhane? A wild woman, and not in a good way like last night. Her pulse settled to a steady rhythm even though her heart was achy-breaky. She'd killed whatever it was they were going to have together as surely as if she'd tied a cement block to the relationship and thrown it off the dock.

Grabbing a tissue, she dabbed away the tears that insisted on welling up. She'd have to salvage this edition and get it out there or she'd be in a worse financial mess. She squared her shoulders and took a deep breath before diving into the computer. She removed Culhane's story and put *Bikini Babes* on page one, fiddled with the photos of the boobilicious star, Scarlett Royale, and double-checked the rest of the edition.

Noah texted her. He said he'd be there with the last of the copies in a sec. She glanced at the clock for the tenth time. Culhane would be at the airport by now, anxious to get home, get away from this latest — what would his Jake Trumbull character call it? Treachery.

Maggie heard the door open behind her. "Noah, sit down. I need to talk to you." Her voice broke, ending on a high note. She snuffled.

The chair by the other desk scraped. She swiveled. "I want — Culhane." Her breath caught. A hundred warring thoughts fought a battle to the death.

He sat in the chair, expressionless, fidgeting with the dog-eared *Gazette* in his hands. "What do you want, Maggie?"

"I — uh, I want…" The battle for comprehension still raged.

"Let me tell you what I want. You."

"You — what?"

"I want you, Maggie Henderson." He smiled.

The ache and break began to mend. He stood and came to her, holding out his hands. Maggie took them and stood on wobbly legs. "But what about the article? My, um, treachery?"

"I had time to read the whole story on the way to the airport. You're such a great writer, Maggie, I could see you wouldn't put that crap in the paper as it was."

Crap? Yes, first draft crap.

"I told the taxi to turn around. Then I met Noah outside the door and he explained—"

"I tried to tell you."

"I know, but I was so angry. Hurt." He touched his lips to hers. "I've been burned by reporters, the paparazzi so many times."

"I would never do anything to hurt you." Maggie wanted another kiss. A real kiss. A toe-curling, brain-frying kiss.

"I know that now. I—"

She couldn't wait for him. Maggie cut him off with a kiss that deepened, went from sizzling to searing. He wrapped his arms around her and molded her body to his. He smelled of coffee and spice and delicious man-scents. Culhane was solid, warm, and apparently, needy. When they broke apart, both were breathless.

"So—" Maggie took in air. "—it's not just my muse you lust after?"

He laughed. "Well, I have to admit, my writing's never been better, Maggie Muse. But it won't keep me warm at night." He kissed her again. "You didn't answer my question. What do you want?"

"My kiss wasn't answer enough?" Maggie smiled into his razzle-dazzle eyes. "I fell for you and your alter-ego, Nick Carraday. I madly want to see where things might lead. But I'm warning you, Culhane, I'm not looking for some casual summertime romance. Are you staying?"

"Well, I bought some real estate a couple of days ago." He held her loosely, his fingers playing with the back hem of her t-shirt.

She held her breath. "What was it?"

"I bought the Moonlight B&B and insisted it come with Karma. I'm going to make the whole lighthouse my home."

"Culhane! That's great!"

"I decided to take your advice. I'm dialing back the hard-partying, author-on-fire. Not doing it for me anymore. Not—authentic."

Maggie tried to keep up with what he was saying. Had she really suggested he make all these life-altering decisions?

"I'm going to finish this book, then renegotiate the deadlines on my six-book contract."

"My gosh. Are you sure?"

"Yep. One other thing, I've become a landlord."

"The B&B?"

"No. *Your* landlord. I also bought this property. Your rent is now a dollar a month."

Maggie squealed. "You have got to be kidding."

"I know you're going to do great things with the *Gazette*. Take the paper to the next level."

The blazing kiss that followed showed him the depth of her gratitude. And it held the sweet promise of much more than a glorious summer fling. Fall and winter and forever beckoned.

Barb DeLong, a long-time member of the Orange County Chapter/Romance Writers of America, is a member of RWA's PRO community. She has been writing one thing or another for as long as she can remember. Her stories have won and finaled in several contests, and she published a contemporary short story in the *Romancing the Pages* anthology (Orange County Romance Authors / 2012).

Barb is currently working on a humorous paranormal romance series called *Charmed by a Witch* as well as a short story for an upcoming anthology. She's excited to share with you the magic of love, laughter, and happily ever after!

You can find her at http://www.NicobarPress.com.

Once upon a Love Letter

by

Jill Jaynes

The taunting cry of seagulls reached Chloe on the breeze that ruffled her hair. She lifted her face to the warmth of the morning sun, and tasted the salt on that breeze. It was a taste from childhood, from days spent running carefree on the beach like the little boy she watched now on the sand below.

Perched at the top of the cliff known as Rainbow's End, she gazed down at the beach: the meeting of golden sand and silver-blue water. It was a perfect day, if a little fuzzy around the edges —it was a dream, after all.

At the far end of the beach, a man and a woman walked slowly together, hands linked, toward the boy. The two of them wore loose white shirts, and the woman wore a peasant skirt that fluttered around her calves in the breeze. The sun glinted off her red curls. The boy ran to them and they reached out to catch him, swinging him between them. She could hear their faint laughter, carried on the breeze as the three of them continued now, winding their tiny, far-away steps towards her. She had the sense, watching them, that they had all they needed in the world in each other. They were complete and happy with nothing more than the sand beneath their feet and each other's hands in their own. It was such a perfect feeling, she ached with jealousy.

Then the woman looked up at her, and as far away as they were from each other, Chloe felt that look to the soles of her feet. She'd never been more seen in her life.

The alarm buzzed her awake. She sat up in the narrow bed and rubbed her hands up and down her arms for a minute, reminding herself of where she was.

Twin bed. Small room. Suitcase in the closet.

Dad's house.

Home again in Moonlight Cove.

Images of the dream wavered and dissipated in the morning sun filtering through the curtains of her childhood bedroom window. The alarm had been a welcome interruption from the dream that had haunted her every night for two weeks since she'd come back here. Every night, the family on the beach was closer to her at the end of the dream than the night before, the woman's features more clear. It was starting to creep her out a little.

She didn't have a lot of these kinds of "visitation" dreams. Most of the dead people she saw came to her in broad daylight when she was fully awake and could deal with it.

And actually, none of that bothered her all that much. She'd never asked for a front row seat to the trials and tribulations of the dead — it was simply something she'd been born with. Like perfect pitch, or a photographic memory. No, she had long ago come to terms with her ability.

Her problem was dealing with everyone else's *inability* to do the same.

She'd promised herself, with this new beginning, that she'd stop worrying about what everyone else thought. People would either accept her — all of her — or not. But she was done hiding who she really was.

She threw back the covers.

Time to get up and go to work.

———

Chloe pulled her shoulder-length brown hair into a ponytail, then ducked through the back entrance of the Honey Bee. She hurriedly tied the strings of her hunter green apron behind her as she joined her boss behind the counter.

"Sorry I'm late, Row." She was only three minutes late, but seven o'clock in the morning was prime "grab coffee on the way to work" time and the line was almost out the door. "Had some trouble with my dad's oven this morning."

"As long as it's just the oven and not your dad," said Row. The owner of the Honey Bee pinned her with a searching look. "How's he doing today? I know these old guys can be a challenge to keep in line. He'd better be following doctor's orders."

Chloe smiled at the tall, willowy woman who looked like she'd be more at home on the art gallery scene with her spiked dark hair and fashionably distressed jeans than in a coffee house in a small town on California's Central Coast.

"He's just fine," she said. "He says 'hi', by the way."

Row smiled, causing the tiny diamond in her nose stud to wink. "Tell him 'hi' back. I hope he knows how lucky he is to have you here helping him. Open-heart surgery's no joke, that's for sure." She leaned closer to Chloe and continued in an undertone. "Don't worry about your schedule — you do what you need to do and we'll work around it. Keep showing up with those amazing scones of yours whenever you come, and I'm good."

Chloe blinked back the mist of tears that clouded her eyes. "Thanks," she whispered. She cleared her throat, mindful of the curious glances from the customers closest to the front of the line. "Got your scones right here," she said, nodding at the container she'd set on the end of the counter.

"Excellent. Go ahead and set those out in the case." Row turned to the gray-haired woman who waited on the other side of the counter. "Here's your change, Joanne. You have a great day."

Joanne looked pointedly at Chloe's container. "Did you say those are scones?" At Row's nod, she dug into her wallet. "I'll take two, please."

"You got it." Row turned to Chloe, who bagged two scones. "See? I told you. I can't keep enough of these on the shelf. You need to double what you're bringing me."

"She needs to do more than that," Joanne said. She turned a sharp gaze on Chloe. "You should think about opening a bakery. We could use one around here." She glanced at Row. "No offense."

"None taken," said Row. She arched an eyebrow at Chloe in pointed emphasis. "Sounds like an excellent idea to me."

"Thanks," Chloe said. The words warmed her heart. "Never know, maybe I will." She hadn't even spoken the dream aloud, but that was exactly what she hoped to do.

She quickly arranged the remaining scones she'd brought onto a tray and set it in the display case. Someday she'd be filling her own display case right here in Moonlight Cove. *Maybe in that vacant store for lease just two doors down from the Honey Bee,* offered the inner voice she was learning to listen to a lot more these days. *Dream big or go home.*

Row stepped away from the counter. "I'll let you take over the line now. I've got some stuff back in the kitchen to see to."

"Sure thing." Chloe turned to the next person in line, her customer service smile in place. "Hi there. What can I get you?"

"Chloe Reiser? I don't believe it. Talk about ghosts of the past."

Chloe blinked up at the guy standing before her. Her glance slid up over the black leather jacket that accentuated his slim waist and broad shoulders, then settled on his face: green eyes, ruffled auburn hair, killer smile complete with dimple. He'd been a heart-throb basketball star in high school, and her secret (okay, maybe not so secret) crush for her whole junior year. He'd apparently grown into the full powers of his charm. "Thomas Stone?"

The smile got bigger, the dimple deeper. "In person. How long have you been back in town? Boy, shows how much can change when you take a two-week vacation. Have you moved back or are you just visiting?"

"Definitely here to stay," she answered. She couldn't wipe off the goofy smile plastered across her face if she'd wanted to. "I can't believe you remember me."

"The girl who helped me pass physics class senior year of high school? How could I forget? I owe my basketball scholarship to you."

A man behind Thomas stepped to the side, flagging her. "Hey guys, nothing personal, but can you catch up later? I'm running late here."

Thomas was instantly apologetic. "Oh, hey, sorry about that." He stepped aside. "Here, Barry, go ahead of me. I can wait."

And he did. He waited for ten minutes while Chloe helped the rest of the customers in line. She learned a lot in those ten minutes. Moonlight Cove was a small town and most of the patrons knew each other. All of them seemed to know and like Thomas Stone, apparent high school history teacher extraordinaire and Varsity Girls basketball coach.

She looked over at him every now and then, catching him watching her as he kept up an easy banter with everyone who greeted him.

He knew everyone's name, and all of their kids. Typical of Moonlight Cove residents—it was one of the things she'd missed most about living here. Yup, he seemed to have grown up well. The girls he coached must all have mad crushes on him.

Every time she caught his eye, her heart did a silly little happy dance in her chest. The teenage crush *she'd* once had didn't seem to know that it should have died a long time ago. She'd better get a grip on her feelings. He seemed like the kind of person who was friendly to everyone. She shouldn't misinterpret his actions as too personal. Surely he had a wife or girlfriend.

Finally, there was no one else in line. Thomas stepped up and leaned an elbow on the counter. "So, Chloe Reiser. I never expected to see you back here in Moonlight Cove." He smiled, gazing into her eyes. "Actually, I'm supposed to meet someone in about ten minutes, so I'll keep it short and to the point while you get me a large coffee and one of your magical scones. If there's any left."

"Oh, of course." Chloe smiled and reached under the counter for the small white bag containing the scone she'd saved for him before they'd all sold out. "Looks like you've done well for yourself, Thomas. I guess I should make that 'Mr. Stone.' Teaching high school and coaching basketball." She grabbed a paper cup and turned to the coffee urn. "Who would've thought?"

He laughed, a deep warm sound. "Yeah. I went over to the dark side. Remember how all the teachers seemed so old to us when we were in high school? And now, here I am." He shook his head. "I've traded in my letterman's jacket for a numbered spot in the staff parking lot. Best decision I ever made."

He pulled out his wallet and slid a credit card onto the counter. "I look at my students now, how they're so sure they know everything and realize I was exactly the same way at that age. But hey, we all outgrow stuff we thought when we were kids—like asking a Ouija board for answers—right?" He grinned.

"Wow, the Ouija board thing. Haven't thought about that in years." She shook her head. Damn, small towns had long memories. One stupid incident in high school at a slumber party and she was branded for life. So much for a clean start.

She set the coffee on the counter and took the proffered card with a silent sigh. "Here you are."

She guessed the seeing-dead-people thing would likely be a problem with Thomas. *For him*, she reminded herself. *Not me*. It was a shift in attitude she was working to cultivate.

She punched Thomas's transaction into the register. "That'll be four-fifty."

He didn't move. Just watched her as a smile played about his lips.

Her cheeks warmed as seconds ticked by. If she wasn't mistaken, there was a whole lot of speculation in that gaze. Very personal speculation. Her heart skipped a beat, ignoring her reservations. "Anything else I can get you?"

"It's really good to see you, Chloe. I always wondered how you'd turn out. Where have you been all this time?"

"Phoenix with my mom," she said, a little breathless at being the focus of all that charm. "After her and my dad got divorced. He stayed here, but I left with her. But I've always wanted to come back to Moonlight Cove, so here I am. I'm staying with my dad for now, helping him recover from bypass surgery, but hopefully I'll get my own place soon." She knew she was sort of babbling, but couldn't seem to help herself. "How's your dad, by the way?"

The sparkle in Thomas's eyes dimmed briefly. "He passed away about six months ago, actually. It was kind of sudden."

Chloe blinked. *Really?* She could have sworn that the figure she'd noticed standing near the window at the front door of the shop was Thomas's father. She rubbed her arms against the sudden chill in the room, and realized that the figure wasn't as solid as it had seemed at first glance.

"Oh. I'm sorry to hear that." She was *really* sorry to hear it. Especially when Harry Stone turned around and looked her right in the eye before she could avert her gaze. If the dead didn't realize she could see them, they usually left her alone. His eyes widened.

You can see me, he mouthed.

Damn. She was outed.

Thomas put a hand over hers, pulling her gaze back to his. "Yeah, well, that's water under the bridge now. I'm much more concerned about the here and now." He leaned closer, crooking a finger at her to lean in as well.

She met him halfway across the counter. God, he smelled good.

"Actually, I was wondering about *your* here and now. Like what you're doing tomorrow for lunch. Do you work Saturdays?"

Well, that seemed to answer the girlfriend/wife question. Unless he was a big cheater, which didn't seem likely.

"I'm working in the morning, but I should be free after eleven if my dad doesn't need anything."

"Good," he said. "Me too. What do you say to a picnic up on Rainbow's End? Give us a chance to catch up."

"Sounds like fun," Chloe said in what she hoped was a calm, adult voice while her internal teenage girl squealed. *Thomas Stone just asked me out!*

"Great." He looked a little relieved, like he'd been worried she might say no. "Why don't you give me your number?" He handed his phone to Chloe. "I'll call you later to set up the details."

"Sure," said Chloe, her inner teenage girl doing cheerleader somersaults while she punched her number into Thomas's phone.

"Okay. Talk to you later." With a last dazzling smile at her, he grabbed his food and headed out the door, brushing past his dead father without a backward glance.

Which was absolutely understandable, since of course he couldn't see him. Like normal people.

———

"You have to help me."

Harry Stone tagged along at her side as she walked the few blocks to her dad's house. He'd been waiting for her, pacing the tree-lined sidewalk outside of the Honey Bee when she'd stepped out at the end of her shift.

Chloe sighed. She wanted to say, "No, I really don't," but that never did any good.

Seeing dead people looked exciting on TV, but in real life, it was often a big pain in the butt.

Ghosts who hung around after they'd died usually had one of two problems. Either they hadn't realized they were dead yet and simply needed to be told, or they wanted help with something. Like telling a relative about hidden jewelry. Or a cat locked in a laundry room. She once had a woman who worried that her oven was still on.

Thomas's father had the second kind of problem. And since Chloe had made the mistake of letting him know she could see him, he would be at her every waking moment until she either helped him or convinced him she couldn't. Once she was sucked in, like now, it was best to finish it out as soon as possible. These guys were on a twenty-four hour clock, being dead and all, and weren't very considerate about her need for sleep.

"Fine. Tell me what you need, and I'll tell you if I can help you."

Harry shoved his hands into the pockets of his threadbare brown sweater. "I've made a terrible mistake with Thomas and you have to help me fix it. I tried to tell him before I died but he wouldn't listen to me at all. He just said it was too late and what was done was done."

Chloe glanced around the quiet neighborhood street lined with pretty beach-bungalow cottages. Except for Mrs. Darby, who was out watering her hydrangeas, the street was deserted.

She smiled and waved at Mrs. Darby as she passed, then murmured to her invisible-to-everyone-else companion. "Start at the beginning. What was your mistake?"

He scowled down at his scuffed brown shoes. Ghosts usually appeared in the clothing they felt most "themselves" in. Apparently Harry hadn't treated himself that well in life.

"I only wanted a mother for my son. I thought I was doing the right thing by sticking out a bad marriage with Miranda after my Abby died." He shook his head. "But I think I ended up scaring him off of marriage. He's had lots of nice girlfriends, but as soon as one starts getting too serious, he breaks it off with them. If he's not careful, he's gonna run out of chances. And it's all my fault."

Chloe frowned, unable to guess where he was headed. She was afraid to ask, but the direct approach was usually the quickest. "So, what do you need from me?"

Harry looked earnestly into her face. "He has to read the letters," he said. "His whole future happiness is at stake. You have to find them and then you have to make him read them."

"Oooookay," Chloe said and sighed. "Still not at the beginning here. Let's keep walking while you tell me. What letters?"

Harry fell into step again beside her. "The letters his mother and I wrote to each other before she died. We were only seventeen when we first fell in love, Abby and me. Her parents weren't crazy about the idea, and we had to sneak around to spend any time together, so we wrote notes and letters to each other and hid them in a book in the library for each other to find. Even after we were finally together and married, we still wrote notes to each other almost every day."

They reached the little house Chloe shared with her dad. She stopped at the steps that led up to the wide covered porch. "Hold that thought and promise me you'll wait here," she said to Harry. "I need to check in on my dad and see if he needs anything. I'll be right back."

After getting his agreement, Chloe slipped through the front door. She didn't have anything to hide from her dad—he'd been accepting of her gift since she'd told him about it when she was ten. She just didn't want to have to fend off Harry's demands while trying to have a conversation with her father.

"Dad?" she called. There was no answer. The house felt quiet and empty. On the kitchen table she found a note from her dad telling her he'd gone over to his friend Glen's house to play some cards with the guys, and he'd see her around dinner.

She smiled, imagining him and his favorite old cronies haggling over poker on Glen's comfortable sun porch. She knew Glen's wife Martha would be fussing over them with snacks while surreptitiously keeping an eye on things.

After taking a minute to pour herself a tall glass of lemonade, she headed back out to the front porch where Harry waited at the bottom of the steps like a lost puppy who smelled dinner.

"Make yourself comfortable," she said as she settled onto the double-seater porch swing. She took a sip of her lemonade. "So, where were we?"

Harry stepped up onto the porch. In a blink he was sitting beside her on the swing. "Talking about the love of my life," he said. "And how you're going to help me save Thomas from an empty, lonely life."

"Well, no promises there," Chloe said. "I'm still not sure what I'm going to be able to do."

"I know you can help me, Chloe. You were always a nice girl, and Thomas listened to you when you both were kids. He wouldn't have passed physics if you hadn't convinced him to buckle down and study. I know you're just the girl for the job."

He leaned forward, his hands on his knees. "My Abby died when Thomas was about three years old. Brain aneurysm, the doctors said." He looked down at his hands. "Just like that, she was gone.

"When I went through her things later, I found that she had saved every one of those letters we'd written to each other. I sat down and read them all one last time, and I knew I'd never love like that again because I'd never find another woman as amazing as her. So, I put them back into the big brown envelope I'd found them in, packed them away in a safe place, and focused on finding a mother for my son."

"Hmm," said Chloe. "I don't remember Thomas ever talking much about his mother, only his stepmother." She glanced at Harry. "He didn't care much for her, from what I gathered."

Harry looked glum. "I know, I know. Believe me, I've had plenty of time to think through all of my regrets since I passed. Hindsight really is 20/20." He gripped her arm, or tried to. He couldn't really touch her, but the energy of his emotion was so strong that she actually felt the pressure of his fingers. "When Thomas reads those letters his mother and I wrote to each other, he'll know beyond a doubt that true love exists and then he'll be able find it too."

Chloe took a pensive sip of her lemonade. "It doesn't sound impossible," she said. If someone handed her a stack of twenty-year-old love letters from a lost parent, wild horses couldn't stop her from reading them. Surely if she could find a way to put the letters in front of Thomas, he would read them. He wouldn't have to know where they had come from. Not right away, at least.

Coward! Accused her inner voice.

Hey, I'm not saying I wouldn't tell him, she argued back. I will if and when I need to. I'm just saying I don't have to lead with the "I have a message from your dead father" thing.

"I think I should be able to help you."

Harry beamed at her. "I knew you would. Didn't I tell you?"

Chloe realized she could see the plaid pattern of the seatback cushions through his scruffy brown sweater. He was fading out, his first mission — to convince her to help him — accomplished.

"Wait!" She jumped to her feet as he blinked out of sight. "Don't go. You didn't tell me where they are." She knew she was shouting and anyone could hear her, but she didn't care. He hadn't told her the one thing she needed to know to perform the task she'd agreed to. She glared around the empty porch. "Mr. Stone! Harry! Where are the letters?"

"Up in my attic," came the disembodied answer, more inside her head than outside of it. Then she felt the air around her go silent, and knew she was alone.

Well, crap. She was going to have her work cut out for her. "Not very helpful, Harry," she muttered under her breath. "That qualifies as barely better than nothing."

At noon the next day, Chloe headed over to Thomas's father's house on Elm Street, just around the block from her dad's place. Thomas had said he would be wrapping up some odds and ends at the property and had asked if she could meet him there to head out for their picnic.

As Chloe approached the white house with dark green shutters, she was struck by how much smaller it looked now than when she'd last been here as an insecure teenage girl. She'd climbed those two front steps and knocked at the door with its intimidating peephole more than a dozen times when she'd helped Thomas study. That was the last semester she'd lived here — his senior, and her junior, year. She'd felt measured and found lacking by the eye watching from behind that closed door every single time she'd knocked.

His stepmother had definitely not been a very pleasant person. At five foot two, she had still managed to look down her nose at everyone.

But now the house sat uninhabited, its power to intimidate gone with the former occupant.

A shiny black, 4-door pickup—Thomas's, she guessed—sat in the driveway with its tailgate down in front of the open garage. The man himself was nowhere in sight.

"Hello?" She stood at the front of the truck and peered into the dim recesses of the garage, which looked to be stacked to the rafters with boxes, bins and furniture. The remnants of a lifetime, down to a few square feet of stuff nobody wanted anymore.

All of *Harry's* stuff, she realized with a jolt. Those letters must be right here, in one of the boxes or bins in front of her. Well, that was a lucky break. At least she didn't have to worry about how to sneak into the attic to poke around. Maybe if she offered to help Thomas move all this stuff, she could manage a little unobtrusive searching in the process.

"Hey! Hi there, glad you made it."

Thomas walked out of the garage into the sunlight, a large box in his arms. His black t-shirt was just tight enough to show off the muscles of his chest and arms as he wrangled the clearly heavy load. Faded jeans enclosed his long, lean legs.

"Sorry to keep you waiting. I'm just loading some of this stuff up. I grab a truckload-full whenever I can." Chloe bit her lip as Thomas slid the box over the open tailgate to rest beside more just like it. What were the chances he might have already thrown away the letters? Well, she would just have to trust that Harry had caught her before the letters had left the property.

Chloe eyed the house. "So what happens to the place now?"

Thomas paused and followed her gaze. "Going up for sale as soon as I can empty it out and make a few repairs," he said. "My dad actually left it to me, but I've got a nice condo down at the beach with a killer view."

"You don't want it? This is such a nice little neighborhood."

"Nope, I'm good," said Thomas, slamming the tailgate and closing the topic. "It can't sell fast enough to suit me."

Chloe clearly read the subtext of that statement. Something to the effect of *never in a million years*. "Got it."

He turned to Chloe with a smile, a breeze playing with his dark auburn hair in a way that made her want to do the same. "I'm ready to go if you are. Picnic basket's up front."

Chloe's insides went gooey under the full force of those trademark dimples. "Okay," she managed a little breathlessly, as Thomas opened the passenger door for her and helped her up into the seat. As he walked around the front of the truck to the driver's side, she admired his easy, athletic stride and the way it showcased all those nice muscles and felt like pinching herself to prove she wasn't dreaming. *I'm on a date with Thomas Stone*.

He slid into his seat and started the engine. "Buckle up," he said, and backed out of the driveway, hitting the remote to close the garage door.

She glanced into the garage as the door swung closed. She needed to find a way to get in there sooner rather than later to look for those letters. "Wow, that's a lot of stuff to go through," she said. "Let me know if you need any help."

Thomas steered the truck through the quiet neighborhood streets, avoiding the main drag to head north to the park at Rainbow's End. "Thanks, but I've pretty much gone through everything already. All that's left either goes to the donation bin or the dump." His fingers tightened on the steering wheel. "My stepmother is living in Santa Barbara now, but she showed up one weekend with a moving van and loaded up everything she wanted before letting me know I could come over and clear out the rest."

Chloe easily filled in the unspoken curse at the end of that sentence. *Bitch*. "Sounds like she hasn't changed much."

Thomas laughed, dispelling the tension in the car. "It's nice to have someone around who understands about all that family drama stuff. And no, she hasn't." He shot a sideways glance at Chloe. "Except that she really went off the deep end the last few years. I remember you used to be kind of interested in psychics and all that when you were in school, but I swear, these people have no morals about lying for a living. I don't have a lot of kind feelings for my stepmother, but it was really sad to watch her blow so much money on that old fraud she hooked up with a few years ago. I don't know why my dad didn't put a stop to it. Oh wait, I know—he was too busy working and being gone as usual." He shook his head as he maneuvered his truck around a stray skateboard some kid had left in the street. "This lady claimed to be communicating with some long-dead relative who apparently had an opinion about everything from when it was safe to travel to what stocks to invest in. For a price, of course." He snorted. "My stepmother practically wouldn't buy a cup of coffee without consulting this nut-case first. Guess she got clearance on what to keep from the house."

Chloe's stomach clenched. *Well, thanks, Nut-Case Lady, for ruining any chance of credibility I might have had.* Her blithe agreement to help Thomas's father was starting to look like a much bigger problem than she had counted on. "Wow. That's too bad."

"You know," he continued, "no matter how much my friends try to tell me how great married life is, I'll never make the same mistake my dad did."

"Which mistake was that?"

"Getting married, of course. Oh, don't get me wrong." He gave Chloe a reassuring smile. "I don't have anything against relationships. But why take a chance of ruining it with marriage? After all, my dad must have liked Miranda enough at the beginning to marry her. I can only assume it went wrong later."

"Told you," said a voice from the back seat.

Chloe turned to find Harry Stone, ratty brown sweater and all, perched on the bench seat behind her. She wanted badly to tell him to get lost in no uncertain terms, but had to settle for shooting him a surreptitious evil-glare-of-death she hoped Thomas didn't notice.

But Harry had a point. She gave an internal sigh. *Another red flag. Big one.*

Chloe frowned, trying to understand his reasoning. Her idea of happily-ever-after definitely included marriage and a family. Hopefully sooner rather than later, with any luck. In fact, here in

Moonlight Cove would be just fine with her. "I've seen some wonderful marriages," she said. "My grandparents have been married for, like, fifty years and they're the happiest couple I know."

Thomas slowed as they approached a stop sign. A pedestrian stepped into the crosswalk ahead.

"And that's great. For them," he said. "For me, I can only worry about the decisions I make, and the effect they will have on the people around me." He leaned his head out the window and waved at a white-haired woman crossing the street in front of them.

"Hi, Mrs. Baker. How're you doing today?"

The woman stopped and peered through the windshield of the truck. Her face lit in a smile of recognition.

"Hi, Thomas." She shifted the books she carried to one arm so she could wave back. "Just on my way to turn these back in to the library." She turned to continue across the street. "You have a nice day, now. And your young lady too!"

"Thanks, will do," he called back cheerfully. He leaned toward Chloe, keeping his smile pasted on and his eyes forward. "Don't take it personally. She keeps hoping I'm going to get married and settle down one of these days. She's always excited to see me with a new girl."

Chloe offered a polite wave as Mrs. Baker made her way to the opposite curb. Thomas tapped his fingers on the steering wheel "Yeah, love is a tricky thing to nail down," he mused. "Seems like a pretty flimsy basis for getting married when you can't really predict how it'll turn out." He turned to her. "Why take that kind of chance?"

Chloe sat dumbfounded. Wow, looked like Harry was right. He really had messed up Thomas's belief in true love and happily ever after. No wonder his spirit couldn't move on. Chancing an over-the-shoulder glance into the back seat, she caught Harry's doleful gaze as he faded out of sight.

Well, at least they had their privacy back. She had a lot to think about, though. Thomas had some serious relationship issues and the message that could help him was coming from someone he didn't even believe in. Alive or dead.

The crosswalk clear, Thomas continued through the intersection. "Mrs. Baker back there is the nicest lady," he said. "She shows up with a platter of cookies at every bake sale the booster club holds." He leaned over to share a conspiratorial smile. "Nobody has the heart to tell her they're totally inedible."

Chloe smiled back. How could a guy who cared so much about everyone around him not believe in love? She could understand a certain amount of caution about the idea of marriage after spending a childhood with a stepmother who was stingy with everything but criticism. But just look at him! He was a teacher and a coach—he basically cared about people for a living. It didn't make sense that he could really build the kind of wall around his heart that he claimed to.

"Sorry I got so serious." Thomas gave a self-conscious laugh. "Didn't mean for that to happen. The good thing is I won't have to ever deal with my stepmother again. In fact, as of this moment, I will never mention her again or waste another brain cell thinking about her." He looked over at Chloe. The twinkle in his green eyes had her name written all over it. "I have something much better to think about right now, for instance." He reached out and took her hand. "It's a beautiful day in a beautiful place with a beautiful girl. Right?" He shot her a ten-megawatt smile that she'd never dreamed would be directed her way. She couldn't help smiling back at him.

"Right."

She looked down at their linked fingers, marveling at how natural his hand felt around hers and how comfortable he made her feel. When she met his gaze, she could tell by the warmth in his eyes that he really meant what he said. And just like that, the adolescent fears and uncertainties that had always colored her interactions with Thomas were gone as if they'd never existed.

Surely he didn't really doubt true love deep down. He was just worried about things he couldn't control. Who wasn't? She pushed down the unpleasant little ripple his opinions had caused in her happy mood, and told herself to enjoy the day one minute at a time. They were only beginning to get to know each other, after all. Time would work these things out.

Hopefully.

She was pleased to find that Rainbow's End County Park had apparently been well cared for during the years she'd been gone. The last time she'd been here, the asphalt in the parking lot had been crumbling and riddled with potholes. Now it boasted a smooth even surface with neatly painted rows of spaces. A sturdy split-rail fence bordered the entire lot. The yellow lettering on the sign at the trailhead listing the hiking trails and their distances looked like it had been recently applied.

Thomas wasted no time once they parked. He grabbed the backpack with their lunch in it and led the way to the trail she recognized as leading to the best overlook of the beach.

Chloe drank in the perfect June day as she followed Thomas along the path that meandered through waving gold grasses and shaded groves of live oaks. She breathed in the scent of salt on the air and wondered how she'd lived so long out of sight of the ocean.

The sun was just hot enough to make the sea breeze feel good against her skin, but not too hot for sitting on the blanket Thomas had brought along when they reached the perfect spot on top of the bluff that bracketed the cove. A little further up, the point of Rainbow's End jutted out in a promontory that fell in a sheer cliff to the rock-churned water below.

"Here you are, my lady." Thomas smoothed the blanket and gestured for Chloe to sit. "Now, you just have a seat and I'll take care of everything."

She settled on the blanket and leaned back on her hands to watch Thomas pull an impressive picnic out of the pack. First came a square, red-checkered table cloth, with matching checkered paper napkins — a nice touch, then paper-wrapped sandwiches, containers of potato salad, Greek olives, ripe strawberries, blueberries, and blackberries, and finally, several big chocolate-chip cookies.

He handed Chloe two wine glasses. "Here, you can be in charge of these." He returned to digging in the pack.

Chloe grinned. "Yes sir." She glanced down at the beach stretched out below them, the same view she'd been seeing in her dreams. Except now it was mainly occupied by the bikini-clad cast of the *Bikini*

Babes reality show, who dutifully trotted up and down the sand under the critical eye of a whole crew of cameramen.

"Looks like Scarlett Royale is earning her paycheck today," she said.

The star of the show was unmistakable even at this distance. If her height and dark hair didn't give her away, her truly impressive, um, feminine charms surely did. There was a lot of buzz at the Honey Bee about the cast and crew of *Bikini Babes* that had set up camp in Moonlight Cove for filming this summer.

"What do you think about all that?" She nodded her chin towards the activity on the sand.

Thomas wrapped his fingers over hers, claiming her hand and her attention as he poured golden wine into the first glass. "I'm only interested in watching one girl at the moment," he said.

"Oh." She dropped her eyes and watched him fill the second glass. She could get used to this.

Thomas set aside the bottle and turned back to face her. The green of his eyes intensified in the sunlight, and she caught her breath at the tiny gold flecks that danced in their depths. His lashes were long and dark, surely the envy of his many female admirers. Would he lower them if he leaned in to kiss her? How would those perfectly sculpted lips feel against hers?

"Chloe?"

She jumped, coming back to herself and realizing that those eyes were watching her with a question in them.

"Sorry. What were you saying?"

"You okay? You seem a little preoccupied."

"I'm fine. Great, actually. I'm just, I don't know, a little overwhelmed right now." She laughed at his frown of concern. "I'm so glad to be back here in Moonlight Cove, and especially glad that I ran into you." She waved one hand at their surroundings. "This is all so beautiful." *And so are you.* "I'm just trying to drink it all in."

"Well, I'm glad you're back in Moonlight Cove, too." His eyes warmed as he leaned in closer. "Let's toast." He lifted his glass a bit. "To being back in Moonlight Cove, and second chances."

He touched his glass to hers with a delicate *clink*. Copying his motions, she took a sip of her wine. The crisp, citrus tang of the liquid swirled in her mouth, while his words swirled in her brain. She didn't know which was more intoxicating. *Second chances.*

She unwrapped a sandwich. Turkey, bacon and avocado. "Yum, Thomas. You know how to throw a picnic."

"Glad you approve, but the credit belongs to Herman's Deli. Here, have some potato salad."

"Was there a *first* chance?" The words were out of her mouth before she could weigh them. Her better judgement tried vainly to snatch them back, but another part of her felt strangely liberated by expressing exactly what she thought.

His lips curved. "I've always had a crush on you, Chloe Reiser. Didn't you know that?"

Chloe felt her mouth drop open. "You did not!" More unfiltered words, but this time her astonishment trampled over her caution unchecked.

He laughed at her shocked expression. "Well, it's true, even though you have every right not to believe me, since I was too young and stupid to act on it." He bit into his own sandwich, then chewed thoughtfully and swallowed. "You were all long brown hair, big brown eyes — and the nicest girl I ever knew. It never occurred to me that you would just leave town one day and never come back." He shook his head. "Boy, I really blew that one."

Chloe blinked, not sure how to respond. "Thomas, don't make fun of me. It's not kind. There's no way you had a crush on me. First of all, you were the most popular guy in school. You didn't even know I was alive until I started tutoring you. Secondly, I think I would have known it."

Thomas reached out to smooth a strand of hair out of her eyes. The spark that jumped from her skin at the touch of his fingers had nothing to do with electricity and everything to do with chemistry.

"It's definitely my fault you didn't know it, Chloe," he said. "But just because I didn't act on it doesn't mean it wasn't true. You're right, I was pretty much at the top of the food chain in high school. I may have been popular, but in some ways, it wasn't a really great time for me and I didn't have many close friends." He looked over the ocean and frowned.

"My stepmother was never intentionally nice to anyone, as far as I ever saw. Actually I wasn't even allowed to have friends over to the house. Ever. Which was fine with me. I didn't want to be there either. I think you were pretty much the only exception because my dad was willing overrule my stepmother to make sure I passed that one class."

Chloe picked up the container of berries and poked at the contents with a plastic fork while she considered how to frame her next question. "What about your dad? I remember he came out and said hi to me a couple of times when I came over. He seemed pretty nice."

Thomas shrugged. "He was hardly ever there. He was always either working or traveling for work. Even when he was home, he barely came out of his office. He never came to a single one of my games when I was in high school. To the outside world, we looked like a perfect family. The inside wasn't so pretty, so I kept that to myself."

Poor Thomas. She'd been aware of a fair amount of tension in his house when she'd been over at that time, but she hadn't realized how deep it went. "I went through a little bit of the same thing, so I know how that feels." Using a plastic fork, Chloe speared a ripe blackberry and popped it into her mouth where it dissolved on her tongue. "My parents fought a lot before the divorce. I didn't even want to be at home, let alone invite anyone else over." Not that she'd had any friends to invite. Her teenage years had been a confusing time for her as she'd struggled to cope with her growing abilities to communicate with the dead. She'd hidden behind her studies in school, keeping well back from most social activities. Getting to know Thomas had been an accidental exception. She tucked her hair behind one ear and cleared her throat. "Actually, that was around the time I started tutoring you. I was glad for a reason to get out of the house."

"Wow, Chloe, I never realized. Of course it makes sense looking back at now. You moved away right after school got out that summer." He shook his head. "Just another selfish kid thing. It was all about me back then."

"Well, you seem to have turned out pretty good for a selfish kid." She held out the container of berries to Thomas.

Thomas plucked a strawberry from the container, then pushed it back to her. "Yeah, well I was lucky. My home life may have sucked, but I had a couple of really great teachers who cared about me and made sure that I succeeded. That's what made me want to be a teacher—to make that kind of a difference for kids who need it."

He caught her gaze. Held it. "I'm sorry I didn't realize you were going through a bad time yourself. I was just glad you were around. I always felt like I could let my guard down around you and just be myself. It was such a relief. I didn't need to impress you. Heck, I couldn't impress you—you were so much smarter than me in school."

Chloe did her best to suppress the smile that fought to break out over her face. Thomas was worried about impressing *her*? Not an idea that had ever crossed her mind.

She waved a dismissive hand. "Don't worry about it. We were both just kids, stuck in the middle of our parents' bad decisions. Plus, I really didn't have it that bad. Once my Mom and Dad split, they were a lot nicer to each other."

Thomas set his glass down and took her hand. "Except that you got dragged off to Arizona. At least I had some choice about where I ended up."

Entranced by the sensation of Thomas's thumb stroking the back of her hand, Chloe dragged her attention back to his words.

"Oh, it didn't turn out so bad for me," she said. "Arizona was okay. After high school I tried some classes at the local college and discovered I had a real passion for baking. There are some great culinary schools in Arizona, and I ended up getting a degree at one of them in Baking and Pastry Arts."

"Wow, culinary school, huh? Like Cordon Bleu or something?"

She laughed. "Actually yes, that's exactly where I went. There's one in Scottsdale."

He gave a low whistle. "I'm impressed. I've never met a real pastry chef before. Have you gotten work in that field?"

"Oh, I've got a long way to go before I'm a chef. School gets you training in all the fundamentals, but it's just a start. It can take years for someone to work their way up to being a real chef. For a while I worked at a high-end restaurant at a resort in Scottsdale. That was a great experience to see how a large place is professionally run. I learned a lot. But after about a year, I got a chance to work for a woman who opened a cupcake shop in Phoenix, and that was amazing. I was allowed to be creative and try new things. I'll tell you, you find out right away what customers like or don't."

"Do you think you'd ever like to have your own business, then?"

Chloe looked away from Thomas's intent gaze, torn. She'd never admitted her dream aloud to anyone, as if speaking the words would dispel the fragile vision she cherished. "You know, having my own bakery is something I've dreamed of for so long, I'm afraid to even say it out loud."

"Why? What are you afraid of?" Thomas's voice was as gentle as the touch of his hand.

She looked down at their interlinked fingers. "I don't know. Have you ever heard that saying that when you say something out loud, if it's bad it happens, but if it's good it goes away? I guess I'm afraid that admitting it will scare it away, or something."

"Sounds to me like your dream is strong enough to take it, Chloe. You just told me. How do you feel?"

She smiled. "Pretty good, actually." She took in an expansive breath, the fear that usually tightened her chest when she looked too closely at this dream gone. "Maybe I should have done this a long time ago."

"I think speaking a dream out loud, especially to someone you trust, makes it stronger. It's like, when you say it out loud you're making a commitment to make it happen. The only scary thing about it, is that now you've taken responsibility for whether it succeeds or fails."

Chloe wondered if Thomas could hear himself. How could he really not believe in love if he understood all about how making a commitment was taking responsibility to make your dream happen?

"It feels more like power to me," said Chloe. "Now that I've said it and owned it, I can't wait to make it happen. Maybe I was the only one in the way of it all along."

Thomas grinned. "I can't wait to see your bakery." His smile faded, and a frown creased his brow. "Wait, it's going to be here in Moonlight Cove, isn't it?"

"Absolutely." Chloe jumped to her feet, unable to contain the excitement that coursed through her as she gave her vision wings.

She could picture exactly what her bakery would look like, inside and out. From the hand-painted lettering arched across the front picture window, to the white wrought-iron legs on the ice-cream parlor chairs beside small round tables. It would be a perfect addition to the other one-of-a-kind shops that graced the brick sidewalks of Main Street.

She leaned down to grab her wine glass, lifting it in a toast. "Here's to making my own decisions. Hopefully good ones." She laughed.

Thomas reached up to touch his glass to hers. "I'll drink to that," he said. He took her free hand and tugged her back down to sit beside him. "As long as giving me another chance is one of them."

Chloe watched him watching her as she took a sip of her wine. Her heart swelled with hope and possibilities. "Well, when you put it that way, how can I say no?"

"Good. Excellent." A smile broke over his face, erasing the little frown lines between his brows. "This is turning out to be a really great day. And there's nowhere to go but up." He drew a fragrant chocolate chip cookie from a white bag and offered it to her. "I'd say this calls for a cookie."

"I'd say you're right," Chloe gave the treat a visual once-over before taking a big bite. She couldn't help it. Her training had become second nature for her. *Not bad.* It was thick and soft and just the right amount of chewy, with plenty of chocolate chips. "Where'd you get them?"

"Herman's Deli gets them from a bakery in Santa Barbara. He never has enough to suit me." Thomas closed his eyes as he savored his bite. "Mmmmmm. These are my favorite."

"Mine are better," said Chloe, taking another bite. "This is pretty good, though."

Thomas laughed. "Well that was fast. From timid to bragging at the speed of light."

"I'm not bragging. It's just the truth. Mine *are* better than this. And I never said I was timid about baking." She wiped crumbs from her palms. "I'm a little nervous about opening my own shop. Okay, maybe a lot nervous. But I'm not going to let that stop me."

After a while they packed up their picnic and meandered along trails that brought them through shady groves of trees, where the tangled underbrush surely housed a zoo's worth of wild creatures, and then walked them along cliff tops for a panoramic view of the ocean.

Thomas needed little urging from Chloe to talk about his work, his students and the girls he coached. The obvious pride in his voice showed Chloe that giving to others, especially to kids, was not only a core value to him, it made him happy. It fulfilled him.

His heart was so full of love and giving that she ached for him. Because as much as he gave to others, she could tell by what he chose to share that there was a big chunk of the equation missing. He clearly didn't allow anyone to give to him. He had kept that vulnerable, secret self locked safely away for twenty-eight years, and clearly had no intention to change.

She longed to be the one to make him want to unlock that carefully guarded door. Because she knew from painful experience that the only one who could open that door was him.

It very well might take something big, something life-changing, to make him change his mind. Change his heart.

Somewhere along the walk, Thomas took possession of Chloe's hand. And when they entered the shelter of another grove of trees, he pulled her to the side of the trail to stop beneath the canopy of a sturdy, gnarled oak.

"It's kind of private here, don't you think?" He took her other hand, turning her towards him.

"Very," Chloe said, pushing the word past the butterflies beating in her chest. She searched his face, trying to read his thoughts. Could she be the one he opened his heart for? Or was she just chasing heartbreak?

"Nobody around to see this," he murmured as he leaned down.

Their lips met, and there was no room for thinking or worry about whether anyone saw them or not.

Thomas's lips were firm and soft at the same time. His kiss was light, caressing. He took it slow, giving her time to get used to him, as if she might spook. Like he had all the time in the world to learn her better.

He tasted, explored, lifted away, and came back for more nibbles, more tastes.

Chloe had been kissed before, plenty of times. But it had never been like this with anyone else.

She held her breath, not thinking, only feeling. Tasting him back. Listening to the hum of her senses build with every touch of his mouth. The only other parts of their bodies that connected were their linked fingers.

He made her want more. So much more.

He pulled back at last. "Wow," he breathed.

"Yeah," she said. "Wow."

Thomas stepped closer, putting his arms around her. "You are kind of amazing, Chloe Reiser."

The feel of his arms circling her, his strong body pressed up against hers, was like coming home. He made her feel wanted. He made her feel safe.

He made her want to do that for him.

"I could kick my teenage-self's butt for letting you get away the first time, but you're back now and I'm not going to waste any more time." He touched the pad of his thumb to her lower lip. "I'm going to kiss you again, if that's all right with you."

"Yes, please —" was all she got out before his mouth closed over hers. She gave herself over to the feeling of completion that came with it.

She wrapped her arms around him, ran her hands over the muscles that tensed in his back, his shoulders. She could feel the answering hum in his body that he had caused in hers. Little shockwaves of pleasure buzzed through her veins, pumped by her racing heart.

At last, he pulled back and rested his forehead against hers. He looked as rumpled and breathless as she felt. "God, Chloe. You make me hot all over." He laughed. "And here I thought you were a nice girl."

"I *am* a nice girl."

He smoothed her hair back from her forehead, then cradled her cheek with his palm. "The nicest," he said, looking deep into her eyes. "And that's the truth."

"So are you," she answered, then smiled. "Nice, I mean."

The afternoon shadows stretched before them by the time they reached the asphalt of the parking lot, and they walked slowly towards Thomas's truck, fingers linked, shoulders bumping.

Chloe basked in the glow of both a new-found feeling of closeness, and the anticipation of more to follow. Judging from the way Thomas literally dragged his feet, he didn't want this date to come to an end any sooner than she did.

They had made a beginning. Of what, they would have to see.

A little cloud prodded at the back of her mind, insisting on spoiling her pleasant thoughts. *How far are you going to let things go before you tell him the truth? Is what he thinks going to be more important than being who you are?* Chloe pushed the thought away. She didn't have to make every decision right this minute. This was only their first date, for goodness' sake.

She looked up. They were almost to Thomas's truck.

Harry Stone was waiting for them, sitting on one of the boxes in the back of the truck, elbows resting on his knees. As soon as she made eye contact with him, he jumped to his feet and began waving his arms.

"Chloe! Chloe! They're here! The letters are right *here!*" He hopped up and down, pointing at the box he'd been sitting on.

Chloe glanced at Thomas, who was unaware that his dead father was doing jumping jacks in the bed of his truck. He met her eye and smiled. She smiled back, her mind racing as she sorted through her options.

As Thomas walked her to the passenger side of the truck to open her door, she stopped and put a hand on the box Harry was fixated on and looked directly at him. *I'll take care of this.* He seemed to get the message, because he faded silently away once more.

"What are you planning to do with these?" She kept her tone as casual as she could manage. "Taking them back to your place?"

"No, these are going to the dump. Just junk." He paused, his hand on the door handle. "You could come with me—just for the ride, that is."

"Um," said Chloe, stalling.

What if she went to the dump with him, then "accidentally" drop the box while moving it, exposing the contents, which she would happen to pick up and discover were long-lost love letters written by his parents? Or maybe she could think of some reason he should open the box to just double-check for something important. Or she could...

Thomas grinned at her hesitation. "Hey, don't worry about it. I'll take care of it on my own time." He pulled the door open for her. "I know, I'm a hopeless romantic, inviting a girl to go to the dump with me. No wonder I'm still single, huh?"

"It's not that—" she said, but broke off when her cell phone began to ring. Pulling it out of her pocket, her heart jumped into her throat at the number on the screen. She'd made sure her dad's friends had her number in case of an emergency. But this was the first time one of them had used it.

"Sorry, gotta take this," she said as she turned away to answer it. "Hi, Glen. What's going on?" She forced herself to keep her voice calm in spite of the panic that clutched her chest.

"Hey, Chloe." The voice on the other end of the line was apologetic. "Sorry to bother you, but your dad has me a little worried. He's here at my place and he says it's nothing, but he keeps kinda wincing and grabbing at his chest every so often. Maybe you should come take him to see someone. He doesn't know I'm calling. You know how he is."

"Thanks, Glen. I'll be there as soon as I can."

She ended the call and turned to find Thomas regarding her solemnly.

"Your dad?"

"Yeah. Sorry, I've got to get home and get him to a doctor. I hate that this happened when I wasn't there."

"Yeah, problems never wait for a convenient time, do they?"

She shook her head and stared down at her phone. "I should have been there. He's the whole reason I'm even in Moonlight Cove right now. You'd think I could keep my priorities straight."

She looked up at Thomas, who was still holding the passenger door open for her, waiting for her to climb into the truck.

Keep your priorities straight, Chloe.

There was just something about a life or death threat to a loved one that put things in their proper perspective like nothing else could.

And everything was perfectly clear and obvious.

Thomas needed to read those letters, or he might not ever get over his fears about getting married.

And she needed to be true to herself. If Thomas couldn't accept her for who she was, all of her, it was better to know now than later, because she definitely deserved a man who could take some of the craziness that was her life. Maybe even support her when she needed it.

She was out of time for diplomacy, so the direct approach would have to do. She plunged in.

"Before we go, there's something I have to tell you. In fact, it's better if I just show you."

"Sure, Chloe. Okay." He frowned. "Don't you need to get going?"

"Yes I do, so we're going to make this quick." Breathing past the painful thump of her heart at what she was about to do, she stepped to the side of the truck, reached over and patted the box Thomas's father had pointed at. "I need to you to open this box."

Thomas raised an eyebrow. "You want me to open up this box of junk I cleared out of my dad's attic," he said in the tone one would use to placate an unreasonable child.

"Yes. Now please."

"Okaaaay." He reached into the bed of the truck, lifted out the box and set it on the ground between them. He pulled open the folded-over flaps, revealing a tossed clutter of papers that filled it to the top. "Now what?"

She swallowed. "Somewhere in there is a large brown envelope. We need to find it."

He frowned. "What is this about, Chloe?"

She wrapped her fingers around the phone in her hand, holding onto her resolve as she watched Thomas slip away from her. He wasn't going to take this well. "I'd be happy to dig for it if you don't want to, but we need to move this along. I've got to get to my dad. Trust me, this is important, or I wouldn't be asking."

"Fine." His lips a thin line, he reached into the box and sifted through the contents until he withdrew a large brown envelope, wrapped with several disintegrating rubber bands. "This it?"

"I think so," said Chloe. "Open it. There should be letters inside."

Thomas pulled out what looked like several bundles of folded pages, each bundle tied with a simple piece of string. He looked at her. "Are these yours?"

"No, they're yours. Or they're yours now. They were written by your parents to each other. You need to read them."

He flung the letters and the envelope back into the box. "I don't need to read anything my dad and stepmother wrote to each other." He shoved the flaps of the box closed, and lifted it to toss it into the bed of the truck. "I had a bellyful of them my whole life."

"Not your stepmother, Thomas. Your mother."

He stopped mid-toss, staring at her. "What do you know about my mother?"

Chloe looked him straight in the eye and swallowed her pain at the wall of disbelief she met there. There was nothing to gain by hedging now. He was as good as gone to her. "I know she died of a brain aneurysm when you were about three. I know that your parents loved each other very deeply. It's in those letters."

"How do you know what she died of?" His tone was belligerent. "I only found out about it myself about a year ago when my dad kept trying to talk to me about love and marriage and a bunch of stuff he never knew *anything* about."

No matter how many times she faced this reaction, it was hard not to take it personally. Right now it was impossible.

At least he had set the box down again.

"I'm sorry this is painful for you." She was really sorry, because painful as it might be for him, it was killing her to lose him like this. But not only had she made a promise to Harry Stone, it was a promise she believed in.

She took a deep breath and hoped he'd be able to hear her over his defensiveness. "I don't think anything about this will be easy, but you need to read those letters so you can see for yourself that your mother and father truly loved each other and made a marriage and a family out of that love."

She pulled the box open and picked up the brown envelope. She held it out to Thomas. "They would want you to have that too, the same happiness they found in each other, but you need to start by believing it's possible. Read the letters—they are what's left of their love." She paused, shook her head. "No, actually, *you* are what's left of their love."

For a moment, Thomas only stared at her. The defensiveness seemed to have moved down a notch to disbelief. She could see an inner struggle taking place as he dropped his gaze to the letters she held out to him.

He reached out and took them.

Chloe released the breath she'd been holding. Thank goodness, curiosity seemed to have gotten the upper hand in the debate she knew he must be having with himself. She watched as he pulled out a letter from one of the bundles, opened it to scan the writing. Then he folded it back up and stuck all the bundles back into the brown envelope. She noted that he held onto the envelope rather than tossing it back into the box. A good sign, she thought. Maybe they could wrap this up. She really needed to get going.

"I have two questions for you." He crossed his arms and planted his feet shoulder width apart.

She squared her shoulders at the challenge in every line of his body. She knew what was coming. "In the interest of time, I'll take a wild guess that you want to know how I knew about the letters and how I knew they were in the box. Right?"

"You don't need to be a psychic to know that."

"I'm not a psychic. I'm a medium. I don't tell the future, I just see the dead. And talk to them sometimes. And the answer to both of your questions is the same. Your father told me."

He appeared to think about this. "Was it one of the times you came over to help me study? I know he always liked you, Chloe. Did he confide in you then and you've just kept this to yourself all these years?"

She turned away, unable to watch the light die out of his eyes when she threw this last-chance lifeline back in his face. "He told me about the letters yesterday, and where they were about ten minutes ago. So, if that's all, I'd really appreciate if we could get going now. I need to get to my dad."

She climbed into the truck and pulled the door closed behind her. She swallowed back the lump of tears in her throat as Thomas walked around the front of the truck to the driver's side, studiously avoiding any and all eye-contact. *We could have been good together.* She wondered which was worse—being honest up front and watching a dream die before it had a chance to come alive or wrecking her heart on another relationship doomed to fail when she later confessed the truth about her abilities. *Surely the second*, she told herself.

Maybe in a couple of weeks she'd believe it.

———————

Chloe sat atop the bluff at Rainbow's End, arms clasped around her drawn-up knees, and watched the sun sink toward the ocean in a blaze of pink clouds. The beach below was empty of all but a few couples enjoying the same view as they strolled the damp sand near the water's edge.

She'd come here a lot in the last week, to walk and try to clear her head when she couldn't outrun thoughts of what had happened, and not happened, between her and Thomas.

Apparently, watching over her dad to make sure he followed doctor's orders and didn't over-do again, working at the Honey Bee five hours a day, and a fair amount of baking-therapy weren't quite enough to banish the events of that day.

She hadn't heard a word from Thomas since he'd taken the letters. She didn't know if he'd read them or tossed them or burned them. He hadn't called and she hadn't seen him at the Honey Bee. Even Harry was curiously silent.

Only the dreams continued.

She guessed now that the family who strolled that dream landscape was Thomas's, a shimmering remnant of his mother's memories.

Well, there were worse places to haunt if that's what one decided to do. Re-living a perfect beach morning for eternity certainly had its attractions.

She sat now in about the same spot where she and Thomas had had their picnic. Her steps kept leading her back here when she came to walk, and she didn't question it. Somehow it was calming.

She'd done the right thing that day, giving Thomas his father's message. She had no doubts about that at all. And being straight with him about her abilities had been difficult, but a huge relief at the same time. Owning the truth, owning her whole self, had been empowering, and she couldn't regret it.

However, she regretted Thomas's apparent choices deeply.

She sighed and blinked back the tears that still hovered just beneath the surface these days. She couldn't believe she still felt this strongly after a week. The two of them had only spent an afternoon together. Shared a few amazing kisses and the beginning of something wonderful.

For a brief moment she'd caught a tantalizing glimpse of what a future could be like with Thomas.

And somehow, the loss of what-might-have-been was the worst heartbreak of all.

She'd been around the block a few times and knew that eventually the pain would fade and she'd feel better. She just had to get up every day and live her best life. Happiness would follow.

She rubbed the tears off her face. She hated crying. She couldn't wait till she stopped.

A familiar looking red-checkered picnic napkin suddenly dangled before her. "Have a napkin," said a voice behind her.

She turned and looked up. For a moment she thought she was imagining things, so present had he been in her thoughts.

"Thomas?"

"Mind if I join you?"

"Sh-sure." She took the napkin and wiped at her face while she watched him drop down to sit beside her. There were a hundred questions she'd like to ask, but this was his conversation to start. So she waited, searching his profile for clues to what he was thinking as he looked out over the horizon.

"Your dad said you might be here," he said.

He'd come to her house looking for her? "It's a good place to think."

"Yeah." He gave a rueful shake of his head. "Well, its main attraction for me is the fact that you're here." He stared down at his hands where they clasped his knees, then tilted his head to look at her. "Chloe, I'm sorry for how I acted that day. I was a jerk."

She sighed. "It's a pretty normal reaction, Thomas. I didn't take it personally." Well, she'd tried not to.

"Don't excuse my behavior, Chloe. I don't. It may be normal not to believe something or not agree with it. That doesn't excuse being rude. Especially when that someone is just trying to help."

Chloe looked at Thomas, saw the truth of his words in his eyes as he waited for her response. The regret and the determination to make his error right.

"Apology accepted, then." The heartache that pressed against her chest eased the slightest bit. An apology for rudeness was more than she usually got from those who were hostile about what she did. She'd take it.

"Thank you." He nodded, relief clear on his face. "I appreciate it." He turned and stared down at the beach again. Chloe stole a sideways glance at him. Was there more?

"I read the letters," he said at last.

"Ah." *Maybe that's why Harry had been silent. Mission accomplished.*

"Yeah," he sighed and rubbed the back of his neck. "It took me a while to decide to do it. I really had a chip on my shoulder about the whole psychic thing. Sorry, *medium* thing. I kept trying to figure out how, even if you knew about the letters in the first place, you could possibly have known they were in that box. I turned my brain inside out trying to come up with a logical explanation, and at the end, I had to admit there wasn't one."

He looked her in the eye. "I packed that box right before you got there that morning by emptying out a bunch of drawers of a desk I'd just moved down from the attic. There was no way you could have known."

She shrugged. "I didn't. Your dad did."

"Yeah. That's what I was left with." He ran a hand through his already wind-tossed hair. "Didn't make me feel any better, to tell the truth."

So what's your point? she wanted to say, but didn't. She'd heard this plenty of times. It was a line of thinking that usually ended at the brick wall of disbelief. It was what people said right before a) it must've been a lucky guess, b) just a coincidence or c) a trick of some kind.

"So I go back to the facts I know. And fact number one, Chloe, is you."

"Me?" Well, that was different. The vote of confidence in these cases rarely came out in her favor.

"I've known you since we were kids. You were a kind, sweet person without an ounce of malice in you then, and from what I've seen of you as an adult, that hasn't changed. You don't really have it in you to lie. So that means you truly believe what you're telling me, and that you're doing it with the best possible intentions."

"Sure, but I could still just be crazy," she pointed out. "Or wrong. Both common conclusions, in my experience."

"True, but I didn't have enough facts at that point to make a judgement. The whole thing was a puzzle. And for some reason, I couldn't just drop it. But I wanted to solve it on my own. I really didn't want to read those letters.

"So I stuck the envelope in my desk drawer. Or I thought I did. But then, every time I turned around, there was that damned brown envelope. First it was on top of my desk, then the next day it was on my kitchen table. I must have picked it up and wandered around with it while I was trying to decide to whether to read them, because the next day when I came home, the envelope was on the table with my mail. The next thing I knew, I was on my couch, going through them, one bundle at a time."

She held her breath. "And?"

"At first, I wasn't interested in the letters my dad wrote, but the letters my mom wrote... well, that was something else entirely." He shook his head, a wondering smile curving his lips. "I started reading one and it was like I could hear her voice in my head. She sounded so sweet and so full of love. For everything, you know? Kind of wide-eyed and innocent." He swallowed hard. "I wish I could have known her," he said in such a low voice she barely heard it sitting just inches away. "How different would my life have been?"

He cleared his throat and continued. "The way she wrote to my dad made me want to read his letters, too. I mean, how could someone like her want to be with someone like him? So I read them. And I was amazed at what a different person he was then, and I pretty much think that she was the one who made him that way. Because the man in those letters, the man who brought home flowers on a Tuesday just because and made silly jokes and kissed her when she talked too much, wasn't anything like the cold, distant man I grew up with. The man he was without *her*. I never knew he had a light inside of him. I only ever saw him after it was gone."

"How sad," said Chloe. "To lose that light. Much worse than if you'd never had it."

"You want to know what's worse?" Thomas reached for her hand.

She let him take it, swallowing hard against bittersweet pain that speared through her even as she savored the way he curled his fingers around hers. Stupid tears threatened again. "What?" she whispered.

"Never having it at all." He looked down at her fingers, then up into her eyes. "I used to think if I never let love in, then it couldn't hurt me. But now, I realize if I don't let it in I'm not really living. I'll never know who I could really be if I had it in my life."

"Oh, Thomas," Chloe squeezed his hand. "That's wonderful. I'm so happy for you." And on an unselfish level, she truly was. On a selfish level though, it was going to take a little longer. "I think you'll be amazed at what can happen when you're willing to give love a chance."

"How about you, Chloe? Will you give it a chance? Will you give *me* a chance?"

She pulled her hand away, mourning the loss of his touch as soon as she did. "I just don't think we'd work, Thomas. I am who I am, and I wouldn't change that for anyone, even if I could."

She looked away, her heart breaking all over again at the stricken look on his face. She took a deep breath and focused on what she needed to say.

"For most of my life, I've kept the real me hidden. I pretended to be someone else, someone who didn't see and converse with the dead. But that just made me unhappy and it always led to complications when the truth came out—and it always came out.

"So when I came back here to Moonlight Cove, I decided I would never lie about myself again. I would be who I am, no more secrets and pretending."

She jumped up, unable to bear his nearness and the puzzled look on his face. Stepping to the edge of the bluff, she faced the beach below and crossed her arms against the cooling breeze. Maybe what she had to say would be easier if she didn't look right at him.

"I know what you think about all of this, and I understand why. But I have a gift." The wind tossed her hair across her face, tangling it in the tears that now ran unchecked down her cheeks. "It's also a responsibility and I can't walk away from it. It's not always easy or convenient. But I know I've helped people and I'm done pretending to be something I'm not." Her voice broke on her last words in spite of her best effort. "Not even for someone as wonderful as you."

"I would never want you to," he said from behind her.

Her thoughts stopped in mid-churn as his words registered.

His hands covered her shoulders, warm and strong. "Chloe, look at me."

She turned in his arms, not caring that her face was a tear-streaked mess and her hair a hopeless tangle. The only thing that mattered were the words beginning to wrap themselves around her heart. "What? What did you say?"

He brushed a strand of hair out of her eyes. "Why would I want to mess with perfection? You have a generous, loving heart. Big enough for everyone, living *and* dead. Don't ever change, not for me, not for anyone." He took her hands and clasped them against his chest. She could feel his heart beating wildly beneath her palms. "Just as long as you have room in there for one more, that is. Me."

She searched his face, looking for shadows, for hesitation, and found none at all. Only the expression of a man waiting patiently, if desperately, for her answer.

"You really mean it," she said, daring, for the first time, to believe it.

He squeezed her hands. "Please?"

She smiled, letting the joy in her heart shine in her eyes. "How could I say no to 'please'?"

In a heartbeat, she was crushed to his chest, his lips hard on hers, his hands in her hair. She smiled against his mouth as she kissed him back, the happiness that bubbled inside of her leaving her fizzy and light-headed.

"I hate to interrupt you kids, but I think maybe I need to get going."

Chloe broke the kiss at the sound of Harry's voice.

He stood a few yards away, on the promontory point of Rainbow's End, facing them with the sunset-lit sky at his back. Behind him, the bluff dropped in a sheer cliff to the water below.

Chloe looked up at Thomas. "It's your dad," she whispered. "He's here."

"There's a really bright light over there," Harry's threadbare brown sweater flapped around him as he gestured behind him. "I think I'm supposed to go to it. You two seem to have things worked out between you now, so I guess I'm probably done here."

He took a step towards her, and cleared his throat. "I wanted to say thanks, Chloe, for getting those letters to Thomas and helping him believe in true love." He gave her a sly smile. "Told you that you were the right girl for the job."

Chloe smiled back at the disreputable-looking ghost. "Glad I could help."

Beside her, Thomas took her hand. "What's he saying?"

"He's saying good-bye."

"You look after my boy now." Harry squinted over his shoulder. "Wow, that's really bright," he said. "Why do I feel like I'm forgetting something?" He patted his hands down his sweater, checked all his insubstantial pockets.

A woman's laugh reached them on the breeze. "Because you always do, sweetheart. That's why you have me — to remember the important things for you."

Thomas looked around. "Who's laughing? I hear a woman laughing."

Harry's eyes grew round. "Abby?"

"Oh my goodness," breathed Chloe. "I think your mom is here."

Thomas stared around him, but Chloe knew he likely couldn't see the woman who had visited Chloe's dreams for the last several weeks. Her peasant skirt and loose white blouse fluttered in the breeze as she solidified. She stepped to Harry's side.

"Abby! It's you!" Harry took her hands, looking her up and down in amazement.

"Oh, Thomas," said Chloe in hushed tones. "She's beautiful. She's come for your father."

"Well of course it's me, silly." She touched a playful finger to the tip of Harry's nose, then placed a light kiss on his surprised lips. Her auburn curls danced as she tilted her head. "Who else would I be?"

Harry stood straighter, shedding his hang-dog demeanor in Abby's presence. In fact, Chloe could swear he grew younger, more vital. The scruffy brown sweater was gone, a soft white linen shirt in its place.

"It's never been anyone but you," he said, opening his arms. Abby stepped into his embrace, sliding her arms around his waist and snuggling against him as he held her close. "Where have you been?" he murmured into her hair.

Chloe felt Thomas squeeze her hand. "What's happening now?"

She turned to see him peering intently at the spot she was focused on. "They're embracing. They're together again."

Thomas swallowed hard and nodded. He put his arm around her and pulled her close. "Good," he whispered. "Good."

Abby pulled back and looked up at Harry. "I've been waiting for you, of course." She sighed. "But you weren't quite ready yet."

"Ready for...?" Harry nodded back over his shoulder, where he'd indicated the light was calling him.

"Of course. What else?" Abby answered.

"Yes, well. About that. I'm sorry I kept you waiting, darling, but I had something important to do before I could leave."

Abby silenced him with a finger on his lips. "I know. And you did exactly the right thing." The smile she gave him was so full of love and understanding that it brought tears to Chloe's eyes. "I wouldn't have expected anything less from you."

"I'm ready now. If you are."

"I think they're going to cross over now," Chloe said to Thomas.

"Cross over to…oh you mean to, like, heaven or something?"

Chloe shot him a grateful look. "Something like that."

"Just give me one minute more," said Abby.

Chloe sensed volumes of meaning and perfect understanding in the look that the pair exchanged.

"Of course, my love."

"So, what's happening now?" asked Thomas.

Chloe felt every hair on her body stand up. "She's coming towards us."

Abby stopped in front of Thomas. Chloe could feel the love she radiated infusing the air, surrounding them in a warm, comforting embrace.

"Tell him I've always watched over him," Abby said as she touched her son's face with ethereal fingers. "And that I love him."

Chloe watched tears fill Thomas's eyes before she could even speak. "Your mother says she's always watched over you and she loves you," she said.

"I can feel it," said Thomas. "I can feel her here."

"I'm so proud of the man he's become." Abby glanced at Chloe. "Tell him."

Chloe swallowed back the tears that constricted her throat. This was important. "She's so proud of you, Thomas."

"Thanks, Mom," he whispered. He put his arms around Chloe. "Thanks, Chloe."

"Take care of each other now. Love each other. It's all that really lasts," said Abby as she stepped back. She turned a dazzling smile on Chloe. "I know you'll help him understand all of that."

"I'll do my best," Chloe managed in a whisper. "Thank you."

Abby returned to Harry and took his hand. "I'm ready now."

Harry smiled down at her, then turned to look back at them. "Bye now. Take care. And thanks again!"

"Bye!" Chloe waved.

Thomas raised his hand and waved as well. A gesture of faith, Chloe knew.

The pair turned to face the promontory's point and took a single step together. A brilliant burst of light flashed around them, and they were gone.

Chloe sucked in a breath of air that felt suddenly lighter, normal again. The soundtrack of a Moonlight Cove dusk resumed as though it had been muted. The raucous calls of gulls and the gentle *bing* of the buoys that bobbed at the mouth of the little marina rode the ocean-salted breeze.

Thomas put an arm around her, pulling her close. "It's our turn now," he said.

She put her arms around his waist and rested her head on his shoulder. "Worried?" she asked.

He smiled down at her. "Not even a little."

———

One Year Later

"Trust me," said Row. "You need to expand Pandora's. You've got a line of customers out your door every day. Think how many more people you can make happy if you double in size."

Chloe rested her chin on her hands as she frowned at the columns of figures on Row's spreadsheet. "I don't know," she said. "You've already done so much for me already. You put up the money for me to even lease *this* place. I hate asking you for more."

Row's lips thinned and she straightened to her full, intimidating five foot ten. Chloe sighed inwardly. She rarely came out on the winning end of an argument when Row went into battle-mode.

"Point number one," Row ticked off on stiff, extended fingers. "You aren't asking, I'm offering. Which brings me to point number two. You paid that loan back six months early. And point number three, the space next door doesn't come open every day. You've got to jump on it before someone else does."

"I know you're right, Row." Chloe laid her hand over Row's with a smile. "And you know how grateful I am for everything you do.

There's just a lot going on right now, and I hate asking you to put more on the line. You've got your own business to worry about."

"Great," said Row, whipping her checkbook out of her bag. "I'm glad we've come to an understanding." She scribbled furiously for a minute then ripped out a check and slapped it into Chloe's hand.

"But—"

"Gotta go." Row was already moving as she slung her bag over her shoulder and waggled her fingers at Chloe. She was out of the back entrance before Chloe could get another word out.

With a sigh, she tucked Row's check into her purse on its shelf below the counter.

The tinkle of the bell over the shop entrance gave its customary half-second warning as the door swung open.

It should really be an air-raid siren, thought Chloe, grinning. Her big picture windows gave her a perfect view of the crowd of uniformed girls about to invade her little bakery.

"We won! Dolphins rule!" A stream of whooping teenaged girls in varsity basketball team uniforms filed in, filling the cozy space as they shouted and high-fived each other.

"Hi, Mrs. Stone!" said a tall, lanky blonde girl who'd reached the counter.

"Hi Erin." Chloe kept her face straight with an effort. "Can I help you with something?"

"Yes ma'am, you can." Erin's grin split her face ear to ear. "We're here 'cuz Coach owes us. He promised cake-pops all around if we won today." She turned to address the crowd. "And we're here to collect. Aren't we, girls?"

Another loud cheer went up, almost drowning out the sound of the little bell chiming again. Thomas's tall frame filled the doorway.

"Coach! Coach! Coach!" The girls chanted, as Thomas made his way to the counter.

It was kind of amazing, thought Chloe as she watched him approach, but somehow the man got more good-looking every day. She still pinched herself once in a while at the thought of how lucky she was that she had him in her life.

"Hi, sweetheart," he said as he reached her.

"Hi yourself," she said, raising her face for his kiss.

The girls broke into more whoops as Thomas lingered over the kiss. As he pulled away, Chloe laughed. "What kind of example are you setting for these girls?" she said.

His eyes were serious as he answered her. "The best," he said. "I'm showing them how a man should treat his wife. Can you think of a better one?"

After a last quick kiss, he turned to face his team. The girls fell silent.

"Great job today, girls. You played like the champions I know you are, and you should be proud of yourselves." He paused, looking out over the crowd. He punched both hands in the air. "Cake pops for everyone!"

After more cheering and high-fiving, the girls fell into a more or less organized line. All except for one lone girl Chloe noticed keeping to herself in a corner of the shop. When she got a clear view of her, she could see the girl wore a uniform, but it wasn't like the others. Her white tank jersey bore the number "12" in tall black characters, and her shorts were dark green, not the royal blue of Amberly High. She clearly wasn't from the local high school. In fact, Chloe realized in a blink, she wasn't even alive.

Well, that explained a lot. Like the streak of black grime down her right shoulder and her too-pale complexion. Duh. *Okay then. Something to keep an eye on.*

Chloe handed each girl two of the special treats she'd prepared for the team. Cake pops decorated in school colors, each adorned with a leaping dolphin, the school mascot.

"You're the best, Mrs. Stone," said a serious girl with brown hair and straight-cut bangs in her second year on Thomas's team. "We're all really glad you married Mr. Stone. He's always been nice, but he's extra nice now."

Chloe smiled as she handed her a plate. "Well, thanks Emily. I'm pretty glad I married him too."

Emily was the last girl in line, and as she walked away, Chloe scanned the room, looking for the girl in the number 12 jersey. Ah, there she was, standing near Emily's table, lips pursed as she eyed the group of chattering girls. There was definitely a negative energy coming off of her.

"Something has your attention. Is it that old woman hanging around again?"

Chloe glanced at Thomas, who had joined her behind the counter, then returned her attention to the girls. "No, I haven't seen her in weeks. I think she's probably moved on." She tapped a finger against her lips. "This is a new one. A teenager, actually. Kinda strange."

Thomas put his arms around her. "Well, I'm sure she's in good hands now that she's on your radar. Just promise me you won't over-do. You've got more than yourself to worry about now."

"I won't," she said, pulling her gaze away from the back of the room to focus on her husband. "I'm too tired these days to worry about much more than taking care of you." She pressed a kiss to his lips, then frowned at the shopping bag he'd set on the counter. "Another one? What did you get this time?"

Thomas grinned and pulled out a mini-foam basketball and hoop set. "Isn't it great? Its Velcro, you stick it on the wall."

"Thomas, the baby doesn't come for another seven months. At this rate, we're going to need a storage unit for all the toys you're buying."

"I know," he said, clearly unrepentant. "I can't wait." His eyes lit with a mischievous smile. "Just think, if we had five kids, we could have our own basketball team."

Chloe rolled her eyes. "Let's see how one goes first, shall we?"

Thomas pulled her close in a hug. "I'm not even worried. As long as I've got you, everything's already perfect."

Jill Jaynes began her love affair with romance when she was a teenager growing up in Southern California, where she spent many a late night under the covers with a flashlight and a good romance novel.

This early addiction stuck, and she discovered one day that telling great stories was even more fun than reading them. Today she writes stories with happy endings her own way—with a dash of magic that means anything can happen.

You can find her at http://www.JillJaynes.com, where you can also sign up for her newsletter. Or you can also find her on Facebook at JillJaynesRomance:

https://www.facebook.com/JillJaynesRomance

Surprise Deliveries

by

Shauna Roberts

Chapter 1

"Do milk cartons ever feature missing fathers?"

Noriko Leonie Hamasaki addressed her poignant question to Puff and Slink, the store cats at Hamasaki Quality Pens and her only friends in Moonlight Cove, California. They looked up from where they sprawled in the sunlight, then yawned and closed their eyes again.

The cats weren't worried, but she was starting to be. When Jake left, she had gotten the impression the father she had only recently met would be gone just a short time. Of course, she didn't know him well enough to know whether four weeks was a short time to him.

It wasn't to her.

Leonie also couldn't shake the uncharitable thought that he was taking advantage of her. Maybe he had invited her here to run the shop while he took a long vacation.

The chimes rang a glissando in b minor, announcing a family of tourists. They strolled in, flip-flops snapping against the wood floor. Grateful for a distraction from the hollow in her gut, Leonie straightened up and smoothed down her red blouse. "Good afternoon," she said, performing the Japanese bow her father insisted they greet customers with. She loved the ritual of that bow; somehow it softened the rough informality of California and made conversations with customers more gracious.

"How wonderful to hear a Louisiana voice!" the woman exclaimed, her pronunciation and intonation revealing she had grown up in southern Louisiana, just as Leonie had.

"Likewise. Some of the accents here are hard to understand." Dozens of accents thrived in southern Louisiana, and Leonie knew most of them. She ventured, "St. Landry Parish?"

The woman nodded and switched to Cajun French. "You're from down the bayou, I think. Are you Choctaw?"

"No, Houma. From Bayou Cane. I'm staying by my father now. This is his shop."

"I have cousins in Bayou Cane! Do you know—"

"Darlin,' we don't have time to compare cousins. My parents are expecting us," the husband interjected in English. He turned to Leonie. "We had coffee at the Honey Bee, and the waitress recommended we come here for postcards."

"We do have the best selection in town." Leonie guided the family to the racks she had put up the previous week. "One day when I was taking tea at the Honey Bee, Chloe introduced me to Erika Archer, a photographer. After I saw her work, I commissioned some postcard shots of Moonlight Cove."

"These are impressive." The man plucked three postcards from the rack—each showing the cliff face at different times of day—and compared them. "Archer has an incredible eye for light."

"These are a hundred times better than the pictures you took, Papa," the teenaged son said.

The father scowled at him, but his eyes twinkled.

"For real," the boy said. "We could buy one of each postcard. Then you could put the camera away and stop complaining about the angle of the sun and how crowded the beach is."

"Zachary has the right of it," the mother said. "These would look great in our scrapbook, and you could pass a good time here instead of always trying to get the perfect shot."

"Some of the postcard scenes are also available as prints." Leonie walked to the bin where the prints stood, each in an envelope of archival-quality Mylar film. "All are exclusive to us."

"Darlin,' pick out what you like. I won't complain about a break from picture shooting." The husband wandered over to the glass case that stretched across the room and held pens and a few pieces of enamelwork.

Leonie kept an eye on him in case he showed any real interest in a pen and made conversation with the wife and son in French. "So you're on vacation in Moonlight Cove. Are you having fun?"

"No." Zachary said, with no sugar coating or soft-pedaling. "Every day the traffic is like an evacuation. The sky is brown. The ocean stinks. The food has no flavor."

Leonie nodded. "That's what I thought when I first got here."

"And now?" the mother asked.

"I'm pretty new here myself, but the longer I'm in California, the harsher and more alien it seems, all thorns and hard angles and sharp sunlight. And much, much traffic, of course." Leonie shook her head. "I'm a traiteuse, but few of my usual healing herbs grow here. I'm always collecting unfamiliar plants and researching them online."

"A traiteuse! Now we know where to go if one of us gets hurt or sick here." The woman added more cards to the stack in her hand and moved to the prints. "What do the locals do for fun?"

"Many like to surf and hang out at the beach. Customers tell me vacationers come to Moonlight Cove to relax because they have fast-paced city jobs."

"If we wanted to relax, we could have stayed home," Zachary complained.

"Hush, boy!" said his mother. "What good fortune you have to spend this time with your Mamère and Papère. Family is the most valuable thing you can ever have."

Leonie's stomach clenched, and she put her arm across it protectively. Her throat clogged with tears she dared not shed in front of customers, neighbors or not. She drew a deep breath and said in English, "True dat. I came all the way out here after my mama passed so I could make a new family with my father."

Leonie had known her father only from Mama's stories. She had never even seen his picture. But everyone needed a family, and he offered one. She wanted to get to know him as much as he claimed he wanted to get to know her and to teach her about her Japanese heritage. Although she would always consider herself first and last a Houma, most Houma folk had a gumbo of ancestries, and she was eager to learn this unknown side of herself.

At her father's invitation, she had sent a delivery truck ahead with her Mamère's dining room furniture, packed some suitcases, and made the long, long drive on Interstate 10 with high hopes.

Her father had called her "Noriko" from the start. What a jolt, answering to her first name after twenty-seven years as "Leonie"! Then after a couple of weeks he put her in charge of the shop and left on business. Secret, secret business. He didn't say when he would be back or how to reach him in an emergency.

Now she was stuck here. When she wasn't running the store or collecting plants, she was planning new ways to make the store more profitable. How her father's business had survived selling only high-end pens to wealthy people from Los Angeles and Silicon Valley was beyond her. Since she had been in charge of the shop, most of the profits had come from the lower-priced necessities and impulse buys she had added.

Speaking of which...

"Miss?" The father stood by the inexpensive plastic fountain pens she had added to the inventory. "Are these any good?"

"They're made for beginners, so the nibs are designed to suit any hand position and writing style. I tested each model when they first came in. All write smoothly without skipping." She gestured toward the other end of the case. "Not everyone can afford a fancy fountain pen, but everyone can afford one that writes well. I love the fun colors! I got a purple one for myself and put purple ink in it."

"Cool!" Zachary exclaimed. He crowded against his father, eyes caressing the pens.

"Go ahead. Try any of the pens you want on that pad of paper. There's a different color of ink in each."

Zachary didn't need a second invitation. He tried each pen, and then so did his mother. Laughing, they drew doodles and wrote their names in huge swirly letters.

Leonie couldn't hold back a smile. *How wonderful it is that some things in life cost almost nothing but bring so much joy!*

The father tapped her on her arm and gestured for Leonie to follow him. He pointed to a detailed cloisonné brooch depicting the Moonlight Cove lighthouse on its rocky cliff above crashing waves and to another, simpler brooch of a flower. "I want to surprise my wife and my mother. Could you wrap those up for me now? Add the price to what my family's buying. I'll pay for everything together."

Both were beautiful pieces. In fact, all the enamelwork in the shop was so gorgeous that Leonie had a crush on the artist without ever having met him. Leonie slipped each brooch into a silk bag and nestled it in cotton in a red box.

The man had just hidden the boxes in his pocket when his wife and son joined him at the cash register. They had chosen a mix of Erika's prints and postcards and several plastic fountain pens in different colors. Leonie rang everything up and dropped a couple boxes of colored ink cartridges into their bag as lagniappe.

As the family left, Leonie bowed. She made a mental note not to order any more standard postcards. She had sold almost none since she had put out Erika's work.

The clock clicked then tolled its melody and seven strokes.

Leonie blinked. Time to close already? Puff and Slink padded out from wherever, pausing to stretch and yawn before beelining toward the door leading from the shop to the living quarters behind.

She shook her head and smiled. "Every evening, the same path. How can it be you two have not worn through the floor polish?"

The cats reached the cat flap in the door and paced impatiently in front of it, mewing and rubbing their chins against the door's frame and her leg. They used the flap without fuss during the day, but at suppertime, they stayed in the shop, making sure Leonie could not forget them.

"Hold your horses, mes petits." Leonie wrote a quick email to Erika to order more postcards. She added a postscript: "Would you like to put some of your framed and signed photos here on consignment? The tourists love especially your postcards with beach scenes and lighthouse scenes. Also the ones with sunsets." She clicked "send" and savored the moment. She had liked Erika immediately. It was gratifying to offer her a chance to make extra money.

And of course, she was helping Jake, as her enigmatic—and truant—father, Kaito Hamasaki, had inexplicably asked her to call him. She sighed and ran her hand through her hair. How much her life had changed in such a short time! Life had been crawfish boils and Saturday night fais-do-does and paddling her pirogue through the bayous for so many years. Bourré and other card games on the kitchen table when it rained too hard to go out. Good times and good friends.

But after the economic downturn and the decrease in oil prices, her friends and cousins had scattered to find jobs elsewhere as so many other people of the Houma tribe had done. She had felt lucky the arts continued to be strong, ensuring the continuation of her job at a small company that provided marketing services for musicians, artists, photographers, and even dancers.

Then Mama got sick. Six months ago, she had died in the room where she had been born fifty years earlier. Before Leonie had composed herself enough to call 911, the phone rang. It was her boss, calling to fire her for having taken so much time off to care for Mama.

Life turned pointless. Leonie went out every day for weeks in her pirogue, paddling and poling aimlessly through the marshes and bayous, slicing through the invasive, jade-green duckweed and making the black-green water underneath swirl. It had seemed a miracle when she received Jake's condolence letter with its invitation to live with him in Moonlight Cove.

At first, she applied for art-marketing jobs in towns around Moonlight Cove, with few nibbles and no bites. The arts did not have the same respect and widespread appeal here as they did at home. As days and then weeks went by and her father remained missing, she gave up her job hunt and instead applied her marketing skills to the shop. Jake might be angry at her initiative when he returned, but he could not dispute she had increased his profits and his customer base.

If he returns. It's getting harder to believe he will.

She was alone here, just as alone as if she had stayed down the bayou. Many nights as she lay sleepless, she debated returning to Bayou Cane and the empty cottage that was now hers. She longed for familiar smells, familiar foods whose ingredients she couldn't buy here, a familiar landscape—lush, shady, and soft, always warm and welcoming. She longed for a familiar way of life. She understood the cultures in Terrebonne Parish in the marrow of her bones, and she spoke their languages—English, Cajun French, and what bits of Houma language still survived. She wouldn't need to go back to marketing. As a traiteuse, she would never go hungry or be without shelter.

But she would not have a family at home, not with her cousins dispersed. She had expected to feel part of a family in California by now, but Jake had left while they were still strangers. Her "family" was only the two cats whining at her heels.

The tourists from Louisiana were the last straw. It was easy to understand what they said, and they had an eye for art that made her like them immediately. Already she missed the sound of their voices.

Waves of cold and emptiness rocked her so thoroughly that even her bones turned cold. Her hands clenched as her body shook. She hugged herself and rubbed the frissons pebbling her arms. It didn't help that summers on the California coast were as chilly as late winter back home; the breeze through the window she had forgotten to close earlier brushed her with cold fingers.

Closing up will warm me up. She gritted her teeth and grabbed the broom. After locking the door and shutting the window, she swept up all the sand that customers had tracked in. Then she swept the floor again because there was always, always more sand. She found it in the kitchen cabinets, too, and sometimes even in her bed.

She put away the broom and slipped her feet out of her shoes before going into the back. It was an odd Japanese custom Jake insisted on, but she would have done it anyway to keep down the sand in the living quarters.

The cats batted her legs with paws as if urging her to hurry. She opened the door to the rest of the house, and as she put on her waiting slippers, the cats raced to the kitchen.

"If it weren't for you two, I'd leave this moment." A warm feeling rose through her body, and calmness enveloped her. She had made a decision without realizing it.

He's abandoned me a second time. I'll give him one week to show up. Then I'll go home.

Chapter 2

The next morning, kibble hit the ceramic cat bowls with a soft patter quickly drowned out by crunching, slurping, and hissing.

Leonie shook her head as she poured, more kibble now bouncing off the cats' heads than landing in the bowls. "You two look just like our cats, Puff and Slink. But I know you cannot be, because you gobble and gorge yourselves like ones who are starved." She set the bag on the cabinet.

Mon Dieu! I completely forgot. Where will I find someone to take care of the cats?

When she decided to go home within a week, she had not taken the two petits into account, and although she had been here for weeks, she had not yet made any friends.

She had tried. Saying "hello" or "good morning" to strangers on the street was plain good manners back home and often led to conversations and then to friendships. Here, though, women responded to her greetings with suspicion, and men, with leers. She had learned to keep her mouth shut and her eyes averted.

"Call vet about boarding cats," she scrawled on a sheet of paper and stuck it to the icebox with a surfboard magnet. The name of the cats' vet was another essential piece of information Jake had not given her. But given the high, high cost of real estate on the California coast, most people in Moonlight Cove had to rent. Surely the town had only one or two vets.

Still, the thought of tracking down Puff and Slink's vet and searching the house for their traveling crates and blankies cast a pall over her day. The idea of pawing through Jake's belongings without his permission made her shudder, and she wondered whether the town had a pet-supply store.

Early afternoon, while Leonie rearranged some items in the counter display, Slink's ears perked up, and he walked toward the door.

"Just another *Bikini Babes* truck," Leonie told him. "Do you hope they come by to cast you in the show, hmmm? You, who has fear of everything?"

The heavy, solid-oak original front door flew open.

A UPS man barreled through the door. A handcart bounced behind him, its package thud, thud, thudding despite his grip.

The wind chimes banged together. The clanging reverberated against the walls.

The man's feet tripped over each other. He let go of the handcart. It hurtled toward the glass counter, package teetering.

Leonie vaulted over the counter and twisted as she landed. The package smacked her shoulder like a beehive full of angry bees. "Oomph!" Stinging pain ran down her arm. She gritted her teeth and clutched the tall, top-heavy package with both arms, meanwhile sticking out her foot to halt the handcart.

It tipped over and crashed to the floor.

The leg that bore her weight wobbled. *I'm not working out enough here.* She thumped the other foot to the floor and lowered the package until it set upright.

As she rubbed her arm, a bead of perspiration trickled down her forehead. She lowered her head to her sleeve to catch it and grinned triumphantly. Nothing had broken! The glass counter was intact, and so was her new display case. "I did it!"

A loud groan came from the floor.

Jorge! Her hand flew to her chest. She'd forgotten the deliveryman. She looked to see how he was.

"You're not Jorge!" This UPS man was a stranger.

The man groaned again and eased himself up onto his elbow. He looked up at her, blinking, his eyes gazing in slightly different directions. "And you're not Mr. Hamasaki. At least, I don't think so." He lay down again, closed his eyes, and took deep breaths.

Leonie rubbed her palms against her black slacks. She was a traiteuse, and he was hurt. *It should be a simple, simple matter—but no one here knows what a traiteuse is, let alone knows the rules.* She would have to guide him.

"Did you bang your head?"

He shook his head "no" without wincing.

"I'm fine." His tone showed his words a lie. He heaved himself onto his elbow again.

"Black waterfall," he mumbled.

"Pardon?"

"Your hair. It looks like a black waterfall on your white blouse." Their gazes caught, and as he stared at her, his eyes darkened.

Heat rose into Leonie's face, and her heartbeat throbbed in her neck. As if she had flipped a light switch, she became aware of him as more than Jorge's substitute. As a man, with male thoughts and male attributes. She dropped her gaze, only to find herself looking at broad, broad shoulders. She shifted her gaze again and this time saw tanned, muscular legs, revealed by the summer uniform. *I'm only attracted to him because I've been alone for weeks. I'd respond to any guy who looked at me with interest.*

"What happened?" Her words came out more brusquely than she had intended. "One moment the store was quiet. The next moment, you charged in like a buffalo."

"What happened?" He raised an eyebrow. "Someone fixed the door and the doorknob, that's what happened. The door's been swollen and the screws in the doorknob stripped for years. Didn't you notice the shiny spot on the door where everyone pushed with their shoulder?"

"Yes, I noticed. I was afraid someone would get hurt, so I planed the door edge and put wood putty in the screw holes." *I did that work for my father, and he may never see it, if he's not planning to come back.*

"You should have put up a sign to tell people the door was working," he grumbled. "You're lucky I didn't crash into your counter and break the glass."

"Do you gripe at all your delivery customers?"

His eyes widened. "What?"

She shrugged. "You're ruder than the *Bikini Babes* van drivers. I wondered whether you are always like this."

He stared at her, and alertness clicked on in his eyes. He sat upright, his face turning red. "I got stuck behind *Bikini Babes* vans three times today and got behind on my route. Now this happens. I guess I better see how bad it is."

He cradled his right arm with his left and brought it in front of him. He took one glance at his bloody elbow and looked away.

"Well, that's revolting!" He swallowed visibly. His gaze flickered briefly to hers, and he smiled wryly. "I'm not making much of an impression yet, am I?"

"Actually, you've made quite an impression." *He can take that however he likes.* She lowered herself to a cross-legged position next to him. "You should be more concerned with your elbow."

She leaned a little closer to the joint in question. The wood floor had scraped his elbow and forearm raw, and blood and serous fluid welled and dripped from countless parallel lacerations and abrasions. Swelling tissue had swallowed his elbow. She glanced quickly over the rest of his exposed arms and legs as well as his head and saw no other bleeding or swelling. His elbow had taken the brunt of the fall.

He was kind of cute. She hoped the pain and the surprise of the fall accounted for his confusion and rudeness.

Puff and Slink came over and sniffed the injury. Puff expanded into a Tribble-like ball of white fuzz. Whiskers twitching, Slink sniffed the arm carefully from the top of the scratches to the bottom. Then, before Leonie realized what he intended, the cat stuck out his tongue and rasped the man's skin.

The man doubled over, his eyes squeezing shut. "Slink! You little orange vampire! No cat treats for you today."

Leonie pulled the tabby onto her lap and held him down. "How awful! I'm so sorry!"

"Me too," he gasped.

After a minute, he slowly rolled up. "I still have my route to finish, and I don't want to mess up my clothes or the packages. Do you have a first-aid kit I can borrow?"

"You won't be able to bandage that yourself." *Take the hint! Please take the hint!*

They sat in silence. A breeze through the still-open door rustled the chimes. The fresh air lifted a few brown waves of his hair and brought his scent to her, a mix of sweat and sandalwood soap and something unique to him. Slink pulled free of her hold and sauntered away.

At last she had to speak. "If you want my help, you have to ask."

His head jerked back. "Never mind. I can ask someone later on my route to help." He struggled to stand.

Leonie rested her hand on his shoulder. He looked at her hand and then sat.

"It's a rule. A person has to request my help. I'm not supposed to tell you the rules for healing, but folks hereabouts don't seem to know them."

He looked at her as if he suspected she were playing a joke on him. She thought pride might hold him back, but he asked, "Please, will you help me?"

"Yes." She brushed her hair back behind her shoulder. "Back in a minute." She uncrossed her legs as she rose. She went to her room in the back of the bungalow and fetched a first-aid kit and a basket.

Again she sat next to him. She cleaned the swelling and abrasions gently with a cloth soaked in an extract of leaves, roots, and bark she had made from a recipe of Nonc Antoine's and brought with her. *I must use it sparingly because some herbs in it don't grow here.* She especially liked to use it on children because the infusion didn't sting and smelled sweetly of bee balm. She tweezed out three splinters and rinsed off his elbow again, trying, but failing, to ignore the zings whenever her skin met his.

Does he feel it too? She didn't dare look into his face. She wrapped his elbow and lower arm thoroughly in gauze and tucked the end in tightly.

He blew out his breath. "That should hold me."

She shook her head. "I'm not done yet." She took from the basket a ball of string, measured out a length from her shoulder to her wrist, and cut it. As she knotted the string in several places and tied it around his elbow, she chanted an old prayer in a mix of French and Houma nine times.

She looked him in the eyes sternly. "Be sure to leave the string on at least a week."

Their gazes caught. His warm eyes pulled her in and seemed to search her soul. They were brown, dark and rich as humus left behind by a river. As their gaze held, his pupils enlarged to engulf the irises.

He does feel something too. Heat again rose in her face. "A week," she repeated. "It's important for the healing."

The antique mantel clock behind the counter clicked as it always did before chiming. She hadn't tried to fix the click; she liked the bit of personality it gave the clock.

But her patient glanced toward the sound. The clock bonged out a melody and then tolled three times.

The deep peals resonated inside Leonie's chest and echoed in the room. Although she knew they had to sound the same everyday, today the peals were poignant, reminding her time ran quickly. She sighed.

"Three o'clock already? I'm even later than I thought. Th—" he began.

She startled at the change in mood in the room and held up her palms. "Don't thank me. My prayers won't work if you thank me. It's another rule."

He looked at her quizzically but again didn't ask any questions. "See you later. I mean, if you get any deliveries before Jorge gets back."

She nodded and bowed.

"Uh, it was good you fixed the door." He stood and took hold of the handcart. As he walked out the door, he slapped his forehead. "I completely forgot. Please remind Mr. Hamasaki he needs to sign the paperwork for our booth at the art show."

Chapter 3

Leonie's heart pounded, and it wasn't from carrying the display-cabinet carton to the side of the shop and cutting it open. Puff rubbed against her legs, which was not like her—but of course! she was wearing black pants today, and every strand of fine white fur showed—and Leonie sank down next to her.

"What did you think of that deliveryman, minou?" She knuckled Puff's bony skull, and the cat responded with a long string of vocalizations. "I guess you're right. We didn't talk long, and he was rude, rude, maybe something of a canaille. At least at first. Then he turned civilized. Was that your doing, Slink? Did you perform some magic when you washed his elbow?"

No answer came from the corner.

The cats might not approve, or her father either, but the deliveryman had made her heart pound. She put a hand on her breastbone. Her heart had not yet slowed. She licked her lips.

"Some people don't make good first impressions, you know? I thought Slink was a sneaky devil when I first arrived, and now he sleeps in the crook of my arm at night." Puff watched her lips with a laser gaze as she talked. "Did you notice his broad shoulders, minou? Those came from real work, not from hanging out in a gym. And his hands. They were... delectable. So large, so well shaped, so calloused and scarred. Hands that have done many things. They show he's not one who is afraid to live life. I think perhaps he's not just another California 'surfer dude' with a high opinion of himself and an empty head. Eh, sha? Do you agree?"

Puff blinked and yawned at the endearment.

"You are lucky you were spayed, petite minou. You don't feel sparks. Just now, with the deliveryman, sparks were leaping between us for sure."

Why oh why didn't I ask him his name? For true, the company should embroider it on his uniform.

Leonie stood, ignoring Puff's complaints, and went to the computer. She stared at it for several minutes. She took the mantel clock down, removed its chilly glass dome, and wound the mechanism, even though it wasn't due to be wound until Sunday. She replaced the dome, wiped away the hint of fingerprints, and set the clock back on the shelf. Then she looked at the computer again.

I will do this.

With damp fingers, she opened the shop's email program and scanned for the delivery receipt. Not there. *How can it not be there yet? We always get them right away.*

She waited, feeling like a girl who languishes from love, who sits by the phone for hours, waiting for a special boy to call.

The computer pinged. She rubbed her damp palms on her jeans and looked at the screen. The receipt had arrived. She opened it, her hand trembling, and scanned it eagerly. Day, date, time, location of delivery.

But not who delivered it.

She sighed, weighing whether she felt more relief or more regret. *Hunky or not, he made a big fuss about a little abrasion. Back home, I treated five-year-olds with worse injuries but more stoicism.*

Not that it mattered one way or the other. Leonie couldn't get involved with a man. Her future was too up in the air and, much as she hated it, it depended on other people. Not least of whom was Jake.

Her stomach fluttered. She might have a second chance to see the man.

She had ordered *two* display cases, but only one had arrived today. UPS would be back tomorrow or the day after. Even if Jorge was back on his route, the man today had business with Jake, business his tone implied was important. What would he do when he didn't get the paperwork he needed from her missing father?

Who do I want this man to turn out to be? Another shallow California guy I can put out of my mind because he has no interests but surfing? Or the man I think he might be, someone hardworking and with dedication in his heart?

Chapter 4

The next day, Leonie passed the time between customers filling out paperwork that took all her concentration. Today she had dressed to impress. Impress the UPS man, that is. Tight black jeans that highlighted her butt, a white shirt that draped and clung flatteringly, and silver beaded earrings that twinkled against her black hair. A simple lily of the valley scent. In the complex Victorian language of flowers, lily of the valley meant a return to happiness.

All this for someone I won't see after next week unless Jake comes back.

The door opened. The chimes jingled their melody with gentle triumph. The hairs on her arms stood up. *I know it's him without even looking.* The thought made her dizzy.

Slink skittered to a corner.

Leonie's hands shook. Slowly she raised her gaze. It was *him*, as she had known. She bowed and stayed down too long.

"Hi!" he croaked.

He sounds as nervous as I feel.

She raised her head and brushed her hair behind her ear. "Hi."

He turned and pulled in the handcart, loaded with her second display stand. "No need to vault over the counter today to rescue your carton. I plan a by-the-book perfect delivery."

"Great. Please set it over by the other one."

After setting the new carton next to the other, he walked to the counter to face her and dragged off his hat. Unrestrained curls popped up here and there on his head. He clutched his hat with both hands, twisting it like Puff and Slink making biscuits.

"I was way out of line yesterday. I'm sorry. I was behind schedule because *Bikini Babes* trucks had blocked several streets I needed, and I was annoyed. Not that my mood was any excuse for how I behaved."

"*Bikini Babes* has that effect on people." She smiled. "Local people who come in complain about the trucks, the crew, and the actors all the time. I hope they all clear out when they're done filming."

Now he wrung his hat like a washcloth. "I know you don't want me to say the t-word. Because rules. At least may I show you my elbow?"

"If you like." She knew from experience what it would look like and how amazed he would be. But people loved to show off her work to her.

He extended his arm and turned it, elbow side up. "By the time I got home, my elbow didn't hurt, and the swelling was gone. Look!" He bent it fully. "My arm's not even tender where the scratches are. Whatever magic you put in that string worked."

"Not magic, and not my doing." She hesitated. She wasn't ready to explain, and he wasn't ready to hear.

He cleared his throat. "I noticed you didn't get your carton completely unpacked yesterday. What if I come back after my route ends tonight and help you take the display cases out and move them where they need to go?"

In truth, she knew nothing about him. She crossed her arms over her chest.

"I'm David, by the way. David Lewys with a 'y,' if you want to call UPS and check on me. I've been with them six years."

The name sounded familiar. More than familiar; it evoked faint feelings of awe. Of liking. Of yearning. Puzzled, she stretched out her hand to shake.

David held it a moment too long, turning it in the light as if counting every scar. "You must be a hard worker. Your palm is as calloused as mine."

She pulled her hand away. "Noriko Leonie Hamasaki."

"Are you the Noriko Mr. Hamasaki is always talking about? The one who markets musicians, painters, and dancers?"

Jake had paid attention to my life? "I... I guess I must be. But please call me Leonie."

"Leonie. That's a pretty name. I thought you lived in Louisiana."

"My mother passed recently, and my father, he invited me here so we could get to know each other."

"Is he here today? We're supposed to share a table at an art show in the fall, but he hasn't signed the application. If I don't turn it in soon, we'll miss the deadline."

"Art show?" She leaned over the case and twisted to look at a piece of enamelwork. It was a brooch whose swirls of greens, blues, and yellows conjured up the grandeur and the terror of the ocean in a place inside her ribs. The small card next to it read, "artist: David Lewys."

Her heart rose into her throat. *I was already crushing on the artist just from looking at his work. Now he turns out to be the only man in Moonlight Cove to have stirred feelings in me.* She swallowed, and the lump in her throat dissolved. "I thought I recognized your name. I love the pieces you have here on consignment."

"I can say 'thanks' for the compliment, right?"

"Yes." She ran her hand through her hair. "I really like your work. If I were still with the marketing firm, I'd ask to represent it." She stared at him, awed by seeing talent in the flesh. "I owe you some money for pieces that have sold since Jake left."

"Jake?"

She shrugged one shoulder. "That's what my father asked me to call him. Can you believe it? A solemn, dignified gentleman who wears conservative suits, polishes his shoes every night, bows to his customers, and spends hours pruning his bonsai and doing calligraphy likes to go by 'Jake.'"

"I wonder what the story behind the nickname is."

"Yeah. Me too." She looked away. "I'll ask him about it if he ever comes home."

"If? Certainly he'll come home. He's a stand-up, responsible guy."

"Is he? I haven't gotten a chance to find out."

"He just up and left? Doesn't sound like him." David's brow wrinkled. "Did he leave the art show paperwork for me? Or any message?"

"He didn't even leave me an emergency number."

David rubbed his face. "Doesn't sound like him," he repeated. "I'm going to ask all my customers today whether they know where he went."

A tightness in her chest Leonie didn't even know she had loosened slightly. "That would be great. Thank you. If your offer to help with the display shelves is still good, I'd be glad of your company. And to hear what you find out today. I close up at seven."

"I'll see you then."

Chapter 5

Gravel crunched outside. Once again, Leonie knew it was David before she saw him. She smoothed her t-shirt, darted to the door, and opened it.

David, out of uniform and in jeans and a gray t-shirt, smiled broadly and came in. Puff meowed and rubbed against his leg. He handed Leonie a tall bag and knelt to scratch Puff's head.

Leonie breathed deeply of the scents, both sweet and savory, drifting from the bag. Her mouth watered. "These smell really good."

David grinned. "Dinner for two. From the Lily Pad."

"Oh my!" The Lily Pad had the best food in town. "On four hours notice? You have more talents than just art."

"One benefit of delivering packages is I know almost everyone in town. Sometimes people do me favors."

"I'll say. Maybe I should apply to be a driver." She made a muscle with her right arm. "Do you think I'm strong enough?"

"You flew over the counter and caught the carton. If that were one of the tests, most of us would have flunked. So yeah, you're strong enough." He brought up his hand and rested his chin in it. "Hmmm."

"What?"

"If you're so strong, you don't need my help. Maybe I should go down to the beach and eat both meals myself."

She propped both fists on her hips and leaned back against the counter. She looked at the bright, happy colors of the painting reproduced on his t-shirt. "Not so fast, Mister Wassily Kandinsky T-Shirt. You came dressed to impress, and as a UPS guy you know how awkward tall cartons are, no matter how strong you are. So I'll put supper in the icebox, and you can help me with the display cases and tell me what you found out about Jake."

"Yes, ma'am." He walked over to the cartons. "I'm impressed you recognized Kandinsky's work." He picked up the box cutter. "Most people look at the shirt and don't get any further than 'Modern Art.'"

"It helps that underneath the picture it says, 'Van Gogh to Kandinsky Exhibit, Los Angeles County Museum of Art, 2014.'"

David looked down at his shirt and chuckled. "Of all my art t-shirts, I had to pick one I got in a museum gift store. You must think I'm really clueless."

"Not at all." In truth, Leonie was impressed he could laugh at himself, unlike most men she had known. "I'm glad you're not one of those 'artists' who pay no attention to any work but their own. We'll have plenty to talk about while we work. Most men who come in the shop and talk to me seem to have no interests except surfing."

"My multifaceted self is at your service." He raised the box cutter. "Shall we?"

"Please, do the honors."

He slit open the seams of both boxes, and together they pulled the cardboard away from the display cases.

Her hand flew to her heart. Flames danced deep in the maple burl veneer. Dark "eyes" of minor spalting contributed to the optical illusion of depth. She stroked the wood and let out a sigh. It was as smoothly finished over the patterned wood as on the tight straight grain. It was worth the extravagant price.

"Seeing wood that pretty makes me want to take up wood turning." David bundled the cardboard together.

"The cabinets look even better than they did online. They'll show off the high-end pens well. Right now, they're so close together, there's no room for an information card or a list of options."

"Are you ready to attach the doors and put the shelves in, or do you want to caress the wood some more?"

She raised her eyebrows and picked up a screwdriver.

He went for the tissue-thin instruction sheet and a bag of screws. "We're off to a good start. The instructions are in English!" He looked at the flimsy brown sheet again and turned it upside down. "Or at least something close to English."

"Together, I'm sure we'll figure it out. But first, what about Jake?"

David sighed. "I've dreaded telling you. No one I spoke to had any idea where he might have gone to."

She hung her head. *Looks as if I'll be going home next week after all.* "Thanks for your efforts. I guess he's not only ditched me but also all his friends."

"Don't give up. I'm not. I still think something's wrong. Or at the very least, there's a good reason for his mysterious disappearance."

Chapter 6

Forty-five minutes later, David wiped sweat from his forehead and announced, "We did a great job together! Should we put the pens in?"

Leonie thought they had worked well together too, barely needing to talk because each had the same idea what to do next. Except for stocking the pens now. "I haven't made up my mind how to organize them. I want to see different placements with my own eyes. It's easy enough for me to play around with the pens between customers."

David's stomach grumbled. He put his hand on his stomach. "Are you ready to eat? I worked up an appetite."

"Me too." She motioned for him to follow her into the back.

"Don't make a fuss on my account," he protested. "We can eat here at the counter."

Her nostrils flared. "What a horrifying idea. I'm going to pretend you didn't say that."

"Or we could sit on the floor here. Really, I don't mind."

"I mind. I'm no Californian. I eat at a proper dining table with a tablecloth, thank you very much. I didn't lug Mamère's dining room furniture all the way here for nothing." She jutted her chin, challenging him to contradict her again.

He raised his hands in surrender. "If you want to pamper me, go ahead." He grinned cockily. "I'll take it as a sign of how much you like me."

"I'm sure you will." The temperature in the room rose, and her face felt hot. She spun on her heels before he could notice and led him into the back.

David walked slowly, peeking into the kitchen and bathrooms and studying the moldings. "This is so cool!"

"As far as I can tell, the parlor and dining room were made into the showroom and everything else left alone."

"It's so rare to see original 1920s tile and fixtures in the kitchen and bath. So many renovators tear that stuff out and put in fixtures that will be trendy for 10 minutes. You must feel lucky to live here."

"Except when I need an outlet for a modern appliance. I make toast in the showroom because otherwise I would need to unplug the icebox." She gestured him into a bedroom, which she had set up with Mamère's furniture as a dining room. She followed him in and placed her hand affectionately on the finely woven white cotton tablecloth with its sheen from years of wear and starch. Jake had installed a small chandelier with rectangles of crystal over the table. As they walked in, it sparkled in the colors of the rainbow and flashed patterns of light on the plaster.

"You look as stunned as I felt the first time someone in California invited me over for supper, and we ate on paper plates on our laps," Leonie said.

"'Stunned' is a good word. 'Stupefied' is even better." He turned in circles several times as if he could not take in everything at once.

It's an ordinary dining room with the usual set of furniture. What's the big deal? But it seemed a big deal to David. She crossed her arms over her chest and chewed the inside of her lip. She had committed some unintentional faux pas and worse yet, didn't know what it was.

"I'm way out of my league. My family always ate in the kitchen on Corelle 'Indian Summer' dinnerware. We had vinyl placemats with ocean scenes." He cleared his throat. "It's okay. I just didn't realize you came from money."

She laughed. "Hardly. We were dirt poor until I got a job at a marketing firm."

"Yet you trust me with your nice stuff already. I'm honored."

She cocked her head. "In Louisiana, we do things civilized. Jake says the Japanese are the same way."

David's face reddened. "Mom was sure if she put out anything nice, I would damage or break it. She picked 'Indian Summer' because it was one of the few Corelle patterns without a glossy white center for me to scratch up with the silverware." He glanced down at Leonie's cutlery. "I mean flatware."

Leonie winced. She looked down and let her hair fall around her face, embarrassed on his behalf and unable to meet his eyes until she had absorbed his revelation.

"Leonie?"

Her fists tightened, and she banged one on the table. How could his parents have treated him so badly?

"Why are you mad at me?" He took a step toward the door. "Never mind. I'll leave."

"David, no! You didn't do anything. It's your mother. Parents shouldn't treat their children like that." Her voice was rising. She stopped and took a few breaths. "She got her comeuppance, though, when you became an artist and made intricate things with precise tool work. I'm glad. I'm sorry, but I'm glad you showed her up."

At last she could look up.

She gasped. His hunched shoulders and puppy-dog eyes stabbed her to the core. His mother had not reformed her ways. She still undermined him. *Not my dog; not my fight.* "Would you like a glass of sweet tea? Or a beer?"

David's body relaxed. "Yeah, sure. A beer would be perfect for this hot night."

Leonie rolled her eyes. "Why don't you have a seat? I'll fetch you your beer and then serve up the food."

She grabbed an Abita Amber from the icebox and popped the cap. She grabbed a tall glass from the cupboard and carried them in.

David had not sat down. Instead, he studied a long silk scroll hanging on the wall. Pasted on the nubby pink silk was a sheet of handmade paper with many lines of calligraphy. As she watched him, he traced the first line with his finger without touching it and then the second line. Slowly he smiled.

She hated to break his reverie, but her curiosity got the better of her. "Is that my father's work?"

"Yes. He was going to exhibit some new pieces at the show I mentioned." He turned toward her. "The chandelier makes the drops of condensation sparkle. What a shame to smear them, but it has to be done." He took the bottle and held it to his forehead. "Ahhh! This is almost as refreshing as drinking it."

"Who would have thought we would get so warm on such a chilly evening?"

"Chilly?" He shook his head. "This is warm for coastal California." He still sweated from their labor.

She grimaced. "I hate to think what winter evenings will be like here. I haven't gotten used to the chilly summers yet." She left again for the kitchen, where she took the food out of Lily's containers and put it on dinner plates. She set them on the dinner table and returned for a third and last time with a tray on which she'd put cloth napkins, more glasses, and a pitcher of ice tea.

David whistled. "I should have worn a dressier t-shirt."

Leonie laughed. "You look fine." She winked. There was no harm in building him up a bit to counter his parents' contempt. "Mighty fine."

He shivered and stuck his hands in his pockets. Then he pulled them back out. "Don't flatter me too much. I might break into song about how I'm too sexy for this tablecloth."

Leonie chuckled. "I'd rather hear about your art."

David grinned. The tension in the room disappeared like clothes flying off a clothesline during a tropical storm. He pulled out her chair for her. As she sat, his hand brushed against her hair, then her shoulder. *Did he do that on purpose?* She hoped so. It felt good.

"Thanks for bringing food," she said. "It looks amazing."

"Yeah!" He stared at his plate with big eyes. "All I asked Lily was to throw together a simple box dinner."

"She went far beyond that." The plates before them held sandwiches of turkey breast and fresh tomatoes on wheat bread, black-bean salad, and Persian cucumber halves with a spiced yogurt dip. Leonie had set the two crème brûlées in tiny fluted ceramic dishes piled with fresh raspberries toward the middle of the table for dessert. Saliva turned her voice sultry. "I'm in awe."

He cleared his throat. "No big deal. I was glad to help you out, and *she* was glad to help *me* out."

Leonie poured herself a glass of tea, picked up her sandwich, and leaned toward him, her eyes mischievous. "So do you actually like art, or do you just get the t-shirts?"

He grinned at her banter and responded in kind. "Just shirts. My friends know when they go to a museum or gallery opening, they should bring me back a t-shirt. Sometimes, though, they try to be funny. I have a box under my bed full of t-shirts that say, 'My friend went to such-and-such and all I got was this lousy t-shirt.'"

"Touché." A grin flitted across her face. "Seriously, I do want to hear about your art."

"Are you sure?"

"I'm not just being polite. I've drooled over your works since I got here."

He blushed and ducked his head in embarrassment. "Where should I start?"

"How about where you want your art to go?"

His smile grew even bigger, and his eyes glowed. "I'd love to be like your dad and have a little shop where I sold things close to my heart. Not pens, of course, but my own art and perhaps friends' art."

"I met a photographer at the Honey Bee and commissioned some postcards and prints. They've been good sellers for the store and bring people in. Some then buy other things."

He nodded like crazy. "Yeah, I did notice the postcards. That's similar to what I had in mind. Good pieces of art enhance each other."

She leaned toward him, eager to hear more. "Do you create anything besides enamelwork?"

"Not much anymore. Some of my musician friends had to try many instruments before they found their soul-mate instrument or instruments, and like them, I had to try many media. I've settled on cloisonné and other enamelwork, although I still do some stained glass."

"Isn't it funny? All the light outside one takes for granted, but go in a building, and the light defines it."

"Exactly! We're on the same wavelength." He grabbed her hand and squeezed it. "That's why I started making stained glass and why I can't stop."

"No reason to when it gives you joy. Where else do you sell your work?"

David's smile became forced, almost a grimace. She had touched a nerve without meaning to. *With that expression, he could pose for a sculptor of gargoyles.*

"I make the craft show circuit on the West Coast every year. People gush over my pieces but…" He trailed off.

"But you don't sell much at craft shows? And you're not in any other stores?"

"Right." He hunched over his plate and forked bean salad into his mouth.

Jake probably invited him to put some enamelwork here in the shop rather than David asking to do so. "It's a common problem of artists, not knowing where to sell their works. I encountered it all the time when I worked in marketing." She spoke matter-of-factly to reduce his embarrassment. "I met many people with art, writing, and music degrees who weren't taught anything about business in their majors. It's no wonder artists often don't know how to profit from their art."

He ate several more forkfuls of bean salad and then slowly looked up at her. "You said that so nicely. My parents would berate me for hours if I admitted to them what I just told you."

She leaned against the chair back and stared at his face for hints he was making a bad joke, but saw none. She opened and shut her mouth several times, changing her mind about what to say. So much she wanted to criticize his parents. But it would not be polite. She struggled to think of something helpful and supportive.

"If artistic talent and business sense always went together, I would not have had any clients. With advice and guidance, artists can learn business sense and increase their skill. Talent by itself is almost never enough."

The tightness left his shoulders, and he straightened up. He pulled a crust off the edge of sandwich and nibbled it while apparently thinking. "I should have talked to the other artists at the craft shows about making money instead of making art, huh?"

"It might not have helped. In my experience, most people at such shows aren't making a living from their art. And that's what you want to do, right?"

"Yes! No question." He swallowed the rest of his crust. "Delivering packages pays the rents for my studio and my attic room at Mrs. Millhouse's, but it's not my passion. I'll do whatever it takes to succeed as an artist. Once I find out what that is." David's speech was rough, loud, rushed. It grated on her ears like out-of-tune bells. The tips of his ears reddened.

How cute he looks when he's embarrassed!

He took a sip of beer. "Do you have anything to suggest?"

"I do, actually." She dotted her mouth with her napkin. "If you want my help," she added to avoid putting him on the spot.

"I'd at least listen to your ideas."

"Relax! I'm not going to suggest anything involving alligators or nude Jell-o wrestling or whatever they do in clubs in California," Leonie said. "First things first: Would you consider putting more enamel pieces here on consignment? Your work is beautiful, and I think it's a good fit with the pens."

He caught his breath.

Success! He wants more of his work for sale here, and I'd love to have his pieces around to look at. To comfort me when I feel everything in California is harsh and ugly.

David spoke slowly. "You'll think this is silly, but when I come into the shop, I crave certain pens. It's as if in some weird way I'm thirsty and looking at them is the only way to satisfy that thirst. Ones with lacy silverwork or sturdy gold overlays. Pens with guilloché work as good as on any Fabergé imperial Easter egg. Pens with hand-painted scenes of fairy tales done in Russian lacquer art."

An adrenaline rush left Leonie breathless and trembling. She felt as if she might dance away on the breeze like a leaf. She covered David's warm, large hand with hers and squeezed it. *Why couldn't I have found such a companion here earlier?* "Me, I understand perfectly. Some days I can't bear to look in the cases for more than a second or two. I drown in the beauty. I get drunk on it and am dazed and dizzy the rest of the day. I'm even sillier than you, yes?"

"Hardly." He squeezed her hand back and chuckled. "As a kid, I once got stuck at the Getty Center in front of a 16th-century pietra dura tabletop for three hours. It seemed like only a few minutes to me. The tabletop had at least a dozen types of stone in it, and the inlay work was so perfect, only the color change gave away where the stone changed. I couldn't stop looking at the patterns within each stone, at the small designs, and at the overall effect. Meanwhile, my parents were frantic and had half the staff looking for me."

She interrupted him. "Let me guess. They found you walking toward the table and backing away from it over and over again?"

"Exactly. You understand." He squeezed her hand again and let go to slide his spoon into silky crème brûlée. "My parents didn't, though, and neither did the psychiatrist."

Talking to David was like talking to a client or to one of the people who worked in the countless art galleries, antique shops, and auction houses in Baton Rouge and New Orleans. Or even to one of the street musicians. *Back home, we're surrounded by beauty. Enthralled and intoxicated by it. Maybe even addicted to it.* She clasped her hands over her heart. *I never knew how lucky I was until I came here.*

"And the worst part of all? My parents wouldn't even get me the t-shirt of the table." David's eyes sparkled with joy and mischief. "Years later, I made one for myself. A t-shirt, not a pietra dura table."

It's a good memory for him, not a bad one. "Have you made a brooch or pendant with the table design in miniature?" she asked.

"No, but that's a fantastic idea." He paused. "I never answered your question. Would I *consider* having my art here with those pens? No way. I'd accept in an instant before you changed your mind."

"Great!" Leonie looked down at her plate and realized she had finished all her food. So had David, despite all his talking. Her adrenaline high plummeted like a hawk, and her body fought gravity to stay upright. She swallowed a yawn. *Can it be late already? The time passed so fast and agreeably.* "We need to discuss your marketing and what pieces you should bring here, but not tonight."

He nodded, all joy leaving his face; only puzzlement remained in his narrowed eyes and vertical wrinkles between his eyebrows. "You haven't mentioned your father."

Her chest tightened, and she ran her finger up and down her ice tea glass. "I get butterflies in my stomach every time I think about ringing strangers' doorbells to ask about Jake as if he were a lost puppy." She grasped the glass with a jittery hand and sipped tea before speaking. "I'll make myself do it. I'm living in his house and eating his food, so I owe it to him. But once I've talked to the neighbors, I have no idea what to do next. Staple 'lost father' flyers on telephone poles? Moonlight Cove seems much bigger when one thinks about knocking on every door."

"I can help. I can introduce you to the neighbors, and then you won't feel awkward. I also know some of the clubs your father belongs to, so we can contact their members. We should be able to find out quickly whether anyone knows what happened to him."

"Tomorrow then? Before I lose my nerve?"

"Sure. And to reward ourselves, why don't we spend Sunday at the beach? We can relax, maybe discuss marketing my art. You could visit my studio to choose what pieces you'd like to carry."

Why do Californians like the beach so much? Leonie wrinkled her nose. "I don't like the beach."

"You don't?" He stared at her. "Are you kidding? Most people move here for the beach."

"I came here to have a family again. With Jake."

"How can anyone not like the beach?"

"The ocean smells bad. The sun is too bright and glares off the sand. The beach is crowded and noisy. It's also boring—nothing but sand, sand, sand."

"Where would you like to go?"

"There probably isn't any such place hereabouts, but I'd love to go someplace quiet and beautiful with lots of trees." Her face was wistful, and her gaze distant. "I know I'm dreaming."

"Maybe not." He leaned back and rubbed his chin. "Have you climbed the cliff at the beach end of the cove? There's a pretty park up there not many people go to. Rainbow's End."

"No, I haven't been up there. But I should see it before I leave. Can we do that?"

A vein in his forehead reddened. "Leave? Why would you leave?"

Leonie tucked a strand of hair behind her ear. "Why would I stay if Jake isn't here?"

"But... but we've only started to get to know... I mean, we're only just starting to look for him."

"He's been gone for weeks! Maybe he isn't coming back. I decided two days ago that if he hasn't shown up in a week, I'm out of here."

"Maybe he's in a hospital somewhere in a coma. You can't give up now. We've only started looking for him."

"He's a grownup. He shouldn't need to be looked for."

"That's cold. He's your father! If we can't figure out where he is, you need to report him missing to the police."

She was determined to keep her voice calm. "There's time before Wednesday to look for him and report him to the police."

David slapped the table with his hands. "I'll come by at 9 to start our search. Be ready." He walked out without saying goodbye. The wind chimes jangled.

Puff strolled into the dining room and jumped on her lap. Leonie buried her face in Puff's fur. "I like him. He seems to like me. Why couldn't we have met in my first week here instead of my last?"

Chapter 7

David arrived the next morning in jeans and a t-shirt showing a Robert Mapplethorpe still life of flowers.

"I didn't know Mapplethorpe took color pictures."

"He didn't very often. He occasionally used color film though." He looked her up and down. "You look like a different person."

Leonie squinted at her reflection next to David's in the window glass. She had decided to canvass the neighborhood in a conservative navy blue dress and with her hair up in a French braid so she would look as respectable as possible. Next to David, though, she looked dowdy and old. She pinched her skirt and twisted the cotton between her fingers. "I look wrong next to you."

He leaned against the wall and rested his chin in his palm. He looked at her in silence, scanned the shop and its furnishings, and looked back at her. "You look exactly how people would picture Mr. Hamasaki's daughter."

She blew out her breath. *I look just right then.* "What about you?"

He looked down at his art t-shirt and back up at her with a grin. "You want people to recognize me, don't you?"

"Yes, but… isn't the picture too upbeat? After all, we're looking for a missing person."

"Hmmm. Good point. Maybe I should have chosen the t-shirt with J.M.W. Turner's *Dutch Boats in a Gale* to underscores the despair behind our quest."

She blinked her eyes. *If we find Jake, I'll suggest we make t-shirts out of one or two of his paintings. It would be a great way to advertise the store.*

"Mapplethorpe's name alone probably conjures up despair, even next to a picture of flowers," she said.

"True. Let's get started."

As she slid on her sunglasses with shaking hands, her heart thumped, and her palms perspired. She, who had worked with famous people and met new people every day in her job, had stage fright. *I've been alone too long, for true. Cats aren't enough.*

"Where should we start?" she asked, locking the door behind them and trying to ignore Slink's wail of abandonment.

"Let's start with Mrs. Itani a few doors down. Your father's good friends with her. If she can't help us, we'll try the rest of your neighbors on this block."

It took only a few minutes to reach Mrs. Itani's house, which was a bungalow much like Jake's house. It had no storefront, though; it was still a residence.

Leonie looked at David, and he gestured at the knocker.

She sighed. She had hoped he would take the lead. She lifted the heavy bronze lion's head and dropped it.

"Coming!" a high, sweet voice called out. The door opened. A woman wearing neatly-pressed gardening clothes and holding a trowel looked at her.

"Mrs. Itani?"

The woman nodded.

Leonie bowed. "I'm Jake Hamasaki's daughter, Noriko Leonie, and I'm looking for my father."

"Come in, come in. Good to see you, David." Mrs. Itani led them into a living room furnished in modern Swedish furniture and decorated with a few large vases bursting with fresh flowers. But they didn't stop there. She took them through the house and out into the back yard, where the air was thick with the sweet scent of jasmine. She gestured for them to sit in the airy, white wicker chairs. "Jake isn't here right now. In fact, I haven't seen him in weeks, it seems. But I'm glad you stopped by. Jake told me he'd bring you over, and I've been waiting. Would you like some tea?"

"Yes, thank you." Leonie answered quickly in case David didn't know it was an insult to refuse. She hadn't known herself until one of Jake's Japanese culture lectures.

Mrs. Itani went into the house and returned a couple minutes later with a tray holding a cast-iron tea set. She poured tea into two tea "bowls" and set down the teapot. Leonie then poured tea for her hostess. Only after nesting the small, scorching bowl between her hands and taking a small sip did she get to business.

"Mrs. Itani, my father left a few weeks ago and didn't tell me where he was going or when he would be back. I haven't heard from him since. I'm getting worried."

David added, "I'm worried too. Mr. Hamasaki and I were supposed to share a booth at an art festival, but he hasn't sent me the signed paperwork, and it needs to be turned in soon. It's not like him to be irresponsible."

"No, it certainly is not." Steam drifted in front of Mrs. Itani's face and softened the ravines of her frown. "He didn't tell me he was leaving, which is odd. On the rare occasions he goes away, he always asks me to feed the cats and bring in packages."

At least now I know who can take care of Puff and Slink if I go home this coming week.

Mrs. Itani looked directly at Leonie. "But of course, he wouldn't have needed my help this time with you there." She narrowed her eyes, and her fingers turned white around the tea bowl. "Still, I would have thought he would have told me he was going away."

"Where has he gone in the past? That might give us some clues about where to look for him." David held his hot tea bowl with his fingertips, which concentrated the heat, Leonie knew. Dots of perspiration broke out on his brow.

"Let me think." Mrs. Itani set down her bowl, steepled her fingers in front of her chin, and bowed her face over them. "Some years he goes to the Los Angeles Pen Show, but that's always in February. A couple of times he's gone to Japan, but I don't remember where or why. Before he takes on a new line of pens, he visits the factory." She looked up. "I can't think of any other place. I'm so sorry."

David said, "He mentioned to me he belonged to some organizations for people of Japanese ancestry… nikkei?"

Mrs. Itani's face brightened. "I'll make you a list." She went inside.

David immediately set down his tea bowl and shook his fingers in the air.

"Hold it like this." Leonie demonstrated the technique Jake had taught her. "It distributes the heat throughout your hands. Did you burn yourself?"

Sheepishly, he held out his hands. *Poor guy.* His fingertips were as red as the feathers of a male cardinal.

"You remember the rules?"

He nodded. "I'll ask for your help if I need it." He examined his fingers. "They're already feeling better. I think they'll be okay." His smile made her feel gooey inside. "Did anyone visit Jake or did he visit anyone that you can remember?"

Leonie stared at his smile. *He has such inviting lips.* They were fuller than the typical white guy's lips, but not so full they didn't go with his face. In fact, all the parts of his face went together breathtakingly well. She sighed.

Dave's eyebrows lifted. "Tired already?"

Her hands involuntarily clutched her tea bowl tighter. "No. Just thinking hard. Jake did go to some meetings. A bonsai club, I think. Maybe a Japanese calligraphy club."

"I think you're right about those two clubs. Let's hope Mrs. Itani knows who's in them."

"What's a nikkei?"

"A person who immigrated from Japan or one of their descendants. I think you probably count." He gingerly picked up and cupped his tea mug the way she had shown him. "You should think about joining one. It would be a good way to start meeting people and maybe make some friends."

She shook her head. "It seems a backward way to meet people. Pushy, too."

"Not in California. People move here from all over. If they want to make friends, they have to make the first move. No one's going to show up at the door with a pie like in some 1950s sitcom."

"You're kidding, right?"

But his expression was open and sincere. *He's telling the truth.*

Tears sprang to her eyes. She batted them back. But one escaped and rolled down her cheek.

Instantly, David leaned over and put a hand on her arm. Warmer than usual from holding the tea bowl, his hand sent a zing up and down her spine. Despite that zing, and despite her efforts to hide the resulting shudder, his touch made her limbs soften and her lax body lean toward him. His touch was comfort. Reassurance. Encouragement. Perversely, her tears flowed freely now.

"Leonie, what's wrong?" He stroked her arm gently.

"I didn't know." She sniffled and managed to slow her tears.

"Didn't know what?"

"I *was* expecting pies. Brownies. Homemade jams. Invitations to visit. When no one came over to welcome me, I assumed people had taken a dislike to me. I didn't know why."

She immediately wanted to take back her words, her show of vulnerability. Most men would respond with a laugh or a patronizing remark making light of her distress.

David was not most men. "Feeling rejected is the worst."

His voice — he sounds half-strangled, as if he's talking about himself as well as me.

She shivered again, this time in pity. Her words had ripped open some painful memory of his. Although she didn't know what that memory was, there was a pain above her breastbone that ached in sympathy.

She put her hand on top of the one stroking her arm. "You've made me feel so much better. Thank you."

She didn't look at him. But she could feel the tension leaving his body and sense his arm slide back to his side.

"How do you know that the rules of *my* healing magic don't forbid you from thanking me?" he asked in his usual good-humored tone.

"I guess I don't. We have such different backgrounds. We're such different people."

Before he could respond, Mrs. Itani came back out with papers in her hand. "I'm sorry to have taken so long. But I wanted to write down the name and phone number of every possible contact I could think of." She handed the papers to David.

He quickly scanned the names and smiled at Mrs. Itani. "This is going to help us a lot. We really appreciate your time."

Looking worried, Mrs. Itani sat down. Her hands found each other and folded in her lap. "It was no trouble. Jake's my friend. If there's anything more I can do to help you, please let me know."

Leonie rose. "Thank you for your help and for the tea and hospitality. May I ask you a question?"

"Of course you can ask." Mrs. Itani's face relaxed, and her mouth quirked. "Of course I can decline to answer."

David laughed, and their mutual apprehension about Jake receded.

Leonie said, "I have — Jake has — a diseased apple tree. Every apple is hard and misshapen, just like the fruit in your apple tree. Is there a way to make the tree healthy again?"

"Apple tree? I don't have an apple tree."

David's sudden cough sounded suspiciously like a muffled chuckle.

Heat rose in Leonie's face. She had blundered somehow, but she soldiered on. "This tree, the one with a bushy shape." She walked over to it and touched a diseased apple. The tree was pregnant with fruit, and every single apple was mottled and hard.

"Oh!" Mrs. Itani broke into a wide smile. "Those aren't apples, they're pomegranates. If you've never had one, you're in for a treat."

Leonie squeezed the pomegranate. It had no give, and the skin was hard and rough like a nut's shell. "How do you eat it? It's too hard to bite into."

"When the fruit ripens, I'll invite you over and show you the best technique for opening them up and separating the membranes from the edible pulp. It takes a little practice, but it's worth it." Mrs. Itani nodded, smiling. "Would you like to come too, David?"

Wistfulness tinged her voice. Leonie looked around the yard for any sign a man lived here and found nothing. *She must be a widow. Is she Jake's girlfriend? Another thing I don't know about my father.*

"I'd love to come over then. You're very kind to invite me."

"It'll be more fun with you here." Mrs. Itani led them to a gate in the yard beneath a trellised arch straining under the weight of glossy-leaved vines studded with thousands of white stars. Jasmine, looking and smelling just as it did at home. Mrs. Itani let them out onto an alley.

The scent of jasmine followed them. Leonie's stomach twisted with homesickness. But before her sick feeling could spread to her mind and sadden her thoughts, David spoke.

"I think you made your first friend."

Chapter 8

By midafternoon, David had lost the spring in his step, and Leonie felt droopy and gloomy. None of the other neighbors on the block had any idea of where Jake could be, and none seemed interested in befriending her. In truth, some seemed riled she had had the nerve to knock on their doors.

"Want to go to the Honey Bee and refuel?" David asked.

Leonie shook her head. Although it was another chilly day, the sun's relentless glare had more than made up for it. Despite her sunglasses, the intense light had given her a headache and sucked out her energy. Her eyes burned from the dry air. "I know it's only a few blocks, but I'm so tuckered they'd feel like miles. Let's get something cold at my place. There should be something in the icebox we can eat."

When they reached the shop, Leonie settled David in the dining room and went to the kitchen to pour glasses of sweet tea. She took David's glass to him and returned to the kitchen, where she drank her whole glass, refilled it, and drank some more.

Puff rubbed against her legs, purring.

"I keep forgetting how fast one gets dehydrated here," she told Puff and finished her second glass of tea. "You should be glad your ancestors were desert animals." Then she opened the icebox and stared into it, slumping against a cabinet. Puff stood with her paws on the bottom shelf and looked inside too.

She had forgotten how much she had cooked this week. She pulled several containers out of the icebox and got down two plates. She put chicken pecan salad, some deviled eggs, and a square of cold cornbread on each plate. Then she loaded them on a tray with her glass and a pitcher of iced tea.

Cautiously, she heaved the heavy tray up from the cabinet and carried it to the dining room, blowing out her held breath when she set it down.

David didn't look up. He had found a notepad somewhere and was writing on it. "I'm trying to figure out an efficient way to reach as many people as possible." The two sheets of names and phone numbers Mrs.

Itani had given them had multiplied into perhaps a dozen sheets scattered over the table.

Leonie set the tray down, refilled his empty glass, and set his plate down, being careful to avoid the papers.

His head swiveled to look at the food. "Oh, wow. Thanks." He drank several swallows of ice tea. "Who could've guessed it would take hours to canvass just one block?"

Guilt stabbed her in the back of her throat. "And you're still here, helping me out. Sorry it's more work than you expected." She took the barrette out of her moist hair.

"No problem. He's my friend and a fellow artist." He raised his eyebrow. "You wouldn't happen to have any art you'd like to exhibit with me at the show, do you?"

"Sorry. I just market art, I don't make it."

"Worth asking." He took a bite of chicken salad. "By the way, do you have any butter for the cornbread?"

"Bite your tongue!" She pretended outrage. "Cornbread done right doesn't need butter."

David drew back from his plate and gave his cornbread the side-eye. "And that is because… ?"

"I put enough butter in it when I made it, of course. Why don't you try some?"

"Not to disparage your cooking—which I haven't tried it yet, I want to point out—but this may be too rich for me. It's me, not you." He picked up his knife and fork and cut a triangle off the corner.

It fell over on its side and lay there. *How can he resist?* The corner was the vivid yellow of an egg yolk and nearly as lustrous. Leonie was tempted to grab it herself before he worked up the courage to eat it.

"Well?" Leonie folded her arms.

"Here goes nothing." He forked the tiny yellow triangle into his mouth. "Oh. My." He chewed a little. "Oh my gosh, this is incredible." He picked up the square and ate all the cornbread. Midway through his eyes drifted shut. Crumbs flaked onto the tablecloth and fell on his clothes and the floor. Butter glazed his lips, and a few tiny yellow crumbs stuck to them.

Leonie, still standing, grabbed the back of her chair. *I really want to kiss him right now.*

He sat still for several moments after he finished chewing. When his eyes opened, they were drunk with pleasure, and his face seemed to glow. His gaze wandered from his plate to her face, and he smiled, his lips parted slightly and seductively.

Leonie swallowed.

"The chicken salad tastes great, and the eggs look heavenly," he said in a voice dripping with desire, "but may I please have some more cornbread?"

"Of course." Leonie rushed to the kitchen and grabbed the cabinet, drooping with both relief and disappointment. *I'm going home soon unless we find Jake. I can't let myself fall for David.*

At floor level, someone meowed, "You have."

Leonie jumped. At her feet, Puff and Slink paraded back and forth in front of their food bowls, tails high, meowing in all kinds of syllables. *Did I hear what I wanted to hear or what I dreaded to hear?*

As she poured out kibble, she considered for the first time whether something besides Jake's return could entice her to stay. She'd now met a man she found appealing, and Mrs. Itani seemed interested in friendship.

As she cut another square of cornbread for Jake, she shook her head. *Such thoughts only show how lonely I am here. One potential boyfriend and one potential woman friend are hardly reasons to live in a chilly town that smells of fish.*

She put the cornbread on a fresh plate and carried it out to David.

He immediately took a bite. "You said you weren't an artist, but my taste buds disagree."

Warmth filled her belly and chest, and for a moment she couldn't breathe. Her heart felt full. *It feels good to be appreciated by someone other than store customers. By someone I care about. I've missed it.*

"Your words are as buttery as the cornbread." She meant for her tone to be light, teasing, a little tart. Instead, her words came out heavy with meaning and rich with emotions she could not herself name but felt embarrassed by anyway. She quickly changed the subject and waved her arm at the papers scattered across the dining room table. "What have you come up with so far?"

Refreshed from the iced tea, she leaned over his shoulder to see his work. David's warmth rose to caress her neck and face. She leaned a little closer.

"The leader of the Shinto discussion group is also the president of the Buddhist relief organization," David said. "We can reach a lot of people by asking him to announce at the next meetings we're looking for Jake."

"When are those meetings?"

"We'll have to ask."

I may be gone by then. Only four days left before I leave unless Jake comes home.

At least, that's what I planned. What if David's right, that something has happened to Jake?

Even if he has abandoned me again, that doesn't make it right for me to abandon him. Mama raised me to be a good daughter.

I don't know what to think or do.

"Earth to Leonie."

"Yeah?" Somehow, her head was now resting on top of David's, the waves in his hair tickling her face. Despite their day outside in the sun and the pollution, his hair smelled clean and fresh. She longed to run her fingers through it. She settled with resting her hands on his muscular shoulders. "Did I miss something?"

"I said I was thinking of going in person to those groups to ask about Jake. Do you want to call the people on these lists? They're the calligraphers and the bonsai makers or bonsai pruners or whatever they're called."

"I don't know what they're called either, but I'll say 'bonsai artists.' That will probably get me the most cooperation."

"Cynic." He held out some papers.

She took them. David had jotted notes about the people he knew, listing their hobbies and interests as well as their sexes, ages, and jobs. Knowing this information would make it easier to establish a connection with the people.

Even so, the density of writing on the pages threatened to make her eyes cross, and she sighed.

David's head snapped up. "Geez, you look tired." He stood and pulled out her chair. "Sit, drink your tea, and have some food. You haven't even touched your plate, have you?"

She sank onto the padded seat gratefully, and another sigh escaped her.

"Don't make any calls until you're feeling better. I can get started on your list while you eat. I want you fresh for our trip to Rainbow's End tomorrow."

Chapter 9

Sunday morning, David led Leonie through the smallest streets and back alleys of Moonlight Cove, but they still had to weave around *Bikini Babes* trucks reeking of diesel fuel, lighting booms that towered over the buildings, men who shouted and waved their arms, and food-service tents smelling of burnt hash browns and weak coffee.

"They haven't even started filming yet, and already I'm looking forward to them leaving." David wrinkled his nose. "I'm glad you didn't want to go to the beach. At the park, we'll be away from the *Bikini Babes* ruckus, and it's a beautiful day to sit outside."

"Beautiful," Leonie agreed, "but a little cool right now." She shivered and shoved her hands in the pockets of her white Tulane sweatshirt with its large Green Wave logo.

David looked up, sighed, and stretched his arms wide as if to embrace the sky. "This is the perfect weather for me." He looked her up and down with an amused expression, just as he had when she had opened the door this morning. "Once the sun is higher, you may be too warm in those hiking boots and heavy pants." He quirked an eyebrow. "If you don't mind my asking, why do you have waders tied to your backpack and a Bowie knife tucked into the lacing cords of your boot?"

"I was going to ask why you didn't." Leonie hadn't yet gotten over her horror at his outfit of flip-flops, camouflage shorts, and a green t-shirt with an image of one of the rose paintings by Redouté. "Aren't you worried a hunter will shoot you or a snake will bite you?"

A grin quirked the corner of his mouth. "Not really."

Leonie shivered. "Me, I hate it when I get snakes in my boots."

David's grin widened.

Leonie's face got hot. "Well, excuse me if I'm too girly for you. I don't mind *fish* in my boots, by the way. Them I can cook." She put her hands on her hips. "Are we going hiking, or are you too disappointed?"

"I'm not disappointed. But you may be when we get to Rainbow's End. Here, let me carry those waders." She mouthed some mild, unconvincing protests, but he untied the waders from her backpack and slung them over his shoulder. A loud string of curses sounded from one of the *Bikini Babes* trucks, and he picked up the pace and turned a corner. "There's a private street here." He climbed over the gate.

Leonie put one hand on the top of the gate and vaulted over. Her gymnastics training had come in handy twice now in the few days she had known David. "Why do you think I'll be disappointed?"

"The park's much tamer than you seem to expect. No marshes, no streams. No large or medium carnivores. Do you know anything about California history?"

She shook her head. "Only that Japanese immigrants have been important in farming since the 1800s. Or at least, that's what Jake told me." She waved her hand at the tiny but beautifully rehabbed old cottages on the street around them. "He also said the Japanese have been in Moonlight Cove since the beginning."

"Then you can guess the habitat and environment around here has changed a lot. The Spanish started building missions along the coast in the 1770s and forced the native people into them to live and work. Many coastal counties quickly became grazing land for horses, sheep, and cattle. The habitat changed, and predators left or were killed."

"That's shameful."

"Were your ancestors treated any better in Louisiana?"

"No." She shook her head so hard that her pigtails slapped her cheeks. "But we at least had the swamplands to flee to."

They both were silent. Then David said, "We're almost there."

They came to the last and most magnificent house of the street, a new house in the style of a cottage but three times as big. While staring at it, Leonie slipped and had to grab on to David's arm to keep from falling. She looked down. Loose sand covered the sidewalk. *What is sand doing here?* She sniffed. Moonlight Cove's fishy, aquarium-plant smell was particularly strong here. She let go of David and jogged in the street, where there was less loose grit, to get past the house and its profusion of bushes.

Sand stretched before her, and the ocean beyond. Children's screams assaulted her ears, barely dulled by the soft, rhythmic roar of the waves.

Her jaw clenched. She turned her gaze to her guide.

"You tricked me!"

"I didn't trick you!" David protested.

She walked onto the beach and turned around. There stood the town's famous lighthouse, high above them… and behind David. Rainbow's End was on the same cliff. For true, they had been walking *away* from the park, not toward it. She put her hands on her hips and glared at him indignantly.

"It's a shortcut," David protested. "I admit, I did want you to see the beach, because I think you could learn to like it. But—"

"But?" *This better be good.*

"But you liked the pieces in Mr. Hamasaki's shop, and I thought…" He swallowed twice and blushed bright red, with his ear tops a particularly flaming color. "I wanted you to see some of my inspiration for those pieces. But it's okay if you don't want to. I'm sorry you felt tricked. I wanted it to be a surprise, and, well, I guess that was stupid. We can go right to the path."

Leonie's face tingled, and nausea briefly overwhelmed her. *I've been smitten with his art since I got here, and now I may have ruined my chance to learn more about it and insulted David in the process.* "I'm an idiot," she said firmly. "I love your art, and I would love to see what inspires it. Please."

He turned away from her and gestured at the bluff. "The cove is roughly a half circle, and the bluff meets the beach on either side of town." He pointed to a spot where the looming cliff ran parallel to the beach before it plunged into the dark, churning ocean. "I want to show you a small piece of the cliff face there. It's very near the stairs up to the park, I promise." When he turned around to face her, his face had returned to its normal color.

She nodded.

With more confidence in his voice, he continued. "The fastest way there is across the sand. I'll stay near you in case you slip again."

"I'll be more careful now I know how tricky sand is to walk on." She sat and took off her boots.

"You won't want to walk barefoot. You'll burn your feet."

"I doubt it." She took off her socks and raised her feet so he could see the calloused bottoms. "I'll balance better if I can feel what I'm walking on." She stood and stepped onto the sand, and David winced.

The sand felt soothing and warm. When she took another step, her feet sank into the embrace of the sand. "Don't faint, but there's something I do like about the beach. I love how my feet feel so cozy in the sand and how the grains tickle the tops of my feet. I also like the shushing sound the ocean makes."

"I knew I'd win you over to beach life!" he crowed.

"Two things I like don't add up to being won over."

"One step at a time." He grinned. "Come on!"

He walked briskly to the cliff, Leonie following. When they reached the spot he had pointed to, she stared at it in wonder, dizzy with euphoria. She grabbed onto David's arm for the second time that day to keep her balance.

"These rocks are crazy. We have nothing like these back home," Leonie said. "What happened here?"

Her words apparently called forth the geeky side of David Lewys. "You're looking at the history of California," he enthused. "The stripes of different colors show deposits from different times. The tan layers are sandstone, and so are these two layers. And *this* pale layer is chert, which often contains millions of skeletons of microscopic organisms. The dark layers are shale, which is clay compacted into rock while underwater."

Leonie's eyes widened. Around her feet, chilly ocean water seethed around rounded knobs of rock that protruded from the sand and massaged her feet. Careful of the slippery stones, Leonie inched closer to the cliff, wading through the low tide, until she could touch the cliff and run her hands over it.

"If you look closely, you can see many bits of rock that don't match what's around them," David said. "Coarse-grained granites that sparkle with tiny quartz crystals. Black basalt pieces so fine-grained that you can't even see the grain at all. Bits of glistening black glass called obsidian that once spewed out of volcanoes as lava."

"In high school, I thought geology was boring," Leonie admitted. "Down the bayou, we didn't have rock formations."

"Here you can see why geology is really cool."

"When you use this cliff for inspiration, how do you translate the different textures and temperatures of the rocks into colors?"

"I don't. Not yet at least. So far, what I capture with my camera provides enough ideas for my work without trying to include the other senses. The colors and patterns you see now will never look exactly like this again. Shadows change during the course of the day and year, rain and tide make the rocks wet, clouds make small differences harder to see, one never looks at something quite at the same angle, the setting sun adds different colors on different days —these and many other things make the cliff constantly change." His voice had gotten louder and faster. "Remember I told you about diatoms in chert? They had silica walls. The chert layer looks dull now, but when the sun hits it, it glows like a band of opal."

"Wow!" Leonie exclaimed. "How do you know so much? Were you a geology major in college?"

He stiffened, and his smile disappeared. "Pre-law."

"You don't seem like the lawyer type."

"I wasn't. It was my parents' idea." Looking away from her, he wiped his palms on his shorts. "I came to my senses in sophomore year and changed to art."

There's a story here. "And your parents?"

"They said I was a huge disappointment to them." He shrugged. "I never fail to disappoint them. I learned long ago not to let it influence what I do." He kicked at a rock. "Besides, I *have* made a few really bad decisions."

"Parents are supposed to have your back. They're supposed to get you on track when you screw up."

He looked her straight in the eye. "I dropped out of college to get married."

She took a step back. "I can see they might have been disappointed. Still. Several kids in my high school dropped out before graduation to get married. Each time, the ruckus died down quickly, and their families rallied around them. That's what families are supposed to do. Or at least what the ones I know do." Her hand flew to her mouth. "You're not still married, are you?"

"No. Not for a long time."

"Good." *What are you doing, Leonie? You're not here on a date. You're here professionally, to talk about marketing.*

"So it's not a deal breaker?"

She licked her lips. He, too, was treating this excursion like a date. "No, not a deal breaker."

He let out a long breath. "Want to see something really unusual? We'll have to squish between some rocks to get into a cave, but it's worth it."

"Sure. I'm starting to like geology. I guess it helps to have an enthusiastic teacher."

He led her along the cliff face to a dark fold of basalt. He sucked in his breath and, to her astonishment, squeezed into an invisible passage between the rough rocks.

She followed him in, and they walked between rocks for several yards. Then the passage opened onto a closed bay lit by sunlight streaming in from gaps in the rocks overhead.

She gasped. "How beautiful! It's like an arm of a bayou, but with rock instead of trees surrounding it. I almost feel at home."

He pointed. "There's what I really wanted to show you."

On the other side of the cove was a masterpiece of nature's art made only of thin layer upon thin layer of pinkish stone. The years had bent and folded and even twisted the stone until it resembled the bark of an ancient, crooked oak, down to the small, knothole-like caves.

Leonie's skin tingled, and she pressed her palm to her chest. "Hoo lawd," she whispered. Being here was like being in the candle-lit church for Midnight Mass on Christmas. Awestruck, she sank to her knees, her gaze never wavering from the formation. The rest of the world disappeared, and she was engulfed by a deep sense of mystery, joy, and privilege. For true, le petit Jésus should have been born here.

Her knee bones ached; the light on the rock was different now. Time had passed, and she had not noticed. She whispered, "Does anyone else know about this?"

"Probably," he said from right beside her, startling her.

"Too bad. This spot is so special, so romantic. Wouldn't it be so very wonderful if it were our secret?" She ran her hand over the rock beneath her, wishing she could gather up a piece of it to carry in her pocket always.

David's fingers touched her chin and turned her face gently toward him. He gazed deeply in her eyes for several moments. "I spoke too soon," he said. "Look around. There's no graffiti, no scratches in the rock from a bear's paw, no woolly mammoth bones on the rocks. No footprints, paw prints, or hoof prints in the sand under the water. Maybe we are the only two ever to set foot in here."

"I like that idea much better." Wincing, she pulled her knees out from under her and folded her legs. "Thank you for bringing me here. I've never even imagined a place like this existed."

He pulled the cap from her head and stroked her hair. "Your eyes are such an unusual color. Like sherry. They're beautiful. Is that color common among the Houma?"

She leaned into his caress. "Your guess about where I got my eye color is as good as mine. The bayous are a melting pot. French Acadians came from Canada. Germans and Spanish wandered by and stayed. So did runaway black and Indian slaves."

He kissed her lightly from her forehead down her nose to her mouth. "It would bother me not to know my roots," he said and then peppered the corners of her mouth with quick little kisses.

It tickled, and she wiggled as she tried to pull away. As she brushed against more of his body, she stopped trying to escape. She relaxed against him and turned her head.

"It's not genetics that determines my roots, it's culture," she said. "Even if I were part alligator, I would still be Houma in my mind, in my heart. When I move back home and tell people about Jake, everyone will still consider me Houma."

His hand stilled. "Wait. Back up. You're still thinking of moving away? Even after today? After what we're doing?"

Something in her chest squeezed painfully at the thought of never seeing David again. "I was so excited about getting to know my father and having a family again. But Jake disappeared soon after I got here. You think something bad has happened to him. I worry he disappeared on purpose, that he's using me as free labor."

"He's not that kind of guy."

"I don't know him well enough to say. My reason for coming was to get a new family, and that didn't happen. Why stay?"

David resumed stroking her hair. "I sometimes get very faint hints from you that you don't like California much."

"You picked up on those, did you?" As always, his teasing relaxed her. "I miss hot weather. The earthy smell of the swamps and their total, dreamlike silence in the mists before dawn. The magical calls of birds. The soft, musical plink of a turtle sliding from a log into the water. The crash of an alligator slapping its tail. Having friends. You're the only friend I've made so far. Most of all I miss trees." She shifted her butt a little until she was leaning against him. "You know what you didn't pick up on? How fast my heart is beating," she complained.

"Yes, I did," he whispered into her ear. He unbuttoned the top button of her shirt and caressed her neck. Then he lifted her, turned her to face him, and kissed and licked the hollow of her throat, shoving aside the collar of her shirt with his chin.

She squeaked, and he chuckled. He leaned back to watch her face as he lightly and slowly stroked a finger from one collarbone to the other and back. Her head tipped back, inviting further exploration.

"I promised you I'd show you some trees on the top of the bluff," he said and then ran his hand over her face. "Do you want to go up there now?"

She smiled impishly, or at least as impishly as possible while breathing hard. "In a minute or two. Or five." Then she pulled his face toward hers and kissed his lips.

David wrapped his arms around her and kissed her back. And in his secret place that was now her secret too, in the mystical stillness and beauty inside that rocky cove, beneath the blue, blue sky, she closed her eyes and clung to him, and they kissed for an eternity.

Chapter 10

Later, they squished themselves through the passageway and out onto the beach and into the normal world where the sun still glared and the ocean still smelled.

"The stairs are this way." Again David led the way, but when they reached the stairs carved into the rock, Leonie ran up them quickly and beat him to the summit. Grinning, she did a Cajun one-step at the top while he stopped to puff before walking the rest of the way.

"That doesn't count as a win, you know," he said. "You're just showing off another of your superpowers."

"Superpowers? What superpowers?"

He shrugged off his backpack and pulled out a bottle of water for each of them. "You can leap tall display counters in a single bound. You can go from standing to sitting in one smooth motion... even when holding a cat. For extra points, I guess. My arms and legs are strong from carrying heavy packages all day, yet your legs held out for the entire flight up."

"I don't have superpowers. Just four years of college gymnastics and a lot of yoga since then." She took several long drinks from her water bottle until it was gone. Once again, she had forgotten how quickly she dehydrated in the dry California air, and she had not brought any water.

"Gymnastics training and yoga don't explain how you healed my elbow so quickly."

He looked around and then pointed to the largest bush in the park—she couldn't call it a tree without being a liar—and they went and sat underneath. As a josh, she did a graceful sink-and-sit with her backpack on.

"Rub it in," he grumbled. He finished his own water bottle and pulled out another two.

"Thanks." She took hers and drank, looking around. The bush might be a stunted runt of shrubbery, but it gave some shade and did a good job of softening the harsh light. She took off her sunglasses to at last really see the ocean. It glimmered and shivered for miles and miles until it merged with the sky far in the distance, and Moonlight Cove looked insignificant next to the power and size of the ocean.

"I know you don't care about the ocean. You're avoiding telling me how you healed my elbow. So what gives?"

She looked him straight in the eye so he would believe her. "I'm a traiteuse."

He looked blank. "I don't know that word. It doesn't even sound English."

"What it means to be a traiteuse, it is hard to explain to outsiders. I'm a healer, but I don't heal people myself. People are healed *through* me. I'm the channel, you could say. My Nonc—my Uncle—Antoine was a traiteur, a male healer, and he had no daughters, so he passed his knowledge on to me. I'll pass it on to one of my future sons."

He looked at her as if she had sprouted horns and a tail. He pulled granola bars from his backpack, dropped them between the two of them, and then ignored them completely. "This, uh, being a traiteuse or traiteur—is it a Houma thing?"

"More a melting-pot thing. I did a paper on its history in college. Online, I found records from France, some four hundred years old, that described healing rituals we still use. Other practices originated among Indian peoples, including the Houma. Others probably came from Africa. Who knows whom God gave these blessings to first?" David's face looked confused and frustrated, and she shook her head. "You and I, we came here to sit under trees and discuss marketing your art. Instead I bore you and make your eyes glaze over."

"I *am* interested. It's just I've never been into New Agey stuff."

She raised an eyebrow. "Louisiana healing techniques aren't new. What we do is hundreds or thousands of years old. Modern Western medicine has developed almost entirely in less than one hundred fifty years. If any healing techniques are 'New Agey,' it's what's practiced in modern hospitals." She leaned toward him. "Did you know that sick poor people who have to settle for 'outdated' treatments have better outcomes than rich people who get the newest, shiniest medical procedures?"

He hooked a finger in the neck of his t-shirt and pulled on it.

I'm making him uncomfortable by questioning his assumptions.

He makes me question my assumptions too. Am I leaving California too fast, without thinking through the pluses and minuses?

"How about marketing?" he asked, relaxing visibly with his change of subject. "Did you research its history too?"

"Yes, and if you don't stop being a smart aleck, I'll tell you about it in minute detail."

He swiped an X across his chest with his finger. "I promise to behave."

"Good." She pulled a pen and a pocket notebook from her backpack. "Let's start with the basics, your customer. Who is the person you have in mind when you imagine and create a piece of art? Who buys your art on the craft fair circuit? How do people react to your art?"

"I'm not sure I understand."

"Whom do you make art for?"

"For myself, of course."

"Of course." *Spoken like a true artist. He's no hack. And I would know; I've had many for clients.* "What I mean is, who are your customers?"

His brow crinkled. "I'm not sure I know. Your father pays me when people buy my pieces, but he doesn't tell me anything about who bought them. Sometimes customers at crafts fairs chitchat, but I don't learn anything important about them."

"Let me approach this a different way. Have you looked for customers to commission stained-glass windows from you? Rich people, churches, synagogues, city halls, those sorts of customers? For the fairs, do you take intricate enamelwork pieces with high price tags and hope to sell one or two? Or do you make lapel pins customers pay a few bucks for and then hope to sell hundreds? When people come to your booth, what do they hope to find, and do they find it?"

Sunlight pierced the shade and encircled David like a giant, full-body halo. He put his hand to his forehead, swaying dizzily.

Leonie grabbed both his arms to steady him. He seemed on the verge of fainting. "Do you need some water? A granola bar?"

He shook his head, closed his eyes, and raised his face to the light. "I feel like Jake Blues in the first *Blues Brothers* movie. And I thought 'seeing the light' was only a metaphor for a revelation."

Darn, I'm good!

She shouldn't get too carried away with herself. She didn't want to take credit for a "come-to-Jesus moment," as her Protestant friends called it. Or for his deciding to get his blues band back together. Cautiously, she asked, "What revelation did you have?"

He took a deep breath, opened his eyes, and leaned toward her. His face was as serious as she had ever seen it. "I finally understand why I don't sell much. Creation has been one process; and selling art has been another, unrelated one. It never occurred to me to analyze what I made and look for the people most likely to buy it." He clasped her hands between his large ones. "Thank you."

Over the next hour, Leonie asked him many questions about his hopes and dreams as well as his goals and plans for achieving them. For almost every question, he answered, "I need to think about it." When he looked completely drained of energy, she took mercy on him and shut up. She wrote down her thoughts and ideas before they could escape.

When she finally looked up, pleased with the progress they had made, she found him staring down at his hands. "I set myself up to work as a delivery guy for the rest of my life and didn't even know it."

"Get in line. There are so many artists like you, I made a living helping them. Did you know ninety percent of businesses fail in their first year of operation? One reason is some people don't have enough savings to tide them over until the business is turning enough profit to cover expenses. You haven't made *that* mistake. Businesses also fail because they don't have a business plan, and we can make one for you.

Together, we can boost your chances of being in the ten percent who succeed."

"If that happens, my mother will faint and conk her head, and my dad will blame me for the concussion."

"That's all you have to say? You should be happy."

He rubbed his forehead with his knuckles. "I will be once everything sinks in. Right now, I'm overwhelmed. My head is about to explode."

"You don't have to do it all today, you know. And you don't have to do it alone. You made a lot of phone calls on my behalf yesterday. I owe you."

"Fat lot of good it did. Nobody knows where Jake is."

"Still, you saved me from having to make those calls," Leonie said. "We'll start your new marketing plan with something small and easy: picking more works for consignment in Jake's shop. Something subtle, elegant, refined, suitable for someone who's will to pay a thousand dollars or more for a writing instrument."

David zipped up his backpack. "Let's go to my studio now."

Chapter 11

David's studio was in the small Victorian part of Moonlight Cove. Leonie had not even known this neighborhood existed, and she looked around with interest. It still contained many elegant Queen Anne houses, each painted in several colors. But there were also brick warehouses, squat 1950s ranches, and two empty lots roped off for pay parking with a bored teenager stationed in each to collect money.

The air here smelled good enough to eat: From the open windows of the homes wafted the aromas of red sauce simmering, garlic frying, and, to her surprise, the nutty smell of a roux cooking. She left David talking to himself and followed her nose to identify the house where someone knew how to make a brown roux correctly. *I need to come back here. There may be other Louisiana transplants in town.*

"Leonie! Over here," David called. He had stopped at one of the warehouses and was unlocking deadbolts on the metal door. Leonie trotted over and put her hand on his arm, corded with years of work.

David pushed the door open and let her go into the open space first.

As she went in, she trailed her hand down his arm to his hand, and he stopped her for a quick kiss.

Guiltily she pulled away. She was here as a professional and should act like it. She smoothed down her blouse and pulled out her notebook; David followed her in and flipped several switches.

The studio brightened, and glass and enamel glittered and shone. Eric Clapton's guitar rang out, his prowess on the covers giving the old songs their due. Songs written by tough men who worked in the red mud of Mississippi fields by day and played in juke joints by night. Songs she had heard performed in bars at home by raw, rough men and women, some of them friends, some of them clients.

"Delta blues. No better music to work to." *Or to make love to.* She tucked that thought away and turned in a slow circle. The former warehouse had a high ceiling, and light streamed in from windows on all four sides, so it was warm and welcoming. A garage door on the street side probably made loading and unloading supplies and art a snap. More than a dozen sturdy wood tables and desks sat in groupings. Those along the walls appeared to hold equipment that needed electrical plugs, with an antifatigue mat in front of each machine.

An old refrigerator hummed evenly but noticeably, a relaxing sound like Puff's purr. The harsh lemon scent of cleaning products lingered, echoing the citrusy perfume of the 'citrosum' geraniums sitting by each window.

"What a fantastic space for creating! I'm impressed, but I shouldn't be. Of course you could turn a warehouse into a flexible, comfortable studio."

"I'm glad you like it." David beamed. "I was lucky to find the space. One of my customers told me about it and put in a good word for me with the landlord."

"People often think of artists as messy, but you keep everything neat, tidy, and organized." She turned around again. "You haven't wasted money on new furniture, tables that match, or things you don't need. You've got a good head for this part of the business."

"Uh, thanks," he said gruffly. "What would you like to see?"

"Everything! In whatever order you like." Her face split into what she feared was a huge, goofy grin, and she rubbed her arms. "It's as if I'm in a new chocolate shop. See, I've got frissons."

"Frizzy whats?"

She tried to think of the English word. "Chill bumps."

He shook his head.

"Goosebumps? Here, feel." She unbuttoned one cuff and rolled up her sleeve.

"Goosebumps. That word I know." He brushed his fingers over the frissons, and the bumps grew higher. "My grandma called them chicken skin."

"Yeah, frissons do look like the skin of freshly plucked chickens. Not very romantic." She let her arm drop.

"More like disgusting." He stepped back. "If we get off track again, I think one of us should say, 'freshly plucked chickens.' Come, I'll show you some finished stained glass." The table he led her to had light boxes on it. "I thought one of my larger panels might look good standing at the back of your front display window, and another could hang in the side window."

"Hmmmm." She jotted some notes and walked to a display of small window hangings. "Are these what you sell most of?"

He nodded and clasped his hands behind his back.

As Leonie peered at the leading and copper foil on several pieces, she felt his presence behind her and then his breath on her neck. She returned her gaze to the suncatchers, doing her best to shut out the tingles running down her spine. "These I know I don't want in the shop. They won't appeal to high-end customers." She tapped her pen against her lips. "You have good technical and compositional skills. I think you squander your talent going to non-juried shows. Their customers want bargains and knick-knacks." She waved her hand over suncatchers in the shape of flip-flops. "These are cute, but why waste your time when you are capable of real art?"

He opened his mouth, but nothing came out. He shook his head and walked to the wall and back. "I should be taking notes too." He grabbed a notepad and pen from a desk and wrote on it. "As I told you yesterday, I do mostly enamelwork now. Do you know much about it?"

"I looked at pictures on Google Images and Pinterest last night and read several articles. My take-away was that enamelwork is an ancient art and that it's not one technique but many, all based on decorating a metal surface with melted, colored ground glass."

"Got it in one! Noriko Leonie Hamasaki, you're a most amazing woman." He brought his hand up to cup her cheek.

She leaned into his large, calloused hand. "You're only just now noticing?" she teased. She turned her face to brush her lips across his palm and chuckled when he shivered.

She drew his hand down and laced her fingers with his. "What are you going to show me next?"

"Cloisonné." He squeezed her hand and led her toward that area of his studio.

"Most of the pictures I saw were labeled cloisonné. Is it the most common enamelwork technique?"

"Probably the most common *art* technique. But overall, the similar champlevé method, in which the artist carves out the base metal instead of laying wire on top, is more common. Those little lapel pins you've probably seen thousands of use champlevé."

She repressed a squeal. "I know those pins! I had a Terrebonne Tiger pin I wore every day in high school. I also wore him to gymnastic meets for good luck."

"I was so gung-ho for my high school's mascot, the cougar, that I had cougar emblems on half my clothes. I never had a champlevé pin to wear, though."

"Do you still know all the words to your high school song?" she asked.

"Sure do. But you're not going to hear me sing it."

"Go on! I want to hear it."

Grinning, he shook his head. "Once you've heard these lips mangle 'Onward Cougars, Fight to Win,' you'll be too traumatized to ever kiss them again."

She pretended to shudder. "You're right. Don't sing. I don't want to take the risk."

"You know, beautiful, you see only the differences between Louisiana and California. But our backgrounds aren't as different as you think. They're just different enough to make things interesting."

Could he be right? Am I focusing too much on the things that separate us and not enough on what we have in common? One difference still left her ambivalent about his prospects as a boyfriend or lover. "I hate that I grew up surrounded by love, and you didn't."

He squeezed his eyes and looked away, letting go of her hand. His hands grew busy turning his pen and fiddling with the pages of his notebook.

Leonie felt his pain as a sharp needle in her heart. She took a breath before she continued. "One of the things I like best about you is you're not too big for your shrimp boots. You can admit you're wrong. You can make fun of yourself. Not many guys can." She hesitated.

"So what's the bad news?"

"I feel… guilty you became a modest, thoughtful person because your parents denigrated you. I hate that if your parents had brought you up right, you might be someone I couldn't… like… as much."

"Sweetie, you shouldn't feel bad. My parents — " He shook his head and ran his hand through his hair. His next words dripped out in globs like too-thick putty applied badly. "My parents thought they were helping a flawed child become… less flawed. But I figured out by high school I wasn't defective. I was no more klutzy and awkward and careless than any other teenage boy. My parents' standards were too high."

More needles joined the one already piercing her heart. "What did you do?"

"I learned to shut them out. If I had to listen, I… listened as if they were talking about someone else, someone I didn't know or care about. And now I avoid visiting them or talking to them."

She clasped his hand and brought it to her heart. Through her shirt, she could feel his warmth and how her heart beat hard against his palm.

"I can't bear to think how much you hurt for years and years," she said. "I can't forgive them for hurting you."

He kissed her forehead. "Would you be the same person if Jake had been part of your childhood? Can you forgive him for not being there?" he asked. "Childhood isn't for wimps. One kid on my block was bullied. Another had terrible acne that left large scars. Two lost their dogs to heartworms. Three kids lost a grandparent. One kid was a teacher's pet and so had no friends. If we wanted to make a complete list of the miseries of childhood, we could stand here all night."

She leaned against him, silent. Her heart sped up its thumping against his hand. Her breaths bounced back from his neck, warm against her lips.

"Everything you say is true," she finally said. "Pardon my saying it, but I reckon that I was tougher as a kid than you were. That I learned to handle things better and earlier. That your parents almost broke you."

"The key word there is 'almost.'" He stroked her hair. "You're probably right you were stronger. I love that you're so gutsy now. But maybe you made yourself tough so Jake's absence would hurt less. Or so you could fight the kids who picked on a girl with no dad for backup."

She trembled against him. "I never told you those things."

"I guessed." He paused, and she thought he was about to tell her something important. But then he continued his thought. "Some parents hurt kids by being gone. Some hurt them by being around. No parent is perfect, so every kid ends up broken, at least a little bit."

She raised her head. "Kids are resilient. They don't need perfect parents, just parents who love them."

"What about us?"

"We're not broken. We may have small cracks and dents, but we're not broken."

"Like the linen shirts with tags that say, 'The slubs and imperfections in your new shirt are normal and enhance its natural beauty'?"

She stroked his back. "Something like that. You're an artist. I'm a traiteuse. Did we turn out the way we did in spite of our upbringing or because of it? Does it matter? We do what we love and we make people's lives better."

"Interesting perspective. I like it."

She stood on her toes and brushed her lips against his. "Why don't we look at your cloisonné pieces and see whether their flaws enhance their natural beauty?"

He chuckled and took her to a table of cloisonné jewelry and other small items.

Leonie sucked in her breath. "Ooooh, shiny. May I touch?"

"Touch your heart out."

She picked up an earring and placed it against her lower lip. The enamelwork was so smooth, even this sensitive part of her body could not detect where stone met metal.

She put the earring down and picked up a small bowl with a lid. She held it closer to the light. "Wow. Just… wow. I love it." She swallowed. "Sha, how did you think of putting coral, straw yellow, and sky blue together?"

He opened a worn black notebook she hadn't noticed for all the beauty. He flipped through Mylar pages of photos and showed her a picture of rock layers.

"I know that rock! We saw it today."

He broke into a grin. "I wondered whether you'd recognize it. Good eye."

She looked between the bowl and the photo several times. "What you're doing is fantastic, fantastic. Marketable, too, if you do it the right way. Pen connoisseurs could use such a bowl to keep paper clips, sticky notes, or thumb drives at hand but out of sight. The Moonlight Cove connection makes it attractive as a souvenir of their trip here."

"I have other pieces inspired by pictures I've taken here." He showed her an envelope opener; a desk tray; lockets and pendants in several sizes; and pins shaped like shells, lizards, the Moonlight Cove lighthouse, and plants native to the region.

Leonie pressed her hand to her heart. "I know many of these things as well from today. They are beautiful, sha. I can't decide which are my favorites." She picked up a pin. "What is this flower?"

"It's a Matilija poppy, but most people call it a fried-egg plant."

"To me, the white, white petals look like ruched fabric. The orange center with its many… thingees… looks like a chrysanthemum in one of Jake's books on Japanese art. I can picture a lady in her best blouse and a blooming mum pinned to it."

"You definitely have a more poetic soul than whoever named them." He stroked his index finger along her bottom lip. "Have any of the artists you know painted you?"

Heat rose from her neck to her face. "We shouldn't waste the last of the sunlight." Her voice was huskier than she intended. She grabbed the nearest pendant and tilted it to see the image. "What about these scarlet trumpets?"

"Hoary California fuchsia."

She tilted her head. "You painted all these flower jewelry pieces with love. It's so evident. I thought rocks were your passion."

"I started drawing and then painting because I wanted to create flowers as pretty as the ones on our dinner plates. By the time I could copy those flowers, I had learned shading, the importance of white space, and some techniques to imply the curve of a petal and the crinkle of a leaf."

His words did not make her think of petals or leaves, but of the curve of his lips, his brows, his ears, and the crinkle of his smile, of his work shirt when he made deliveries. She swallowed. "What do you think of making copies of your photos on cardstock and attaching each piece to the photo that inspired it? Your name would be on it, along with something like 'Your little piece of Moonlight Cove.' We could put the price, the technique, anything else you wanted on the back of the card."

He rested his hand on the table. "You know better than me how to present them. But I like the idea a lot."

"Good. What about your non-cloisonné enamelwork?"

He pointed to a table and went to it. "I've fooled around with techniques, but I always come back to painting in enamel on glass or ceramic."

"Tell me about some of these pieces."

David scanned the pieces and picked up a pendant. "I've made many pieces based on that warped sedimentary formation in our secret cove. I painted this particular pendant with enamels of the same colors as the rock with no effort to be precise. Rather, I wanted to emphasize

153

the impressions and feelings the rock creates. Even the silver base isn't a perfect oval."

Leonie took it from him and held it up to the light. "It's not perfectly flat, either. Amazing, how slight irregularities create movement." A shiver went down her back.

David picked up another pendant. "Here, I've used the same photo and rendered it more formally. I've inset a rectangular blue topaz at the bottom and another at the top for the water and the sky. In-between, cloisonné details the swirls and folds, with the colors intensified for emphasis."

He placed the pendant on her palm next to the other so she could compare. "And *this* pendant is a more affordable version of the second one. Still cloisonné, but fewer wires." He placed the third pendant next to the others, grazing her palm with his fingertips.

His art made her shiver; his touch made her shiver. She felt as if she was about to jump out of her skin. She could not bear to look at him. She stepped away to study the three pendants and then looked at other pieces on the table. "You often render one photo in many styles and shapes."

"I like to try new things, and customers have different tastes. Some like jewelry that's subtle, soft focus, impressionistic. Others like sharp edges and bold colors."

"But sha, what about your own tastes?"

"Each year I take thousands of pictures and winnow them down to thirty or forty favorites. My own taste shows in what I choose to photograph and which shot I pick. I work only with photos I love. I want to recreate the images in so many ways that everyone, no matter what their tastes, can share in their beauty."

"Interesting perspective," she quoted back to him.

He took back each pendant one at a time, grazing her palm with his fingers each time.

She leaned over the table. "The more I look at the pieces made from the same photo, the more I see—even though I saw the original rocks today. The different renderings enhance each other. I'd like to display these in groups of three or five so the customer can be enlightened in the same way."

"You like some pieces enough to take them on consignment?"

"Yes, if you're willing. You know I may leave. We don't know when — or if — Jake is coming back."

"I'm willing. It's not as if other stores are begging me for pieces to display."

"Great! Your pendants and pins should appeal to the same people who want a unique pen. The hard part is choosing which ones to take." She rubbed her eyes and glanced at her watch. *Look how late it is! My head is swimming from looking at so much splendor.* "I can see your stained-glass work from here, but I want to look at it up close again."

At the wall where the mirrors hung and other pieces lay on light boxes, she glanced over everything. "I still don't want any pieces meant to hang in windows. But I would like some of the intricate mirrors. The copper foil in the stained glass echoes the wires in the cloisonné, so the pieces would resonate with each other." Her shoulders felt heavier and heavier, and she yawned. "That one, that one, that one, that one, if you're willing."

"Yes. Certainly." He took each down and set it on an empty table.

"Now let's pick some similar pieces in the cloisonné and enamelwork."

David's long legs got him to the tables first. "Given the mirrors you chose and your idea for grouping pieces based on the same photo, I'd suggest these." He pointed at pieces, setting aside the ones she nodded at.

"When would you like to bring them to the store?"

"Would tomorrow night be too soon?" David asked.

"Tomorrow night would be fine. Between now and then, think about how much money you want to make on each piece. We'll mark each up a percentage for our commission." She sighed. "There's more to do, but we'll talk about it later." She ran a hand up her forehead and over her hair. It stuck out all over. The wind had tugged strands from her braids all day.

Their gazes met. His eyes darkened.

"Your hair. It's like a storm cloud. No, you look more like an old Eastern Orthodox icon with a dark, tarnished-silver halo." He leaned toward her, caressed her face. "Your skin is so smooth and perfect it could be enameled. You are… sumptuous."

She felt weightless, fearless, full of joy. She felt as if she were glowing. She raised her face, drawn to him like a sunflower toward the sun and wrapped her hands around his neck. Bristles of cut hair teased her palms. She stood on tiptoes with her lips close, teasing him, inviting him, basking in his warmth.

He stroked her face. "Like velvet," he murmured. He wrapped his other arm around her waist and pulled her tightly toward himself.

She shivered and ran her hands up into the wind-tousled waves and curls of his short hair. *Kiss me, kiss me, kiss me!* Her fingers tightened and tugged his head, but he resisted, teasing her by blowing softly on her lips and nose. Her knees wobbled; her legs turned to gelatin.

His hand ran slowly down from her waist over the jut of her hipbone and the broad curve of her hip and stayed there. Then, at last, when she was afraid she would melt into a puddle, he pressed his lips against hers.

His lips. They were hungry and eager and swollen and sparked fire in her lips and then over the rest of her skin.

She drew one finger down his neck and across his jaw. As he shuddered against her breasts and she gasped in response, she explored his face. The bristly stubble on the cheek that had been baby-bottom smooth that morning. The smooth angle of his cheekbone. The perfection of his nose, straight and just the right size and proportions for his face.

He pulled his face back, his breath ragged. "I'm always happy when I'm with you. I never feel you're judging me or my work and finding me lacking."

She stroked his face, feeling her heart stabbed again by his pain of never being good enough for his parents. "Sha." She drew out the endearment. "Darlin'. You are a great artist and, I reckon, a man worthy of the art he makes."

"No woman has ever made me feel this way," he murmured before he devoured her lips as he had her cornbread.

It felt so good, she stopped kissing back and instead twined her arms tightly around his waist, savoring each sensation his kisses produced.

A car drove by outside, crunching a can and kicking up gravel.

The studio was silent, the blues CD over. Leonie half-opened her eyes. It seemed they had kissed for only moments. But in those moments, the sunlight had disappeared; the studio windows reflected wavering images of the two of them and the sparkling pieces on the table.

Thoughts of hungry cats and getting the shop ready for Monday shattered her single-minded focus on David's body. Leonie pulled away and backed up until she bumped into something hard. A desk.

They stared at each other, eyes wide, breath loud.

David picked up the nearest brooch and polished the silver edges and back.

Leonie perched on the edge of the desk. She had known a lot of artists and seen a lot of artists' relationships fail. There were questions she needed to ask David before their connection got stronger. "David?" She licked her lips. "Was your art the reason your marriage broke up?"

He reeled back as if she had punched him in the gut. The brooch fell from his hands and landed on the cement floor with a loud crack. David didn't even look at it. His eyes focused behind her.

She swallowed the lump in his throat and walked over to him. She put her hand on his cheek. "I'm sorry. Maybe it's too early to be any of my business."

David took a step back, breaking her touch. "It's better you know before things between us get more... serious." He pulled at the neck of his t-shirt as if it had gotten too tight. "Many artists pour their entire souls into their work and save nothing for their families. Paul Gauguin, for example. Georgia O'Keefe."

"Gauguin and O'Keefe both spent long times away from their spouses. Is that what you did?"

"No! Never." He swallowed and looked toward the icebox. "I was happy to settle down, be married, have a baby. I did my share of the chores. I always remembered Jessica's birthday and our anniversary. We went a lot of places together."

A baby! Another surprise. "So what happened?"

"I'm not sure. Before we got married, I made sure Jess knew I would have a day job and do art during what was 'free time' for other people. I thought she understood."

"You were wrong?"

He nodded. "She wanted all of me, all the time—every evening, every Saturday, every Sunday. I suggested she and the baby come with me to the studio. She could read a book or do some embroidery, and we'd all be together. She refused. She only wanted to do things that kept me from my art."

"Didn't she know anyone else here?"

"She had many friends in Moonlight Cove, and she Skyped with her family several times a week." He swallowed. "She wasn't lonely. Just jealous. Jess saw the part of myself I gave to art as something taken from her."

"She wasn't interested in going with you to take photographs? Helping you choose the ones to make into new pieces? Giving you feedback and encouragement?"

"Not at all." He rubbed his chin. "Before we married, she was always going to this club or that meeting or was out with her friends. I had no clue she thought the bonds of marriage should be made of superglue."

"Myself, I would expect to spend some fun time with my husband. Just saying."

"We did do fun things. I loved Jessica, I loved the baby, and I treated them the opposite of how I was treated. It ripped me apart when they left." He bent and picked up the dropped brooch. After examining it and dusting it off, he set it on the table. "What about you, Leonie? You talk about going back to Louisiana. I don't want to develop... feelings and then have you leave. I don't want to be ripped apart again."

"I'm not independent, and I don't want to be." She hugged herself. "I need to be part of a family. My decision depends on how things work out with Jake." She exhaled a long breath. "If I have to be alone,

Moonlight Cove is not where I'd choose to be." The room was suddenly stifling, and the abundance of sparkling items felt oppressive. She collected her notebook and backpack and headed for the door. "I'll see you tomorrow night."

David didn't try to convince her to stay, and her heart warmed with gratitude. His keys clinked when he pulled them from his pocket. "I'll walk you home. Don't want any TV producers stealing you away to star in *Bikini Babes*."

As if. She played along, patting the knife stuck in the webbing of her boots and then pulling up her sleeve to reveal large, round scars on her arm. "No need to come with me. If I can fend off an alligator, I can fend off a producer."

For a moment, he was speechless. "I insist. It wouldn't be polite to let you walk alone when you spent all day helping me."

She placed her palm against his chest, over his heart, her eyes soft. "Sha, I have a lot of thinking to do. You'd be a distraction." She stretched up to kiss him quickly and went out the door.

She walked slowly, thoughts tumbling through her head and bumping into each other. So involved was she in her thoughts it took her two blocks to hear stealthy steps behind her. *I should have known he wouldn't let me walk home alone. He gave in too easily. Should I stop and wait for him to catch up? No. I need to think without him around. Should I leave? Should I stay and get involved with him when he's an artist?*

She sped up. No need for him to spend more time shadowing her than necessary. Besides, someone might see him tailing her and call the police.

She also pulled her knife. This wasn't tiny Bayou Cane, where everybody knew everybody and watched out for each other. What if a robber, not David, followed her? She should be prepared to teach him the same lesson she had taught the alligator.

But the footsteps stayed the same distance behind her. Her chest felt a little gooey that David wanted to protect her. When she reached the shop, she turned and located a jiggling bush. She waved and blew a kiss.

Sheepishly, David stepped out from behind the bush and waved back. Then he stuck his hands in his pockets and trotted away.

She shut the door, locked it, and leaned against it, looking around the shop. Little paws padded on the floor as the cats ran toward her. She scooped up Slink and rested her chin on his head. She had an extra complication to consider. *Am I stepping into an ethical quagmire by mixing business and pleasure?*

Chapter 12

The next evening, Leonie stood in the showroom, hands on her hips. The cold evening breeze raised frissons on her arms. *Did California ever have nice weather?* Still, she left the windows open despite the odor of the ocean and the cold air. She and David would heat up once they started climbing ladders and pounding nails. And, she had to admit, the sound of ocean waves had grown on her; it was different from the soft lapping of the water against plant stems and the banks of the bayou, but just as calming.

Now she needed to choose the best places for the mirrors before David arrived. Although she had hung her father's framed calligraphy pieces only a few days earlier, she was already immune to their presence. She couldn't decide whether adding mirrors would make the room look crowded.

I should err on the side of caution and replace four calligraphy pieces with the four mirrors. She took down four frames and took them to the back living quarters. Then she checked the supplies on the card table set up in the middle of the room. She had forgotten to look at the back of David's mirrors to see how he had prepared them for hanging, but she had equipment for however they needed to be hung.

Puff rubbed against the gleaming new aluminum telescoping ladder, a jarring note in an otherwise harmonious room of woodwork with softened edges and plaster whose peaked brush strokes had mellowed into molehills. Leonie crouched down and dug her fingers in the plush white fur of the cat's scruff, as much to keep her from knocking over the ladder as to enjoy her softness.

She looked at the mantel clock. 8:30.

"Where do you think he is, Puff?"

Puff butted her forehead. Slink yawned. Leonie bowed her head, letting her forehead rest against the summery warmth of their bodies. "If only Jake and David were as simple to understand as you two."

A tickle ran up her back. *David's here.* She wasn't sure how she knew, but she was right: Seconds later, he rapped.

Slink wriggled free and ran, low to the ground, behind the counter.

All Leonie's plans for calm, businesslike efficiency vanished. Beaming uncontrollably, she pulled open the door so hard that the chimes jolted off their hook and clanged to the floor.

David seemed nervous too. He closed his eyes briefly, and his Adam's apple bobbed several times above his t-shirt, this one showing a Vincent Van Gogh painting of sunflowers in a vase.

"Come in, come in!" Leonie didn't kiss him or even touch him. Her mouth was too dry and her palms too damp.

David pulled in a handcart loaded with several boxes, which he unloaded onto the card table.

"I thought we'd put the mirrors up first." She pointed out the four spots she had cleared. They unwrapped the mirrors. As they hung them up, Puff jumped and twirled and pounced on the kraft paper, and they laughed together at her antics, breaking the nervous tension between them.

Two mirrors worked in the places Leonie had picked out, but they both agreed the other two spots did not do the mirrors justice.

"What about moving that dusty frame somewhere else? It's in a prominent spot, but doesn't match anything." David walked behind the counter and lifted a frame off the wall. He brushed ancient dust from the glass with the corner of his t-shirt. Slink sneezed.

"What's in there?" Leonie held a mirror up between the two new display cabinets. *No, this doesn't look good either.*

"A newspaper story about the store's opening."

"That was a long time ago." She tried the mirror up in another place. "What do you think of this spot?"

He didn't answer.

She turned.

He cleared his throat and looked at Puff. "Leonie, you should see this."

The strain in his voice made her scurry over like one of the cats. "Are you okay, sha?"

David held out the frame, back side up. A photograph was wedged in the corner. When she took the frame from him, a musty smell rose from the photo.

As Leonie fumbled for the switch for the lights over the counter, her stomach tied itself into a knot. She placed the frame on the display counter's top, and they stood shoulder to shoulder.

The old picture's colors had faded and changed hues. In it, a Japanese-American man in a rumpled, dirty Navy uniform slouched on a plaid sofa. He was drunk, skunk drunk, given his glazed eyes and the amount of his drawers showing above his pants. A cigarette dangled from his lips, and ash littered his pants. He had his arm around a beautiful black or Creole woman. She held a dark-skinned baby.

Leonie's hand flew to her throat. "No, that not be Jake!"

"The man looks a lot like him." David cleared his throat and turned the picture over. "Look at the writing on the back. 'Jake, Naomi, and T-Jake, Gulfport, Miss.'"

She flipped it back to the front and stared at the man's face in the photo, unable to talk. Could it really be her father?

"T-Jake. That's a pretty strange name," David said.

"It means Little Jake or Jake Junior," Leonie answered mechanically. "'T' is short for petit, which means 'little.'" She tore her gaze away from the man's face and turned the picture over again to read the inscription for herself. When she reached the date, she gasped.

Stomach roiling, face hot, she raced into the back into the closest bathroom and vomited. Up came everything she had eaten for supper. And for dinner. And maybe what she ate for breakfast too.

Afterward, her face was as red and sweaty as if she had run for miles. She turned on the cold-water tap and splashed her face and rinsed her mouth until the sour taste went away. She pressed her forehead against the coolness of the mirror.

"Leonie?" David called back. "Do you need help?"

"I'll be right out." Hands trembling, she pulled the hand towel from its hook and dried her face slowly, one portion at a time. She stared at her reflection, sighed, and went to face David.

"You're really pale. Are you sure you're all right?" He reached out and wrapped his arm around her shoulder.

She tapped a finger on the faded blue date he hadn't read aloud. "This is two months after I was born. If this is Jake, then he was cheating on Mama."

David became rigid as a post. "But... I know him. We've talked about more than art. We've talked about you, the time he spent in Japan, all sorts of things."

She pulled away from his embrace. "Did you talk about when he was in the Navy?"

"No, he never mentioned it." David ran his hand through his hair. "I don't know what to think."

"We have to think he has many secrets he doesn't want us to know."

He hesitated before answering. "I guess."

"We wondered about his nickname, remember? 'Jake' certainly suits the man in the picture." She took a deep breath. "The more I look at the photo, the more I see Jake in his features. It has to be him."

"He didn't trust you, his daughter. He didn't trust me, his friend." David's brow crinkled. Softly, he said, "He was more than a friend. He was the kind, encouraging father I never had." He shook his head like a horse trying to shake off flies. "But it was a lie."

Leonie's eyes warmed with tears. "He lied to my mother. He lied to you. He deserted me when I needed him more than anyone else did." The tears spilled out and ran down her face.

"You were better off without a father like that!" David turned the photo over to the front again. "Look at him! A drunk, a two-timer, a man who can't even be bothered to keep his uniform clean. He would have hurt you."

Mon Dieu! David, he has so much anger in him. On my behalf? On his own behalf?

Maybe I too will be angry, but right now I just feel betrayed. Betrayed and confused and lost. Her tears continued. She twirled a strand of hair around and around her finger. "Sha, I still wish he'd stayed with Mama. Any father is better than no father."

"No." He shook his head hard. "You wouldn't say that if you'd grown up in my family." He spit out the words. "I would have been better off an orphan. I'm glad Jake abandoned you so your life turned out better than mine."

Her head snapped up, and their gazes locked. She wrapped her arms around him, and he pulled her tight. The muscles of his back were in knots, and her touch didn't loosen them. They clung to each other like children, swaying as if dancing. For true, her head reeled, and his probably did too.

"I'm sorry for your childhood," she said. "I can't know what it was like to grow up in California. But down the bayou, family is important, maybe the most important thing in life. Jake should have been there for me. Clearly he lacked some fatherly traits. But that, that was no excuse."

She reached for the photo and ran her finger over the names on the back again. They were slightly indented. "Jake wrote these words a ballpoint pen." Not a fountain pen, but a ballpoint. Her shoulders felt heavy, and she felt her backpack on her back even though she knew it wasn't there. "The worst part is, now I don't know whether anything he told Mama was true! Was their marriage legal? Why did he really invite me out here? Why did he leave me so soon?"

David at last relaxed into her embrace. Puff's claws clicked as she landed on the counter and strolled to join them, casually as if she did not pick up on their moods—or, catlike, assumed her presence would fix everything.

Leonie stroked Puff. After a moment, David turned and petted the cat too.

When at last David spoke, it was with carefulness and certainty. "Your father may not have stayed around because he knew he couldn't be a good father. He knew you'd be better off without him as he was back then. His current behavior could be an act, but I can't believe that. I *refuse* to believe that. It would hurt too much."

Tenderly, she said, "Sha, you can't disbelieve something because it would be painful."

"I got angry without thinking. He's not like my parents. If anyone could have seen cruelty in him, it would be me."

She knuckled the tears from her eyes. "What are you saying? That this picture is not of him?"

"I think it's him. But that was almost thirty years ago. Some people change and grow as they get older. I hope I do. I think Jake changed. I think Jake believes he can now be the father he should be."

Anger at last exploded in her stomach, and her teeth clenched. "No! He pretends to be so proud of his Japanese heritage. His calligraphy, his bonsai, his desire for me to learn about Japan. It all felt real," she snapped, jabbing her finger at the photograph. "Look at that! His drawers are sticking out of his pants! This Jake, he could not have changed into the one I know."

"How do you know? How can anyone know what a person is capable of becoming?"

"I so wanted a family again. I told Jake that. Why didn't he tell me about my half-brother? Why did he leave me here alone?"

He reached for her. She jerked away. She wanted to hang on to her righteous anger. She was too tough to give in to self-pity. "Jake betrayed me. He should have found a way somehow to be a father. I longed for him every day."

"Leonie, do you really believe the man in the photo could have been good for you? I don't believe it. I think he would have harmed you, as my parents harmed me. Every moment, I have to fight to feel I am a worthwhile person. Every moment, I have to remind myself I don't have to be perfect, that it's okay to make mistakes. And I've made some doozies. The Jake in this photo? He would have bent or twisted you in some way, maybe even broken you."

He put his arm around her, and this time she didn't pull away, but leaned into him. She wished he would kiss her and make everything okay for a few minutes. "I don't agree with you, sha. *Not* having my father around nearabouts broke me." She paused, then decided to soften her words. "I'm glad you're here with me, for sure. I would have been tore up bad if I had found this picture when I was alone."

He drew Puff across the counter and into his arms. "I have to tell you something." His voice was so quiet she had to strain to hear. "I

165

haven't seen my daughter, Ysabel, in six years. I miss her every moment, but Jessica says until my art pays well, my daughter is better off without me."

"Your wife is full of crap! She's punishing you for being who you are, a talented, hard-working artist. She's twisting you just as your parents twisted you. Children need love, not money!"

Then the implications of his words sank in. She jumped back, repulsed by his touch.

"You abandoned your daughter?" she whispered, incredulous. "How could you? How could you?"

"I want Ysabel with me, but what kind of life can I give her?"

"You could give her what really matters in life. Love. Art. Beauty."

"Jessica says I'm not mature enough, well off enough, stable enough, to be Ysabel's father."

"And you believed her? How could you?" Leonie repeated. "Your child needs you. She needs to go with you to see the things you love, the ocean and the lighthouse and the beach. She needs you to tell her stories of the rocks and the town. She needs to have a table in your studio where she can work on projects and be proud to be like her daddy. Haven't you been listening to me, sha? Not having a father warped my childhood. I would have rather had that saleau in the picture than no father." She paced behind the counter, clenching and unclenching her fists.

"First my father turns out to be something other than he seems. Now you, too. I don't like you anymore. I don't ever want to see you or your things again. Pack up your mirrors and haul your boxes and your child-abandoning butt out of here."

David stood his ground. "We both had some shocks tonight. Neither of us is thinking straight. Don't say things you'll regret tomorrow. I'm doing what's best for Ysabel so she can grow up without my harming her the way my parents harmed me."

Leonie rounded on him and scowled. "Says your lying barnacle of an ex-wife. And you went along with it! You. Abandoned. Your. Child. Get out."

"I didn't abandon her. I made a huge sacrifice for her benefit. When you calm down you'll see that. Maybe you'll also see that Jake too may have sacrificed to give you a better life."

"Stop talking. My head hurts from trying to understand your reasons. They're not reasons. They're justifications for not seeing your daughter. Please leave."

"Leonie, please."

She turned her back on him and stared at the place on the wall where the photo had been hidden. She blinked furiously to hold back her tears, but a few escaped and rolled hotly down her cheeks. *I have no reason to stay now. As soon as I can make arrangements for Puff and Slink, I'm catching a plane home.*

The bell tinkled. Air whooshed into the room and chilled her back. Cart wheels clattered as they rolled over the threshold.

"I'm sorry, chère," David said softly.

The door closed with a decisive thud.

Chapter 13

The next morning, head throbbing, Leonie stumbled to the icebox to grab an Abita Amber. But there were none.

She groaned. "No wonder my head, it hurts. I drank every beer last night. Way to be a fool, Leonie." She looked inside the cabinets and moved around the contents of the pantry. At the back of a shelf she found a white box covered with Japanese letters. Inside was a cobalt-blue bottle of sake. She peeled off the gold seal and opened the bottle. She sniffed. It smelled fruity and burned her nose. *It must have a lot of alcohol.*

She held the bottle to her chest. This would take away her pain for a while, both her hangover headache and the pain of loss and betrayal, which felt like a cave had been excavated inside her chest. She smelled it again and closed it up.

She needed more alcohol like she needed another Jake or David in her life. She put the sake bottle back in the pantry. Then she wrote "closed today" on a thick sheet of calligraphy paper and taped it outside above the "closed" sign on the door.

She lugged her suitcases from the back of a storage closet, but her head pounded too much to pack. So she chose an art book from Jake's bookshelves and sat on the bed next to the window to look at the pictures.

Two hours later, her head was better, and her mind had cleared. The dishonor of her actions the previous night made her cheeks burn. She rubbed them with her hands and then flopped onto the bed in a fetal position.

David had said things would be clearer in the morning, but he was wrong. Confusion vied with anger, which vied with guilt to control her.

How can I have been so unprofessional? I let my feelings ruin a good business deal for the shop. If anyone back home hears about this, my reputation may be ruined. Jake may be a jerk, but it's still my duty to leave the shop in the best possible financial condition in case he comes back.

Both cats jumped on the bed, saw her lying down, and climbed on top of her, purring and kneading her flesh.

She closed her eyes and focused on the rumbles from their chests and the pinpricks of their claws. It was a good meditation, and she gave herself to it for a long time.

When she sat up, she knew what she had to do. She went back out to the shop, booted up the computer, and opened the email program.

"David," she typed. "It is good for both the shop and you for your art to be here. I was foolish to let my anger interfere with what should have been pure business last night.

"I'm sorry, but I still don't want to see you. If you still want to display and sell your pieces here, bring them back later and leave them by the back door. There's a gate in the alley behind the house that leads into the yard. You'll see the door. Ring the bell, and I'll bring your boxes inside as soon as you leave so nothing will happen to your pieces.

"I promise, I'll display them as well as they deserve. Your art is still genuine, even if you are not who you pretended to be.

"Noriko Leonie Hamasaki"

She stared at the letter, then cut the second half of the last sentence and replaced it with, "even if you are not the man I believed you to be. That was my fault."

She read it twice more and then clicked "send."

She sighed, and the tightness in her head disappeared. It felt good to do the right thing. She could never trust David as a boyfriend now, knowing he had abandoned his daughter. But he had done many favors for her and been her only friend besides the cats. He had helped search for Jake. He had been truly and sincerely kind.

I hope he does well with his art, for true.

She packed her suitcases with a light heart.

Chapter 14

That evening, while Leonie was eating some leftovers for supper as part of cleaning out the icebox, the back doorbell buzzed.

She jumped at the noise, and her disobedient heart pounded. She looked down and said "Stop that!" to her dusty t-shirt. But her heart paid no attention, and a strong envie rose in her to see David one last time.

She slid along the wall of the kitchen to the window and peeked out without pulling back the curtain. David was nowhere in sight, and the gate was closed.

She had been too slow. She had missed him.

She pressed a hand to her abdomen. It seemed impossible for emptiness to hurt, but it did. *Like the mind's version of phantom limb pain.* She hoped it went away more easily.

She opened the kitchen door. The same stack of boxes from last night sat on the stoop. *Hard to believe how different I felt then.* She knelt down to pick them up. The stack was tall. She better take them in in batches so she didn't drop any.

"They're awkward. I'll carry them in." David walked around the corner of the house.

Her hand flew to her mouth. *David!* Her spirits rose to the sky.

But nothing had changed since last night. Nothing could change. She stood to confront him. "I don't want you here."

169

"I don't care. I made you a promise to help you find Jake, and I did. I talked to him this morning, in fact."

"Go away!" She pointed toward the gate. "Wait. What?"

"May I come inside and tell you about it?"

Tongue-tied, she nodded.

He carried the boxes in, set them in the shop, and then went into the dining room. He sat down at the table and pulled out his cell phone and a thick manila folder with a rubber band around it.

She sat down across the table and clasped her hands together, trying not to twist them or her t-shirt. "You found Jake? How?"

"You want the long version or the short?"

"Long version. After you tell me whether he's alive or dead." She squeezed her hands so tightly together that her knuckles were white and bulging.

"Don't worry. Jake's alive."

A whoosh of breath escaped Leonie's throat, and her hands shook. Her relief surprised her; she still believed he had left her alone so long on purpose and still was angry about it.

"I left here last night pretty angry with myself, maybe as angry as you were. You were the last person in the world I wanted to disappoint.

"This morning, when I was calmer, I realized we had an important new clue: the existence of T-Jake. I decided to start with the obvious—the White Pages for Mississippi—and expand out to other states from there if necessary. How many people named Hamasaki could there be in a small Southern state? Or in the country for that matter?

"But I got it in one. I found a number for a Kaito Hamasaki in Mississippi.

"I didn't call right away. What if Jake had abandoned Little Jake as well? What if Kaito H. were yet another by-blow from Jake's wild years in the South? I might turn over an even bigger hornet's nest.

"Finally, I punched in the number. An answering machine answered. When it dinged, I left a mangled, doofus-y message introducing myself saying I was trying to track down T-Jake Hamasaki on behalf of his sister, Noriko Leonie Hamasaki. That I was also looking for Jake Hamasaki of Moonlight Cove, who's been missing.

"Someone picked up the phone, and a deep voice interrupted me. Leonie, you're going to like your brother. At least I did.

"He said, in a deep, growly voice with a Southern accent, not like yours but more like what you hear on TV, 'This is T-Jake Hamasaki, and if you're from the collection agency, I am going to track you down and stuff my paid receipts down your lying throat.'"

Leonie leaned forward. "What did you do?"

"I've had plenty of rude customers. At least T-Jake answered. I said, 'Nice to meet you, T-Jake. I'm trying to arrange a family get-together between you and your sister Leonie.'"

Leonie drew back. "I'm not ready to meet him yet. I only learned he existed last night. I need to get used to the idea."

"Then T-Jake said, 'Aww, man, not you, too. Pop's been camped out here for weeks, ragging on me to go meet this girl. Pop goes on and on as if she pees gold, or whatever it was that damn goose did in the fairytale. What's your angle?'"

David took a deep breath. "I said you feel as if Jake has deserted you twice. I asked for his help in getting Jake back here.

"He wasn't sympathetic, not at first. He said, 'Good ol' T-Jake, always ready to help out a friend or a friend of a friend or a friend of a friend of a friend. Sure, I have plenty of time to do you a favor even though I don't know you from a hole in the ground. Even though Pop is sick, and I'm taking care of him after working all day.'"

"He's sick?" Leonie looked down at the tablecloth. She had been so angry that he had left her again, and it wasn't his fault. "I'm ashamed of myself. I never considered he might be sick. I should have called the local hospitals. Now we know he wasn't there, but I should have called."

"It's not your fault, Leonie. I didn't think of it either. Anyway, I said to T-Jake, 'I have one question for you. Why don't you want to meet your sister? What do you have to lose?'

"He didn't answer for a while. Then he said quietly, 'That's two questions.'

"I just waited.

"Finally, T-Jake said, 'I'm afraid she's like Pop.'

"'Which one?' I asked. 'The father he was when you were little? Or the man he is now? You're a grown man. Haven't you figured out how to handle him yet?'

"'Now I almost wish you were the damn collection agent,' he said.

"'Pretend I am and hang up on me,' I dared him.

"'You'll just call back. I hear it in your voice. 'Get them back together' my ass. You got something else up your sleeve.'

"So I told T-Jake that Jake and I were supposed to do an art show together, but Jake hadn't signed the papers yet. I also told him you were a traiteuse and perhaps you could help Jake even if the doctors couldn't.

"T-Jake heaved a big sigh. I could almost hear him throwing his hands up in the air. Then he told me Jake was too sick to travel."

"Mon Dieu!" Leonie leaned her elbows on the table and rested her head in her hands. "It's a lot to take in. Jake so sick. Jake planning to come back here with T-Jake. He didn't desert me after all." She lifted her head. "I should have trusted him."

David pulled the rubber band off his manila folder. He scooted several printouts across the table.

Leonie glanced through. David—or T-Jake?—had bought her a ticket to Mississippi for the next day.

One way.

She looked up, and he handed her a sticky note. "That's T-Jake's phone number. You can call him." David tapped his cell phone. "Otherwise, he'll pick you up at the airport when your flight gets in. I can take you to the airport here if you like. If you're not still so angry at me."

Leonie's head reeled. "I should be more angry at you for railroading me into flying to Mississippi."

"You don't have to use the ticket. I could fly out myself, get the art-show papers signed, and make sure T-Jake can afford a good doctor for your father."

She sat silent. She may have been railroaded, but she had been railroaded into getting what she wanted: a family.

It was all so sudden she couldn't think straight or make a decision.

"I've already talked to Mrs. Itani." David's voice held deep sadness. "She'll take care of Puff and Slink until Jake comes home."

He's not expecting me to come back. In truth, she couldn't tell him otherwise.

"I reckon I need to thank you for fixing everything."

"I haven't fixed anything. I wish I could have. Jake is still sick. T-Jake still doesn't want to meet you. If you want to have a family, you're going to have to use your superpowers to make one yourself."

"I wish it were as easy as jumping over the display counter or fixing your elbow." She straightened up, everything in her mind clicking into place like a puzzle working itself while she watched. "I'll go. I'll accept your offer of a drive to the airport. Thank you for being so... bossy."

He grinned. "You encouraged me to go after what I wanted. I'm only returning the favor." He stood up, and his smile faded. "I'm going to miss you, Noriko Leonie Hamasaki."

Chapter 15

Leonie stepped out of the over-air-conditioned airport into what felt like a steamy oven. As always, it was a shock, one she knew would only last a few minutes. She tipped her head back and breathed deeply, letting the heavy, damp air moisten her eyes and nose. She parked her suitcases next to herself, pulled off her cardigan, and rolled up the sleeves of her blouse. She looked at the scratch marks on her dry skin and stretched her arms out. She had bought several bottles of moisturizers in California, but none had worked. Now she didn't need them.

"Ahhhhh," she sighed.

A fellow passenger, an elderly black lady in a tailored light-pink suit, smiled at her. "Always great to come home to our climate, isn't it, darlin'?"

Leonie smiled back. "For true! Today it's double great. I'm about to meet my brother for the first time."

"Good on you. I hope you have a wonderful reunion."

"Noriko!" A man bellowed. A force of nature, large and bearlike and wearing a pork-pie hat, thundered across the roadway on legs like telephone poles. He stopped right in front of her. "You're Noriko, all right. You look like Pop. You know, Japanese-y." He tipped his hat to the elderly lady in pink. "Ma'am! Isn't this a glorious day? May I help you with your bags?"

Without waiting for either woman to answer, he picked up both of Leonie's bags and stacked the elderly woman's three bags on top. "My truck's this way." He strode on long legs back across the roadway into the parking lot and didn't look back.

Leonie and the lady exchanged bemused looks, and Leonie burst out laughing. "It may take me some time to get used to my new brother. In the meantime, I think we should follow him before he drives off with our bags and leaves us stranded."

Chapter 16

T-Jake had dropped the elderly lady, Miss Evelyn, at her house with her bags after persuading her to come for supper the next night. The cab of the truck was silent as he tore out of her driveway, hurling gravel every which way. Startled chickens launched themselves into the air, and Leonie hung on to the door handle for dear life.

But after they reached the county road, she asked T-Jake a tentative question. He made a surprisingly shy reply. Soon they were chatting about food and fun and the other usual topics of conversation she was accustomed to. She learned T-Jake worked as an orderly in a hospital and loved to fish in a creek behind his house.

T-Jake didn't bring up Jake, so she had to. "What's wrong with Jake? Why haven't the doctors been able to help him?"

He glanced over at her. "The doctors don't know what's wrong. They done a lot of tests. They didn't find nothing."

Leonie frowned. Diagnosing some diseases required going beyond blood and urine tests. "Did you get him a second opinion?"

"Ain't no other general doctors in town or anywheres nearby. We got a specialist in hearts and a specialist in feets, but his are fine, the doctors say."

"Does he look sick? Does he feel bad?"

T-Jake rustled in a mess of junk by the gearshift, found a toothpick, and stuck it between his teeth. "He looks mighty pale. But he don't go outside. I keep telling him and telling him it ain't healthy to look at walls instead of trees and to walk on carpet instead of good healthy dirt and pine needles. He won't take his shoes off neither except to go to bed."

"Is he in pain?"

"He say he feel bad all over."

"What do you think?"

"I think it mighty good you a traiteuse. You know the right prayers and the right herbs, and you his daughter besides. Maybe you can get him well and out of my damn house."

She poked his upper arm. "T-Jake! What kind of son are you?"

"The kind that git fed up with people moping about and needing cooking for. You should just call me 'Bro' or 'T.' Too many 'Jakes' flying around elsewise." T jerked the wheel, and they left the blacktop for a rutted dirt road.

"You can call me 'Leonie.'"

"Leonie, we almost home now."

She had expected T to live in a rusty double-wide sitting on cement blocks, with maybe some goats in the yard to keep the grass short. Instead, he pulled up in front of a white, recently painted center-hall cottage with a lawn in front and a white picket fence along the road. Fruit trees clustered on one side of the house, and a large, neat rectangular garden lay on the other side. Behind the house, a line of willows showed where the creek must run.

"I built it myself," he said proudly. "Like it?"

"Yeah. I feel right at home already."

"Well, don't you be staying here forever like our daddy," he said darkly. "He old, so he get cut some slack. You, I just kick your butt out when I get tired of it."

"I promise my butt will behave." She giggled.

He lowered his fierce eyebrows at her. "Don't you be poking fun of me neither. I know you a college girl. But this my house, my rules."

"Sorry, Bro. I'm nervous, and I'm worried about Jake."

"Yeah. Me too." He shut the truck off. "Go on in. I'll bring your bags."

She walked slowly to the house. The pine forest across the road made the air smell fresh, and many species of birds sang from all around. She didn't recognize some of the songs, but that made sense. They were a little farther north here, and that little distance made a big difference in the things that mattered to birds, such as trees and landscape.

She climbed the steps to the stoop, pulled off her shoes and socks, and set them by the door. She wiggled her toes and rolled her head to get the kinks out from the flight. "Feets, don't fail me now," she muttered. She pulled the screen door open and went in.

Jake sat on the sofa, an unopened newspaper on his lap and a full mug of tea in front of him. "Noriko! You're here." The dull, even tone of his voice saddened her. They had never touched before. She took his hand and squeezed it, then hugged him quickly.

"Believe it, Jake. Father. I missed you. So have Puff and Slink. They want you home."

He looked down at her hand but didn't pull away. "The doctors didn't make me well. Will you try?"

"Yes. Of course. I know several things that will make you feel better. Soon you'll be up and around." She touched the mug. As she suspected, it was cold. "First thing, I'll make you a fresh cup of hot tea. Tea is good for everything. I'll cut up a tomato for you too."

"I'm not hungry."

Her chest tightened, and her eyes squeezed half-shut. "I know."

Traiteurs were supposed to treat, not diagnose. But Leonie couldn't help thinking Jake was depressed. Maybe dehydrated and enervated as well from not eating or moving around.

T came in with her bags and set them side by side on the floor, bottom ends lined up like soldiers.

"T, could you fetch a fine ripe tomato from your garden for Jake?"

"Sure. There still some left on the vine that the heat ain't overtook."

"Thanks. I'm going to make Jake some fresh tea in the kitchen." She held her brother's gaze, and he nodded.

"Kitchen's in there." He jerked his thumb toward a door.

Leonie took her time with the tea, not only to make sure she made it just the way Jake liked it but also so she could talk to T. He arrived quickly from the garden, opening and shutting the kitchen screen door without a sound. He set two huge, purple-black tomatoes on the cabinet, and her mouth watered.

"One's for you," he whispered. "What you think about Pop?"

"He's certainly not the man he was in California. Did the doctors ask you or him about his sleep, his appetite, or his interest in doing things?"

"No. They only interested in his blood and piss. Can you make him better?"

"I'll try. Will you help me?"

"Sure thing." He poked her in the upper arm as she had done to him. "Anything to get Pop out of my favorite spot on the sofa."

Chapter 17

Leonie coaxed Jake to drink his tea and eat his tomato by telling him stories about customers and funny things Puff and Slink had done. He laughed a couple times and told a story of his own about Slink.

Then she insisted they go out onto the stoop for his treatment. Jake refused until T made it clear he would carry Jake out if he didn't walk on his own.

Leonie settled Jake in a bright red metal lawn chair and pulled up a stool to sit next to him. "Jake, tell me how you're feeling. Where do you hurt? What doesn't feel right?"

"It's hard to describe. At first, I felt bored. Not just my mind but my whole body. I know it doesn't make sense for a leg or a finger to be bored, but that's what it was like."

Leonie nodded. "I understand. Go on."

"I didn't want to do anything. I thought the feeling would pass but it just got worse. Then my body felt guilty and ashamed. I lost my appetite. It was as if my body thought I didn't deserve food or drink or any other pleasure."

"Do you have pain anywhere?"

"Not at first. But now I'm stiff and it hurts to move around."

Common sense tells me what will make him better, but it's my authority as a traiteuse and the rituals that will make him follow my advice. She stood, laid her hands on his head, prayed for several minutes, and then walked around him. She repeated the ritual two more times.

She sat on the stool.

"I feel better, but not back to my usual self."

"There's more. I've started things, but you must finish them. Listen. Each day, I will make special teas for you, and you must drink them. Each day, first thing in the morning, you must weed T-Jake's garden for an hour. Each day, for an hour, you will either walk with me in the pines or go fishing in the creek with T-Jake. Do these things for seven days, and then I will repeat the ritual."

Chapter 18

A month later, after getting five treatments, catching a lot of fish, and muscling up from daily weeding, Jake was back to the dignified, self-possessed man Leonie had met when she went to California. Leonie and T-Jake had become siblings in truth as well as in blood, and Miss Evelyn came over once a week to eat or play cards or just tell stories. Sometimes she brought friends, and T's house would fill with music and laughter. Although Leonie had only a tiny room to sleep in, she was content and happy and in no hurry to make any decisions about her future. Her here and now was enough for a while.

But one Saturday morning, instead of going out to weed, Jake woke both Leonie and T up and insisted on a family meeting. He had them sit on the sofa while he stood before them, legs slightly spread and his hands clasped behind him.

"I have a great shame to confess," he started.

"You don't have to confess to us, Pop," T said.

Leonie said, "That's right."

"I'm the father, so you two will sit still and listen." Jake cleared his throat. "I understand now why I became sick. It was a punishment for being a bad father.

"As I got to know you both, I saw you had grown into honorable people with good characters, and I knew I had no part in it. Your mothers made you what you are.

"I was not a good man when I was young. Even the Navy couldn't straighten me out. I was ashamed of being Japanese and tried to be the opposite of everything I thought a Japanese man was.

"Then my father — your grandfather — sent me to Japan to visit my aunts and uncles and cousins. I learned about my heritage and what it really meant to be Japanese.

"I came back to California a changed man. But I was too embarrassed to contact your mothers. My old Navy buddies who stayed around here sometimes told me about your lives. When your mothers died, I had a duty to step up as your father so you wouldn't be orphans, even though I didn't feel worthy.

"Now I want to go back to California, to my life and friends there. I want you both to come with me. I want to finally be the good father you deserve.

"Please tell me your answers tomorrow. I must go weed now."

"Didn't see that coming." T chewed harder on his toothpick.

"What are you going to do, T?"

"What are *you* going to do?"

She closed her eyes and rubbed her forehead. "This is tough. I want to stay here by you, but I also want to get to know my father at last. The weeks I spent here don't really count; he wasn't himself."

"I know what you mean." He picked lint from his pajama bottoms. "I haven't used vacation time. I can take time off. I guess it the right thing to do."

"Well, at least he gave us plenty of time to make a decision," she joked lamely. "We don't have to tell him until tomorrow. And you get an extra day of no weeding."

He scowled at her. "Feeble. Real feeble. You plain shouldn't be making jokes."

David would have laughed. He would have even thought she was funny. Her stomach knotted, and she stared at her toes. *I was so self-righteous. I sent him away, yet he still helped me find my family.*

"Bro, I'm going with Jake to California. I really want you to come too."

"Such short notice," he grumbled. "Is it as great in sunny California as they say on TV?"

"Not at all. But *Bikini Babes* films in Moonlight Cove"—T perked up at the mention of his favorite show—"and we'll be together. We'll be a family. Does it matter what California is like?"

T grinned and spit out his toothpick. "Naw."

Chapter 19

They had been back in Moonlight Cove for two weeks, and the cats were still showing displeasure at their having been gone. Leonie knelt on the wood floor, her knees getting tender despite her work jeans, cleaning the glass where one of the petits diables had peed on the display counter. Puff washed herself calmly in a pool of light by a window, and Leonie called to her, "Diable! You are one for true, even if you don't have horns."

Puff stopped washing in midstroke, her tongue still sticking out and her leg in the air. She gave Leonie a long, haughty look and then resumed her bath.

Leonie sighed. She had already put a thick layer of baking soda paste on the wood floor but didn't know whether it could take out such a great stink. She could still smell cat pee, but she suspected it was her clothes she smelled, not another, undiscovered marking site. *I should probably rinse my clothes out in the backyard. If I put them in the laundry, we may all smell like urine.*

The chimes tinkled as the door opened. T had hated the chimes from the first moment. He thought they were too girly for a sophisticated store, thought they should be given to a toy store or a dress store, but Jake had over-ruled him. In fact, Jake liked nearly all of the changes she had made and was surprised and pleased she had increased profits so much. He had even told her how proud he was of her. The warmth in her heart she had felt then came back just as strong.

"Uh, hi." The voice was familiar. "I came to check out your new stock."

Leonie gasped, and her heart leapt into her throat. *I'm wrong. I'm hearing what I want to hear.* But her tingling skin and the growing warmth of her lips confirmed her original thought. Still facing the counter, she brushed baking soda off her knees and cat hairs off her work jeans and work shirt. She elbowed a strand of hair off her face.

She couldn't delay her greeting any longer. She swung her legs under her, sat on her heels, and bowed. "Welcome."

Two pairs of feet stood in the store, one small pair and one large pair, both wearing pink Hello Kitty flip-flops. She raised her eyes higher. Two pairs of blue shorts. Two white t-shirts with a Renaissance still life of flowers on them. One smiling face, one nervous face.

She looked at the little girl beside David, holding onto his hand tightly. "You must be Ysabel."

"Yes." She bowed stiffly, and Leonie's heart melted that Ysabel had copied her greeting. The little girl had wavy brown hair like David's. Two pink Hello Kitty barrettes held her hair back from falling in her face. "I'm Ysabel Lewys and this is my father, David Lewys. I am pleased to meet you." She looked up at her father.

David smiled proudly and ruffled her hair with his free hand. "Good job."

Ysabel's face glowed with joy.

"I thought about everything you said. You were right," David said quietly. "I now have temporary custody of Ysabel and hope for permanent soon. Maybe shared, but I hope full custody. Thank you."

"You're welcome." She licked her lips. "Are you still living in the attic?"

"No. The warehouse is zoned for mixed-use, so we're living there. I built a couple of bedrooms and put in a kitchenette. My workspace is smaller, but it just means I don't have to walk as far. It's great. I'm very happy there." He looked down at Ysabel and smiled.

"My room has a window with two geraniums," Ysabel said proudly. "My futon has Hello Kitty sheets and a Hello Kitty bedspread."

"Sounds as if you have everything you need."

Ysabel nodded.

"I see you like art like your papa."

"I don't have a papa. I have a daddy," Ysabel said with great seriousness. "He likes modern art." She scrunched her face. "I like the great masters. The picture on our t-shirts is *Bouquet* and it was painted by Broo... Bruh... Brueghel!"

"You made a great choice." Clearly, David had been telling her about art, and the girl had wolfed it down.

Leonie looked down at her cleaning clothes and winced. *What a day for David to show up!* She stood anyway. "I have to thank you too. I have a family now because of you. It's not only Jake and me. T-Jake is staying by us for a while."

"I'm glad." His warm smile confirmed that he truly was happy for her. His eyes took on the puppy-dog look she could not resist.

"I said some terrible things to you," Leonie said. "I'm sorry. Jake helped me understand how you felt. I know you probably can never forgive me, but if one day you do"—her mouth was so dry she had to stop and swallow—"I wouldn't mind picking up where we left off."

"I was hoping you'd say that," David said. "Ysabel?" He winked at his daughter.

The girl dropped his hand, ran outside, and came back in holding a bag with two hands. She shoved it at Leonie. "Here! This is for you."

The bag made a crinkling noise as she opened it. Inside was something soft and white. She pulled it out. It was a t-shirt. She unfolded it. It was a t-shirt of the painting *Bouquet* by Brueghel.

"Oh, sha!" She hugged the t-shirt to herself, then remembered she was covered in cat pee. She quickly tossed the t-shirt on the counter. Tears ran down her face. She tried to explain, to thank him, to say how happy she was to see him, but her nose was running so hard that her throat was clogged.

"Daddy, she doesn't like it!"

"Yes, she does, Ysabel." He took Leonie's hand. "She likes it a lot."

Tears did not keep Leonie from smiling the biggest smile she had ever smiled.

Shauna Roberts is a graduate of the Clarion Science Fiction and Fantasy Writers' Workshop and a past winner of the Speculative Literature Foundation's Older Writers' Grant. She has had three novels published. Two are historical novels set in ancient Mesopotamia; *Claimed by the Enemy* won the 2014 National Readers Choice Award for Novel with Romantic Elements and the 2015 Romancing the Novel contest in the category "Ancient-Medieval-Renaissance."

Her newest novel is the fantasy *Ice Magic, Fire Magic*, set in a sentient world in which men and women wield different types of magic.

She invites you to sign up for her newsletter at:

http://eepurl.com/Fr3Hf

and to visit her website at:

http://www.ShaunaRoberts.com

Second Time Around

by

Janna Roznos

Patrice stumbled over the uneven sidewalk. Maybe wearing her stiletto sandals wasn't a good fashion choice this morning. She took a deep breath, filling her lungs with the early morning fog-filled air of Moonlight Cove.

She needed coffee.

Checking the time on her phone, she still had a good half-hour before her meeting with the real estate agent. Perfect. A light breakfast, couple cups of coffee, and then tackling the job of selling her dead sister's house. Slipping her phone back into the back pocket of her jeans, she made her way to the Lily Pad.

Her reflection in the bistro's front door stared back at her. With only four hours of sleep plus the three-hour drive from L.A. this morning, she looked like something her dead sister's cat dragged in. This was going to be the longest week of her life. Better get it started. She yanked the door open and walked into the bistro.

The bell above the door rang and several patrons eyed her over.

"One? Breakfast?" The waitress asked, carrying two plates on her arm and a coffee pot in the other hand.

"Uh? Me? No? I mean. Yes. Yes. For breakfast, but I am expecting someone."

"In the back." She motioned with her head to the one empty booth.

Patrice slid across the naugahyde seat, ignoring the postcard-worthy scene of the Pacific Ocean, the boats bobbing in the harbor and the seagulls posing on the balustrade of the board walk. She checked her phone.

"Coffee?" The waitress set a mug and a menu on the table.

"Huh? Yes. Yes. Thank you." The coffee smelled good. "Do you have cream?"

She gestured to end of the table. "So, you're Debra's sister from L.A."

Patrice hesitated. Had she met this woman ten years ago during her one and only visit to Moonlight Cove? "Yes, I am or I was. I drove up this morning."

"Long drive."

It was and it was a drive Patrice was reluctant to do. She had ignored her sister in life. She couldn't do that in death. The first sip of coffee seemed to revive her a bit. "Have to clean out Debra's house and get it on the market." Apparently, news of her arrival had traveled fast.

"We'll miss Debra. She was a good friend. It happened so fast. One day she was fine and then the next…" Her voice cracked and she looked away for a moment before saying, "I'll be right back to take your order."

Patrice opened the menu. However, her sorrow engulfed her. Unable to focus on the array of breakfast combos, she set the menu aside. Debra's death had happened fast. A late night voicemail—I'm being admitted to the hospital in San Luis Obispo, and then the hospital advocate—I'm sorry to inform you of the death of Debra Miller. It seemed surreal. Debra was only forty. She was healthy. She shouldn't have died.

Wrapping her hands around the mug of coffee, Patrice hoped the hot liquid would burn away the sadness that seeped into her bones every time she thought about Debra. The coffee was good, but even it couldn't scorch the guilt she felt for not being there for her sister.

"What can I get you?" The waitress said, pen in hand and notebook ready to take her order.

Patrice glanced at the menu again. She was hungry. But a whole week without the gym would play havoc with her waistline. "Toast would be fine. Just some dry wheat toast, please."

"Okay. Coming right up."

Scrolling through her emails, Patrice tried to concentrate on the work she had left behind in L.A. But the remorse she felt about her strained relationship with Debra kept interrupting her thoughts. Her search through her emails proved fruitless. Laying her phone aside she ran her hands through her hair. Her celebrity client, the one she dressed for every major award show still hadn't responded. Sitting back in the booth, she stared at the boats in the marina, drumming her fingers on the table. If she lost this account... new clients wouldn't want to sign with her. Of all the weeks to be out of Los Angeles. Award season was just ramping up. She couldn't dress, polish and promote via text messages—she needed to be in L.A. She read the real estate agent's email again, hoping the promise of a quick, lucrative sale was true.

The ring of the bistro bell rang through the din of the morning breakfast crowd. Patrice leaned over to see who had arrived.

She gasped.

Not the real estate agent, but someone she wanted to avoid while in Moonlight Cove. Jackson Barrell.

Hunkering down in the booth, Patrice hoped he didn't see her. He strolled in, greeting several patrons with a handshake or a pat on the back. He was just as she remembered him. No, that wasn't true. He was even better. His tan complexion radiated his good health and she could almost taste the tang of his skin. His t-shirt, stretched across his broad chest, and his jeans molded to his every muscle. A fleeting memory of being held in his arms, his body molding to hers seared through her thoughts. The tingling sensation of his calloused hands caressing her skin made her shift uncomfortably in the booth. A moist heat simmered within her. She wiped her finger across the screen of her phone looking for anything to distract her thoughts.

"May I join you?"

Patrice hesitated, not wanting to acknowledge him, but also wanting to speak to him. His intense gaze raked over her. She swallowed, wondering what to say to the man she had left ten years ago. He didn't wait for her response, sliding into the booth on the other side of the table.

"Good."

"JB." The waitress appeared with Patrice's toast and another mug. "Wasn't expecting you this morning. The usual?"

"No. Just coffee this morning, Lily. Thanks." He flashed her a smile as she filled his coffee cup.

She nodded, her speculative gaze traveling from JB to Patrice and then back to JB before walking away.

"Heard you were in town," he said, cupping the mug of coffee in his hands.

"Yeah." Her voice sounded small in her head. "You, and apparently everyone else." Patrice picked up an unappetizing piece of dry toast.

"You look great, Patrice. You look better than I remember. Been awhile, hasn't it?"

Warmth crept into her cheeks. She stared into his eyes. "Yes, it has."

"How's L.A.? Still loving it? Business been good?"

Noisy, crowded, and congested is how she would describe her West Hollywood neighborhood. Her business was shrinking and she had no clue how to reverse the trend; she hoped the money from the sale of Debra's house would tide her over for a while. "It's great," she lied. "My apartment is in this old art deco building. Rent controlled, too."

He nodded, splaying his hands flat on the table. A warm jolt spread through her. Would his caresses still be as heady today as they were ten years ago?

"You were missed at the memorial service."

With the toast half way to her mouth, Patrice paused. Memorial service? She vaguely recalled an email about it. "Yeah. Well. I couldn't take time from work." The toast tasted like sawdust in her mouth. She gulped a mouthful of coffee to wash it down.

"Even for your own sister? The whole town showed up to remember Debra."

"The whole town? What did they do roll up the sidewalks for the day?" Patrice glanced at her phone—still nothing.

He shrugged. "Almost. Schools stayed open, I don't think the police station closed, but just about everyone else who knew Debra came."

That would have been a lot of people who knew Debra and had come to say their good-byes. "Sounds nice. I'm glad. Sorry I couldn't make it."

"Work?"

"Yeah, it's my busiest season. Debra would have understood."

"No. Is that work?" He pointed to her phone.

"What? Oh. Yeah. One of my clients. One of my famous clients. I'm dressing her for the Emmys."

He nodded and sipped his coffee. Patrice scrolled though her emails. Nothing.

"It was at the lighthouse. You know, you see it first when you drive up Highway 101."

Patrice looked up. "What?"

"It was Debra's favorite spot."

She sat back in the booth. Dumbstruck, she had no idea Debra had a favorite spot. Suddenly she realized, once again, how much she really didn't know her sister. They were virtual strangers, other than they shared the same last name.

"Yeah," JB continued. "Everyone reminisced about her. She was a great asset to the town. A good friend to everyone."

"Even you?" Patrice voice was small.

"She was a good friend. I'll miss seeing her around. She was too young to die. Way too young."

Patrice pushed the toast away, and gulped in a few shallow breaths. She was moved that Debra was so well liked. She wanted to ask what people said, but didn't. Couldn't JB just leave her alone and go sit with someone else? Did he have any idea that she too missed her baby sister?

"It would have been nice if you had been there, Patrice. You should have kept in touch with Debra all these years. You know she missed you. She was your sister."

Patrice stared at him. Was he serious? What did he know about her? Or her sister, for that matter? "Debra knew I thought about her. We just—"

"Did she?" He motioned to her phone next to her plate. "Did you ever call her? She was your family, Patrice. You ignored her. Now she's gone."

She recoiled; his words were a slap in the face. She surely didn't need him, an old lover, to point out what she already knew for herself: she had ignored her baby sister. She should have called. She should have visited. She should have made the effort to keep in touch. But she hadn't, and now with Debra's death, she couldn't.

"JB, I appreciate your thoughts," Patrice steadied her voice, trying to control her anger "but what happened between me and Debra was —"

"The only thing that happened between you and your sister was that you were too busy to care. Too busy in your own life to think about anyone else."

"You don't know what you're talking about." She tapped her finger on the table pressing home her point. "You may think you know all about Debra and me, but you don't. You really don't." Patrice swallowed the last of her coffee. Where was that waitress? She needed a second cup of coffee.

"Looking for a way to escape the truth?"

"What? No. I'm not leaving."

"This time?"

"I was looking for the waitress. I could use some more coffee." She held up her empty mug, but she knew what he was referring to — she left ten years ago. She had driven out of town and never looked back. It wasn't just Debra she ignored. It was him, too.

JB let out a long breath and looked past her. His expression was unreadable.

She had forgotten how he could make her become unglued; he had ten years ago when they had first met, fallen into bed together, thinking that was just a weekend tryst. Something to pass the time, but it been more than that. He had touched her in a way that no one ever had before, and no one had since.

"You know," Patrice said, breaking the silence. "I wasn't expecting to see you. I am selling Debra's house. Are you interested?" She dabbed her napkin to the corner of her mouth, trying to sound somewhat nonchalant as if their history shouldn't affect them now.

"No."

"Know anyone who is?"

"You know, it's a small town, Patrice. We were bound to run into each other." He stretched one arm across the back of the booth.

Patrice had a flashing sensation of how it felt to tuck herself up against his body.

"I take it you eat here a lot." Patrice surreptitiously glanced at her phone, again. Where was the real estate agent?

"I sell abalone to Lily who owns this bistro. It's one of her signature dishes."

Patrice nodded, carelessly tapping her fingers on the table. The conversation had dried up between them. Ten years was a big divide filled with unanswered questions and hurt feelings that bubbled just below the surface. They were two strangers who just happened to be at the same booth together.

"Coffee?"

"Yes, please." Patrice pushed her empty cup, eager for another jolt of caffeine.

"So I hear," the waitress said, "Aurora won big at the county fair. Good for her."

JB saluted her with his now full mug of coffee, "Yeah. Thank goodness she got Alana's brains, and not mine?"

"You got lucky there, JB."

Patrice forced herself not to choke on her mouthful of coffee. Aurora? Alana? He had a family? She glanced at his left hand. It was empty—no wedding ring; but a lot had changed in the last ten years.

"So Patrice, how long are you here for?" JB asked as the waitress left.

"Just a week, I hope. Award season is starting up; it's the busiest time for me. I need to be back in L.A."

"Tough business being a shopper for famous people?"

"Stylist. I style clients for red-carpet events, personal appearances, and editorial photo shoots, I try to show them off in their best light. You'd be surprised to know that some of these actors think getting dressed up is putting on a clean t-shirt and long pants." She shook her head in disgust.

JB grinned. "Working with all those famous people sounds exciting. I bet you're good at it."

Patrice felt the pride of realizing his implication that he was proud of what she did. "I've been in the business for a long time. I know what colors photograph best, what styles work on what body types—when a client is praised for her appearance and it goes viral, of course, it all seems worth it." She sipped her coffee, looking at him. A yearning inside that she thought had gone dormant, was slowly and methodically coming to life as she glanced at JB over her coffee. She really needed to squelch that yearning. She could easily slip back into bed with him, and that would complicate anything and everything. She didn't need that right now in her life.

"So," she cleared her throat. "I take it you have a family now?"

He grinned and leaned forward holding her with his gaze. "I knew you were itching to ask me that!"

Patrice pulled a face. Only one weekend, ten years ago and he seemed to know her better than anyone else she had met since.

"Aurora. My daughter. She's seven. Beautiful—father's privilege! Smart, creative, too."

"And… your wife?"

JB's demeanor changed. He looked down at his hands and then at Patrice. The open expression he had worn was now closed off.

"Only me and Aurora."

Was it pain or sorrow she heard in the tone of his voice? She wanted to reach out and grasp his hand in hers to assure him that whatever happened, it all would be okay. She just knew instinctively that he had to be a good father. There was a lot between them—ten years' worth of living that couldn't really be bridged with a quick squeeze of his hand.

"Hey! Patrice Miller, right?" A middle-aged man, in a rumpled Hawaiian shirt lumbered up to the table.

The real estate agent? "Yes. Yes, I am. You must be—"

"Harry Hamrock. Prestige Realty." He offered her his hand. "Great to meet you in the flesh, so to speak!" He chortled at his own joke, pushing his bulk into the booth.

Patrice slid over, making herself as small as she could. "Thank you for seeing me on such short notice. I just got the details of the will and need to get this house situation resolved as quickly as possible."

"No problem. Glad I could make it. Phew. Traffic on Highway 101 was a bust. How was it coming up from L.A.? Bet it was crazy. L.A. drivers are cracked, right?"

"No. No, the traffic wasn't bad at all," she responded, but he wasn't listening as he clawed through his oversized briefcase, pulling out a fistful of papers and depositing them in front of her.

"These here are the papers mentioned in my email. You need to—"

JB's low laugh, rumbled from the other side of the table, interrupted Harry's instructions.

"By God! JB. JB Barrell. Didn't see you there!"

"Harry. It's been awhile." JB took Harry's offered handshake.

"Hey! You interested in this Victorian that Patrice is selling? It's really sweet. Good investment property. Previous owner took excellent care of it and was in the restoration process."

JB shook his head. "No. Not interested."

"You two know each other?" Patrice interrupted, looking from one man to the other. Of all the real estate agents she could have contacted, she hired the one that JB knew.

"We've met." JB said over the rim of his coffee cup.

"Met? Oh come on. Class of '96. Us two." Harry made a wide gesture with his arms.

"High school?" Patrice asked.

"Yep," JB responded. "But it was a long time ago. I thought you only did business in Santa Barbara?"

"Oh! I travel up and down the central coast. Go where the opportunities are. Especially for prospects like this one. Top dollar for this sweet Victorian," Harry tapped his finger on top of the documents and grinned at Patrice.

Patrice eyed the stack. "What is all this?"

"Boiler plate stuff. The usual contractual language when selling. Nothing to worry about. Standard stuff."

Standard stuff? How many trees were felled for *non*-standard stuff! Something stronger than coffee would be required to mow through this stack of papers.

"So review it. Initial and sign where marked. We'll be official." Harry pulled a pen from his shirt pocket and laid it on top.

Her plan of returning to L.A. by the end of the week looked a bit hazy.

"So JB. How's the fish business?" Harry asked.

"Mollusk, Harry. Abalone are mollusk. Not fish."

"Yeah. Yeah. Sure. This area around Moonlight Cove is sort of an untouched jewel. Just between us, this stretch of coast is ripe for development." He leaned forward and acted like he was whispering it to JB.

"And you're the man to do it?" JB asked.

"It's a new economy, my old friend. Got to change with the times, as the old saying goes."

"Part of this new economy," JB said, "is balancing progress with heritage, or at least it is here in Moonlight Cove."

Harry let out a belly laugh and slapped the table. "Man. Oh! Man. I forgot how stuffy you can be. Better be careful or this new economy will pass you by."

JB shrugged. "Thank goodness people still need to eat. I won't run out of business yet. I have to be going."

"So soon?" Patrice asked. She really wanted him to stay and maybe help her read through these papers and help her understand them.

"Have to get back the farm."

"You know, if you are ever interested in selling, you've got a prime piece of coastal real estate there. What is it five acres? Ten?" Harry pulled out his business card and tossed it in front of JB.

"I'll keep that in mind, if it ever comes to that," JB said, unfolding himself out of the booth and tucking five dollars under his coffee cup.

"JB, you don't have to do that. I'll get it," Patrice said, wishing he would stay.

"I pay my debts. I honor my commitments, Patrice."

"Ha! Spoken like a true old salt of the sea, right?" Harry said, jabbing his finger in the air.

"It was nice seeing you again, JB." Patrice said, hoping he didn't hear the longing in her voice.

He paused. A grin played on his lips and he finally said, "I doubt it."

Harry laughed. Patrice watched JB walk out of the restaurant, waving a good-bye to Lily. The bell rang over the door and he was gone, absorbed in the morning sunshine. Harry's business card was still on the table.

"So," Harry said, rubbing his hands together, "let's talk about selling this house."

Patrice nodded, feeling numb, like another death had just occurred.

———

Parking his truck in front of Debra's house, JB ran his hand across the stubble on his chin. He could just call. He didn't need to do this in person. Not tonight. Practicing his apology over and over again was one thing, but apologizing to Patrice in person was another. He could just call. Just like he could have avoided going to Lily's Pad this morning, after he had heard that Patrice was in town. What was he thinking confronting her like he did? Seriously? What good had come from it?

Memories from their shared weekend ten years ago still resonated with him. She had imprinted on him like no other woman. Even her refusal of his impromptu marriage proposal didn't deter his desire to reconnect with her.

He grabbed his cell phone. He'd call Debra's home number; Patrice was bound to pick up. But Aurora's smiling face on the screen stopped him from making that call. "Fear," he had told Aurora earlier in the week, "it's what keeps us from doing the right thing." Calling Patrice would be the chicken way out. He had to speak to her face-to-face.

Grabbing the two shopping bags, he got out of his truck and pushed open the gate. The geraniums, their pungent scent mixed with the sea air, met him at the corner of the house where the kitchen light glowed in the window.

He paused, glancing through the back door window. Patrice paced back and forth, speaking into her cell phone. The real estate documents were splayed across the kitchen table. JB's heart skipped a beat. She was still beautiful—even under the glare of the kitchen light, dressed in an old sweatshirt, with her hair piled on top of her head, and obviously agitated by whomever she was speaking with.

Watching her traverse back and forth, JB realized that Patrice moved him like no woman ever had before or since. Even Aurora's mother, who he had loved, never took his breath away like Patrice.

If only... he pushed those thoughts aside. She was a friend. That's all he could ask for. Honestly, right now in his life that's all he could handle. She was here for just the week. Only a week. She deserved more than just a phone call.

He knocked on the kitchen door.

She looked over and JB held his breath for a brief instant — what if she ignored him? But she didn't. She unlocked the door, still speaking into her phone.

"Listen, I have to go. I'll call you tomorrow. Text me if you hear anything and I mean anything — okay? Thanks." She tapped her phone off, leaning against the doorjamb, crossing her arms over her chest. "I wasn't expecting to see you again, after this morning."

"Yeah. I know." He dropped he eyes. He was still embarrassed by his behavior this morning. "May I come in?"

"JB, I'm busy. It's late. I have all of that real estate mumbo jumbo to read through and sign and I'm — "

"I brought dinner." He held up the two shopping bags. "And a bottle of central California wine, which I think you'll like."

Her stomach growled in response, but she didn't budge from her stance.

"Patrice you need to eat. I know you. You probably think the toast from this morning and a couple cups of coffee was enough." He hoped she didn't hear the desperation in his voice.

She rolled her eyes and then stepped aside. "I suppose so. And since you're already here."

"Best invitation I've had all day." Setting the shopping bags on the kitchen counter, JB stepped back just as a grey and white tabby cat jumped up and strolled over to him. "Hey Dante, how you doing old boy?" The cat responded with a deep, vocal meow and head bumped JB's hand for some affection.

"Dante? That's the cat's name?" Patrice asked, glancing at her cell phone before setting it down.

"Yeah. Debra said it was from a book or something." JB continued to pet the cat, being rewarded with a deep satisfying purr.

"Epic poem," Patrice mumbled. Her expression clouded as if she had turned inward, withdrawing from the moment. "It was one of Debra's favorites. Dante's Inferno." Her voice cracked and she carelessly wiped the sleeve of her sweatshirt across her eyes.

"I'll feed him," JB said, "so we can eat in peace."

"No. No. I can do that." She opened the pantry door, staring at the contents before pulling out a bag of dry cat food. Dante leaped from the kitchen counter, weaving in and out of Patrice's legs as she filled his empty food bowl. Patrice, wearing a faded Moonlight Cove sweatshirt and a pair of sweat pants, reminded JB why he was so attracted to her. She seemed to mold and fit into any situation. With her face clean of make-up and her hair piled atop her head, she was still comfortable and confident.

"So what's the occasion?" Patrice asked, closing the pantry door.

"Thought you might be hungry," He slowly took the containers of food from the shopping bag, hoping she hadn't noticed him staring at her. "And I wanted to —"

"You got dressed up to bring me dinner?"

He glanced down at what he was wearing. "No. I came from work."

"You dress like that for work? You wear wing tips to farm abalone?"

He chuckled, fidgeting with his tie. "No. Teaching. I teach a night class at the community college. Aquatic and Marine Biology."

"You're kidding?"

"Is that so odd?"

"What? No. No, not at all."

Had he embarrassed her? Maybe she was more vulnerable than he remembered.

"It's just that when I knew you before, just had the farm and well, this morning you looked like you were dressed from the farm and..."

"A lot has changed since we knew each other, Patrice. I'm not the same man I was then."

And neither was she, he realized, as she watched him; there was an edge to her that wasn't there ten years ago. If he touched her, would her skin still feel as intoxicating as he remembered, or would she be prickly and tart, as she seemed right now in front of him? He pulled out the chair. "Why don't you sit down? I'll get it ready."

She hesitated, and then threw her hands in the air, as if she had lost some argument and plopped down, her shoulders slumped. Folding up the real estate documents, she pushed the bundle away to the far side of the table, tossing her reading glasses on top of the stack. JB wondered if she was just running on reserves. She couldn't keep this pace forever, although knowing Patrice, as he once did, she would certainly try.

"Plates?"

"I think they are in that cabinet." She pointed and he found the plates, cutlery, and two wine glasses.

"If I remember right, you like red wine." He uncorked the bottle, pouring her a glass.

A faint smile played on her lips. "I do. I was thinking earlier about how good a glass of wine would taste." She took a sip. "This is good. Very good. So can I ask you something?"

"Of course."

"Don't you have to feed your daughter dinner?"

He paused as he dished up their meal. "She's with the sitter when I'm teaching." He set down two plates of food and joined her at the table.

Patrice picked up her fork and took a bite. "Mmm. Delicious."

JB steepled his hands over his plate. "Patrice," he said. "I owe you an apology."

She laid down her fork and stared at him. "For what?"

"For being a jerk this morning at Lily's. I said some things I shouldn't have. Seeing you just... well, I'm sorry and I'm embarrassed by my behavior. I wasn't much of a friend to you."

"And dinner?"

He smiled. "I thought you would be hungry."

She didn't respond, but just stared at him. She blinked. Her eyes filled with tears. He hadn't wanted to upset her. That surely wasn't his intention. He laid his hand over hers. "I'm sorry about Debra. I'm —"

Her tears rolled down her face, and sitting back in her chair, she pulled her hand from his. "I'm okay. Debra's death is a shock to us all. Thank you. This means a lot."

"I hope we can still be friends." He held out his hand.

"Of course." Laying her hand in his, a bloom of heat spread up his arm. He gazed at her tear-stained face, wondering what she was feeling right now. Her eyes were wide and he squeezed her hand, wanting to reassure her. She pulled her hand away, tucking it under the table, and cleared her throat.

"So, what is this?"

"One of Lily's specialties. Abalone Marsala."

Patrice took another bite. "This is your abalone? What you grow?"

He nodded. "Raise. I *raise* abalone."

"Whatever. This is really good. No, this is better than good." She punctuated the air with her fork.

A tentative meow came from the floor, and Dante launched himself onto the table. "None for you, old man," JB gathered up the cat and placed him back on the floor.

"Sorry Dante, I'm not sharing mine," Patrice said, as the cat continued to meow. He finally stalked off into the other room.

"So how did you know it was Debra's cat, and not some random cat hanging out in the garden?"

"The bowl on the floor says cat, so I assumed that this is the cat. Besides, he was howling at the kitchen door when I got here this morning, so he must be Debra's. I do find it odd that she would even have a cat."

"Why? She wasn't an animal lover?"

"Debra was allergic." Patrice tucked a wayward strand of hair behind her ear. "When she lived in L.A. she went to an allergist and an acupuncturist. She was especially allergic to cats."

"Maybe she left all that when she moved up here. Stranger things have occurred."

Patrice rolled her eyes at him. "You don't really believe that do you?"

He shrugged. "Moonlight Cove has a way of affecting people. Remember what we did when you were here?"

Patrice's face turned bright red. Instantly JB knew he misspoke. "Patrice I'm sorry. I shouldn't have said that."

"It's okay. I probably deserved it." She took another swallow of wine, and JB refilled her glass. "Oh, no more for me." She held her hand up for him stop. "I've got paperwork to review and sign." She popped another mouthful of abalone into her mouth. "I had to call Harry three times today regarding this stuff." Pointing to the stack of documents shoved to the end of the table, she rolled her eyes. Little red tags, denoting required signatures, stuck out of the document like sticky tongues mocking anyone who tried to understand or comprehend their legalese.

"I wish I could help," he said, "but legal documents aren't really my thing."

"Yeah, mine either. I'm more of a would-a-stiletto-or-a-mule-look-better sort of person."

"Not sure what that is, but I'll take your word for it. It would take me weeks to read through all of that," JB said.

"Yeah, well I don't have weeks—just a week."

He swallowed the last of his abalone. The deliciousness of his dinner had changed, because in seven days, she'd be gone, again. "Was Harry able to answer your questions?"

Patrice shook her head, refolding her napkin. "I was more confused after I got off the phone with him than I was before I called."

"Why did you hire him? There are real estate agents here in Moonlight Cove"

"I don't know. Harry contacted me first. Sent me an email, then this handwritten letter. When I agreed to let him have the listing, he sent me a dozen yellow roses as a thank you. I was so busy with work, I just didn't have time to look for anyone else. And besides, he said he could get top dollar for this house." Patrice polished off the last of her wine.

"And the money is that important?"

She nodded, her eyes downcast. "I know it sounds mercenary, but my business isn't doing so well. I've lost several clients—good ones, too. Not only did they pay, but they paid on time. The industry has changed so much. Anyone with a smart phone and a few well-placed 'selfies' on social media can call themselves a stylist nowadays. Nobody wants a designer look anymore. Nobody cares who they're wearing, either. Everyone just wants to wear what's in or what's hot. The more shocking the fashion, the more free publicity. Going viral is a good thing. I can't compete with that."

"Can't or won't?"

"Isn't that the same thing?"

He heard the defiance in her tone. Was there more going on here than just the death of her sister? If her whole industry was evolving faster than she could keep up, what would happen to her? He had seen this within the commercial fishing industry; the coast is overfished and then industry collapses, leaving behind unemployment and bitterness. He swallowed the rest of his wine. Tonight was not the time for a discussion of sustainable economics. "So, what will you do with Debra's stuff?"

"Not sure yet. I contacted the local thrift shop. You know, I couldn't figure out why she would fill every room in this huge house, until I found this in her office." Patrice grabbed an oversized notebook off the side counter.

"Did you know she was planning to turn this place into a B&B? I found her business plan." She opened the notebook, flipping through the pages. "It seems that was her intent when moving here in the first place."

"You didn't know that?"

She looked up at him. "No. She never told me. Did you know?"

He shook his head. He had considered Debra a friend. However, maybe they were more like just casual acquaintances.

"Everything is here: business plan, hospitality procedures, advertising, applications for credit, a brochure mock-up, notes on a website design. She has recipes for breakfast. Abalone-style eggs benedict, her signature dish."

"Now it sort of makes sense why she would have bought this three story Victorian House. It would make the perfect B&B."

"Yeah. Wouldn't it? This was her reason for moving here." Patrice sat back, the remnants of her dinner abandoned. She ran her hand across the page of Debra's dream, encapsulated in a three-ring binder.

"She never told you why she left?"

Patrice stared at the notebook, shaking her head. "No. Never. We argued when she moved, and when I came up to visit her that one time. You know, I accused her of being irresponsible. I thought she would make partner at that accounting firm. She told me she hated being a CPA, and that there was more to life than crunching other peoples' numbers. I didn't understand what she meant. I should have listened to her. I should have called more often. I should have…" Patrice closed the notebook and tossed it onto the empty chair, her tears swallowing her words. JB placed his hand on her arm, unable to voice any words of comfort. Patrice leaned into him. JB pulled her into his arms as her body shook with sobs.

"Why? Why?" She lamented. "She was my baby sister."

Holding her tightly, JB wanted to absorb her pain and sorrow, except he couldn't. It was her pain and hers alone. He rocked back and forth ever so slightly, murmuring into her hair.

"I never thought she'd die." Patrice wailed through her sobs. "She was my baby sister."

"I know. I know. No one did." Her body softened in his embrace. He tucked her head under his chin, still rocking back and forth, rubbing her back in small circles until her tears were spent.

Patrice disengaged herself from his embrace and sat up, pushing her hair back, taking in big gulps of air. JB pulled his handkerchief from his pocket and dabbed away a few errant tears still clinging to her red cheeks.

Enclosing her hand over his, Patrice took the handkerchief he offered. "This," she held it up, "and the wing tips. JB, you're full of surprises."

He laughed; hoping the wave of sadness had passed.

"Aurora's sitter told me that all well-dressed men should carry handkerchiefs. I surely wasn't going to argue with a 70-year-old woman who lectures me on the accoutrements of a gentleman."

A faint smile spread on her lips. "You know JB, you're the first person not to say everything will be okay. I've heard that from everybody back in L.A. It will all be okay. Everything will be fine." She waved her hand around in a circle. "As if Debra's death is just some blip in my life, and in time everything will be right in the world, once I have closure. I'm not sure what that even means."

"I don't know either."

She laughed. "I appreciate your honesty."

JB got up and cleared the table of their plates and glasses. "No. But I do know I brought red velvet cake for dessert."

"Great. I'm going to roll back to L.A. if I eat this way the whole week."

"Patrice," he sat back down and took both of her hands in his. "I wish I had some answers for you, but I'm just swimming through life like everyone else."

She leaned toward him. Her eyes sparkled and he sucked in his breath as she ran her hand along his cheek. "I know. You're a good friend. You're actually a best friend. Thank you." She brushed her lips across his. He gripped the side of the chair, forcing himself not to reach out and pull her into an embrace.

"Patrice," he whispered, waiting for her to speak, only she didn't but continued to hold his gaze. The memory of their last time together, ten years ago, flashed across his mind. However, rather than pulling away, he leaned closer.

Patrice laid her hands on his chest. Her touch burned his skin through his dress shirt. He ran his hands along her legs, up her hips and under the hem of her sweatshirt, exposing her soft skin. His body warmed as he ran his hands up her back. She felt as good as he remembered—even better. She shimmied onto his chair, squatting in his lap, encircling his neck with her arms, their bodies fitting together with ease.

"JB." She breathed, her breath cascading across his face. An invitation? He leaned back and looked up into her face. She grinned, touching her nose against his, before she gently kissed him. Any doubts about seeing Patrice again vanished as her lips melted against his.

Cupping his hands under her, he scooped her up onto the table, disregarding the real estate papers. She straddled him, wrapping her legs around his waist. He buried his face in her neck, drinking in her intoxicating scent. He trailed kisses up to her chin and pulled back.

Her eyes were filled with mischievousness and something else he wasn't able to identify. He captured her mouth, tasting her deeply, ignoring the warning bell echoing in the back of his mind. Her hands raked through his hair. Her legs tighten around him, melding his body to hers, igniting his dormant desire.

The shrill ring of the cell phone broke into his thoughts. What the — He stood up, stepping back away from the table. "Patrice" His voice was hoarse and hardly recognizable.

"My phone!" Rolling off the table she lunged for her cell phone, frantically swiping the screen before saying hello.

JB leaned against the sink, rubbing his head, and mentally kicking himself. He should have called.

Patrice stood in the empty kitchen, clutching her phone, reading Harry's text again, letting the news sink in.

The house was sold.

Sure there were some details that had to be finalized. Harry texted he'd send an email outlining what still needed to be done. As far as he could tell, it was a done deal.

Patrice squealed; soon this house would belong to someone else and she could return to L.A., Debra's notebook lay open on the table. Her sister's dreams were tied up in this old house. Dreams she didn't live to fulfill. Patrice shut the notebook, pushing it aside. She couldn't bring her sister back, so lamenting over her unfilled dream was fruitless.

Dante jumped up onto the table, sitting just out of arms reach, fixing his green eyes on her.

Patrice stared back. "This is crazy." She needed to get out of the house. She'd spent the day cleaning out Debra's closet, packing the kitchen, and boxing stuff up for the thrift shop. A change of scenery was in order.

Closing the kitchen door behind her, Patrice walked through Debra's neglected garden. The night jasmine, overgrown and choked with weeds, filled the air with its pungent aroma. Patrice gave it all a passing thought as she headed for town.

Plucking her phone from her purse, she scrolled through to JB's number. She wanted to share her good news. She halted. What would he say? How would he react? She dropped her phone back into her purse. As much as she wanted to speak with him, there was a part of her that was hesitant to tell him her good news. Besides, if she saw him again before she left Moonlight Cove she could tell him then. That is, if she did see him again.

Main Street was closed up for the night except for the Lily Pad and the Marlin Bar, which was squeezed between the Crystal Experience Rock Shop and the Massage Therapy Spa. Its slim door, resplendent with peeling paint leaked a sliver of noise from within into the still night.

Patrice stepped inside, pausing as her eyes adjusted to the gloomy interior. A '90's pop tune blared from a jukebox. Several patrons glanced at her and then returned to their drinks; in the back of the bar a spirited game of billiards was in play. Climbing onto a barstool, she caught the bartender's attention, "Wine. Merlot. Please."

He nodded, fishing a bottle off the back counter, filling the glass to the rim and setting it in front of her. "House Merlot. A local winery. You're Debra's sister." He slipped the cork back into the bottle.

Patrice hesitated with her wine glass half way to her lips. "Yes."

"Nice gal. Sorry about your loss."

"Thank you. It's nice to know she was so well liked here."

"Know what?" JB stood behind her. Patrice felt a momentary wave of confusion. She had wanted to talk to him—didn't she? And he was dressed for work on the farm, not the classroom. Under the gloomy light of the bar, Patrice noticed he avoided making eye contact with her.

"Hey JB, what would you like?" The bartender asked.

"Bourbon. Rocks." He took the bar stool next to Patrice. "You don't mind, do you?"

"No. Not at all." She sipped her wine, looking straight ahead. The bartender returned with JB's drink.

"Heard your good news." He held her gaze in the mirror on the back of the bar.

Patrice smirked. "Everyone knows everybody's business around Moonlight Cove, don't they?"

"Not everything. There are plenty of secrets, but selling Debra's house is not one of them."

She turned to him mocking his seriousness. "Really? And what secrets are you keeping?"

He stared at the amber liquid in his glass for a moment before replying, "None that I am able to divulge at the moment."

Patrice ignored his comment and stared at his profile, hard and handsome, he betrayed nothing. Was something troubling him? Patrice brushed off her doubts. She was reading more than what was there. That was the trouble with spending so much time alone with only Dante for company; she started to see things that weren't there. JB smiled. His eyes focused on her, and a wave of warmth spread through her body. She shifted, trying to get comfortable on the barstool.

"You have a secret I've been wondering about?" JB asked.

Patrice laughed. "Nope you got that wrong. I have no secrets."

"What you see is what you get?"

"Something like that. Yes."

She held his gaze, drawn to him. He pulled away and stared into his drink.

"Debra. What did she die from?"

Patrice ran her hands back and forth along the bar before answering. "Streptococcal toxic shock syndrome."

He raised an eyebrow in question.

"A sore throat. My sister died from a sore throat." Patrice gulped a mouthful of wine. "I thought everybody knew that."

"I didn't. I wanted to ask you before, but I didn't want to upset you."

She laid a hand on his arm. She felt the radiant heat of his skin on her palm.

"You know the funny thing is, cleaning out her house, going through her closet and boxing up her clothes and her books, and being here," she waved her hand around. "I think I've learned more about my sister and who she was in her death than I ever knew in her life. You know, we never really got along, even as kids."

JB nodded. "I remember. I was around ten years ago."

Patrice shuddered to think of all she had said, their arguments and criminations to each other. "After our parents split, we never saw my dad again, except for a check that arrived promptly on the first of every month. Then when mom died, Debra and I just drifted apart. I guess Mom was what held us together. Without her, we had nothing in common."

"I know Debra was proud of you."

"Yeah, well. Being proud of someone's accomplishments and actually liking them as a person aren't the same thing." She drank more wine, wondering if she should order another glass.

"I wouldn't be so hard on yourself. You did the —"

"The best that I could? No. I didn't. I didn't make amends with Debra. We argued when I was here before, and I left without getting it resolved. That was wrong of me. I should have apologized. I should have tried to stay in touch with her. I've missed out on seeing her because of my pride and my stubbornness. It's a regret that I will always carry." She stared into the red wine. "You know, the only upside to all of this, is that I discovered how much Debra was loved by people here. I had no idea she was so well thought of. Driving up here last Monday, I was so angry and frustrated having to deal with selling her house and being away from L.A. at this time of year. But, since being here and hearing all the nice things people have said, makes me feel better. In some crazy way, it warms my heart to know she wasn't lonely. That she had friends here who cared about her."

"You're a good person, Patrice." He raised his glass.

"Thank you. That means a lot." Patrice acknowledged his toast.

They were both silent, staring into their drinks. Patrice felt the all familiar rush of being so close to JB. Noticing how the tendons of his neck twisted and his hair shorn so close on the back of his head, she itched just to run her hands along his hairline, feeling the strength radiating from him.

He sipped his drink and then carefully aligned it in the middle of his napkin. "So, when are you heading back to L.A.?"

Patrice didn't hesitate. "End of the week. Like I had always planned. I still want to box up a few of Debra's things to take them with me and then ship the rest."

"That's a pretty quick sale."

"Yeah. I know. I'm getting the asking price, a short escrow, and they waived the home inspection. Seriously, I feel like a huge weight has been lifted from my shoulders."

"And Dante?"

"The neighbors want him. Apparently, they were feeding him until I arrived and they told me that he has eradicated every mouse in their garden. So he's welcomed there."

"Everything has worked out perfectly for you, hasn't it?"

"Yes. Yes, it has. The money from the house will really help. It will help, a lot. Keep me solvent for a while as I re-tool my business." She ran through a mental list of what she would do first.

"Sounds like you have it all planned out." He ran his thumb and forefinger up and down the condensation on his glass.

She looked away, feeling a bit undone. Plan? She had never really planned anything in her life—just run by the seat of her pants. He surely wasn't sharing in her enthusiasm, but he wasn't criticizing her plan either. Sipping her wine, she asked, "So, what brings you into town tonight?"

His mouth twisted. "Meeting over at city hall. Went by your place—I mean Debra's. You weren't there and—"

"Did Dante suggest you come here looking for me?"

JB gave a lopsided grin and shook his head. "No. I figured I just needed a drink before I drove back to the farm."

"And where is your daughter while you're here?" She bit her lower lip, wondering if she should even ask.

"With the sitter."

Patrice grinned. It was still early.

"How's the wine?" JB asked, gazing back at her, although his smile didn't reach his eyes.

"Good. Actually, it's quite nice. I never knew the central coast had such good wines." Patrice looked at the glass in her hand.

"Central coast has a lot to offer."

She laughed. "You sound like the tourist board."

He shrugged, sitting back. She sucked in her breath, eager to touch him, but more eager to move past this unspoken barrier between them.

Her phone buzzed. She scrambled, pulling it from her purse and staring at the screen.

"Work?"

"Yep." Tapping her reply, she said, "I have a couple of clients lined up. One in particular could really help. She's very influential."

"You love it. Your work? Don't you?"

Patrice hit Send and laid the phone next to her half empty glass. "Yeah. Yeah I do. I mean, I'm good at it. I really am, if I do say so myself." She laughed at her own bravado. "But yeah, I like making the client happy. Making her feel fantastic in a gown or an outfit that I've put together. Making her look her best. If the client feels great then I know I've done my job well. It's always changing. One day is never like the last one. I like the change, the excitement."

"Good. I'm glad. I'm glad you're happy." He downed the last of his drink and stood. "I've got to get going. It was good to see you again, Patrice. I hope everything works out for the best. I truly do." He pulled out a wad of bills.

"No. No. No way, I've got this one." Patrice dug into her purse, pulling out her wallet.

"You don't have to do that."

"Yes. Yes. I do. You've been a good friend to me these last few days and you were a good friend to my sister. The very least I can do is buy you a drink." She tossed some bills onto the bar, gathered up her stuff and slurped down the last bit of wine. "I'll walk out with you."

He followed her out, his hand on her lower back. His touch singed through her blouse, warmth spread through her body, and just as they stepped out of the bar, he moved aside dropping his hand. Patrice shivered.

"Smells like rain." JB took a deep gulp of the night air.

"You're kidding. You can smell that?" His face was shrouded in the darkness of the evening, but she could feel him staring at her.

"Yes," he said quietly under the muted hubbub from the bar and the undulating sound of the crashing waves on the beach.

The tension between them was different. Patrice wasn't sure why. Some sort of shift had occurred and she felt a bit off kilter.

"My truck is up by your house. I'll walk you home."

He fell in step beside her, but she didn't walk up the street towards Debra's house. She walked in the opposite direction. She slid her hand in his, which was rough and calloused, and she itched to feel his caresses across her body.

His profile, murky in the cloudy night, was hazy. However, his presence overwhelmed her. She knew that tonight, she'd follow him anywhere, if only he'd ask.

The bark of sea lions in the distance and the methodical chant of the moored boats in the harbor were the only sounds. She let go of his hand and carefully made her way down the stairs to the beach, JB close behind her.

Stepping onto the sand, she kicked off her shoes. Wiggling her feet deep into the flesh of the beach, feeling the granules between her toes, Patrice let out a sigh. "This is the first time I've been to the beach since I've been here."

JB picked up her discarded shoes. "Usually this is the first thing people do when they come to Moonlight Cove. They walk along the beach."

She had, so many years ago when she had come to see Debra. She had walked down those stairs, tossing off her shoes to feel the sand. She remembered that now, enjoying that moment.

"JB, I—" she stopped, suddenly unsure, afraid of the possibility of rejection. His being with her, was intoxicating enough, but would he be willing to follow her. She was unsure.

Never taking his eyes from her face, he asked. "Care to go around the rocks?"

Patrice nodded. JB offered her his hand and she slipped her hand in his. "Lead the way."

He led her over the craggy outcrops, helping her through the roughest part to a secluded area just in sight of the Moonlight Cove lighthouse.

He sat down on the dry sand and pulled her down next to him, wrapping his arms around her, pulling her close. He smelled of soap and aftershave, and she nestled up against him, feeling his body pressing against hers. She closed her eyes, concentrating, trying to imprint his presence on her memory, ignoring the star-filled sky and the rolling waves.

"This is where we started." His voice sounded far away, even though his breath tickled her ear. "And this is where we'll end."

She shuddered. "JB, I know you must think I'm a—"

He didn't let her finish her sentence but twisted her around, capturing her lips. Patrice opened herself to him. He tasted of caramel drenched in desire and she melted in his arms.

As his ragged breath cascaded over her, she snuggled closer, tucking her head in between his chin and shoulder, cocooning herself in his embrace.

"No regrets, this time," she said into his chest.

He laughed. She felt it more than heard it.

"Then, I guess this is good-bye."

His words were blunt, pregnant with meaning. It was good-bye, truly their final farewell. This would be the last time they saw each other.

"Yes. It is." The finality of her words even struck her as hard and harsh. But she wasn't going to make some empty promises of returning to Moonlight Cove. She dug her feet deeper into the sand, hoping to find some stability, but just the opposite occurred. The deeper she pushed, the more unstable she felt.

He leaned back and cupped his hand along the side of her face, holding her gaze with his. She didn't hesitate. Wrapping her arms around his neck, she pulled him closer, capturing his lips with hers, rolling onto the sand.

A barrage of emotions crashed over her, but she ignored them, as he covered her body with his.

Opening her eyes, Patrice gazed up as JB hovered over her.

"Patrice," he said, "I've never forgotten you. I've tried, but when I heard you were in town, all of those memories I had let fade away were infused with life again, and I haven't been able fight them off."

Patrice touched his cheek. It was warm and rough from the day's growth of his beard. "I haven't forgotten you. How could I? You've lived in my dreams of long ago."

He kissed her lightly on her lips again. "I should walk you back." He started to roll off of her, but Patrice held tight to his outstretched arms.

"No," she said. "I don't want to just remember what was, I want to live what is, right now."

"Are you sure?"

She nodded, more sure about this than anything else.

"I don't have any protection."

"You don't need any from me," she whispered pulling his head down to hers and kissing him hard.

Patrice tugged his t-shirt free, running her hands up his back, feeling each valley and peak of his muscles. His tongue danced through his kiss and Patrice arched her body up wanting to feel every single inch of him. Desire fueled her movements; she pushed JB up and over, rolling him onto his back. Climbing on top of him, she straddled him, pressing down, feeling his arousal through his jeans.

"Patrice," he whispered, "look at me." JB cupped his hands over hers, as she fumbled with the fly of his jeans.

She looked at him just as the beacon from the lighthouse swirled, stretching high above their heads. His eyes burned with desire and Patrice swallowed, wanting to satisfy her thirst for him.

"They're buttons," he said, glancing at the fly of his jeans.

Patrice took a closer look. Buttons. She heard him laugh and she silenced him with a kiss. "Just for that. I'm not giving up my place on top."

He held her by her hips, his hands snaking up her flank under her blouse. "I wouldn't dream of usurping you. Ever."

Arching back, she relished in his touch. His hands caressed her skin, igniting the smoldering fire that burned within her.

He bent his knees forcing Patrice to lean back against his thighs as he tugged the elastic waist of her leggings down, slipping his hand into her underwear. He probed her with his fingers slowly and methodically back and forth; letting each movement, each touch, speak for itself.

Leaning back, and overcome by his ministrations, Patrice felt her body, asleep for so long, awaken by his touch. Her wet response increased as his tempo intensified. He pushed deeper and she clung to his hand, pressing her body down, arching her back even further. His name died on her lips as her body spasmed. She opened her eyes in the star filled night, floating, weightlessness, her limbs liquefied. Euphoria bubbled deep within her, floating up, pulling with it a searing heat that burned through her, searing to the end of her extremities.

The moonlight cascaded over her, cool and brilliant, as it rose over the weather-beaten rock cliffs, coating them with its luminousness.

Holding her by her arms, JB slowly guided her forward, laying her on his chest as she caught her breath. His heartbeat, loud, strong and reassuring, echoing against her ear.

His body was still rigid, strung tight beckoning her to move. She pushed herself up and looked into his face. His face raged with passion under the moonlight. She rubbed her nose against his and he laughed. "Your turn."

Leaning back, she methodically unbuttoned his jeans; his eyes never left her face. She caressed him through his briefs. He sucked in his breath just as Patrice rolled up to her knees, tugging at his jeans. They tumbled over, a disarray of arms and legs, stripping their clothes off until they both were naked. Patrice pushed his legs apart, wrapping her hand around his erection.

Leaning over, she ran her tongue up to its head. JB shuddered, arching his back. Patrice did it again, this time concentrating on the top, swirling her tongue back and forth licking each droplet of cum. Slowly closing her mouth over him, she braced herself with her hands on either side of his body. Curling her fingers deep into the sand, she sucked slowly at first and then increasing the rhythm as he grew harder.

JB squirmed and moaned, a deep guttural moan redolent of pleasure and pain, which encouraged Patrice to pick up the tempo. His hands interweaved in her hair as she continued to move up and down. He grew larger, stretching the confines of his pleasure; his cum salty and sticky came faster and denser.

"Stop. Please," he said, his breath ragged. "God. Patrice. You. Are. Amazing." He ran his hands down her arms, holding on to her.

"One of my many talents." She sat up, watching the waves of emotions flow across his face.

"Oh God," he exclaimed again, as she slowly lowered herself down guiding him inside her. His girth pulled at her and she grimaced as a shot of pain radiated through her body. She slowed her descent as her body became more and more comfortable with his intrusion.

Finally, resting on top of him, she slowly rocked back and forth, undulating with the sound of the waves crashing on the beach.

JB gripped her hips, his fingers holding her tight. Under her motion, he grew harder within her; she could feel him straining against the inevitable just struggling to hang on.

He raised his hips, a final push, filling her. He let out a yelp and Patrice lost her inner control, as her body shattered. Falling forward, she rested on his sweat slick chest. JB gently wiped her hair from her face, before kissing the top of her head.

She breathed deeply, experiencing the luxurious state of being with him once again. She listened to the beat of his heart and was struck by the thought that she loved him. There had been many before and many after, but never someone like him: he was the only man for her, even though she knew she could never have him.

Coldness crept over her back as she forced her eyes open. She was naked, still a top of JB. The lighthouse beacon swirled across the sky overhead. JB was sound asleep, his mouth slightly open just breathing below a snore. He was still in her and she carefully maneuvered off of him and rolled to the side, the sand cold and wet against her bare skin.

"What?" JB sat up on his elbows, looking at Patrice.

She shivered, fumbling with the tangle of their discarded clothes.

"You're freezing." He rolled up, yanking on his jeans, grabbing her blouse and shaking out the sand. "Here."

She slipped it on. Piece-by-piece they dressed, without speaking, trying to combat the cold. Patrice shoved her bra and underwear into her purse and grabbed her shoes. JB helped her over the rocks back to the main beach.

Patrice wondered what time it was, since the full moon was now high in the night sky, but her phone was buried in her purse and besides, did it really matter what time it was? All that mattered was that it was the last time she would be with JB.

Reaching over, JB took her free hand and brought it to his lips, "I'll walk you back."

She nodded as they walked in silence up the staircase leading to Main Street.

Under the glow of the streetlight, Patrice stopped; mustering up her courage to speak. This might be the last chance to say what was on her mind, to tell him how she really felt. "JB?" Her voice seemed loud.

He didn't stop, but kept walking, "We'll talk later. You need to get home and so do I."

Home. That was what she felt. She was home with him, whether it was on the beach or across the table at Lily's Pad, being with JB was home—where she felt safe, secure, but more importantly, loved.

She felt every crack and imperfection with her bare feet on the rough concrete. Remnants of sand was still buried in the creases of her body and clung to her mess of hair, but rather than being cold, she was warm and satisfied and content, like she had never been before. Her stride was in perfect cadence with his and in the far recess of her mind, she dared to think that Moonlight Cove could really be home.

———

JB sat in his truck in front of the dance academy, watching Aurora enter the building with other little girls dressed in pink tights and black leotards. He had an hour to wait until she was done. He picked up one of his student papers. He flipped through the first one and then tossed it back on the stack on the passenger seat. He couldn't concentrate. His mind kept circling back to Patrice. He ran his hands over his shorn hair. His desire was to drive over to Debra's house, take Patrice in his arms and confess all. But of course, he couldn't do that.

Last night was amazing. She was everything he remembered and even more. Having sex on the beach was great. But more so, it was just the reminder he needed that he could easily lose his heart to her all over again.

The pain of her leaving ten years ago was one thing. But could he withstand a second time? He needed to keep his feelings under wraps. How could he when the woman of his dreams climbed on top of him and seemed to know his body better than he did.

His phone buzzed. Good news. The restaurant in San Francisco got their special delivery of abalone. The chef sent a thank you and a personal invite; if you are ever in town… JB thought how he'd like to take Patrice there. He bet she would dress up and be stunning, although she could never be more beautiful than she was last night out on the beach.

Was he a coward? He should have told Patrice about the house and the planning commission last night when he walked into the Marlin Bar. He should have told her right then, but seeing her there made his heart flip-flop. What good would it have done—ruin her evening? He was a coward.

He glanced at his watch. He had an hour before he had to be back for Aurora. He started his truck and threw it into drive.

He had to tell her. He needed to be honest with her. He knew she was going to be angry but he would never forgive himself nor be able to live with himself, if he wasn't honest with her and tried to help her.

The house was quiet. For some reason he had thought maybe she would be storming around, yelling and swearing. He had to admit as he got out of his truck, he never really ever knew how she would react.

Take last night. When he saw her he wasn't expecting to have sex on the beach. That was the thing with Patrice. He just never knew. Maybe that's why she made such an impression on him those ten years ago. He just never knew what to expect with her, and that intrigued him.

He slammed the truck door and made his way along the side garden to the kitchen door. The garden was overgrowing. The geraniums spilled out over the brick walkway, and their fragrance lingered in the night air.

He looked into the window. The kitchen was deserted. Even Dante wasn't around. He tried the door and it was unlocked.

"Patrice?" he called out, before walking in. He got no answer.

On top of the table was the letter from the planning commission, his signature in bright blue ink. He didn't need to look at it to know what it said. He knew. They had debated and argued about the issue, and one of the members had even accused him of sleeping with the enemy. But in the end, he had to agree with the final assessment. The sale of this house couldn't go through without planning commission approval.

"What the — You're not welcomed here."

Patrice stood in the doorway. Under the kitchen light, her face was sharp angles and deep shadows.

"I came to —"

"Gloat? Congratulate yourself? You don't need me to do that, do you?"

"Patrice I know this looks bad. The commission is only protecting Moonlight Cove from predator developers. It's nothing personal."

"It's my house. Mine. A probate judge told me so. I can do with it what I want. You can't stop me. I can sell this house to whomever I want. I own it. It's mine. I have rights as the owner."

"The house is on the state historic registry. It's a protected state —"

"Just stop. Just. Stop."

"You can still sell the house, but the planning commission has to approve the —"

"Or I could just abandon it and you have a nice piece of blight here in your precious Moonlight Cove?"

"You don't mean to —"

"Maybe that's what I plan on doing. Throw away all the restoration work Debra did. You can sue me for it."

"Patrice. Don't be ridiculous. This can all be resolved."

"Me? Ridiculous? Are you kidding? This letter is ridiculous. I can't stay here. I can't go to your precious planning commission meeting. I've got to get back to L.A. I have a job. A life, a whole existence that doesn't include any of this."

"The commission doesn't meet for another two weeks. You can come back then and present the issues and —"

"I can't. You don't get it. It's award season. I have to be in L.A. Stylists don't do their work over the phone or via Twitter. Can you raise and sell abalone driving across the country?"

"Patrice —"

"No! Don't. You have staff, employees and probably students you teach who work for you. I have no one. It's just me. I do it all. And, now —" She pulled out the chair and sat down "I can't do any of it."

JB sat down next to her. He wanted to reach over and wrap her in his embrace, making the hurt go away. He knew she wouldn't welcome his empathy, so he waited as she fumed before asking, "Is this more than just the letter?"

Patrice pulled out her phone, swiping her finger across the screen and held it in front of him. "Read it."

He wasn't quite sure what it said, but he got the meaning of it. Whoever sent it had fired Patrice.

"You know her." Patrice tossed her phone on the table. "She's been a regular on the soaps and just made the jump to the big screen last year. She is or was my biggest client. I've been dressing her for years, even before she had money to pay me. I used to take credit from her. I trusted her. I knew she was going to make it in the industry. I just knew it. I know her shape, her coloring, and her style better than she does. She doesn't just wear clothes. She breathes life into them. Her first Emmy nomination, she wore this no-name designer gown. You know what? Because of her, that designer is now designing at a Paris Fashion house. All because of me. Me. I chose the dress, the shoes, and the jewelry. I convinced her to wear it. Assured her she looked great."

"What happened?"

"She's going with someone else — probably someone she found on Instagram, some fashionista with a smart phone and the knack for 'selfies,' who has a hundred-thousand likes so everything she does goes viral."

"What about your other clients?"

Patrice reached over and grabbed her cellphone. "They didn't leave quietly"

JB took the phone and scrolled down one by one reading.

"Yep, there's nothing better than being ignored—especially in social media."

"There must be others. You're good at what you do. You—"

"Spare me the pep talk, please." Patrice got up and paced back and forth.

"What are you going to do?"

"Go back to L.A. I know a guy who works at one of the studios. His partner lives in the same complex that I do. I'll see if he has any leads for me."

"Patrice, I'm sorry."

"Don't be. Seriously, Don't. I should have known this. I should have seen this coming, being dumped by not only the up and coming famous clients, but the client clinging to fame trying to reinvent herself for a younger audience." She picked up the letter. "This just adds to it. Adds to the whole crap that I'm dealing with."

He didn't know what to say. He realized that maybe it was a bad idea to come here tonight, but she shouldn't be alone. However, was he really the best company? He checked his watch to make sure he wasn't late for Aurora.

"See, even you have some place better to go," Patrice observed.

"No. I've got to pick up Aurora from dance practice."

She shrugged. "You *do* have some place better to go."

He got up from the table; sliding his chair in. "I'll be at the meeting in two weeks. I'll answer any questions you have. I won't recuse myself from the commission because of our relationship, but I won't grant any favors. Someone else will want to buy it and keep it as is."

"You don't get it, do you? Everyone in this little seaside town doesn't get it! I can't afford to keep this house. I need the money from the sale—"

"For your business?"

"Yeah. And my rent, my cell phone, and my car insurance…" She ticked off her financial needs one by one on her fingers.

"If you need money…"

"You'll just hand it out to me? That will look great on your commission won't it? While you guys are undermining my sale, violating my property rights, you're going to loan me money? Just for curiosity sake, how much does a loan from you cost anyway? Do I get a low interest rate since I put out last night?"

"I know you're angry, but last night has nothing to do with any of this."

"It doesn't? Was it just some coincidence that we were both at the same bar at the same time?"

"Just how many places in Moonlight Cove can you get a drink at 9 o'clock at night?"

She ran her hands through her hair and let out a long breath. Dark circles hung under her eyes. The faded t-shirt and the sweat pants she wore had a thin layer of dust and grime.

"I was wondering what was going on." She ran her hand back and forth across the back of the chair. "I thought you were a bit off last night. Oh, not on the beach—no that was great, better than great. No, there was something else that I sensed last night about you, but I couldn't really grasp at it. You never once said anything to me. You had every chance to at the bar, but chose not to."

"I wanted to. I did. I went there just to have a drink and think. You were there. Excited about the sale and—"

"You lied to me."

He rocked back, momentarily stunned by her accusation.

"You had every chance to tell me what was going on. That this high and mighty commission that you're chairman of, was going to stop the sale of my house, but you didn't."

"Patrice, I—"

"You lied. You lied to me and took advantage of me, too."

"Patrice, it wasn't like that. I—"

"Get out."

Her words, tinged with venom, slapped him.

"Get out. I never want to see or hear from you again." Her face contorted and turned red. JB opened his mouth and then closed it again. He didn't know what to say and so it was better not to say anything.

He pulled open the kitchen door, ready to turn around, ready to go back and comfort her, but he didn't look back. He didn't even pet Dante who was perched on the kitchen counter looking regal and dignified. JB just stepped out into the night and closed the kitchen door quietly behind him. His shoes crunched on the sand-spewed bricks. The image of Patrice's face was still freshly imprinted on his mind. He drove back into town in a daze, trying to regain a bit of control so not to upset Aurora. But the pain lingered, as if she had punched him and punched him hard, because he knew in the depth of his heart that what she said was true. He had lied to her. He had lied to the one and only woman he had ever truly loved.

———

Patrice flopped down, digging her toes into the wet sand. In JB's company, the sand was inviting and somewhat invigorating on her bare feet. Now it was cold, gritty, and annoying. She hugged her knees to her chest, burying her feet up to her ankles. The sun would be up soon. The eastern sky just above the rocks was already glowing pink, announcing the new day. On the other side of the rocks, was where she had had sex with JB. The memory of his body under her warmed her from the inside out. She let out a long breath. She and JB were over, over before it really began. She stared out into the dark ocean, trying to organize her chaotic thoughts.

Could she go back to L.A.? And to what? A paltry client list, a cramped apartment? The thought of trying to re-ignite her career filled her with dread. She knew she was good at what she did, but women her age weren't honored in Hollywood.

Grabbing a handful of sand, she let it slowly fall from her grasp. Her meager savings weren't going to go very far. Her future was as obscure as the night still clinging to the western sky.

Moving her feet back and forth, she knew she couldn't go back to L.A. Hustling for work, trying to revive her faltering career wasn't an option.

Selling the house was the only solution. However, how would she be able to attract another buyer with the commission restrictions?

She dropped her head into her hands, just as her tears filled her eyes and ran down her face. Her body shook with her sobs as her despair crashed over her.

The sun broke over the rocky ridge, burning away the vestiges of the night. Patrice rolled over, sitting up. She had shed her last tear sometime earlier and was too spent to return to Debra's house; she had simply lain down in the sand.

The beach drenched in the morning light, was vibrant. Gone were the murky shadows that lurked amongst the outcrops of rocks. The only remnant of the night was the coldness that still hung in the air. Patrice breathed deeply, filling her lungs, surprised to discover that her anger and frustration had dissipated in the morning light. She only felt renewed eagerness to figure out how to deal with the house.

Debra's house.

Why had Debra left the house to her? She must have had some reason. Debra could have left the house to anyone she had wanted to, but she had chosen her errant sister. Inheritance was a gift, not an obligation. So why? Why had Debra given the house to her? It had to be more than just some sort of familial requirement.

Patrice ran her feet back and forth in the sand squinting into the sun. A second chance? She realized that her sister had given her a second chance at life. Debra's notebook. The plans for a B&B. The resort town of Moonlight Cove.

Patrice didn't need to go back to L.A. She could stay here; open the B&B like her sister had planned. She could grab this opportunity and make the most of it. She had one chance at life—she had taken it years ago by becoming a stylist. Fashion was a fickle mistress and no longer wanted her; now her sister had given her another chance. Patrice was someplace that needed her. She got up, brushing off the sand; the lighthouse caught her attention, its whitewash conical beacon shone in the morning light. She shook away the coldness of the night and made her way up the wooden stairs. Her future started today.

─ ◆ ─

He was sitting in the back of the bistro, staring out the window. Patrice paused before going over to him. What seemed only a few hours ago like the best idea ever, now seeing JB, she wondered if this was the wisest choice. But she had come this far. She couldn't let her own self-doubts stop her.

"JB?" Patrice uttered. He turned, looking at her almost as if he was expecting her. His face was ashen, dark circles hung under his eyes. His shoulders were slumped as if exhaustion weighed him down. She knew the feeling. She could use a few more hours of sleep, too. "May I?" she motioned to the chair. He shrugged, stacking up the papers he had strewn over the table.

"I thought you'd be at the farm this morning." She watched him neaten the stack before slipping it into his brief case.

"Had a meeting at city hall this morning," he responded without even looking up at her.

"And those?"

"Student papers. Sustainable marine life propagation." His voice was flat, his face, expressionless.

Patrice shifted uncomfortably in the chair. "JB... I... we... need to —"

"When are you leaving for L.A.?"

"What? Oh! Well, I'm —"

"Coffee?" Lily stood at the table with a coffee cup and coffee pot in hand, and a menu tucked under her arm.

"Yes. That would be great. Thank you." A jolt of caffeine was probably what she needed after a sleepless night.

Lily filled the mug and looked at JB. "And, you?"

"Sure. Thanks, Lily." He pushed his mug towards her.

"Breakfast?" Lily asked.

Patrice's stomach lurched. Food would be good. "Yes."

Lily reached for the menu, but Patrice shook her head. "Tell me what's good. What do you recommend?"

Lily glanced at JB before responding. "The eggs *à la* Moonlight. Made with choice abalone. It's quite good."

"Okay, I'll have that and a glass of orange juice."

"Coming right up."

Patrice poured cream into her coffee and took a tentative sip. "She does make the best coffee."

"You've had coffee at every restaurant in Moonlight Cove?"

"No. Not yet." The caffeine elbowed her attention, clearing her thoughts. She was right to come here this morning and speak to JB. She had to. She just did.

"Aren't you leaving? You're going to hit all the Highway 101 traffic, if you don't leave soon."

She shook her head. "No. Not today, at least."

JB eyes widened. He leaned forward and opened his mouth to speak just as Lily came up to the table.

"Here you go. Eggs *à la* Moonlight. Anything else?"

Patrice eyed the oversized plate with two eggs upon a filet of abalone, lined with spinach all neatly arranged, on English muffins, and drenched in hollandaise sauce.

"No, thank you. This looks delicious." Patrice picked up her fork and took the first bite. And it *was* delicious. She inwardly sighed.

JB was still staring at her; she could feel his gaze on her as she ate.

"This is good. Really, really good." She waved her fork in the air. "Do you think Lily would give me the recipe for how she prepares the abalone? Debra's notebook didn't have specifics about that."

"I didn't know you cooked?" He sipped his coffee.

She smirked at him. "One of my many talents."

He set his coffee cup down with a bang. "Have a safe drive back to L.A. I hope everything works out for you, Patrice." He moved to get up from the table.

"Wait. Don't go. Please." She swallowed her last mouthful.

He shook his head. "There is nothing more I need to say and I surely don't need to hear anything more from you."

His words hurt, as if their past held no significance for him. "I suppose I deserved that. But I think you may want to hear what I have to say." She twisted, retrieving her temporary Moonlight Cove business license from the front pocket of her jeans. She tossed the folded piece of paper onto the table.

"What's this?"

"Read it."

JB glared at the folded paper. Patrice watched him under her hooded eyes as she continued to eat. Reaching over, he unfolded the paper, running his eyes across it.

"I applied for that business license this morning. It's the temporary copy. The real one I'll frame and hang behind the front desk. Well, when I get a front desk." She wiped her mouth with her napkin.

He let the paper slip from his hand. "Is this some joke?" His glare hardened.

"No. I thought you'd at least say congratulations. Or best of luck, or something encouraging like that." She reached over and snatched the paper out from him, and jammed it back into her pocket.

He braced himself against the table. "You're staying? Here? In Moonlight Cove? What about—"

"My job in L.A.? I'm giving that up. Sure, I'll need to go clean out my apartment and stuff. My lease isn't up for another six months so there's no rush on that."

He blinked, crossing his arms over his chest. He stared out the window, his mouth a straight line.

"You know after you left last night, I was angry, really angry. I went and sat on the beach—"

He turned to her and raised an eyebrow in question.

"I just sat there alone and cold, thinking about what I was going to do. It dawned on me. Debra had to have left me this house for a reason. She could have left the house to anyone, but she left it to me."

"Maybe because you were her sister?"

Patrice shook her head. "We ignored each other for the last ten years. You know that. But this town was her friend and her family. I realized she left me more than just a piece of property. She left me a chance: a chance to have a different life."

"It takes money to open a business. Capital investment and—"

She waved her hand in the air. "Already taken care of. I called a friend of mine in L.A., and she's going to help me get some private investors. I'm going to start an internet funding campaign to finish the restoration that Debra started. I know a lot of people in the entertainment industry. They may not want to hire me as a stylist, but

I bet they'll invest in my B&B and even better, I bet they'll want to come and stay here, too."

He shook his head, rubbing his hand over his face. "Patrice, what do you know about running a B&B? Besides reading Debra's notebook?"

"I've stayed in a few over the years."

"So that makes you an expert?"

"No. Of course, not. I've worked in the service industry all my adult life. As a stylist, I dressed people to look good. I provided a service with my expertise in clothing, makeup and fashion. Running a B&B is sort of the same; I'll provide a nice place to stay, a tasty breakfast and information about the area."

"So your career that you've spent you whole adult life on—you're just going to toss it aside."

Patrice shook her head, wiping up the last bite of egg with the edge of her toast. "You know, this was the best meal I've had in a long time."

"You're not even listening to me."

She popped the last bit of toast into her mouth. "I heard you. I'm not throwing my career away. I'm transitioning from one career to another. I'm grabbing an opportunity where I didn't see one before."

"Are you just doing this because of the planning commission? They'll want—"

She held up her hands. "No. I'm not doing this to skirt around a bunch of nosy public servants. I'll be at the meeting. I'll have Debra's business plan, if there are questions. There are a few things in it that need to be updated, but it's solid. It will be my business plan."

"I wouldn't refer to the members of the planning commission as nosy public servants."

"Why? Are there any of them in here?" Patrice looked around. The bistro was almost empty. The breakfast rush must have come and gone, and the lunch crowd hadn't arrived yet.

With a partial grin on his face, JB shook his head. "Only me."

"Good. You're the only one I'm interested in."

JB sat back in the booth and shook his head before letting out a shallow laugh, "Then I guess all I can say is congratulations."

"You still don't sound convinced that I can do this."

He let out a long breath, before answering. "I'm not. You came here with the sole intention of selling and now you're staying. What happens in a week? Or a month? Or a year? Will you still be here? Or are you going to bail out?"

Patrice gripped her hands in her lap. "I know you think I'm crazy, but—"

"I didn't say that. Are you doing this because it's a sound business opportunity or are you doing it for some other reason?"

Patrice sniffled. The tears were just below the surface. She took a deep hard swallow trying to gain control. "My regret in life is that I never patched things up with Debra."

"Patrice—"

"No. Let me finish."

"JB, I don't want to live my life with any more regrets. I want to live my life to the fullest. I think I can do that here in Moonlight Cove. I truly do."

JB nodded, holding out his hand, Patrice laid her hand in his. Security, warmth and happiness spread through her as he wrapped his fingers around her palm.

"Patrice, I lost you ten years ago. You left and I didn't know how to stop you."

Patrice nodded. "I know. I had to leave. I had to figure things out. Funny, it's taken me ten years to figure things out."

JB laid his other hand on hers and smiled. "Patrice, I've never stopped thinking about you. All I felt I just bundled up and hid away until I heard you were back in town, and now I—"

"JB," Patrice said, her heart thumping in her ears. "I didn't just think about changing careers when I was out on the beach this morning."

He pulled his hands from her grasp, as a worried look passed over his face.

"I've been a fool. Not just ten years ago, but many times since, and I probably will make foolish decisions in the future, too—"

"Don't be so hard on yourself. You're only human."

Patrice laughed. "But, the hardest thing is right now. Like I said, I don't want to live my life with regrets. I don't want to wonder about the 'what ifs'."

JB didn't respond, but continued to stare at her. Patrice took in a huge gulp of air. It was now or never, so she trudged on. "I love you. I loved you ten years ago and that among other reasons, is why I left and never came back. I was scared. I had never felt that way about anyone before, and I've never felt that way about anyone since."

JB smiled and leaned his elbows on the table. "Patrice—"

"I love you." She repeated herself, her voice cracking. "I truly do. And, I have no reason for you to return my love for the way I behaved. But I hope that you will give me another chance. I'll admit I don't know anything about being a mother or a stepmother, but I hope you and your daughter will give me a chance."

JB's eyes grew wide.

Patrice took a deep breath, plunging forward, "Jackson Barrell, will you marry me?"

He didn't respond, but stared. Patrice's heart was in her throat. She wiped her sweating palms on the legs of her pants. "JB, I know you may think I'm—"

"I'm not the same man I was ten years ago." His eyes glimmered with unshed tears.

"I know. I'm not the same person I was ten years ago, either."

His downcast eyes confirmed her biggest fear: the uncertainty of living the rest of her life so close to the man she loved. She shuddered to think that every time she saw JB she would be reminded of what her foolishness had cost her.

JB cleared his throat, laying his hands on the table. Hesitantly, Patrice reached over, sliding her hands into his. His touch was warm and inviting and instantly she wanted to make this all right, to fix whatever she had done wrong, but she couldn't voice a response.

"Yes." His voice was choked with emotion.

"Yes?"

"Patrice?" His thumbs danced back and forth across the tops of her hands "Yes."

Letting out her breath, Patrice squeezed her eyes shut trying to stop the tears that ran down her face. "I'm so happy. I so—"

"You know what this means, don't you?"

Patrice frantically shook her head back and forth, wondering what he might say.

"You'll only buy abalone from me for your B&B."

Patrice laughed. "It's a deal." She wiped her face with her napkin and blew her runny nose.

"Good. Come on." He stood up, offering her his hand.

Brimming with excitement, Patrice whispered to JB, "Are you going to tell Lily?"

He shook his head, pausing at the door before escorting her outside "Why? She already knows."

Patrice squinted against the mid-morning sun, which had burned away the misty fog. The blue sky was dotted with circling seagulls, and the sea lions that lined the rocky abutments of the boardwalk were barking.

"How would she know?" Patrice asked looking back at the bistro.

JB put his arm around her and pulled her close, his face just a mere breath away from hers. "That's one of the many secrets of Moonlight Cove."

Janna Roznos is a native Californian who shares her home with a former professional athlete—a retired greyhound racer—two grumpy cats, and one very supportive husband.

When she isn't out fly-fishing or sewing or searching used bookstores for vintage Harlequin romances, she is tapping away on her keyboard.

This novella is her first published work.

You can find her at http://www.NicobarPress.com.

Lily's Pad

by

Kathleen Rowland

Chapter 1

Most everything in Creed Taylor's life came easily. Women? Anyone he'd wanted, but he saved his animal urges for Scarlett. Lately, those urges presented a problem. Was now the time to cut her loose?

After deployment, the former Army Ranger gripped a cane. Scarlett couldn't look at his busted up knee, but he'd be damned if he let it hold him back. His woman was slipping, but he'd never lost a man. After the gunshot wound, he was off the ground, didn't run, didn't hide, and kept fighting. Now he limped, but humble didn't work for the new second grade teacher in town.

His heart swelled with pride over his newest award. On a sticky note, the principal, Mrs. Dovey, wrote, "Congratulations for the most well-attended parent conference."

A hot, gusty wind howled through coastal live oaks. Echoes of the closeness he and Scarlett once shared competed with free-floating anxiety. His rational brain took over as he shed his jacket and folded it over his arm, burdened with a longing to end things. They'd attended premarital conferencing. On paper their personalities interlaced with perfection, but who lives on paper? Not him.

This summer he'd made a habit of breakfasting at Lily's Pad. His retired army canine veered toward the beach bistro along the boardwalk next to Port Drive. As expected, the filming of the reality TV show, *Bikini Babes*, took over the staged beach next to it. Beyond

231

the sea wall, sailboats cut across blue waters. The scene was fucking perfect.

His longtime girl, Scarlett Royale, splashed from the shore. She stood out in her red swimsuit and waved, but not at him. The glare of sunlight glanced off cameras and the sheen of her glossy black hair as it bounced over her tan shoulders. He squinted at the woman who'd versed him in beachwear selections, mixed, matched, and sanctioned for a PG audience. With other goddesses in tow, she strutted in a halter top and mid-rise bottom. Wasn't his heart supposed to thump?

Sweat prickled on his forehead, and he wiped off ambivalence. It wasn't her competitive streak that caused his desire to wane. It matched his, but her unchecked obsession for stardom ate at him.

Like most reality TV stars required to fund their own publicity, Scarlett rose to producers' expectations. She modeled along the Main Street and appeared in every possible side event. He admired hard work, but the egotist's do-anything commitment was dark and cunning. Yesterday she destroyed a colleague who designed her swimwear in watercolor tones. Scarlett wore red. Like a spider, she climbed along a steep-angled web. In front of the producer, she shredded and dangled the woman. Today a new designer took her place.

His Belgian shepherd heeled alongside him, touching his good left leg. He bent to stroke his dog's fur. "Good dog, Fritz." Heeling was a difficult skill to master, but intense repetition perfected an army canine's tasks. His own repetition to support Scarlett's happiness bucked against him.

With Fritz's affected leg in a partially bent position, it was easy to see his ACL was acting up. Creed slowed the pace, but knowing this about his dog, relief loosened the concern rising in his chest.

Fritz barked a greeting and shuffled toward Scarlett.

Scarlett raced for his shepherd. "What's wrong, buddy?" She surveyed the area and then spotted Creed coming from behind a bottlebrush hedge.

"You know Fritz is okay." He watched her, but she stood her ground as stiff and tough as anyone guarding a reality TV empire.

"Maybe not." The reality faker yanked her long hair into a ponytail, threw on a crocheted tunic, and loaded Fritz into the passenger seat of her red Boxster convertible. "You'll shut your big mouth now?" Scarlett focused over his head.

Behind him, Creed heard a familiar voice and turned.

The director, Dan White, powered up his most stern expression. "Hold on there, Scarlett," he said in that clipped almost rude tone of his, the one that turned a request into an order.

"Film me, Dan." The brunette groped into her beach bag for keys. The tendons in her graceful neck stood out. She cared, and when she did, his heart warmed, but genuine situations came once in a blue moon.

"Good stunt if your love interest were into it." White gave her a curt this-isn't-working nod. "We can't have negative. Cut."

Out she came, bootie first.

"Too bad," White said. "View is nice."

Fritz bounded out and resumed his heeling position against Creed's leg.

"Come on, boy. Let's go." He fisted his free hand and continued on his way.

A second grader stood by an ice cream truck and flashed an easy grin. "Hi, Mr. Taylor!"

"How ya doin' there, Stuart?" Even while teaching, he used a laid back tone. "Nice fishing pole." Grateful for the distraction, his hand relaxed from its battering position. They chatted about casting lines from the jetty. "Got a bucket of live bait?"

"Sure do." There the kid was, ice cream dripping over the cone, heading for the shore. He'd never met a finer bunch of anglers than the kids in his class.

Creed scanned the town sprawling from the shore up the rugged cliffs. Moonlight Cove, founded in 1888, carried legends and secrets. Mr. Valentine was a mysterious summer visitor from out of town. Most residents were permanent. Moonlight Cove, built with bricks and U-shaped archways, was remote and only accessible by boat and two roads. There wasn't a single high-rise, nightclub, shopping mall, or Starbucks in sight. Townfolk preferred coffee at the Honey Bee.

Down-home described his destination, Lily's Pad, except today the place was packed with *Bikini Babes* fans of all ages.

He made his way to the only empty table, propped his cane against an empty chair and sat with Fritz at his feet. The pet-friendly outdoor area drew him for the food, welcoming ambiance, and in the recent past, nearness to Scarlett. Now saddled with less desire, he tipped up his water bottle and swallowed back a dilemma.

His mind raced, jumping from one idea to another, never settling on one. There was no kind way to tell her. The earth hadn't moved. Not even a wiggle. She wasn't wrong, he wasn't right, but they were wrong for each other.

"See that? The *Bikini Babes* are artists!" A teenage girl squealed.

Posing as artists was more like it. Dan White had purchased paintings from college art students. At the moment the babes were setting up easels on the grassy area between the boardwalk and the ocean. He glanced at his watch. Nine o'clock was opening time for their art sale on reality TV.

Behind him, the noise in a nearby throng kicked up an octave. Coming from a different direction, a towering, androgynous person with spiky white hair rushed toward him. "Aren't you the new teacher in town?"

"Yes, I am. Hello. Creed Taylor." He'd never rock Scarlett's publicity boat. "And you are?"

"Marcella. Is there an engagement ring?"

He cupped his hand and whispered, "I bought one." He injected enthusiasm which didn't come naturally.

"You must be thrilled." Marcella deadpanned and winked with one of her big blue eyes.

"Thrilled to death." He gripped his water bottle until the plastic crinkled and water drenched his hand. "Who are you?"

"I work for Mr. Valentine. He actively observes." Marcella stood with elbows akimbo, tipped her head back, and laughed. Was he the butt of a joke?

"Is he a love guru?" Creed asked.

Marcella turned her back and disappeared into the crowd which leaped to attention when Scarlett took the microphone.

"Here's my rowboat painting," she cooed. "I signed it." She brushed her hand to where her initials stood out in red. The crowd applauded, and then another starlet took her place.

Fans dragged metal chairs across the stone patio. As more people clambered to face the set, screeching was worse than nails on a blackboard. With the relentless clicking of digital cameras, the excitement and anticipation grew bigger by the second.

Scarlett was the reason he'd taken the teaching job in Moonlight Cove. She wasn't just a passing blip on the radar. They'd grown up next door. She was the daughter his parents never had and served as an anchor for both sets of parents. Once, after a breakup, they wanted nothing to do with him. Without Scarlett around, their parents were aimless islands. They became angry and confused.

Their mothers wanted to announce their engagement. Naturally it would be filmed on the show, and he was to show up at the doorway with a dozen red roses. He recalled the words of the stage manager: You're handsome, sexy. He, the perfect prop, faced the guilt trap from hell. What had he gotten himself into? How could their families survive? Two very good questions that he couldn't answer right now.

His dog stirred and gave him a long-suffering look.

Creed ruffled fur behind Fritz's ears. Hearing footsteps shuffle up behind him, he turned to see Lily.

He marveled at the owner, friendly but never personal. Hustling and bustling, she dressed in jeans and an old T-shirt advertising the bistro. Scarlett wouldn't be caught dead in her wardrobe. "Good morning, Lily."

A faint smile played at the corners of her lips.

His dog bumped into his cane.

She grabbed it and placed it flat on the ledge of a lily pond. In her other hand she cradled a huge pickle jar. "This lid is super tight. Open this?"

He took the gallon jar, braced it against his chest, and gave it a hard twist.

"You're my handiest customer."

"Yeah, yeah." He waited in anticipation to hear her rattle off breakfast specialties.

"Care for a tomato tart? It's made with organic egg whites, heirloom tomatoes, Fontina cheese, chopped—"

"—yes, I remember. Bring two."

"Sure, big guy." Lily stepped away to get coffee, freshly squeezed orange juice, and the double order. Fritz relaxed and spread out under the table.

Creed's phone pinged with a message from "Mrs. Taylor," the title Scarlett gave herself when she'd messed with his phone months before. He read her text. "Dan White says the diamond you gave me is too small for the camera."

She's giving it back, breaking free. His blood boiled with the insult but then cooled down. What better time to end things? He sent her a smiley face with a text message of okay.

Ping. Mrs. Taylor again. "Do not misunderstand. I'm buying my own ring. For the show."

He cursed under his breath, punched in her number to talk rather than text. He wanted to tell her to hock his diamond for the bigger one.

"Hi, this is Scarlett." Her voice mail picked up after four rings.

Lily returned.

"Where's your son? It's Saturday." He expected to see Max playing around the pond and feeding the koi.

Her eyes narrowed into a squint. "Max is, was, my foster son. His mother picked him up yesterday." Her upper lip wobbled.

"I'm sorry."

"I dreaded this day. I knew it would come sometime."

"You knew what would come?"

"His mother was released from prison. I'm glad for that, but—"

"—it's rough on you." He recalled seeing her volunteer in Max's third grade classroom. "When school starts up, how about helping out in mine?" Creed hoped his offer didn't extend her brooding. Better and healthier to look toward tomorrow. "If you want to, let me know."

"I'd like that." Lily turned toward her pond.

"Don't swan dive. Your pond is shallow."

"Good depth for a broken neck." She bent toward a yellowing lily pad. "The plants get crowded." She yanked out the pad with spent flowers and pressed her face into them. "Their smell is subtle, sweet." She wiped tears with the pads and then dropped them into an aluminum recycling can.

He glanced up at the wall where her blue kayak hung on a rack. "Going out today?"

"Not today." She nodded toward volleyball nets. "Big tournament this afternoon. Business will be brisk."

"You know the tricks to attract customers." Creed observed other restaurants begging for activity. The Lily Pad wasn't the only place with a good location.

"Believe me, I work hard at marketing." Her long eyelashes flanked hazel eyes. She was one of those lucky women who didn't require makeup.

"Yeah? What's your method?"

"I email every coach within a twenty-mile radius and attach my menu. I give them a discount." The marketing guru weaved her fingers through her brown hair.

"What food is their favorite?"

"Hands down, it's fish tacos, melon of all kinds, and gallons of lemonade."

"Hydration is everything. Look, you're busy. I don't want to keep you."

"Nonsense," she said. "Oh, and I didn't forget about your class's field trip on Monday."

"Thanks."

She looked into his eyes. "What are you up to, Creed?"

"Heading to a reunion. Army Rangers." He couldn't tear his gaze from her. Scarlett hadn't affected him this way in a long time.

"Here in Moonlight Cove?" Her hazel eyes sparkled with gold, and he saw the possibility that she found something worthy in him.

"Yup, Vinnie's," he said. "It reopened after reconstruction. Actually, we prefer seedy bars."

"Vinnie's is less ratty now." Lily picked up Max's Hot Wheels truck, dropped it into her apron pocket, and smiled as best she could. "I peeked into Vinnie's. Upscale nautical." She shifted her gaze around the area, checked for customers' hand signals, and then back to him. "At your Fort Benning shithole, what went on?"

"Fights. One night my cousin, Finn Donahue, insulted some Hells Angels. We got the crap kicked out of us."

She glanced at his knee. "That's not when—"

"—my knee? No." He placed a hand over it. "This baby was gunned."

"Tell me. Do you miss combat?" Her question required conscious thought.

"I miss the ability, and—"

"—that cane is a damn good jabber. Right between the legs." She stretched a hand over the table, and ran fingers up the ketchup bottle.

He smiled with appreciation for her rowdy humor.

"Somewhere along the way," she said, "you chose to be a teacher."

He felt his breath catch at the intensity in her eyes. "It's the best job in the world. Doesn't feel like work. Everything I value is in that classroom, in my backpack, and right here." He gave his dog a gentle nudge with his foot.

"You're a minimalist." She glanced to the east, past the church, at the gated Coastline Condos. "Didn't you buy one of those?"

"Had to, sort of. The school district prefers teachers to be permanent." Buying the model home meant not thinking about furnishings. "Fritz has a small yard."

"Bet he has a doggy-door." Lily turned and sashayed her hips. "Call me Foxy."

He chuckled. Once, long ago, his attraction to Scarlett was as potent and pervasive as a sand storm. Regret seeped through his brain and left him with a throbbing headache. At that moment it hit him. The last time they kissed, he'd put his heart and soul into it. The kiss left him feeling nothing.

Lily dropped off his food and pressed her face close enough to reveal freckles across her nose. "Sorry, I have to scurry." She stepped away, but then turned back and smiled.

He whiffed the basil on top of the tomato tart and took a bite. Damn good.

Music drifted from the set. The cheerful beat of Jake Owen's song, *Beachin'*, evoked a dancing ruckus. He blinked to clear his vision. Looking out at Scarlett made his chest hurt from wishing he wanted the woman who gazed into her own eyes and eluded his. Fake eyelashes required her full attention. He took a shuddery breath and bit down on his lip. On hold. The story of his life.

Chapter 2

Creed dropped Fritz off at home. He backed his car out of the driveway and looked through the rear-view. Fritz smashed his furry face against the front window.

Moments later, on the corner of Port Drive and Main, he stood outside Vinnie Cappelli's Bar and Grill. He leaned on his cane for a moment and faced the endless blue surf. Rough waves tossed against the shore and dragged back gritty sand. In back and forth confusion, he scrubbed his face with his hands before stepping inside.

The establishment lacked its usual musty scent. He inhaled a whisper of fresh paint and gazed around the transformed surroundings.

Reclaimed decor came from maritime origins. He ran his hand along ship parts and booths covered with old sails with the Elliott/Pattison logo. Chair barstools were upholstered in U.S. Navy blankets. He walked on the thick oak flooring. The former rattrap was now vintage-cool.

His cell phone chimed with a text message from Mrs. Taylor. "Are you getting cold feet?"

He typed, "No." He didn't have cold feet. He was frozen all the way through. Today he'd explain.

Behind him, two male voices shouted in anger, one tenor and one baritone.

Creed angled sideways. The raspy baritone belonged to Vinnie.

"I hate this contract. Know what you are? A true idiot." The owner spoke to a man on his left.

Dick Sloan. There was no question about his identity. Creed hadn't seen him for a decade. Dick graduated from Cerritos High School in his and Scarlett's class. After selling non-existent carnival rides, his pinball capers landed him in the slammer. Today, his Boglioli blazer was the con artist's attempt to appear prosperous.

What the hell was he up to now? Creed anchored himself behind a mast and listened to their bickering.

Dick shrugged. "Who are you calling an idiot? Read the small print."

Vinnie paused for a long moment and then walked away. Not saying anything confirmed what Creed hadn't been able to bring himself to believe. Vinnie had taken out a loan, and his place was about to be stolen from him.

Rage tumbled through Creed in a continuous stream, vibrating through his lungs. He worked to keep his breathing even before facing Dick. "Well, shit, man. Long time, no see."

Dick frowned. "Creed, eavesdropping? So you know. I'm a bona-fide licensed moneylender with Kwik Kash."

"Is your company regulated by the FCA? That's small print I'd like to see." Creed kept his emotions hidden in his lack of expression. If Dicky had a middleman, he'd gained money as well. Or someone could be a woman, serving as a sexy distraction. High-end partying preceded signing on the dotted line.

Creed weaved his way toward Finn at the bar. Despite his knee, he was in better shape than the guys who'd been drinking since sunrise, were already stinking drunk, and could barely high-five him.

His cousin smiled widely and then turned to the hungry-eyed waitress. "Make it two."

"Thanks in advance."

"Hooah." Finn back-slapped him. "Hey. Thanks for making it to our wedding."

"Have to say," Creed said, "it was super short notice." Much had changed in the last five years. Finn had gone from a jaded, bitter man to a husband and father.

"My dad spread the word." Finn was big, bossy, and sullen at times. Also loyal and utterly supportive. "Bloody hell. Is it true?"

"Is what true?"

"Your engagement will be announced on the *Bikini Babes* show?"

"Scarlett puts her life on social media." Creed tried to drag air into his lungs. The upcoming engagement party worked his lungs like a Chinese finger trap.

"A toast to the childhood sweethearts." Finn raised his glass, making it plain. When he saw Creed, he thought of Scarlett. "Hey. Look happy." Finn couldn't picture them apart. "PTSD resurfaced, right?"

"It's not that." Creed drew a breath to calm down. "Symptoms aren't the same. I'm not emotionally cut off." He had new interests and cared about different things. "Scarlett and I matured in different ways." He didn't say Scarlett was stuck in mean-girl adolescence. His mind spun to Lily. He pictured himself being with her more, whatever that meant. He pictured their fingers tangled together. Candlelit dinners. Her face on his chest. His lips descending to hers as the sun set behind them in Moonlight Cove. What was wrong with him? Why was he fantasizing about Lily all of a sudden?

"I recall your moms gave birth to you and Scarlett in the same hospital." Finn looked at him.

"We were knitted together. Two rooms apart, two days apart." Creed forced his thoughts to emptiness.

"Like two little pack animals," Finn laughed, but Creed shuttered over his reservations.

Army Rangers were pack animals and worked together as a unit. That was what he missed most. His pack was his second graders, and they were under his protection. In a surprising way, their parents looked out for him. Creed felt this when he gave Billy's dad, P.I. William Bradford, a call.

"Mr. Taylor," Bradford said. "Are you calling in the favor I'd promised?"

"Actually, yes. Is this a convenient time?"

"Sure," Bradford said, "shoot."

"I'm at Vinnie's and overheard him bickering with someone who loaned him money. It sounded like he couldn't make payments, and he might lose his establishment."

"Vinnie isn't the only one. My wife is an old friend of Patrice Miller, and—"

"—Dick approached the celebrity stylist from West Hollywood?"

Bradford said, "Yeah, well, she's originally a home-town gal. Now Patrice is outfitting and accessorizing women here. Anyway, I've taken the liberty to do a little checking on Dick Sloan. He makes big promises to increase business."

"Those promises are not in writing," Creed said.

"Correct. Patrice asked me to take Sloan on. I have a forensic accounting firm to track financial dealings. My guy is expensive, but Patrice paid up front."

"Great, I'm sending you money. For Vinnie." Creed clicked off, and then wired five hundred to Bradford through his PayPal account.

After filming ended, Scarlett ditched fans and phoned Creed. No answer. She tried again. And again. She slid into the driver's side of her car, made a U-turn, and spotted his economical four-cylinder Honda parked diagonally in front of Vinnie's. Then she remembered his Army Ranger's reunion.

The smiley face in his text message threw her off. Truly his stubborn-ass side surfaced. He wanted to talk. Talk needed to be happy talk. In anticipation of speaking to him about the engagement party, she strung together some random excuses.

She'd done a good job of hiding her secret venture. Salt water had splashed and smeared her eye makeup. One of her fake eyelashes fell off, and she ripped off the other one. Catching her tearful reflection in the new fancy doors, she pushed her way through.

The bar looked like an old ship, thanks to the smooth operator. The loan went through, and Vinnie's updated establishment would soon belong to Dick. She'd get a hefty commission. Wide wooden planks paneled the walls, and patrons sat on ancient steamer trunks covered with travel stickers.

"Scarlett?"

She heard Creed come up behind her. His footsteps matched throbbing vibrations across her forehead. She smelled his familiar aftershave, Dior Eau Sauvage, but no longer wanted to lean against him. When she visualized doing the deed, it was with Dick, and she didn't have to fake orgasms. She turned and waved with her pinky.

"Let's find a spot." Creed's too-handsome-for-his-own-good face used to make her heart race. His reddish hair was freshly cut, the cleft in his chin deep, his jaw set. The problem? His walk changed him. No, he didn't walk, he hobbled, his bad knee buckling with every other step.

Hit with a case of fight or flight, flight won. "It's so cold in here." Going in and out of the cold ocean wasn't the only thing wreaking havoc on her. A lover's triangle required attention.

"AC is on high. Here, take my jacket." He draped it over her shoulders, but his voice roughened. "So, what's going on?"

"Business is going on." It seemed to Scarlett the messy eyes didn't work. He didn't trust her. Week by week, the divide between them deepened, and now he was steeped in suspicion. He was right to be suspicious. Her instinct was to share as little as possible and shut up before he guessed she was two-timing him. "You wanted to talk?"

He said, "You won't want to advertise our discussion."

"There's a vacant steamer in the corner. Let's sit there." She dug into her purse, pulled out a piece of salt water taffy, placed it in his hand, and squeezed. "Blue raspberry, your favorite." She needed to string him along.

"Thanks." Taking the candy, he led the way but lost his balance just once while angling through people. He set his cane against the wall and lowered himself onto the trunk. Instead of pulling her to his side, he unwrapped the candy and popped it into his mouth. "Scarlett, we're wrong for each other."

"You didn't think so before." She bristled. This couldn't happen now.

"There's a whole lot not right between us." He took her hand and frowned at the ring he'd given her.

She tugged her hand back. "Don't nurse a grudge."

"Give me the ring." He sounded relaxed. "I'll hold onto it."

She tugged it off and handed it to him. Not that it mattered. As soon as she walked out, she'd slip on a three-carat solitaire. Anyway, she was so over his clumsiness and his itsy-bitsy stone. Looking at the way he rolled the candy around in his mouth put butterflies in her stomach. Memories, how he'd once tasted and how hard his body had felt, collided with previous thoughts of Dick. Oh, brother. Maybe she thought she was over him. "Creed, please understand. I want to be loved, admired. I have clear goals." She wasn't going to let him shake her off. His wholesome image was a necessary scaffold.

"We're way too different. I'm a teacher." He swallowed the candy. "I like my ordinary life. You're in the glittery world of Tinsel Town. And you're just getting started."

"That's right, thank you very much." She'd put up with his controlling ways far too long. "*Bikini Babes* is not my peak." She straightened her back, adjusted her tank top to show a bit of cleavage. Closing her eyes, she tilted her head back, letting the dim light caress her face. Sure enough, a flashbulb went off.

He frowned, his lips sneering.

"Please be patient. *Bikini Babes* will be in a movie." She neglected to keep him in the loop. "I forgot to tell you. Sorry for the oversight." Her stomach pitched like an elevator drop.

"Congrats. What's the plot?" He moved, and his knee bumped into her.

Scarlett took a breath to ease the general nausea from bumping his bad knee. "It's a haunted house movie. Did you know there's one in Moonlight Cove?"

"Sure, the Victorian, up on White Star Lane. It belonged to Martin and Stella."

"That's the one." Her mind whirled over the excitement of 3-D.

"Supernatural demons? Ghosts?" Clearly, he wasn't impressed. That was his problem.

Her scream matched that of the scream queen, Jamie Lee Curtis. Plus, horror movies made money. "We'll have our serious talk. I promise."

"Fine."

"Not now," she said. "Let's hash things out after the engagement party." Her fans had expectations, and Creed Taylor fit them. Dick filled her needs. The way he scooped her up, took her upstairs to his bed, and slid deep inside her. Best of all, afterward, they cuddled and talked about money. After money-talk, wet heat and soft power thrilled through her, giving way to another go around.

Chapter 3

"I don't believe in miracles." Lily Holmes gazed at her new friend, Scarlett Royale. Mid-morning sun shone on her tan flawless face, making her look like a mannequin. The reality-TV star increased business to her bistro. For this her grateful heart warmed, but for the last ten minutes, Scarlett was pushing her to take out a loan.

"The miracle you need right now is money." Scarlett brightened. "You don't want *Bikini Babes* filmed up there." She nodded toward the Lighthouse Bed and Breakfast. "Well, do you?"

"No, but I've attracted celebrities. Like you, for instance." She didn't mention the volleyball and surf competitions, her dinner menu featuring abalone from Jackson Barrell's Abalone Farm.

By now, Lily was whipped. She'd started her day with the breakfast crowd. Her staff took over while she spoke at a YWCA lunchtime fundraiser. Later, she MC-ed a foster care charity event. She wanted to climb the stairs to her apartment, kick off her shoes, put her feet up, and watch funny cat videos.

Scarlett's proud-of-you smile faded. "You could do better."

Looking at the star's uncompromising face, Lily knew she wasn't taking no for an answer.

"Listen to me." The brunette leaned across the table. "In another month our producer will choose, down here or up there. What about a neon sign, maybe in the shape of a lily pad?" She sipped the on-the-house tropical smoothie.

"Sounds cute." Large neon signage ran around ten thousand, and a voice in Lily's brain told her to think for herself. She rubbed her aching temple and shoved back the opportunity Scarlett was promoting.

"How did you end up with this joint?" Scarlett leaned back a bit.

"This joint? My Grandmother Lillian made it into a social hub on the beach. She willed it to me." She resented Scarlett's demeaning tone. "Too shabby for your taste?"

The raven-haired stunner with high cheekbones was as dark, tall, and worldly as Lily was pale, mousy, and short. "Sweetie, it's far from shabby chic."

Lily gazed around the patio. The lattice cover sagged a bit. Underwater pond lighting lacked sparkle. She'd bought paint for the rusting bistro table and chair sets.

"With a loan, guess what? You could quadruple the profits. I have connections." Scarlett stretched out her long legs. "Another thing. I won a contract for a movie."

Ambition stirred her heart with the idea of doing better. Then again, she didn't want debt.

Scarlett said, "I can set up a loan for you."

Over her tall glass, Lily forced a smile. Leave it to Grandma to plant insecurity about owing money.

"Show me a little enthusiasm," Scarlett wailed. "Don't be a ninety-year-old choosing your coffin. You're thirty. A loan won't bury you." She reached into her bag and brought out papers.

Lily took the papers but dropped them. They swished onto the table.

"I'll introduce you to the officer." Like a miracle worker, she clasped Lily's shoulders and squeezed. "Is this afternoon good?"

Damn. She hated feeling dumb and helpless. Looking around the barren patio, she shrugged, not knowing what to say.

"Honestly? I don't know how you stay in business. At all." She smoothed a hand down her slender thighs. "Four o'clock, right here."

"Okay." Lily slammed a palm on the table with an attempt to rally. "Is the loan officer a friend of yours?"

Abruptly, Scarlett stood up. "Dick Sloan and I share a lot of things, from his loan business to the color of his socks."

"You're sleeping with him."

She narrowed her eyes and didn't answer. "I'm about to marry someone else." She stretched out her hand to display a huge solitaire diamond.

"Oh, Scarlett."

"My fiancé was an Army Ranger in Iraq. A bullet had its name on his knee. Shattered it to smithereens."

"You're describing Creed Taylor." Until now, she hadn't made the connection. "Busted knee, but I bet he's good in bed. Lucky you to be marrying such a brave hunk."

Scarlett waved it off. "Over there his claim to fame was saving kids from terrorists. The Purple Heart is a bigger honor. It's the one worth a mention."

"Creed's a teacher." Pain strained the muscles across her forehead. His injury didn't strip from him a powerful persona. Not for her, anyway. Drat her libido and the fun she had flirting with him.

"We grew up together. Our parents are best friends." Scarlett stood, curled a hand over hers. "Our future together? Predictable."

She pulled out car keys and pressed a button. A cherry-red convertible chirped.

Scarlett's words swirled in Lily's brain. A ring, no zing. With a hand over her heart, she thought it best to change the subject. "What's the name of the lending company?"

"Kwik Kash." Scarlett's dark eyes lit up again, and she blew her a kiss on her way out the exit gate. "Dick and I will see you later."

"Later," She echoed and gathered up the glasses, wiped the table with napkins, and headed inside. A thousand questions cropped up in her mind, but she shoved them back to work alongside her team.

At exactly four o'clock, Scarlett and Dick Sloan showed up at Lily's Pad.

Lily invited them to join her around the pond.

"Lily. Isn't he good looking?" Scarlett elbowed the loan officer.

"Sure." Lily assumed it was a rhetorical question, otherwise she would have said he looked like a dressed up pit bull. Ready for their visit, she pushed a cart with an icy pitcher of lemonade and glasses to a table. "Please sit."

Dick snort-laughed and pulled out two chairs. Turned out one was for Scarlett, and the other for him.

"Really," Scarlett continued, "he's a bastard. Rich beyond imagining. As a human, he's not worth much."

"So," Lily joked back, "you're one of his belles after his money." She poured lemonade for them.

Scarlett grinned. "Now he's here for you."

Dick handed Lily a white Mont Blanc fountain pen, engraved with Kwik Kash in black script.

The pen felt heavy with pen-snobbery.

He took a sip of lemonade. "You can keep the pen, Lily. After you sign, I have a couple of other gifts." He set out a Cartier watch and a Louis Vuitton bag. Both glistened in the dappled sunlight. Under the table, Lily noticed he nudged Scarlett's sandaled foot with his Venetian loafer. Were his thoughts traveling down a salacious path?

Lily pulled the brim of her hat down, more to shade her seething expression than her eyes. How could Scarlett treat Creed this way? She placed the unopened pen with the watch and bag. "These are beautiful gifts, Dick."

"Jeez, Lily," Scarlett said. "Don't make an ass of yourself. Come on, tackle the paperwork."

Vulnerability vanished. "I paid off my college loan. I'm still making a monthly auto payment." She nodded toward her Mini Cooper. "Before taking on more, I need to be debt free."

"Pardon me," the beach star said. "You have to spend money to make money."

"The interest rate is high." Lily pointed to the fine print. "Fifteen percent."

"We can make an adjustment." Dick tapped his fingernails on the table.

"With a balloon loan," Lily said, and Dick stopped tapping.

Scarlett jerked to attention. "Your place needs some TLC. Money is good for that."

Lily stiffened. "I've decided against it."

"Don't do this to me, Lily." Scarlett shook her head.

"Do *what* to you?" Lily took a sip of lemonade, closing her eyes briefly as she swallowed.

"Not rising to the occasion. I can bring you more business." Scarlett's persistence rubbed Lily the wrong way. Usually the loanee courted the loaner, not the other way around.

"It's a business decision. You have your answer," Lily said without apology. "I need to head inside."

"Move from that seat, and you're dead," Scarlett said levelly.

"A death threat, even in jest, isn't funny." Lily folded her arms across her chest.

"What if I give you a solid," Scarlett said. "My parents and Creed's have a twenty-thousand dollar budget for our engagement party. Let's have it here."

"You might not remember," Lily said, "but last month you booked a date to have it here."

"Well, I'm canceling."

"Fine." Lily couldn't understand why she was marrying someone other than Dick Sloan who seemed to drive her mad with desire.

Scarlett coughed, choked on the mouthful of lemonade. She reached for a napkin and pressed it to her mouth. "You're going to be sorry. As far as I'm concerned, you're dead."

"I'm sorry we're not friends." Lily couldn't help but frown at the bitterness in Scarlett's voice and hostility in her eyes.

Dick gathered up the pen and other gifts. Scarlett gave her a sidelong glance. "Goodbye, Miss Shabby."

Lily bit her lip to shut down a sassy retort. Except for the plane crash taking the lives of her parents, she'd enjoyed a happy childhood with her late grandparents. They'd attended Our Redeemer Church on Grace Street. Tomorrow, Sunday, she'd head there and count her blessings.

Chapter 4

At eleven in the morning, Lily headed from church where she'd prayed for understanding. Suddenly she understood many things. She wanted Creed to kiss her but understood the danger in a kiss. She yearned for him to kiss her, and she'd kiss him back with the heat and the power and the lightening she felt for him. She stepped faster down the hill toward the shoreline. With thick fog hanging low, she nearly bumped into Maggie Henderson. "Hey, Maggie."

"Hey, you." The publisher of the *Moonlight Cove Gazette* had a column going about helicopter noise. Noise resulted from the *Bikini Babes* filming.

"So, Maggie." Lily's curiosity had gone way past the need-to-know stage. "Who authorized the helipad?"

Maggie let out a slow breath. "The FAA agreed to use a field twenty years ago."

"For the fire, correct?"

"That's right. For natural disasters we need one, but we didn't plan on jackhammer-racket." Noise from twin-engine helicopters rattled windows and knocked pictures off walls.

"Bummer!" declared a loud male voice. Dan White directed *Bikini Babes* and everybody else in town. "Don't get your panties in a tangle, gals."

Once again, Lily thought, how fitting. The last time Lily had the ear-numbing pleasure of this guy's company was when he'd raged with a UPS guy who'd parked in front of Hamasaki Quality Pens. The UPS guy happened to be David Lewys, a struggling artist who made deliveries part-time. That day, White had his crew filming the babes as they picked out supplies to send cards to fans.

White seemed to argue with everyone in Moonlight Cove. Wait, correction. It didn't *seem* that way. It *was* that way.

He said, "We're getting new choppers. You'll notice a change. With a lower subsonic frequency, they'll sound like electric fans."

"Liar," Maggie said, unfazed.

Lily's phone rang, and she looked at the caller ID. "Hey, Lupe," she said to her head waitress. "What's up?"

"A truck is parked near the garbage cans in the back. The marine layer is dense. I don't recognize it." Lupe's voice carried, and Maggie cringed.

Maggie latched her hands on her hips. "A truck parked behind the motel just before it was sprayed with paint. A private investigator told me about it. I'll call him."

"Wouldn't hurt, thanks." Lily shot toward the bistro.

Creed thought it something of a coincidence when he saw Lily dash across Port Drive. She'd just appeared in his mind. Out for a stroll with Fritz, his dog tugged at the leash. As soon as Creed unlatched it, Fritz tore into the dense fog, and Creed raced to keep up.

A bark came from behind the bistro.

Creed spotted Lily standing beside the trash bins. Fritz growled a warning of a hostile target.

It was then Creed recognized Dick Sloan on the ground. "What did you do to him, Fritz?" Creed peered down into a pair of closed eyes. Only a throbbing pulse on the side of the loan shark's neck gave any indication of life. "How badly are you hurt?" Creed asked.

"Bloody hell, your dog knocked the wind out of me and ruined my back," Sloan gasped between clenched teeth.

Lily screamed, "Creed. Are you okay?" Other things she said didn't make sense. A string of words about Scarlett and Dick were only remotely connected to what was happening until he saw Scarlett.

She held a spray can of red paint. Behind her, scrolled on the bistro wall were the words, "You're dead."

An outside observer stood by. Private Investigator William Bradford commented on the play-by-play. "Scarlett Royale and Dick Sloan, you will face charges for vandalism."

"Drat, my ratings will sink," Scarlett said, her face filled with anguish.

Lily stepped forward. "Scarlett, I won't press charges if you do two things for me."

"Anything," she muttered. "What's the first?"

"Every Kwik Kash loanee gets a new rate of five percent."

Scarlett looked at Dick, now up from the ground.

Dick bore the agony radiating from his back. "Vinnie. He's the only one, and yes."

A whisper of wind rustled Lily's yellow dress. Fog lifted a bit, and she smiled at him. "Are you ready to hear the second thing, Scarlett?"

"Go ahead with it."

"Let Creed go. You're with Dick." Lily turned to Creed. "I want a crack at the new second grade teacher in town."

Creed looked into her eyes, and they sparkled like stars.

"No problem, our engagement is off." Scarlett walked away, followed by Dick.

"Hold on, you two," P.I. William Bradford called after them. "First we make a stop at Vinnie's."

"Well done." The excitement within Creed was more than he could contain.

Lily, with her head high and glorious aloofness engraved on her pretty face, said, "I've got paint."

"I can paint," Creed said.

"Let's get started. Your class field trip is tomorrow. I don't want the kids to see that graffiti." She curled her hand around his arm, the other on his nape. "I'm making sure you won't pull away."

He kissed her and didn't stop.

"I feel something hard pressing against me." She obviously knew what it was in his flash of heat.

He broke the kiss and shifted, pulling his hips back. His gaze flickered over her body, and she blushed, perhaps from his attention and from the knowledge of what she felt.

She ran a hand over his chest and looked further down, to where a bulge gave away what they both were aware of.

"I'm sorry. I don't know what happened," he said.

She giggled. "Creed, I'm pretty sure we both know that's bullshit. I know what happened. So do you. We kissed, and you got... excited."

Creed sighed. "I did. This changes everything for us, doesn't it?"

"I hope so." She ran a tongue over her bottom lip, and he knew she was thinking about kissing again.

He beat her to it.

Chapter 5

Ten o'clock, Monday morning, marked the beginning of the field trip. He'd invited his parents along, and they filed in with the kids. Last night, after learning Scarlett was marrying Dick Sloan, their world flipped on its axis and rotated the other way. He figured out the best way to right it was to give them chaperone jobs. Spotting Lily, he said, "Mom, Dad, I'd like you to meet Lily Holmes."

Lily shook his mom's hand, and then his dad's. "Thank you for helping out, Mr. and Mrs. Taylor."

Creed handed her a hundred-dollar bill. "For expenses, Lily."

"It's not—"

"—it *is* necessary. Please take it." Lily was one independent woman, Creed thought. Guess she had to be, living upstairs and running the bistro. It seemed to kill her when he'd handed her money.

Lily pushed back the hair escaping from a rubber band over her ear. "Welcome, second graders!" She beamed as his thirty students lined-up. "Thank you for not touching anything."

"No harm looking," Creed said, "but why will we use the 'no touching' rule?" He saw Katie's hand shoot up. "Katie?"

"It could be hot or sharp." Her red hair could use combing, and she wore the same T-shirt as yesterday.

Lily's quizzical eyes shifted around the room. "Is anyone lactose intolerant?"

Billy Bradford raised his hand.

"Good to know," she said. "Who wants a tuna and who wants a grilled cheese?"

"Mom and Dad," Creed said, "would you please get head counts?"

Within minutes Lily, wearing a crisp white apron with a lily pad motif, had two food stations set up. "Who can help me name ingredients?" She waited while the kids called out answers.

The class gathered around the counter in admiration of the restaurant-size tuna cans, gigantic jar of mayonnaise, and big bowl of chopped cucumber, parsley and lettuce. Leaving space between stations, she set out slices of American cheese and thin slices of tomato. "Both sandwiches are made with this flax and sunflower bread." She held up a whole loaf. "I buy bread from a local baker."

"Notice, class," Creed said. "The loaf is not sliced. Sliced bread goes stale faster than loaves left unsliced."

"Correct, Mr. Taylor." She dropped the loaf into a commercial slicer and spoke above the whirring grind. "I slice a loaf at a time."

A man in a chef hat sauntered in. "Who loves a great sandwich?"

"We do." Creed answered for the class.

"Please meet Chef Moreno, everybody. He will make sandwiches for us." Lily said. "Follow me to the smoothie machine." She waved them over. She placed bananas, blueberries, honey, and orange juice into the gigantic blender and then dropped in ice cubes. "Scrumptious smoothies coming up! Hold your ears." The blender roared, and after she pushed stop, she said, "A smoothie is like a magic potion. It makes you feel great."

She's engaged, interested. Not all about herself. Ever since he'd met her, Creed felt as if he were spinning in a seasick blender, filled with salty roaring sea air, wave noise, and an oddly claustrophobic sensation of his upcoming engagement. Now he was free.

Lily's eyes twinkled. "We're lining up to wash our hands, Mr. Taylor." As she squirted dish soap in their hands, little bubbles rose in the air.

Creed said, "Class, let's sing *Hippo in my Tub* while you wash up." Creed sang with them while he gazed around. The bare wooden floor hadn't been refinished for ages. The incongruous lace curtains hung for privacy from the street. The room had a claw-foot table in the corner for eating. Surfaces were spotless.

One by one, Lily and Chef Moreno passed out sandwiches and smoothies.

An older waitress introduced herself as Lupe. "Follow me. We'll eat here." She gestured to the shady side-yard.

"Mr. and Mrs. Taylor, we have a table set up for you. It's right next to the lily pond."

His parents were all smiles and thanked her for the best seats in the house. Lupe served them sandwiches.

Lily said, "Class, you can sit on the ledge. If you look closely, you might see a koi fish." Turning to Creed, she grinned. "Here are two extra sandwiches. Pick the one you want."

"I'd like to try half of each. Thank you, Lily," he said.

"As hard as you worked painting yesterday, you deserve three halves." She took a half grilled cheese for herself and then moved to nestle between kids on the ledge.

Lily was just what he needed. She made him happy and made him laugh. Creed turned his attention to the class. "What's that noise?

Anybody?" No one answered. "Can you help us out, Miss Lily Holmes?"

"Flipping tail-fins," she said. "The fish swim fast when nibbling on my lily pads."

He'd like to nibble on her. "How can you prevent the fish from eating all your lily pads?"

His parents stood to look.

"I sink the pots holding the plants deep," she said. "There's some nibbling, but the larger pads survive better underwater."

"I learned something today," his dad said.

Creed had a sixth sense when I came to danger. "Katie, careful you don't fall in," he warned before her face smacked the surface. Water splashed over the ledge.

His mom was the closest and darted over. Her arms came around Katie's shoulders, and she pulled her close.

"Good save, Mrs. Taylor," Lily said. "I have T-shirts for all of you. Katie needs hers now." She glanced at Creed. "Go ahead and let the class feed the fish. Everybody can give them a tiny bite of crust." She took Katie's hand. "We'll be right back."

In her absence, he and the two chaperones organized the fish feeding party. A few minutes passed before Lily appeared with thirty T-shirts and Katie with hair in two ponytails.

Lily was like coming home, and his heart skipped at that smile of hers. "Put those on my tab."

"The hundred-dollar bill more than covers it."

"It's time for us to head back to school. Mom and Dad, thanks for helping out."

"Super fun," his dad said.

"It was just great, Lily." His mother looked like there was no place she'd rather be. Mom looked nice in a summer red dress that gave society women a run for their money. She cuddled in close with Dad as they waved goodbye.

Creed had so much to tell Lily. They'd make time for that.

"Thank you for coming." Lily glided around, high-fiving the kids as they filed out.

He gave her a high-five as well but wanted to give her a hug. "Can I drag you to dinner tonight?" He watched her hazel eyes rove over the beach. There was a light mist hanging over the water.

"It touches me deeply, you asking me out. What time?"

"Seven. Can we meet at Vinnie's?" A productive step after kissing, he thought, and a dinner date moved their budding attraction to another level.

Chapter 6

Creed checked his watch and stirred in his chair at their table for two at Vinnie's. He straightened his tie with one hand and smoothed his hair with the other. Scowling, he took a sip of his scotch. If she didn't show up in a few minutes, he'd go looking for her. The past twenty-four hours nearly killed him. To have been so close to Lily while painting, but not touching her because delivery people arrived, and then the dinner crowd nearly killed him.

He knew the moment she entered the restaurant. He felt the nearly magnetic charge in the air. His gaze locked on her, and when she smiled, everything inside him tightened. Tonight she wore a lilac dress with skinny straps that snaked across her shoulders. The black pumps she wore had three-inch heels. Her legs looked amazing.

She took his breath away.

He made his way to her and pulled her in for a kiss. "You look beautiful." She placed her purse on the table.

"Thank you. You make me feel beautiful." She lifted one hand to his lips. "I like the kiss you left there."

"There will be more." He couldn't imagine how he'd kept from touching her for so long. His heart filled, his mind raced, and he said, "I had the idiotic idea to go slowly with you. All I want to do is snatch you up and never let you go."

"Creed, Lily." Vinnie hurried up to them. "Bradford told me."

"It worked out?" Lily asked.

"Sure did." Vinnie shoved a hand through his thinning hair. "The interest rate went way down. Bradford said you both had a hand in that."

Lily smiled. "We stick up for each other around Moonlight Cove."

"Let me get you some wine," Vinnie continued, and his voice softened. "Dinner is on the house."

"Serving gnocchi with prosciutto?" Creed asked. "I've been looking forward to that all day."

"That does sound good," Lily said.

"Coming right up," Vinnie said and was off and running.

Creed looked at her, and she said, "God, you look good."

"I've been thinking about us." He took a deep breath and held it. "I'm going to get it right this time."

"We're already connected." A smile hovered at her mouth, and she took his hand and squeezed. "I don't mind if we rush things."

"I don't want to take my time either. I'm going to tell you how it's going to be between us." He laid both hands on her shoulders. "I love you. I always will."

"Creed."

"Let me finish." His heart was beating so fast it was a wonder she didn't hear it. "I'm not a minimalist anymore."

"No?"

"There's a house for sale on a cliff overlooking the cove. The view is stupendous and leads down a moonlight path. If you want kids, we'll have plenty of room. Want to take a look tomorrow?"

"Of course I do."

He yanked her in close, so close he could feel her heart thundering as fast and furiously as his own. "I want you with me always."

"We need each other." She held him tight. "I'm going to love you... so hard." She smoothed her hand down his hip, and it stopped over his pocket. "What's in there, besides you?"

Drat. These were the pants he wore when he asked for the engagement ring back. "A ring. Scarlett—"

"—returned it? If you bought it, I'd love to have it." Lily extended her delicate hand.

Creed pulled it out, slipped it onto her fourth finger, and said, "Will you marry me?"

"Ask me louder."

"Will you marry me, Lily Holmes?" he shouted. "Is that loud enough?" He pulled her in for a deep kiss.

She opened her mouth just a little for a tongue tangle. "Marrying you is precisely what I want. Wake up every morning with you in my bed."

He kissed her again and then took a breath. "I'm supposed to get down on a knee and ask you."

"No need for that, Creed Taylor." She reached up and cupped his cheek in her palm.

He turned his face into her palm and kissed it.

Soon everyone in the bar surrounded them.

Mr. Valentine was the first to offer his good wishes. "It's good to see you two are reveling in the promise of love." Following him, Nick and Maggie, Thomas and Chloe, David and Nori, and Jackson and Patrice stepped up and offered their good wishes.

Creed thanked them for their sentiments.

Lily smiled up at him and turned to their friends, "This is more than I could have ever dreamed of. Creed, let me get my purse."

On the pier under a full moon, Lily lost herself in his kiss. Adrenaline coursed through her, powering her with hot energy. She clenched her fists in the hair at the back of his head, then caught the neck of his shirt, and her palm slipped under the cotton to stutter over bare flesh. She gasped at the heat of his skin, at the electricity zinging through her body at the feel of his skin.

And then he touched her. Oh, God. His fingers reached for the zipper, unzipped her dress, and as he palmed the hot flesh of her back, unsnapped her bra. She arched her bare breasts against his touch, felt his tongue dart to taste hers, drowning wonderfully. She brought her hands around, feeling the ridges of his abs and muscles on his chest.

He slid his hands around to trace her belly with his fingers. Their kiss broke, leaving their lips touching, eyes open and sparking intensity between them. She held her breath as he cupped her breast.

Nude from the waist up, her nipples hardened under his touch. His hands roamed her belly, her sides, and returned to her breasts. He explored her breasts with his palms and fingers.

"God, you're hot," he breathed, taking in her pale skin and the dark circles of her areola and the pink nipples. She bit her lip as he cupped one breast and rubbed the nipple in circles with his thumb.

She squeezed her eyes shut in a rush of nerves, wanting him here and now. Her heart swelled, remembering how it ached every time she was near him. "I love you, Creed."

"I love you so much, Lily. I want to take you right now."

A bolt of need shot through her. "Not here, though. You're the second-grade teacher in town."

His eyes brightened. "That's another reason why I love you. The decency you show." His hands roamed up her sides, and he gently played with her breasts as he replaced her bra and dressed her.

They walked hand-in-hand along the dock and stepped onto the boardwalk. A car engine rumbled along Port Drive, headlights bathing them in a swath of brightness.

"That scared the crap out of me." She clutched his arm and walked the rest of the way to his beachside condo. "I'll always remember this night. The night you proposed to me." She stood on her tiptoes and kissed his cheek.

He turned and kissed her but not as long as he normally did. They were getting carried away again and needed to get inside.

Book Buyers Best finalist **Kathleen Rowland** is devoted to giving her readers fast-paced, high-stakes suspense with a sizzling love story sure to melt their hearts. Some are sweet: *Lily's Pad* and the Intervenus Series: *A Brand New Address* and *Betrayal at Crater's Edge.*

Her Under the Wire Series is ultra-hot. *Deadly Alliance* and her work-in-progress, *Unholy Alliance*, are contracted with Tirgearr Publishing (http://www.tirgearrpublishing.com/). Other romantic suspense books are available.

Kathleen used to write computer programs but now writes novels. She grew up in Iowa, where she caught lightning bugs, ran barefoot, and raced her sailboat on Lake Okoboji. Now she wears flip-flops and sails with her husband, Gerry, on Newport Harbor but wishes there were lightning bugs in California.

Kathleen exists happily with her witty CPA husband in their 1970's poolside retreat in Southern California, where she adores time spent with visiting grandchildren, dogs, one bunny, and noisy neighbors. While proud of their five children who've flown the coop, she appreciates the luxury of time to write. If you'd enjoy news, sign up for Kathleen's newsletter at http://www.KathleenRowland.com.

You can also find her at:

http://GoodReads.com/author/show/786656.Kathleen_Rowland
http://twitter.com/rowlandkathleen

Valentine's Vacation

(epilog)

by

A.G. Reid

Chapter Five

Valentine entered the hotel, followed by Marcella, with Sahayak riding inside Valentine's jacket pocket. Valentine stopped to brush the raindrops from his clothing just inside the entrance.

The lobby floor was a polished brown red tile that gleamed in the soft white lights overhead. Large arches defined where the lobby ended and various areas of the hotel began. Dark oak tables held large vases of flowers and greenery at the juncture where the arches met.

"Do you think Erica and Brett are here?" Marcella asked.

"No, the storm hit first further north. They'll need to return this way from where the road washed out to find the hotel." Valentine walked toward the front desk.

The reservation attendant at the desk smiled as Valentine approached.

"May I help you, sir?"

Valentine handed the attendant his reservation. "Yes, I have two rooms reserved."

"Yes sir." The attendant glanced at the document. "Would you like to keep the charges on the same card?"

"That will be fine," Valentine said. "I expect your establishment will be busy tonight due to the storm."

"As of your check-in we are completely full."

Sahayak pulsed his wings from inside Valentine's jacket pocket. The reservation attendant jumped because of the loud noise. He stared at the moving pocket of Valentine's jacket.

Valentine placed his hand over the pocket that continued to move. "Phone," was all he said.

He knew what worried Sahayak. Valentine had checked the sequence of events in Venus's library before his Vacation. Sahayak had also confirmed that one room would be available for Erica and Brett during the storm. Someone had changed that. Whether that was incidental or on purpose, it should not have been possible.

The reservation attendant coughed. Valentine's attention flooded back to the present. He looked down at the golden card keys that were on the counter.

Valentine slid one of the keys back toward the reservation attendant. "I'm sure, due to the storm, you'll have at least one more party looking for accommodations."

The attendant began to shuffle papers behind the counter. "Well, I don't know, I need to speak with the manager."

"Yes, I would hate the thought of someone turned away on a night like this." Valentine glanced at the name on the office door behind the counter. "Tell her my concern and that I expect to keep the charge for the room on my card."

When the attendant left, Valentine turned toward Marcella. "Remember, in an emergency, money can be a useful tool but the method must be subtle."

"In all situations?" Marcella asked.

Valentine drummed his fingers on the counter. "People have an interesting saying. It's a cliché by now but still useful. 'Money talks but don't let it talk to law enforcement.'" He smiled. "To answer your question, in most situations."

The reservation attendant returned, same smile still on his face. "We'll be happy to accommodate you, Mr. Valentine."

"Thank you, could you please have a rollaway bed delivered to my room?"

"Yes sir, but the couches in your suite fold out into beds. Extra bedding will be in the closets."

"That will be fine," Valentine said.

"Is there anything else I can do for you, sir?"

"No, you've been quite helpful."

Valentine walked toward the stairway. The polished redwood glowed in the light that shined on it.

There was an elevator at the base of the stairs. Its elaborate twisting and winding wrought-iron bars made Valentine think of it as a large birdcage.

Sahayak poked his head from Valentine's pocket. "Are we going to take the elevator?"

"No, not tonight. Someone is keeping Erica and Brett in sight and I suspect they are here. It would be best not to use the elevator. It could become a trap."

Sahayak frowned as he watched the elevator ascend to the upper floors.

Valentine had begun to take the stairs when Sahayak tugged on his lapel. "Venus, look."

Valentine turned as Venus came through the inner set of lobby doors. Raindrops dotted her braided hair. Caught in the lights overhead, he thought they sparkled like diamonds.

Venus was wearing skinny black jeans and light gray hiking boots, both items appropriate for the local terrain. The emerald green silk blouse was an item more to her liking, Valentine thought.

She slipped off her black leather jacket and draped it over her shoulder. Her head jolted back when she caught sight of Valentine.

Valentine had already begun walking towards Venus and they met just inside the lobby.

Venus frowned, then whispered. "The Transition left me miles from Moonlight Cove. When I tried to reenter, it wasn't there."

At that revelation, a tingling fluttered through Valentine's chest. It ran down both arms to his hands. He looked into Venus's eyes. "Are you unharmed?"

"I'm fine." She said as she shook her head.

Marcella put a hand on Valentine's shoulder. "The Transition, that's not possible."

"Yet it is." Valentine said as he kept his eyes on Venus.

Venus gave Valentine a quick nod. "There is more happening here than you know."

Valentine became still. Holding his chin between his thumb and forefinger for a moment before he spoke. "Apparently."

———

Valentine slid the gold key card into a slot above the doorknob. He heard the sharp click when the door unlocked. He let Venus enter first.

The light-green carpet felt firm as they walked into the room. He noted that the living room had enough space, and it would accommodate him and Marcella once the couches folded out into beds.

A short hallway, its polished wood floor gleaming in the warm light of the suite, led to the main bedroom that Venus would take. Valentine felt the suite was compact but adequate.

Valentine walked over to the window and looked out. He could hear the soft whisper of the rain beat against the glass. "I believe our assailants who took out the Transition are here."

"Just because of a taken room. It could be a coincidence," Marcella said.

"It's no coincidence, not tonight," Valentine said.

Marcella looked at the ceiling and let out a breath. "I wish they would stop playing around."

"There's been no playing. Incompetence or impatience, maybe, but not playing." Valentine closed the drapes.

Venus hung her leather jacket on the back of a chair, then sat down at the dining table in the suite. "What happened in Ireland wasn't because of you, Valentine."

Valentine walked over to the table and sat down looking at Venus.

"We have evidence of the Vehementem's use in Is Brea. That spontaneous love was the outcome implies unfamiliarity with its operation."

Valentine raised his eyebrows. "Who do you think is using it?"

Venus tossed a few loose braids back over her shoulder. "Unknown. A cloaked figure, definitely female."

Marcella walked to the front door. "I'm bringing up the rest of our bags. Do you need something from your car, Venus?"

"Yes, front passenger seat." She held up her keys as Sahayak swooped in and took them. He darted into Marcella's coat pocket as she left the suite.

After the door closed, Venus looked down at the table. She dropped both hands to her lap and interlaced her fingers.

Valentine walked over to the counter at the room divide. He held up a bottle of wine and two glasses. "The hotel has provided this, red and a rather good year."

Venus looked up. "Thank you, yes."

Valentine filled both glasses half way and set one in front of her as he sat down again at the table.

She swirled the red wine in her glass, then took a sip. "Yes, a good year." Then took another longer sip.

"Valentine, I need to apologize. I knew of the Vehementem's use in Ireland before our meeting. I should have told you. I'm sorry."

Valentine relaxed back in his chair. "It seems unimportant now."

"The Vehementem requires strong emotional force to spread its effect. I hoped that by limiting you to observing there'd be no repeat of what happened in Is Brea."

"Yes, about that…" Valentine started.

"I appointed Marcella as your apprentice to keep your attention on her training. Not the new project you planned while on vacation."

"Yes, about the first point…" Valentine began.

"I put my library off-limits. Then you wouldn't have access to information to start the project with that couple. Eric and…"

"Erica and Brett. Yes, about that…"

Sahayak flew through the open door into the suite as Marcella began to open it. The Cherub landed on the table between Venus and Valentine. "Erica and Brett are here."

Venus raised her eyebrows while looking at Valentine. "The same couple you mentioned this morning?"

"Well, yes. About that…"

"Is this coincidental? If so, how could that be?" Venus asked.

Sahayak flew up and hovered in front of Venus. "We were actively observing. Marcella told me all about it."

"Actively observe?" Venus shifted in her chair so she could look around Sahayak to see Valentine. "Is there anything else I need to know?"

Sahayak hovered into Venus's line of sight. "I'm on the project too."

Venus remained looking at Sahayak. "A project now."

Sahayak thrust out his small chest. "Yes, I went to your library."

Marcella coughed loud enough and got everyone's attention. She blushed. "Sahayak, let's check the situation outside."

The hum from Sahayak's wings got louder. "More project?"

Marcella was already opening the door. "We'll talk about it outside."

Sahayak darted out the door and Marcella stepped through and closed it behind her.

Venus took another sip of wine before she spoke. "I'm not surprised you know." She set her wine glass down and moved it in small circles on the tabletop. "You tend to bend the rules."

Keeping her eyes on the wine glass she then spoke. "It won't work you know. Maybe short term, but no."

Valentine sensed she had moved onto something else: them. "All right, that sounds reasonable. Tell me what works."

"Is that an offer to tell my life story?"

Valentine remained silent.

"It's a short story." Venus began. "I like predictable, safe, steady."

Valentine crossed his arms. "Keep going, I'm listening."

"That's all. Oh, what's the use? I should never have encouraged you, but I…"

Valentine raised his eyebrows. "You encouraged me? I like that."

"No, I meant…" Venus began.

Valentine cupped his hands behind his head. "You admitted it."

"You're the least predictable man I know." She finally said.

Valentine grinned. "I like it when you say it that way."

Venus drew her eyebrows together, looking at Valentine. "It wasn't a compliment."

Valentine brought his hands from behind his head and laid them on the table, one over the other. "I think there have been many predictable characters in your life."

"You don't know anything about me, Valentine."

"I've got a good idea already." Valentine said, his voice deep and steady.

Venus squinted her eyes at him. "No you don't. I came here to make you feel like a fool."

Valentine cocked his head. "Many would tell you that would be easy."

"Instead, I'm the one who feels foolish." She whispered.

Valentine leaned forward. "Venus…"

Venus looked up at him. "I've never felt this way before. Please, Valentine, before I make a complete fool of myself."

Valentine got up and gently touched her cheek. "I understand. I see the hurt you remember and hate myself for it."

Venus placed her hand on his. "Sometimes, you make me so mad. Then there are other times like this…"

Valentine smiled as he looked into her eyes. "Only sometimes? I'm encouraged."

Venus looked down. "You can take your hand back now."

"You're the one holding my hand in place." Valentine leaned in closer. "You're trembling."

Venus swallowed. "It's been a long day."

"Is that all?"

Venus remained silent.

Valentine leaned in closer and breathed against her neck. "I'm predictable when it's about you, Venus." He could feel her warm breath quicken against his cheek. He turned towards her and his lips ever so lightly brushed hers. A slight gasp, almost a whisper, almost a sigh escaped through her parted lips.

They both rose in an embrace.

Valentine tightened his arms around her. "I want more, so much more."

Valentine felt a shiver quake through her body. Then she pressed her lips more fully onto his.

Their kiss deepened. Valentine felt his heart ache, its pounding so powerful, he was afraid it would stop from one beat to the next.

Venus then looked down. "I'm, I'm afraid."

Valentine put his fingers under her chin so she would look up into his eyes. "Of me?"

"No, don't think that. Never that. Of, myself."

Valentine smiled, "Then we'll go slow."

Authors' Notes

We hope you enjoyed reading *Secrets of Moonlight Cove*. We all enjoyed writing it and hope to visit again soon.

Please consider leaving a review of this book at the site where you purchased it because reviews are the best way for other readers to discover new books. We'd love it if you would like to share your thoughts.

Visit http://www.NicobarPress.com to learn more about all of the authors who contributed to this anthology as well as to post your thoughts and comments.

You can also visit the following additional author websites or social media pages to subscribe to their newsletters and get more information about other releases:

- **Jill Jaynes**: http://www.JillJaynes.com
- **A.G. Reid**: http://www.WhatIsLove.zone
- **Shauna Roberts**: http://eepurl.com/Fr3Hf
- **Kathleen Rowland**: http://www.KathleenRowland.com
- **Janna Roznos**: http:/facebook.com/JKRoznos and https://twitter.com/JannaRoznos

47798491R00172

Made in the USA
San Bernardino, CA
08 April 2017